Sept '15

PARADISE VALLEY

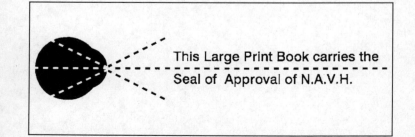

This Large Print Book carries the
Seal of Approval of N.A.V.H.

PARADISE VALLEY

DALE CRAMER

THORNDIKE PRESS
A part of Gale, Cengage Learning

GALE
CENGAGE Learning™

Detroit • New York • San Francisco • New Haven, Conn • Waterville, Maine • London

Copyright © 2011 by Dale Cramer.
Scripture quotations are from the King James Version of the Bible.
Thorndike Press, a part of Gale, Cengage Learning.

LIBRARY OF CONGRESS CATALOGING-IN-PUBLICATION DATA

Cramer, W. Dale.
    Paradise valley / by Dale Cramer.
        p. cm. — (Thorndike Press large print Christian historical
    fiction)
    ISBN-13: 978-1-4104-3471-5 (hardcover)
    ISBN-10: 1-4104-3471-0 (hardcover)
    1. Amish—Fiction. 2. Amish teenagers—Fiction. 3. Frontier
and pioneer life—Fiction. 4. Large type books. I. Title.
PS3603.R37P37 2011b
813'.6—dc22   2011001442

Published in 2011 by arrangement with Bethany House Publishers, a
division of Baker Publishing Group.

Printed in Mexico
3 4 5 6 7 15 14 13

For my sister,
Fannie Wengerd

FAMILY OF CALEB AND MARTHA BENDER
JANUARY 1922

ADA, 27   *Unmarried; mentally challenged*

MARY, 24   *Husband, Ezra Raber (children: Samuel, 5; Paul, 4)*

LIZZIE, 23   *Remains behind in Ohio with husband, Andy Shetler (3 children)*

AARON, 21

AMOS   *Aaron's twin brother; deceased*

EMMA, 20

MIRIAM, 18+

HARVEY, 17

RACHEL, 15+

LEAH, 13

BARBARA, 11

CHAPTER 1

In January of 1922 the Salt Creek Township in eastern Ohio was a pastoral haven of rolling hills and curving country lanes lined with horse fences and dotted here and there with the spartan farmhouses of the Amish. Perched near the road in a little bend above a creek valley sat the home of Caleb Bender, a plain white two-story saltbox with a tin roof. Across the gravel drive to the right of the house lay a long, low five-bay buggy shed, and rising from the knoll behind the house a massive T-shaped barn with a tall grain silo attached to one corner. Though nothing about the farm was ostentatious in any way, the whole of it — from the sleek, fat livestock to the neatly trimmed front lawn and flower beds, to the freshly whitewashed board fence around the yard — spoke of order and loving attention to detail.

By sunrise young Rachel Bender and her older sister Emma had already milked the cows and fed the chickens. There were no eggs, for they had been gathered the evening before to keep them from freezing in the night.

The heavy frost turned barbed wire into guitar strings. Rachel's breath came out in clouds, and brittle grass crunched underfoot as she followed her sister up to the silo after breakfast to throw down fresh silage. The patch of cow-churned mud in the barn lot had frozen solid during the night, and now her toes burned and threatened to go numb, even in boots.

Normally, this would be a boy's job, but in the Bender family there weren't enough boys to go around, so the girls grabbed pitchforks and bent their backs to the task. Rachel could handle a pitchfork well enough, though ten minutes of throwing down silage still made her puff a little. Warmed by the effort, she paused for a second to unbutton the neck of her heavy coat.

Emma kept working, humming an old tune, not even breathing hard. Strong, that one was. Neatly parted light brown hair peeked out the front of the black wool scarf covering her head, tied tightly under her chin.

"Are you and Levi going to be married?"

Rachel asked, out of the blue. Approaching sixteen, she would soon be old enough to date, so lately she had spent a great deal of time thinking about boys. Levi Mullet had been courting her older sister for almost two years, but so far there were no wedding rumors. At twenty, it was getting late for Emma. Amish girls were always secretive about wedding plans — it was a tradition — so if Levi and Emma were indeed thinking of getting married, it would not be announced until a month before the wedding. Rachel wanted in on the secret *now* — if there *was* one.

Emma stopped and leaned on her pitchfork, grinning at her younger sister's bold intrusion.

She sniffed. "Well, we *could* be. But don't you think that would be up to Levi?"

"*Jah,* I suppose, but I'd think you'd know his mind by now. Wouldn't you?"

Emma smiled and averted her eyes, a clear hint. "I do, and it's a good mind. He's a fine man. I'd be proud to be his wife — he already knows that. But he's also a practical man, and he wants to be sure he can support a family. Anyway, there's plenty of time. It's only the first week of the new year, child, and marrying season isn't until after harvest in the fall."

Rachel knew her sister well, and the merry glint in Emma's bright blue eyes told her all she wanted to know. Obviously, Emma and Levi had already discussed these things privately, but it was not yet a matter for everyone else's ears. The things Emma hadn't said brought a bold grin to Rachel's face, her suspicions confirmed.

Emma wagged a finger at her. "Now, don't you go spreading rumors to all your friends, girl. I'll thank you to control your gossipy tongue." But she was smiling as she said it.

That was when they heard the engine.

They froze, listening. Rachel couldn't see, for there were no windows in the silo, but she could hear what was happening. The automobile coughed twice as the high-pitched clattering slowed to a warbling rumble, and she heard the faint but unmistakable crunch of gravel as rubber tires turned up into the Bender driveway.

She seldom saw an automobile out here in the heart of Amish country, though they had become common in town. Only rarely did a car pass by on the road in front of the house, and none of them had *ever* turned into their driveway before. Dat would not like this. To him, these motorcars were the work of the devil — noisy and smelly and ignorant. Even a *stupid* horse could be made to see reason, but not so a machine. *"Good horses make more good horses, and they eat hay. The land feeds the horse, and the horse feeds the land,"* Caleb Bender was fond of saying. *"Gott made it so."* The automobile, Dat said, was just another assault on the family — like most modern contrivances, a wedge to drive them apart from each other and from the land.

Emma leaned her pitchfork against the wall. "What on earth could *that* be about?"

The noise stopped abruptly, the automobile's motor clanking and grinding to a halt. Emma backed through the hatch, scrambled down the ladder and ran to the barn door with Rachel close behind. Rachel bumped into her when she pulled up suddenly at the edge of the door.

"Be still," Emma whispered, peeking out. "It's probably just some lost Englisher asking directions to Shallowback's store."

Rachel giggled at the inside joke. An Englisher passing through recently had stopped an Amishman on the road, asking, "How do you get to Shallowback's store?" There was a new Amish grocer in town, and the sign over the door read *Schlabach's.* Englishers' linguistic offenses were an endless source of amusement.

"You stay here," Emma said. "I will go

and see what it is they want." She stepped out into the sliver of sunlight between the barn doors, her blue eyes focused and fearless, then turned and gave Rachel a warning glance, shaking a finger at her. "Don't you move from this spot!"

Rachel's eyes followed her sister across the barn lot and through the gate before she finally turned her attention to the driveway and took a good look at the automobile parked there. It was the fancy new patrol wagon used by the police — not that different from a surrey except for the small air-filled rubber tires and the funny-looking horseless front end. In place of a tongue there was only an odd-shaped box, like a little coffin, with bug-eyed headlamps. The back half of the vehicle was all enclosed with wood like an ice wagon, except there were rows and rows of holes along the upper part, so if a prisoner was locked inside he could get air. She had seen this monster once or twice before from a distance. The boys called it "Black Mariah."

The doors opened, and two policemen climbed out of the paddy wagon adjusting their strange, flat, top-heavy hats. The driver's hair was neatly trimmed and combed, and he was clean-shaven except for a big broom of a mustache. They wore

14

brass buttons on their uniforms. She'd grown up with stories of soldiers with mustaches and brass buttons who persecuted the Amish in the old country, which was why Amishmen would not wear them to this day.

As soon as the two policemen disappeared around the front of the house, Rachel slipped out the barn door and ran across the lot, her ankle-length skirts fluttering in the wind, her heart pounding as she crept past her mother's dormant kitchen garden and along the side of the house until she could peek around the corner.

Policemen on her front porch! What would the world do next?

Rachel couldn't make out what they were saying, but as the two policemen stood on the porch talking to her mother, she could see the growing fear in Mamm's eyes, the trembling of her fingers as she covered her mouth to cough. Rachel heard quite clearly, though, when her mother turned and voiced one simple command to someone standing just out of sight in the doorway.

"Go get Dat."

A minute later Rachel heard the back door slam, then hurried footsteps heading for the barn. Within seconds, hoofbeats charged out of the barn lot, and Rachel knew without looking that it was Miriam, the horse girl of the family — the only one who would even think of jumping on a bareback horse and taking off to the woods. Dat had gone out that morning with a neighbor to the fallow field beyond the creek, hunting rabbits.

Mamm disappeared into the house, and the two policemen after her. In the ensuing silence Rachel could hear the murmuring of voices, but they were not coming from the house. Confused at first, she turned her head about, listening, until she finally figured out that the voices were coming from the back of the police wagon.

Someone was locked in there.

Timidly, she tiptoed from the shadow of the house and inched closer to the Black Mariah, but despite her best efforts, her feet made crunching noises on the gravel and the murmuring from the paddy wagon instantly stopped. She froze, ten feet away, fear gripping her heart. She did not know what desperate criminals might be restrained there.

"Wer iss sel?" a hushed voice said — from the wagon. A Dutch voice. *Who is there?*

She took a deep breath, swallowing her terror. "Rachel," she finally answered, frozen in a crouch, prepared to bolt.

"Caleb's Rachel? Bender?"

She straightened, relaxed a little. "Jah. Who are *you*?"

Fingertips appeared through a couple of the holes in the side of the police wagon.

"Jonas Weaver," the voice said softly.

The Weaver farm lay two miles down the road, and she knew Jonas well, an upright Amishman and a deeply good man. The world had truly lost its bearings if Jonas Weaver had been arrested. Rachel rushed forward and spread her hands against the wagon, trying to see inside. There was more than one man in there.

"Why are you locked up? How many are in there?"

"With me are three other men. They arrested us because we wouldn't let our children go all the time to the consolidated school. They come for Caleb."

It was as if a mule had kicked her in the stomach. Her knees buckled and she sat heavily in the gravel, trembling, unable to catch her breath. Her face fell into her hands and she wept, overwhelmed with fear and remorse. She couldn't even think. The police had come to take her father to jail — on account of her and her sisters!

"Rachel, you must get up. We don't know what they will do yet. You must get up and go. Run and hide so they don't take you, too. Go!"

The voice of Jonas Weaver rang like a beacon of reason in a world gone mad, so she did as he said. Her heart was pounding, her head spinning and her vision blurred with tears, yet somehow she found her legs and fled toward the barn, stumbling over frozen clumps and nearly falling twice.

Once inside the barn, Rachel rolled the heavy door nearly shut, leaving only a crack large enough for her face so she could watch the house.

"Rachel."

She jumped and spun about, barely stifling a scream, startled by the hushed voice coming from someone standing behind her in the darkness of the barn. But then a face and a broad dark hat appeared in the sliver of light coming through the door, and she saw that it was only Jake Weaver, the son of Jonas.

"Sorry," he said. "I came to warn you. They took my dat, and I thought they might come here next. But I couldn't outrun them, so I hid in the barn. I saw you out there . . . at the Black Mariah."

"Jah," she said, only now beginning to recover her voice. "I talked to your dat. He said this was because of the school."

"Jah, that's what the policemen said."

18

"They're going to put our fathers away?" she asked, her voice quivering.

He nodded gravely.

"How long? How long will they have to be in jail?"

Jake's head wagged slowly and he sighed. "I don't know."

Jake was fifteen, the same age as Rachel, and she had known him all her life. His young face was full of fear and guilt and confusion, the same things she felt. Shocked and disoriented, in that moment Rachel did not know whether she would ever see her father again. She knew one thing for certain: If getting out of jail depended on Dat changing his mind and agreeing to send his three youngest daughters to "the school of the world" five days a week, then he would remain in jail for life. Caleb Bender was a man of principle.

They both heard the hoofbeats at the same time and knew that it was Caleb Bender returning on the horse Miriam had taken. Together, they put their hands to the heavy door to slide it open, and a moment later her father rounded the corner of the barn and steered his horse into the barn. He dismounted, put the horse in a stall and walked calmly over to the two of them, his shotgun still cradled in his arms.

19

"Jake," he said, nodding to the boy. "Miriam said they have come for me. I'm thinking that if you ran all the way up here, then they must have took your dat, too."

Jake nodded.

"Well, thank you for trying to warn me, but it won't do any good. Me and your dat, we'll just have to face this thing and see how it comes out."

He put a gloved hand on Rachel's shoulder and gave a reassuring squeeze. "It's all right, daughter. Gott straightens the path of those who mind Him."

Eyeing the Black Mariah parked in his driveway, her dat handed over the shotgun with a low chuckle.

"Could you put this away in the tack room for me, Jake? I'm thinking it might not be so good for me to go in that house with a gun in my hands yet. And it's probably best if you two wait out here until they're gone, just in case they might want to take you, too."

Undaunted, Caleb Bender walked out of the barn with his shoulders squared and his head up.

Rachel was filled with a dark despair. Her father's calm strength only served to sharpen her fears, and double them. He was a chunk of granite, her father — the center of her world, the pillar of strength and guiding force that held the family together, their decision-maker, their protector.

"They are in trouble because of us!" she cried. "What will we do?" She turned away from the door, put her face in her hands and wept.

It shocked her a little at first, when she felt Jake's hands touch lightly on her shoulders and then slide around to her back, drawing her close and enfolding her in a gentle hug. The boy had never once touched her in so familiar a manner. She looked up at his face and met with another shock.

For years she had sat in the same little red schoolhouse with Jake once a week, seen him every two weeks at church services and did work frolics with his family at harvesttime. Each of them had grown up as an everyday part of the other's world, like cousins, so her image of him was that of a bright and mischievous child who sometimes irritated her but on the whole was a dependable friend.

Until now. Now the boyishness was gone from his face, along with all fear and confusion, and his eyes suddenly reminded her of her father's. Now she saw in Jake's eyes a tender compassion and an iron strength that she had never noticed before.

"It will be all right," he said. "Our families will be strong and wait for them to come back. The police will see they have made a mistake and let them go. Everything will be good again, you'll see."

Rachel noticed too, almost absently, that she had stopped crying. A warmth flushed through her, despite the bitter cold, and her fears subsided as she stared at Jake's face. His arms felt as strong as trees, and yet he did not press her. She knew that she had only to step back if she wished — if she felt this was too close, too personal — and he would let her go. But again, she surprised herself.

She laid her head softly against his shoulder.

CHAPTER 2

Five days later, still wearing the same work clothes and winter coats they'd been wearing when they were arrested, the five Amish fathers filed into the courtroom with hats in hand, led by a uniformed deputy who directed them all to sit behind the cherry table down front. They had a few minutes to look around the room. Four of their wives sat in the pews behind the rail, but all they could do was wave to each other. When they tried to speak, the deputy ordered them to be quiet. Shortly, the "All rise" command was given and the Honorable Charles Etheridge of the Superior Court of Holmes County swept into the room and took his place behind the bar.

The defendants remained standing before him.

"Gentlemen," he began, once he had settled into his big chair, "your cases are identical — same charges, same penalties —

so in the interest of saving everyone's time we'll try them all at once, if no one has any objection."

Silence. No one objected.

The judge nodded curtly, then picked up a piece of paper and studied it through the wire-rimmed glasses perched precariously on the end of his nose.

"Do you have representation?"

The five men standing before the bar glanced at each other in confusion.

"A lawyer," the judge clarified. "Do you have a lawyer?"

They shook their heads, no.

"Is there one of you who would like to be the spokesman for the group?"

No one moved. Not a single expression changed.

The judge sighed. "Now, I honestly don't know if what I'm seeing is stubbornness or humility, but if we're going to get to the bottom of this, *one* of you is going to have to talk."

No words passed between them still, but all of them squirmed a bit. Four of the men cut their eyes toward the bald-headed one in the middle, the oldest of the group. Caleb gave a small nod of resignation, cleared his throat and said, "I will speak."

"And you are?" Again the judge glanced

at his paper, going down the typed list of names.

"Caleb Bender."

"Mr. Bender, in a court of law it's customary to address the judge as 'Your Honor.' "

"I'm sorry, sir — Your Honor. It's chust I never been in a court before."

"Mr. Bender, the five of you are each charged with neglecting the welfare of your children and contributing to the delinquency of a minor. How do you plead?"

Caleb thought for a moment and said, "Your Honor, if that last thing you said means we kept our children home from your school, then yes, we did that."

"Then you plead guilty."

Caleb's brow furrowed. "I don't know whether we're *guilty* of anything, but for us to say we neglected our children, why that would chust be a lie. We kept them home because it was right. To send them to the consolidated school every day, *that* would make us guilty."

The judge laid aside the piece of paper, propped his chin on his palm and, with obvious amusement, asked, "Do you feel it's right to deprive your children of an education, Mr. Bender?"

"Oh no!" Caleb answered, earnest and sincere. "We keep them home to *give* them

25

an education. Our children grow up to be farmers, and farmers' wives. We teach them the ways of the farm, and the ways of Gott. Surely some schooling is *gut,* but if they learn to read and write and figure, what more would they need?"

"I see." The judge's face was still propped in his palm, one finger tapping absently against his cheek. A faint smile played at his lips. "So your argument is that subjects such as history, geography, and hygiene are not only entirely unnecessary but in fact detrimental to your children's character in some way, and further, that one day of schooling a week is adequate, since all they need is the three R's."

The judge looked down his nose at the papers in front of him, waiting for an answer.

"Is that your argument, Mr. Bender?"

Caleb nodded, shifting his feet uncomfortably.

"Yes, sir . . . Your Honor." His eyes narrowed involuntarily, his jaw clinched and his nostrils flared. He could already see how this would go.

The judge's lips pursed and he stared over the top of his glasses, all traces of amusement gone.

"Well, Mr. Bender, I can see that perhaps

we need to advance *your* education a little. Maybe a civics lesson is in order. You see, gentlemen — you *are* gentlemen, are you not?"

The five glanced at each other. "We are Amish," Caleb answered.

Chuckling, the judge resumed his lecture.

"Gentlemen, we are a nation of laws. Ohio, likewise, is a *state* of laws. The way this works is, the citizens of Ohio elect representatives who enact laws to advance the well-being of the citizens who elected them, and who, incidentally, agree to *abide* by those laws.

"One of the laws enacted recently by our chosen representatives — the Bing Act — stipulates that all children shall attend public school five days a week from the age of six until eighteen with a possible exemption at sixteen, providing they obtain a valid work permit. Now, it's not an easy thing to draft and pass a law — it's an awful lot of trouble, a lot of work. Mr. Bender, do you have any idea why our esteemed legislators might have felt that it was worth all that effort to pass such a law?"

An honest shrug. "No."

The judge waited a beat and prompted, *"Your Honor . . ."*

"No, Your Honor."

"Well then, let me tell you. They did it in an effort to curtail child labor practices. It seems a great many people have been subsidizing their family income by putting their own children to work as early as eight or nine years old. We had eight-year-old boys losing fingers working on factory assembly lines, ten-year-old girls plucking chickens or sweating over sewing machines twelve hours a day, six days a week. Last year in West Virginia, boys as young as eleven died in the coal mines."

The judge clasped his hands in front of him and peered for a few seconds at each of the five men.

"Let me ask you one question," he said, "and I want each of you to answer it individually, yes or no."

The five Amishmen stood shoulder to shoulder, Caleb Bender in the middle. Caleb looked to his right. Reuben Miller would be first. Reuben's eyes widened and his face, already ruddy, flushed even redder at the prospect of having to speak out loud in a courtroom.

The judge pointed to Reuben.

"Mr. . . ."

"Miller. Reuben H. Miller."

"Mr. Miller, I see here you have three

children between the ages of six and sixteen."

Reuben nodded.

"Now, specifically regarding these three children that you are accused of keeping home from school in contravention of the Bing Act — did you work them on your farm during the days when they were supposed to be in school?"

Reuben Miller's brow furrowed in confusion, staring at the judge, and he hesitated. Caleb was afraid he might have to explain the question to his friend, whose English was worse than his own, until Reuben Miller finally found his nerve and stammered out an answer.

"Well, yes I did, but —"

The judge threw up a hand instantly, palm out, cutting him off.

"No *buts,* Mr. Miller. A simple yes or no is all I want. Just the truth."

Caleb sensed a trap. In his experience the truth very often lay not in the yes or the no, but in the *why* behind it.

The judge moved on to the next man, who also stated that, yes, his children were indeed expected to work on the farm on the days they were not in school. Caleb answered the same. They all did.

"So," the judge said, with an air of smug

finality, "now that all the cards are on the table it seems that you have violated not only the letter of the law but the spirit of it, as well. If you men need farmhands, I would suggest that from now on you *hire* them."

Caleb Bender looked up sharply, his jaw set, a dangerous amount of white showing in his eyes.

The judge glanced at him and apparently noticed the look on his face.

"Mr. Bender, I get the distinct impression there's something you'd like to say."

"There is more to it," Caleb said.

"There's more? Well then, by all means, enlighten us!"

Caleb Bender was not an eloquent man, but he was as he chose to be — a simple man who saw eloquence as a delicate flower, shriveling in the sunlight of plain truth.

He glanced sideways, waved his hat toward the men standing with him and said, "We are here because we are fathers and we want to teach our children what is best. Who is better to decide what to teach a child than his father? The Bible tells us we are to bring them up in the nurture and admonition of the Lord, so this is what we try to do. We teach them to love Gott and neighbor, to work hard, to care for the land, to provide for their family, to cooperate with their neighbors and to help widows and orphans. A little schooling is gut, but your consolidated school is full of the world. If we leave our children so much time in the school of the world, they learn other ways. They learn . . ." Caleb leaned his head toward Jonas Weaver, who stood at his right, and whispered, *"Konkurrenz . . ."*

"Competition," Jonas muttered.

"They learn competition," Caleb continued. "Not working together, but *against* one another. They learn to be selfish. So then it seems to me we are bringing them up in the nurture of the world. We fear for our children. We fear for their minds and hearts because we don't know what they will be taught in your schools."

Caleb Bender's eyes had grown sharp and fierce, his breathing heavy. His jaw worked as if he were chewing small seeds.

"So much time in your school," he finished, in a voice hard as iron, "makes them greedy and lazy, and fills their heads with foolishness."

The judge removed his glasses and rubbed his eyes with a thumb and forefinger, then sat staring into space for a moment, his chin resting on his fist. Finally, he put his glasses back on and spoke to Caleb Bender and his brethren.

"Gentlemen," he said, with a curious mixture of anger and regret in his voice, "I suspect we are at a cultural impasse, and that is a pity. The thing is, there will be others who will no doubt wish to do as you are doing, and what we decide here today will have a bearing on how those cases are treated. So I will explain the law and its consequences to you as best I can and then let *you* decide how you wish to respond.

"Unless they are sick, the *law* says — not me, not the sheriff, but the *law,* voted upon and approved by the good citizens of Ohio — stipulates that *for the good of the children,* they must attend school and study the prescribed subjects. This law — and it is a *law,* Mr. Bender, with concomitant penalties for noncompliance — applies to every citizen of the state, regardless of religious affiliation."

The judge paused for a moment to let this sink in, and then asked, "You *are* a citizen of this state, are you not?"

Caleb couldn't help noticing the twinkle in the judge's eye as he drove home the question like a nail. Judge Etheridge's delivery made it clear he considered this the very linchpin of civilization.

Caleb hesitated. His head, bald but for the ring of graying hair dutifully cut in a straight line below his ears, tilted down. His troubled gaze studied his own plain clothes, the coarse white shirt, the broad suspenders, the black wide-brimmed hat hanging in his work-worn hands, the scuffed black work boots on his feet. A chasm of history yawned wide between his brethren and the officials of the state — a history of persecution wrought by worldly governors terrified of the Amish because they did not understand them, because they mistook simplicity for anarchy and so felt threatened by the least threatening people on earth. The judge had unwittingly asked the one question that did in fact pierce straight to the heart of the matter, and yet, like Pilate's ironic question, it was one whose answer the judge would never understand. In the end, life had taught Caleb Bender it was not his responsibility to be understood, but only to speak the truth. The eyes Caleb raised to the judge were clear and calm, inscrutable. His wispy gray-tinged beard kept time with his words.

"Your Honor, I am not a citizen of this *world*."

The judge sighed heavily.

"Then you leave me no choice." His voice contained only sadness and resignation now, the anger all but gone. "I'm going to find all of you guilty as charged and sentence you to sixty days in the county jail unless and until you each pay a fine of twenty dollars per child, plus expenses, *and* submit a signed statement agreeing to comply with the conditions of the Bing Act by seeing to it that your minor children attend public school five days a week, henceforth."

His proposal drew nothing but blank stares from the five men.

"Do you understand what I'm saying?"

Caleb nodded once. "We understand you want us to sign a paper promising to send our children to school every day." The rest, in Caleb's opinion, was trivial.

The judge peered warily over his glasses.

"And will you agree to do this?"

Caleb did not hesitate, nor did he need to confer with his brethren. There was nothing to discuss.

"No, Your Honor. We will not."

"Sixty days," the judge pronounced, and banged his gavel. "Gentlemen, I'm very disappointed. You should think more of your children's futures. Rest assured, you have not heard the last of this. Bailiff, remove the prisoners."

They were allowed to stop on the way out and speak, only for a moment, with their wives. There were a few tears, but mostly what Caleb saw in the eyes of his wife, and the others, was pride.

CHAPTER 3

Three days had passed since the trial. Fifty-two days remained until Rachel's father could come home. There was a little more work to do with Dat in jail, but not so much that the family couldn't split it up and make light of it. It was a small price to pay. Rachel was up well before daylight doing chores — feeding the livestock, helping Emma with the milking, forking down fresh hay through the hay hole in the mow while her brother Aaron cleaned out the stalls.

After breakfast she rode with Aaron on the wagon when he went to spread the manure on the winter-brown stubble of the cornfield. Some steel part had broken in the spreader and they would have to do the job by hand until they could get a part made by the smith.

Working alongside her twenty-one-year-old brother, Rachel was always vaguely aware of standing in the shadow of his departed twin. They had been like a team of matched horses, Aaron and Amos, working shoulder to shoulder right up until the Spanish flu felled Amos three winters back, and left Aaron to grieve.

They were identical. The family had been able to tell the twins apart most of the time, but others found it easier to identify Amos by his harmonica. No one knew where he'd gotten it, but Amos loved to play the harmonica when he and Aaron were out working in the fields or riding someplace in the wagon, and Aaron loved to hear it. Their particular Old Order sect maintained a strict ban on musical instruments, but Amos never played his harmonica anywhere near the house, and if Caleb ever knew about it, he chose to look the other way. Right or wrong, Aaron loved it. Only Rachel and Emma knew that Amos went to his grave with his harmonica in his pocket. They were the only ones who saw Aaron put it there, and they would never tell.

Even now, after three years, Aaron would occasionally pause for a second, his head would come up and his eyes would scan the horizon as if he'd heard some distant music, but then he would close his mouth without speaking and darkness would cover him for a while. They had laughed constantly, Amos and Aaron, always playing pranks. If they weren't playing a joke on one of their sisters, they were doing it to each other.

When Amos was alive.

Aaron didn't laugh much anymore, and he always seemed to be looking for something, as if part of himself had gone missing. He could have easily handled his chores alone, but Rachel had gotten in the habit of keeping him company when she could see the loneliness on him. Anyway, it wouldn't have made sense for her to be inside helping wash dishes and scrub floors while her father was in jail. Aaron and Harvey had the men's work to do all by themselves now, and there were six sisters still living in the house.

Rachel and Aaron were in the north field, slinging straw and manure as far as their shovels would throw it, from opposite sides of the wagon. The horses, a pair of old Belgians long accustomed to this work, plodded straight down the row at a snail's pace exactly as they had been trained to do. Rachel could hear the rhythmic scrape of Aaron's shovel, and she matched it. It was more difficult for her because she was smaller and weaker, but her dat had always said hard work only makes you bigger and stronger. She tried to match him toss for toss.

But then he stopped. The sound of Aaron's shoveling ceased, and in the next few seconds she heard the soft whistle meant for the horses' ears. The two big Belgians halted in their tracks, heads down. When Rachel turned to see what was the matter, Aaron was leaning on his shovel gazing across the fields to the road, staring at a spot a half mile away, down by the cow pond.

"What is it?" Rachel asked, glad for the small breather but too proud to admit it.

Aaron pointed, and then she saw him — an Amish boy, running. He was charging up the slight grade toward the Bender house, one hand pressing his hat to his head, running as if his hair were on fire.

"That's Jake," she said, and her pulse quickened. She thought again of that day in the barn when their fathers had been arrested, when Jake had held her in his arms and comforted her. Like a man. The look in his eyes, his genuine heartfelt concern for her, brought the butterflies to her middle even now, and made her face flush. Since then, except for her dat in jail, she had thought of little else.

"Jah, I think mebbe it's Jake, all right,"

Aaron said, "but he should be home doing chores at this hour. Especially now, with his father away."

"Look how *hard* he's going!" Rachel said. "He must be bringing news."

Aaron nodded slowly. "That must be it. Something has happened. You go and find out. I'll finish here."

Rachel hit the ground flying, hitching her skirts up so she could run flat-out.

She arrived at the back door at almost the same moment Jake arrived at the front. Her mother and sisters brought him into the living room, where he stood gasping by the wood stove, bent double. He was still trying to catch his breath when Rachel came running in from the back. She was winded too, and she stopped in the kitchen doorway with her hands on her hips, her chest heaving, waiting to hear what Jake had to say.

He straightened, still panting, and scanned the roomful of women's faces watching him. Flushed with exertion, he stammered between gasps, "They came . . . for Lydia."

Mamm's brow furrowed. "Who came?"

Jake gasped like a fish, holding up a forefinger, asking for patience. "Sheriff," he managed.

"For Eli's Lydia? Stoltzfus?" Eli Stoltzfus was one of the men in jail with Rachel's father. Lydia was the eleven-year-old daughter whose name had been listed in the charges against Eli.

A vigorous nod, and then Jake finally gained control of his breathing. "They came this morning," he said, taking a deep breath, "but they didn't get her yet. Eli-Mary was afraid this would happen, so she sent Lydia to her sister's in Lancaster. Yesterday."

Mamm's shoulders visibly relaxed, and something approaching a smile came to her plump face. "Well, that's good then. All is —"

"Oh no!" Emma's eyes went wide in alarm as she was the first to see the whole picture. The rest of them stared at her.

Emma grabbed Jake's shoulder. "What did he say?" The desperation in her voice was bigger than the breach of etiquette. "The sheriff! Did he say *why* he came for Lydia?"

Jake nodded. "He had a paper. It said Eli neglected his children, and words about how he was not fit to be a father, so they were going to take away Lydia and put her in a home."

A chorus of cries went up as Rachel and her sisters saw what Emma had already seen: If the sheriff came for Lydia, he would come for the others — all the school-age children of the five men now in jail.

The list included Jake Weaver and the three youngest Bender girls, including Rachel.

"They can't *do* this!" Mamm cried, her voice rising in panic, and the exertion set her to coughing. The two youngest daughters crept in from the kitchen wiping their hands on dish towels, wanting to know what all the fuss was about.

"Jah. They can," Emma answered quietly. She had already calmed herself, already begun thinking. "They are the government. They make the laws and they have the guns. They can do whatever they want."

"Then we will run away like Lydia did!" Rachel cried out. "We can go to Aunt Susie's in Geauga County. They won't find us *there!*"

Mamm collapsed into her rocker, coughing, unable to talk. None of the men were here at the moment — Aaron was in the north field, Harvey was way down by the creek clearing a stump, and Caleb was in jail. All eyes eventually turned to Emma. They all knew — she was the one closest to her father's mind.

She shook her head sadly. "They should not go." Emma would not say "cannot go" with her mother sitting right there, though that was how Rachel heard it.

"But *why?*" Mamm asked between coughs, her eyes full of tears, her two youngest gathered under her like chicks.

Emma looked around the room from her mother to her sisters, and a great sadness came into her eyes.

"Because it's not right. Oh, sure, they could run and hide in Geauga County, but what good will come of that? Will the problem go away? No, it'll only be up to someone else to deal with it. Would you have someone else do your work, bear your burdens? That's not our way, and it's surely not Dat's way. That's why he sits in jail right now, because he had a problem and he wouldn't run from it. He would want us to stand up and face this, no matter the cost."

Her words wrenched Rachel's heart with guilt, but not enough to conquer the fear. She was terrified by the thought of being hauled away to some strange place and separated from her family.

She didn't have long to wait. A moment later they all heard the sound of an automobile motor chugging up the road. The two youngest daughters ran to the window to watch as for the second time in eight days an automobile turned into the gravel driveway and pulled up between the Bender house and the buggy shed.

Rachel's eleven-year-old sister peered out the window, then turned to the hushed crowd in the living room and said, "It's not the same one that took Dat. This one has a *star* on it."

They waited, quaking in terror, no one moving or speaking. Rachel's breath quickened. She could feel her heart pounding in her chest. She looked at her mamm's face, hoping for permission to bolt out the back, but Mamm's tear-filled eyes were on the front door.

Emma caught Rachel's attention and, as if she were reading her little sister's mind, shook her head. Then she pressed her palms together in a clear message: *Trust Gott.*

Mamm's coughing attack had abated by the time the knock came at the door, but she still didn't get up. Emma was the first to move. She opened the door to find the sheriff standing alone on the porch with a yellow paper in his hand.

"Is this the home of Caleb Bender?" he asked. The sheriff was a portly, cherry-faced man in his mid-forties, wearing a brown uniform with a badge and a hat that looked sort of like a cowboy hat. A pistol hung from his hip in a holster, and the mere sight of it sent a chill through Rachel.

Emma smiled politely and glanced around

the room at her sisters' faces. Every one of them was staring at that pistol.

"Jah," Emma said pleasantly, "this is the home of Caleb Bender. Could I please speak with you alone? Chust for a moment, please."

He hesitated for a second, but clearly no one there was trying to run or hide.

"Sure," he said.

Emma stepped out onto the porch and closed the door behind her. Rachel could hear the buzzing of soft voices but could not make out what was being said. Then she heard footsteps leaving the porch, and in a moment, coming back. The door opened again, and Emma ushered the sheriff into the room.

His gun belt was gone. Emma had talked him into leaving it in the car. Dat had always said Emma could talk the devil out of his pitchfork.

The Bender girls stood more or less in a circle around the room, their hands folded in front of them and their fear only half hidden on their faces.

"This is Martha Bender," Emma said, introducing their mother. "Wife of Caleb Bender, who is not at home right now."

"I know," the sheriff said, remembering only now to remove his hat. "I want you to

45

know this wasn't really my idea, but I have orders. Mrs. Bender, do you have a fifteen-year-old daughter named Rachel, a thirteen-year-old named Leah, and an eleven-year-old named Barbara?"

Mamm nodded and glanced up at Rachel. "Jah. They are here," she said, stifling a cough.

"I'm afraid I have to take them in."

Mother and daughters all looked pleadingly at Emma. Emma nodded, gently pressing her palms together.

Suddenly, Jake Weaver, who had remained silent until now, stepped forward and stood directly between the sheriff and Rachel.

"Take me instead," he said. "I am Jacob Weaver, son of Jonas Weaver. I'm thinking you have my name on that paper, too. Take me, and leave them go."

Rachel was stunned, and now a host of other emotions fought against the fear inside her. She could feel her face flush with the strange new excitement she had felt in the barn that day, only this time it overwhelmed her, sweeping away her fears like dry leaves in a gust. In that tumultuous moment an image flashed across her mind for the first time, clear and beautiful — a picture of herself all grown up and married to the handsome, gallant Jake Weaver.

The sheriff looked for a second as if he might waver, regret written plainly on his face.

"You're right, son, I'm afraid I have to take you, too. But the fact is, all four of you are going to have to come with me. I'm sorry, but there's a bench warrant. I have no choice in the matter, I'm just following orders. When we leave here we're going straight to your house and pick up your little brother."

Mamm grabbed her two youngest in her arms, clinging to them, and for a moment there was some question as to whether she would let her baby daughters go. This time it was Rachel who spoke to her.

"It's all right, Mamm. I'll watch over them. Emma is right. We should not run from this."

Turning to face the sheriff, Rachel buttoned her coat, checked to make sure her unruly red hair was tucked into her *kapp* properly and said simply, "I'm ready."

Rachel and her sisters rode in the back seat of the sheriff's Model T, while Jake and his brother shared the passenger seat up front. It took a half hour to reach the county children's home, a sprawling seventy-five-acre compound out in the country four miles east of Millersburg. The sheriff turned onto a long paved driveway that curved gently up a grassy hill dotted here and there with winter-bare oaks and dominated at its crest by a large, rambling one-story house, red brick trimmed in white. The car swung around the teardrop driveway in front of the house and stopped. Wide brick-lined steps led up to a shaded front porch stretching nearly all the way across the front, where a few ladder-back rocking chairs and a porch swing tried to make the place look homey. It didn't work. The grounds were clean, the grass neatly cut, but even though it was January and nothing would be in bloom anyway, Rachel couldn't help noticing the absence of flower beds and shrubs. To her Amish eyes this was clearly no home.

The sheriff herded the five of them up the steps to the front door, where they were greeted by the superintendent, a tall man in a suit.

"Good morning," he said with a smile that seemed painted on, and then he gave a small dismissive nod to the sheriff as if to say, That'll be all. I'll take it from here.

The sheriff tipped his hat and headed back down the steps to his automobile.

"Right this way," the superintendent said, ushering them into the front room, where there were comfortable chairs and hard-

48

wood floors, oil paintings of flowers on the walls. Two Englisher girls and a boy, all of them in fancy clothes, stood talking to a woman there, but they stopped talking and stared at the five Amish children as they filed past. The boy, who looked to be about twelve, flashed Rachel a curiously sinister smile, and then, when he was sure neither of the adults would see him, grimaced and dragged a forefinger across his throat.

They followed the superintendent through a door, down a long hallway and into a rectangular room off to the right. Wooden chairs lined the walls, like a doctor's waiting room, and sitting in them were seven other Amish children. An older woman dressed in white sat behind a desk in front of the window at the far end of the room. Her hair was plastered into some kind of tall hairdo with a little white nurse's hat pinned to the top. She wore a lot of makeup, and when she smiled, something about those neatly painted bright red lips seemed vaguely sinister.

"I believe you all know each other?" the superintendent said, grinning as if he thought finding friends in the same predicament would somehow make it easier to adjust to his pretty prison.

Rachel did know them. They were all there

— all the school-age children of the five men being held in the Holmes County jail — except for Lydia Stoltzfus, who had gone to Lancaster. They jumped up from their seats when the new ones came in and greeted them as if they had not seen one another in years. Rachel noticed that all of them were between the ages of ten and fifteen. For some reason the county had not taken any children younger than ten.

The nurse let them chat for a minute before she rose from her desk, spread her hands and herded them back to the chairs along the wall.

"You all need to settle down now," she said. "I don't mind if you talk a bit, but do it quietly."

The superintendent stepped out the door and closed it softly behind him. Listening, Rachel was sure she heard the click of a lock.

From long habit, the children segregated themselves — boys together on one end of the row and girls on the other, the older girls trying to console their younger siblings. Rachel, who sat nearest the boys, turned to Henry Hershberger and asked, "What is this place? What are we doing in this room?"

A shy one, Henry was reluctant to answer at first, but after he took a cautious glance at the nurse he said, in Dutch, "I'm not sure, but they said they were going to clean us up. I guess they think we're dirty."

This seemed strange to Rachel, but then everything here was strange. Suddenly it dawned on her that Henry's older brother Mose was missing. Mose was Rachel's and Jake's age and should have been taken along with his brother and sisters. Maybe he had gotten away.

Rachel leaned close and whispered as quietly as she could, "Where is Mose?"

Henry raised his hand only a few inches from his lap and timidly jabbed a forefinger toward a closed door on the other side of the room. "In there," he whispered. "They took him first."

Oh. Mose was in the next room being cleaned up, whatever *that* meant. Rachel sneaked a glance at the nurse, who seemed to be paying them very little attention. All of their talk to this point had been in Dutch, and Rachel was fairly sure the woman hadn't understood a word.

They waited for an eternity, full of curiosity about what was happening on the other side of that door. Finally, after they had sat quietly for so long that the younger ones were starting to squirm, the door opened and an Englisher boy walked through it

51

wearing matching tweed pants and coat with a white cotton shirt underneath, and a tie. There were brown city shoes on his feet. His hair was trimmed very short on the sides, left a little longer on top, and slicked down, parted in the middle. He seemed terribly upset and embarrassed, and most of them didn't know why until he came and took a seat next to Henry, his head hanging nearly in his lap.

Only then did they recognize Mose Hershberger.

His little sister began to cry. Even the boys recoiled in horror, but none of them said a word. Rachel didn't know what to say to this. Never in her wildest dreams had she imagined that such a thing could happen to Amish children in America.

She didn't even notice the two men standing in the doorway until one of them spoke.

"Who's next?" the man said. They were big men, and they wore no coats or ties, their sleeves rolled up as if for work. They looked very strong.

The girls cowered. The younger ones were all crying now. The boys shrank back against the wall, the whites of their eyes showing.

"Well then," the man said, "if nobody wants to volunteer, we'll just pick one. You!"

He pointed at Henry and crooked a finger.

"Come with us."

Poor shy Henry shook his head and looked almost as if he might start crying himself. When he didn't rise from his seat, the two men came and took him by the arms, lifting him, half dragging him into the other room. The last Rachel saw of him, he was looking back over his shoulder at his brother as if there were something he could do.

And then the door closed.

Mose would not look up. His shorn head hung low, his eyes on the floor in front of him, his hands limp in his lap, utterly humiliated. What thoughts must have been going through his head! He had taken the empty seat next to Rachel, and she turned to him now to try to console him.

"It's all right, Mose," she said in Dutch. "There was nothing you could do. It's not your fault. You did nothing wrong."

He gave his head the slightest shake, a deep and genuine grief lining his young face. He would not speak, and she knew it. There were no words.

Then she looked down the row and saw Jake's face. His jaw was set. There was fire in his eyes. His younger brother sat next to him, huddled against the wall and leaning to one side, trying to hide behind Jake. It was all too clear to Rachel what was on

Jake's mind. He would not worry about himself. Jake could endure anything, but his younger brother had always been his to watch over and it was a responsibility he did not take lightly. Jake would think only of his brother, of the humiliation that awaited him. He was searching for a way out.

Rachel followed Jake's gaze. At first she thought he was staring at the nurse behind the desk, but then she realized he was looking at the window — and the woods beyond. An ordinary window, with an ordinary latch, on the first floor. Beyond the window, the edge of the woods lay no more than a hundred yards distant. Jake and his brother could both run like the wind. If they got a three-step head start, there was not a man in this place who would be able to catch them.

But the nurse was in the way. If Jake made a move toward the window, she would call out and the men from the other room would be on him in an instant.

The nurse raised her head and smiled compassionately at Mose. "You know, you really shouldn't be upset, dear." Clown red lips cracked her powdered face in a disquieting smile. "I think you look quite handsome in your new clothes. Very nice indeed."

There was no hint of insincerity in her voice. She meant it. She had no idea what she was saying.

Jake had moved to the edge of his seat. His left hand was behind him, squeezing his little brother's knee, making sure he was paying attention. Rachel saw the desperation in his eyes. Any second now he would bolt for the window, his only thought to get William out of this place — but he hadn't thought it through. He would never make it.

Rachel thought, for the hundredth time, of that moment in her own living room when Jake had stood between her and the sheriff. *"Take me instead,"* he'd said.

Jake coiled himself on the edge of his chair, planting the balls of his feet squarely under him. She had to do something, and quickly.

Rachel pressed a hand on her younger sister's knee and mouthed the word *Stay!*

Then she stood up.

When the nurse looked up, Rachel smiled demurely and crept closer to the desk.

"I'm very sorry to bother you," she said meekly, "but I have to go."

"Go? Oh no, dear, I'm afraid you can't go. You have to stay here and wait your turn like —"

"No, I mean I have to *go.* You know . . ." Rachel pointed discreetly to the window and her voice dropped to an embarrassed whisper. "To the outhouse."

The nurse chuckled. "Oh, you poor child, we have no outhouse here. This building has indoor plumbing. The facility is just down the hall to the left. I'll unlock the door and let you go if you promise to come right back, okay?"

Rachel's face twisted in girlish confusion. "Indoor plumbing? But I wouldn't know what to . . . I've never even *seen* one of those. I don't know how it works."

It was a small lie — two of them actually — but she could repent of it later. Rachel had *seen* an indoor toilet, though she'd never used one, and she *did* know how it worked. Nevertheless, the nurse took pity on her, which was precisely the reaction she had hoped for. Rising from behind the desk, the nurse pulled a ring of keys from a drawer.

"Oh, all right," she said, laughing. "Come on, I'll show you. It'll only take a second."

She unlocked the door and followed Rachel out, locking the door behind them before hurrying down the hall. After showing Rachel the toilet she even pulled the chain and flushed it once to demonstrate how it worked before she scurried back to her post.

The scream reached the bathroom, even with the door closed, and Rachel smiled.

When she got back to the waiting room the only people in it were the nurse and the superintendent. Cold air poured in from the wide-open window, and in the fields beyond she could see a bedlam of grown men chasing Amish kids through the tall grass in every direction.

"I don't know *how* it could have happened," the nurse was saying. "I was only gone for a *minute!*"

The superintendent stood with his back to her, glaring out the window with his arms crossed on his chest. Even from behind she could see his jaw working. Rachel tiptoed into the room and took a seat, folding her hands innocently in her lap. She had promised to come straight back, and she had kept her word.

Ten minutes later her friends and sisters had been recaptured and returned to their seats in the waiting room to await their humiliation — all except for two.

Jake and William Weaver were still missing.

Chapter 4

The Holmes County jailer never had to feed his Amish inmates. He wouldn't have been able to feed them even if he had tried, for the five Amish fathers refused to accept anything from the hand of their jailers. Every morning just after daylight a buggy would pull up to the hitching rail, and one of their wives or daughters would bring a basket of food sufficient for all five men for the entire day. She would visit for as long as the jailer allowed, and then take her basket and return home. On Saturdays they received a double portion, for no wife wanted to dishonor the Sabbath with so much work, nor would they willingly miss *gma* if the biweekly services happened to be held that day.

Early on a Saturday morning Caleb's wife arrived at the jail lugging her large basket, her steps leaden, her face lined with grief and fatigue. There were dark circles under her eyes from lack of sleep and she was constantly fighting that rattling cough. It was unusual for her to come. Usually she sent Emma with the meals. Something was wrong.

"Mamm, are you all right?" Caleb asked her as the jailer unlocked the cell. She nodded weakly, handing him the cloth-covered basket and fussing with the handkerchief in her hands, unable to look him in the eye.

"You shouldn't have come," he said. "You don't need to be out in this weather. What is it? What has happened, Mamm?"

"They have taken the children," she wheezed.

Caleb nearly dropped the basket as his eyes widened and he gasped audibly.

"*Who* took them?"

"The sheriff."

"Which children? Tell me."

She named them, one by one, ending with her own. "They took them away to the children's home," she said, "and they cut the boys' hair."

"No!" The four other men, two in the cell with Caleb and two in the adjacent cell, all clung to the bars as the jailer closed the cell door in front of Martha Bender.

"They cut the boys' hair?" Reuben Miller cried out. "My boys, too?"

Martha nodded, barely able to look up. "And they took away their clothes. They dressed them in fancy clothes yet, all of them." Then she remembered, and caught the eye of Jonas Weaver. "But not your boys, Jonas. Jake and William got away."

She eyed the jailer suspiciously, and Caleb read her thoughts. Even though she was speaking Dutch and was fairly certain he couldn't understand a word, she would say no more regarding the whereabouts of the two Weaver boys. Nor did she need to. Jonas knew her well, and he would know from her tone of voice that she had spoken to his boys. They were safe, either at home or at a nearby Amish farm.

"What will we do now?" John Hershberger asked quietly from the other cell, his knuckles white on the bars.

"I think we all know what we must do now," Caleb said. They were out of options, and he knew when he was beaten.

"Mamm, listen to me. On Monday morning you must go to the courthouse and ask to speak to the judge."

"Oh no, I couldn't do that!" she said, shaking her head in horror. "What would I say to him? He wouldn't talk to me anyway."

Caleb nodded gravely. "Jah, he will speak to you. This man knows one of us will come to him. Who do you think ordered our children to be taken away? Tell him we will do what he asks. He knows we have no choice now."

Eli Stoltzfus laid a hand on Caleb's shoulder. "We cannot do this," he said, his voice thick with anger. "It is against the *ordnung*."

Caleb's burning eyes leveled on Eli, and he thought for a moment of saying to him, It is mighty easy for you to talk about the ordnung when your daughter is safe in Lancaster. But he held his tongue. Such words would only cause strife now, and they could not afford to be divided.

"We have no choice," he repeated, as calmly as he could manage. "Before, we chose to be in jail rather than have our children go to the consolidated school. Now we have a different choice. We must choose whether to let our children be in the worldly school five days a week, or to let them be raised in the children's home *all the time.* We must choose the lesser of the two evils."

"The lesser of two evils," Eli said, "is still an evil."

It seemed cruel and punitive beyond measure, but when Martha Bender finally met with the judge, he gave orders for the five men to appear in court again on a day nearly two weeks off, and in the meantime the children would remain in the children's home.

The minutes and days were as an eternity for the men in the jail, but the day finally came. They stood once again in court, this time with their heads hanging in abject defeat. The judge levied fines against them all, and they were made to say out loud in front of the court that they would agree to send their children to school and allow them to study the prescribed subjects. And then, right there in the courtroom in front of their wives, they signed a paper agreeing to do this. They had no choice. They were utterly defeated.

The next day, on a Saturday in late January, the children came home. Caleb was standing on his front porch watching, and he saw the automobile chugging up the road from a long way off. He called out to Mamm, and by the time the automobile stopped in the driveway of the Bender house, the entire family had gathered on the front lawn to welcome the girls home.

Rachel got out first, from the passenger side of the car, with her copper hair hanging down her back in long braids. She was wearing shiny black leather shoes with brass buckles, and a green gingham dress that came up almost to her knees. Her younger sisters followed her like ducklings, hiding in her shadow, clearly ashamed of the way they were dressed. The three of them walked around the car with their heads down, unable to look anyone in the eye, angling across the yard toward the steps, heading directly for the house with the obvious intention of bypassing their family while they were in such a state.

The whole family shared in the humiliation, but no one spoke. No one moved. Caleb's heart burned within him and he was filled with a desire to lift his baby daughters off their feet in a great roaring bear hug right there in front of everybody, but he didn't do it. It would not have been proper, and it was not what they expected of him. As Rachel passed he couldn't stop his hand from reaching out to her, and her shoulder just brushed under his fingertips. She didn't look up, even then, but kept walking quickly, resolutely. As the car backed out, Caleb and his family fell in step behind the girls.

As soon as they were inside, the three girls asked to go up to the room they shared. Mamm went with them, and ten minutes later Rachel came back down the stairs looking like herself. Gone were the green dress and the downcast gaze, and her hair was once again neatly pinned under her prayer kapp. Smiling contentedly, she carried three Englisher dresses bundled in her arms, and when she got to the bottom of the stairs she turned left instead of right. Without a word, she passed through the kitchen on the way to the back door, lifting a box of kitchen matches from a drawer on her way out.

Chuckling softly, Caleb followed her. He picked up a can of kerosene from the back porch and fell in behind his beautiful red-haired daughter as she marched straight to the burn pile down behind the barn.

CHAPTER 5

The next morning Rachel and her family huddled together under a pile of buggy robes in the surrey while Caleb drove to the home of Uri Mullet up near Apple Creek. The horse's breath chuffed little clouds on the frosty air as it trotted, head high, glad to be running on such a morning. Mamm was not with them. Unable to breathe lying down, she had sat up all night next to the stove in her rocker. Dat told her to stay home and rest rather than make the drive on such a frosty morning in an open buggy. He was uncharacteristically silent while he drove, his face lined with worry.

After two weeks in the children's home, Rachel's first morning at church felt almost as good as her first day back home. All the familiar things — the pile of black hats on the mud room table, the backless benches, the dark curtains tied back to let in clean winter sunlight, the singing, the old bishop's singsong preaching, and especially the faces of all the people she loved — all of it felt as fine and warm as home itself.

Jake Weaver was there, sitting across from her — and so was his hair, she noted with a twinge of selfish pride. The other boys had not been so lucky, but it was only hair — it would grow back. No one blamed them for what had happened.

She hadn't seen Jake since that first day at the children's home, nor had she bumped into him before the service began, but he was here now, sitting alongside his father and brothers. The mere sight of him filled her with joy. Once, before the minister got warmed up, she caught Jake sneaking a glance in her direction. She averted her eyes quickly, but she knew. He was looking for her. She sat a little straighter, held her head a little higher and took pains not to let her gaze linger on him. Until she turned sixteen, even such innocent flirtation would meet with dire disapproval. Besides, even now she suffered the natural insecurities of a fifteen-year-old girl, and Jake had really said nothing of his feelings. How could she be sure that Jake's gentle caress that day in the barn hadn't merely been brotherly consolation over her father's arrest?

■ ■ ■ ■

After the service Rachel and her family went outside to wait for a bit while the Mullets and their kin prepared lunch. She lined up at the privy with the rest of the women. The men, in order not to make the line at the outhouse uncomfortably long for the women, gravitated to the barn to use the unoccupied stalls.

Rachel kept an eye on the group of men going in and out of the barn, but she didn't see Jake. He must have stayed behind with some of the men and older boys who remained in the house to help set up tables.

A short while later everyone went back inside for lunch. Each of the long tables held three big bowls of *bohnesuppe* — it was called bean soup, though it consisted of mostly bread and milk — enough so that everyone could reach one of the hot bowls without having to pass them around. There were loaves of fresh homemade bread and newly churned butter, and for dessert what the children called "moon pies" — half-moon-shaped fruit pies, usually filled with apple snitz.

For Rachel and the others who had been the last two weeks in the children's home eating strange food, it was wonderful. To be back among family, breaking bread in a warm Amish home with so many who had shared so much, Ida Mullet's weak bean soup was a feast for which Rachel was truly grateful. School or no school, life was good.

After lunch she went outside with a dozen girls and wandered down to the other side of the kitchen garden to catch up on the latest gossip. Lovina Hershberger was there, along with the others who had been imprisoned with Rachel and her sisters in the children's home. Lovina had always been like a sister to Rachel and Emma, and on this day the girls who had been in the children's home were the center of attention. Everyone peppered them with questions, endlessly curious about life in that awful place.

"Did they beat you?" a little girl asked. There were several smaller children with them, including a toddler or two. The older girls were expected to help tend the little ones.

"Every day, twice," Lovina said, her eyes twinkling with mischief. She leaned close to the little girl and added in a whisper, "With barbed wire." Then she burst into hysterical laughter.

Rachel wagged her head. "No they didn't.

You shouldn't scare the poor child like that, Lovina. Really, it wasn't that bad. Most of them were nice. We had warm beds to sleep in, and a hot bath on Saturday."

Still chuckling, Lovina said, "The worst of it is now we have to go to school every day."

"I won't," a six-year-old said, stamping a foot. "I'll run and hide in the loft."

"No you won't," Rachel warned. "Our fathers gave their word. They made a promise. Would you make a liar of them? Besides, if you don't go to school, the attendance officer will know and then they'll come and put your dat in jail."

Tears welled up in the little girl's eyes. "But *why?*" she whined. "Why must we do this?"

"Because they don't understand," Lovina answered patiently. "You know what they said? One of the women in the children's home told me we had to go to school because it was cruel of our parents to make us work on the farm."

They all laughed at that. Home was home. They had seen enough of the world to know they were far more likely to encounter cruelty in the consolidated school.

"Cruel?" the little girl giggled, her eyes wide in disbelief. "How could anyone think that?"

"I don't know," Rachel said. "I think they only know how to look at us the same way they look at each other. My dat says a prideful man thinks everyone is vain, and a deceiver thinks everyone is a liar. Anyway, most Englishers are in such a hurry they don't want to take the trouble to understand someone who is different from them. They don't think the way we do, that's all."

Caleb Bender stayed at his table when lunch was over, as did most of the men. The women chatted happily, busy with cleaning up, hustling dishes to the kitchen and wiping the tables clean.

The minister sat down next to Caleb and asked after Martha. "I noticed she is not here this morning," he said. "Has she gotten worse?"

"Jah," Caleb said. "I even took her to the doctor once, but he didn't give us much hope. There was nothing he could do. He said she needs to go and live someplace where the air is dry and warm, like Arizona."

The minister nodded gravely.

What Caleb did not say, *would* not say, was that the doctor had told him she would die if he did not do this. Though the doctor would never understand it, Caleb knew that moving to a place with no Amish community was not an option. He could only pray that Gott would not allow her to die, but when she left the bed in the night to sit upright by the stove, the doctor's words tormented him.

Caleb twisted his water glass on the table, staring at it. "What will we do now?" he asked, mostly to change the subject. "About the schools, I mean."

"We will trust Gott," the minister said firmly. This was always his first answer.

"Always," Caleb agreed. "Still, there are choices we must make. Will we be content to send our children to the consolidated school forever? I think it would be the end of us."

Eli Stoltzfus, the man whose daughter hid in Lancaster, rolled his eyes. "*Neh*. I say we ignore them and do as we have always done. In time the government will get busy with something else and forget us. They always do."

Caleb shook his head. "No, they won't forget. We have already seen what comes of that thinking. Anyway, we made a promise. Now we must keep it."

"Then you have no choice but to honor your word," the bishop agreed, one fist stroking his long white beard as if he were milking it. "But just because we have no

71

choice does not mean we become complacent. For now, we must pray and ask Gott to show us a way. We must think of our children, the future of our people and our way of life. If we bring them up in the way they should go, when they are old they will not depart from it. But if we let them be raised by the world, why it's only a matter of time until they leave us and go their own way. No matter how we love them, most of them will jump the fence. Caleb is right. If we let this go on, in twenty years there won't be any more Amish."

"It won't last forever," John Hershberger said. "Things will change, you'll see. We just have to endure for a time."

Caleb Bender shook his head sadly. "For how long a time, John? I say only until we can find a way to change things. This is a new problem, one we have not dealt with before, at least not in this way. We have to learn to think in new ways, to see a new path. We have to think bigger and wider and be willing to pay any price to save our children. We can even leave here if we have to, and start another settlement someplace where the law is not against us."

"Oh, I could never do that," Jonas Weaver said. "My grandparents were born here and they are buried here, along with my first wife and two of my children." He wagged his head, deeply aggrieved. "It is too much of a price to pay, Caleb."

Caleb laid a hand on Jonas's forearm and replied gently, "What price would you put on living as Gott would have us live? What is heaven worth?"

The bishop and the minister nodded somberly. The results of such decisions could be the difference between heaven and hell for many.

One of the men who was young and sometimes a little hasty said, "Mebbe we could get our people to vote, this once, to elect public officials who think as we do and who will change things for us."

Caleb had heard this argument before. Some of the more liberal sects did not prohibit voting, but this branch of the Old Order Amish was firmly against it.

The bishop leveled a hard gaze on the young man, and for a moment Caleb thought there would be a tongue-lashing, but the bishop was old enough to be patient with the young.

"Would we try to rule as the greedy do?" he asked. "Will we try to grab power over other people's possessions? What fellowship has righteousness with unrighteousness, and what communion hath light with darkness?

On the day we do such as that we become like everyone else, and the battle is already lost."

"There has to be a way," Caleb Bender said, shaking his head. "Mebbe Gott will show us."

The boys split up into cliques after lunch as well, the younger ones playing some kind of chasing game up near the house and the older ones in a group down beside the barn. Rachel could see Jake from a distance, leaning back against the wall of the barn, one foot planted against the boards, his hands in his pockets. She could tell just by watching the other boys in the group, the way they all looked to Jake, he'd gained a new stature among them by virtue of his harrowing escape from the children's home. By now he'd probably told the story a dozen times. He was a hero.

In midafternoon Rachel saw her father coming around the barn with the surrey, so she said a quick goodbye to her friends and followed her sisters up toward the driveway. She didn't see Jake until she was crossing the yard behind the house and he casually stepped out from behind a tree, nearly bumping into her. As if it were accidental.

Their paths only intersected for a second,

and Jake was glancing around, looking everywhere but at her. She didn't know if he would even acknowledge her until he whispered, with his eyes elsewhere, "Will you be here tonight?"

The singing. The youth always gathered on the Sunday evening after church services for singing. She had heard Emma say she was coming.

"Jah," she said, and their eyes met for a split second.

"Gut." Jake nodded, and moved on. He barely even smiled, and then he was gone. She understood his caution; on Sunday, among the church crowd, nothing went unnoticed.

But sometimes, after the singing, the chaperones looked the other way.

Bundled with her sisters in the back of the surrey on the way home, Rachel could hardly contain her excitement. Though only for a moment, he had made contact. He had spoken to her. That was all that mattered.

CHAPTER 6

There were chores to do even on Sunday, so Rachel kept herself busy most of the afternoon, although it didn't help all that much. She hummed constantly as she went about her chores, counting the minutes until she could go back up to the Mullet farm for the singing, and every time she thought about Jake Weaver it seemed her feet barely touched the ground. She dreamed of a time when they would be older and able to be together, perhaps to hold hands in the back of a buggy on a chaperoned date. She dared not think of kissing. Even the thought, at her age, was surely sinful.

Time dragged by until finally the hour came and Emma called to her. There would be three others with Rachel in the surrey — Emma, at twenty practically engaged to Levi Mullet; then Miriam, eighteen and still unattached; and Harvey, the mischievous seventeen-year-old brother who had always considered Rachel the spoiled baby of the family. Leah and Barbara were too young, and Aaron had not attended a singing since the death of his twin.

Harvey took the reins, and Rachel sat up front beside him. There was mischief in his eyes, and halfway to the Mullet farm he leaned close to Rachel and whispered, "I saw you making eyes at Jake this morning."

"You did not," she said firmly, but she blushed the color of her hair and his grin widened.

Just like in the morning service, the boys sat facing the girls, though this was a much smaller gathering because most of the adults were absent. The grown-ups stayed home with the infants and toddlers who needed to get to bed early, giving the teenage girls an evening off from baby-sitting duties. The singing was a time specially set aside for the teenagers, and there were social nuances that they all learned very quickly. A boy who was interested in a girl would jockey for a seat directly across from the object of his desire and try to catch her eye. During the singing, the girls all watched to see who was smiling at whom. Any new infatuation would be the object of endless whisperings over the next two weeks, until the next meeting.

Rachel sat in the second row next to Emma, watching. When Jake Weaver wandered in among a throng of older teenage boys and ousted his cousin from a seat directly across from Rachel, she noticed. Emma noticed, too. Leaning forward a little she smiled knowingly at the flush of excitement on Rachel's face. Secrets did not last long among people who knew each other so well.

With so few adults in attendance Rachel was able to steal discreet glances in Jake's direction occasionally, and twice during the singing she caught him looking directly at her.

Something in the way Jake looked at her felt completely different from the other boys his age. Subtler. There was nothing brash or childish in the gesture. Even at fifteen, Jake's countenance held something she had not seen in the others. Where most teenage boys tended to boast and challenge, strutting their colors like a peacock, Jake's face held only a calm knowing, a patient confidence. It still surprised her to see a man where there had always been a boy before, as if overnight he had grown taller and become something very different.

It was dark outside by the time the singing ended. Despite the cold, the young people drifted outside and mingled, although they did it so slowly and cautiously that the pairings seemed purely accidental. Groups of boys and groups of girls began to break apart almost imperceptibly, and individuals drifted toward each other. While all the adults were in the house pretending not to notice, boys and girls who didn't even appear to see each other at first somehow found themselves standing beside each other. Then they spoke, just a word or two of simple greeting. Then, two by two, they eased away toward the barn or to the back of the buggy shed, or out behind the smokehouse.

Rachel turned around and Jake was there. His back was to her, but then he glanced over his shoulder as if surprised and said, "Oh, hello, Rachel."

"Jake." She nodded, straining with the effort of sounding nonchalant. She could hear her heart thumping.

"I haven't seen you since that day at the children's home," he said casually. "I hope they didn't treat you too bad."

"No," she said, fiddling demurely with the dangling laces of her kapp. "It was nothing."

Casting a backward glance across the

yard, he began moving slowly toward a dark corner of the house where the light from the windows didn't reach. She found herself walking beside him.

"We have to take care who sees us," he said softly, an unnecessary explanation. "We are too young."

"We're almost sixteen."

"Jah, but only almost."

In the semidarkness around the corner they stopped, facing each other but not touching. She could barely make out his face. He was silent for too long, and kept peeking around the corner at the backyard, lit only by a kerosene lantern hanging by the door, as if he wanted to say something important and was afraid someone might hear. Her mind spun off all sorts of possibilities while she waited. Finally, he stammered out some words.

"I . . . Rachel, I can't get it out of my head. I just wanted to say thank you for what you did at the children's home."

"What? I didn't do anything."

"You got that nurse out of the way for me."

She blushed. "I needed to go, that's all."

"You did not. And you shouldn't lie on Sunday."

"You shouldn't lie anytime," she said.

"But I went, just the same, so I must have needed to."

"Well. I'm not dumb. I know what I saw, and I knew what you were thinking. You did it on purpose, and you did it for me. I thank you for that."

He was definitely not dumb.

"You would have done the same for me." This was not idle flattery. *"Take me,"* he had said to the sheriff.

Again, he fell silent for too long, thinking.

Finally, out of the darkness his voice said softly, "I would do a great many things for you."

Rachel was too stunned to reply. She could feel her face flushing deeply red and was glad for the covering darkness.

He had not so much as offered to touch her hand up to this point, behavior quite unlike what she expected from a boy. Now, without the slightest hint of haste or childish uncertainty, he slowly removed his wide hat, and lifting her hand very gently in his, he brushed a kiss, light as a spider web, on the backs of her fingers.

Then he snugged his hat back on his head and, without another word, turned and walked back into the light.

She remained where she was for a moment because she didn't trust her legs.

"And I you," she whispered to his back, but only after he was too far away to hear.

As the host family, it was the Mullets' responsibility to chaperone the teenagers on the night of the singing, and they could only look the other way for so long. Soon the adults filed out the back door, three of them carrying kerosene lanterns. They talked and laughed loudly, swinging their lanterns and making a general ruckus so everyone would hear and know that it was time to go. Within a minute, little groups appeared from all directions, merging into the lantern light to shake hands and say their formal goodbyes.

The evening was officially over. Riding home in the darkness huddled under a blanket in the back of the surrey, Rachel said nothing. A million questions swirled through her mind. She owned none of the answers, but the questions consumed her.

CHAPTER 7

The consolidated school was more than three miles from the Bender house, an hour's brisk walk each way, and unless the weather was harsh — in which case Emma would drive them to school in the buggy — Rachel and her two younger sisters would have to walk it five days a week, lunch pails in hand. She might have been able to talk her father into letting her hitch an old horse to the hack and drive it to school but she never brought it up. The walk was good exercise and it would have been hard on the horse, having to wait all day tied under a tree. And though she would never have said it, there was another reason Rachel didn't mind the walk.

She would be going right past Jake's house.

As it happened, the first time she walked to the consolidated school, Jake and his younger brother set out from home at the

very moment Rachel happened to be passing by.

It was almost as if he'd been watching for
her.

The boys fell in step with Rachel and her
sisters.

"Morning," the younger brother said.

Jake just sort of nodded.

"Good morning," Rachel answered, shooting Jake a cautious glance. After last night
she couldn't help wondering — was he only
being shy, or had the light of day already
changed his mind about her?

She got an answer soon enough. Jake
looked around her at the others and said,
"Don't let us hold you back. I know you
children would rather walk a little faster."

His little brother glanced at him twice in
confusion before he took the hint.

"Oh, *now* I see!" He snickered, but then
he broke into a trot and quickly opened up
a fifty-yard space between them. Rachel's
sisters took the hint too and ran after him.

Still, Jake didn't say anything for a while.
After a few minutes Rachel couldn't take
the silence anymore.

"Jake," she said hesitantly, "about last
night. What exactly did it mean?"

"Oh, that," Jake said, and then went on
another few paces while he thought about

it. "I meant what I said. I thought you did a brave thing and I wanted to thank you for it."

She stared at him for a second. "I wasn't talking about what you *said*."

"Oh. The other thing, then."

She waited patiently.

"I'm sorry if I was too bold, or I embarrassed you or something." He shrugged, but he avoided eye contact and his face flashed crimson. "I didn't mean nothing by it."

Now she had inadvertently painted herself into a corner and left herself no way to answer. If she said she was glad he didn't mean anything by it, he might think she didn't like him. But if she told him she *wanted* it to be something more, he would think she was too forward. This romance business was entirely too complicated.

"Okay," she said flatly.

Walking to school beside Jake every day was a gift from heaven. They only walked and talked — they dared not touch or hold hands, because William and Leah and Barbara were there. They would have told and then there would have been trouble. But being able to spend an hour walking with Jake was almost worth having to go to school every day.

Almost. Up to now they had always gone

to a little one-room schoolhouse near home where all the children were Amish, but at the consolidated school the classes were mixed — that is, there were a few Amish children and a great many Englishers. She had to learn to deal with a fair amount of teasing about her Amish clothes, yet Rachel counted her own trials as nothing compared with what the boys had to face. Some of the English boys brought with them the rantings of fathers who said the Amish were cowards because some of them had refused to wear a uniform or pick up a gun in the recent Great War. More than once Jake came home with his clothes torn from being shoved around on the playground. He would not fight back, which only served to reinforce the other boys' suspicion of cowardice and make things worse for him.

"And all of this," Jake said bitterly, walking home nursing a black eye one afternoon, "because the government thinks it would be cruel for us to work with our fathers on the farm."

It didn't last long. Three weeks after they started going to the consolidated school, Jake turned sixteen. The next day his father acquired a work exemption for him and he didn't go to school anymore. At the singing that Sunday night he and Rachel managed to slip away for a minute.

"I miss walking to school with you," Rachel told him, "but I'm glad you don't have to go anymore. I only wish I didn't have to."

Caleb Bender watched his daughters leave the house every morning, strolling down the road on their way to school, swinging their lunch pails. When he saw them, no matter where he was or what he was doing, he stopped, took his hat off and held it against his chest while he said a brief, earnest prayer asking his Gott to show him another way. And it wasn't just his own children he prayed for, but all the others who were being trained and immersed in worldly ways every day, abducted from their parents' upbringing against their will. He could see no end to it. It would never stop. This would go on and on, with his children's children, and their children too, and so on until there *were* no more plain people. To outsiders it seemed innocuous enough, but Caleb was wise enough to see that if Amish children were forced to spend most of their time in English schools, in a generation or two there would be no Amish left.

It broke his heart, and it hardened his resolve.

When he had finished his brief, hard prayer he would put his hat on and turn his hands to whatever the day demanded of him. But Caleb Bender had been a farmer all his life and his hands, like a well-trained mule, knew their own way. His work seldom required much of his mind, so while he walked a fence line with a pair of pliers and a roll of wire, he was free to think about the school dilemma. While he chopped up a dead fall for firewood, he was probing, and while he worked a new horse or roamed the woods hunting deer, his mind was ranging far and wide searching for a way to rescue the children from the grip of the world without breaking his word. In time it became inescapably clear that as long as he stayed in Ohio he would be bound by the law, and by his promise.

He was not averse to leaving Ohio — after all, it was persecution that drove the Amish to America in the first place. But history also told him that even a move to another Amish settlement in Pennsylvania or Indiana would provide only a temporary solution. If one state passed such a law, sooner or later they all would.

He just couldn't see a way out.

Caleb's mind was occupied with these things on a Thursday morning in mid-

February when he hitched up his buggy and drove down to Kidron for the livestock auction. At the auction he spoke with at least a dozen brethren he knew very well, and all of them were scratching their heads and wagging their beards over the same issue. It was the main topic of conversation at the sale, yet none of them could see a way out.

Caleb found nothing he wanted at the auction — it was always a little slow this time of year — but when the sale ended he was deep in discussion with his good friend the blacksmith, so he walked with him over to the hardware store. The blacksmith needed to buy a new knife for trimming hooves. He weighed various knives while they talked, hefting each in his hand to gauge the strength and balance of it, and when he had made his choice he went to the counter to pay for it. Caleb waited for him by the door, staring absently through the glass. As he stood there an Amish girl passed by on her way home with a lunch pail in her hand, and from the back she looked so much like his Rachel that he instinctively pulled the hat from his head, right there in the store, and sent up a silent, fervent plea for his Gott to show him another way.

Then he put his hat back on his head and

turned to his right where he saw his reflection in the glass case covering a bulletin board. It was just a cork board with pieces of paper pinned to it announcing horses and mules for sale, offering the services of cobblers and tinkers and well diggers. But there in the middle of his face, as his eyes refocused to see the board behind the glass, was a folded piece of paper bearing a bold one-word headline that caught his eye and would, he knew instantly, alter the course of his life.

MEXICO.

Underneath that, in smaller letters, were the words LAND FOR SALE.

It was an answer, a sign — he recognized that still small voice, the incendiary subtlety. A little shiver ran through him.

Caleb swung the glass door open by its wooden knob, and his hand shook as he reached in and pulled the tack from the pamphlet. He didn't wait for Irvin. Holding the paper close to his face with both hands he hurried outside into the bright sunlight so he could read the small print without his glasses. The front page said:

Paradise Valley — five thousand acres of prime, flat, fertile farmland nestled in the Sierra Madre of northeastern Mexico, only a hundred miles from the American border.

Five thousand acres. Enough for *many* Amish farms. Before now, he had not thought in terms of a whole group of Amish migrating to another place, but if there was plenty of land, why not? There were lots of others who felt the same way he did.

And then another thought struck him, and it brought a tear to his eye.

Martha.

Mexico was a dry place! In Mexico, his Martha might be able to get better!

This was too good to be true, too perfect. Opening the pamphlet he read the finer print on the inside, skipping and scanning in a feverish search for hard facts.

Ten dollars an acre, it said. Cheap. There had to be a catch. Probably desert land, where they would all starve.

Green pasture. Elevation six thousand feet, spring-like weather year round, long planting season. Warm days, cool nights.

Green pasture. Caleb looked up with a kind of wonder in his eyes, and his lips worked silently over words from the *Heilige Schrift,* words in High German so ingrained he could not remember a time when he didn't know them.

"Er weidet mich auf einer grünen Aue."

He maketh me to lie down in a green pasture.

Flipping over to the back of the brochure, his forefinger traced a line to the bottom, where he found what he was looking for.

Laredo Land Brokers, Ltd.
Laredo, Texas
Local agent: Avery Fiedler
Morgan-Fiedler Real Estate
109 Main St.
Kidron, Ohio

Less than two blocks away. Caleb headed down Main Street with a fire in his heart and a purpose in his stride, the pamphlet clenched tight in his fist. Only when he laid his hand on the doorknob of the Morgan-Fiedler Real Estate offices did he look back up the street and remember that in his haste he had simply walked off and left his friend in the hardware store.

Avery Fiedler was not what Caleb expected in a real-estate agent, a man who sat behind a desk and made his living by selling other people's homes. He was a tidy, clean-shaven little man in a three-piece wool suit, but despite his prim appearance and his office job, Fiedler gave a firm handshake. The office was neat and clean too, the desktop clear but for a blotter and inkstand. The walls were mostly covered with maps of the surrounding countryside dotted with stick-pins, marking, Caleb assumed, the properties Morgan-Fiedler represented.

"What can I do for you?" Avery asked. He asked this quietly, sincerely, without the proud, brassy tone Caleb had come to expect from salesmen.

Caleb held out the brochure. "Can you tell me about this?"

Avery took the pamphlet from his hand and opened it.

"I sure can. A Mr. Marlon Harris, from Laredo, came by here on his way to Canada last week and left this with me. I figured the best thing to do was post it at the hardware store where some Amish farmer might see it." He smiled at Caleb, and it seemed a very genuine smile. "It appears I was right."

"This Paradise Valley," Caleb said, "have you seen it?"

"Oh no, I haven't been to Mexico, but Mr. Harris said he went down there and looked it over. He had nothing but good things to say about it. There's a road right down the middle of the property, longways. Lots of road frontage on both sides. Perfect climate. Even though it's south of the border, it's not too hot because it's so high up, but not too high to grow crops. Mountains on three sides and good black dirt, he said. Volcanic origin, if I understood him right. He said you could grow just about anything there if you knew how to irrigate. If there's a drawback to the place, I guess that would be it — there's not much surface water. No creeks or rivers on the land at all."

"How much rain do they get?"

"Enough, I suppose. All I know is it's not desert. From what I understand the really arid country is in the lowlands, not the mountains. Right now this parcel belongs to some Mexican cattle baron who used to use it for pasture, and Mr. Harris said it was greener than anything around Laredo. Big ranch called Hacienda El Prado."

"Why would this Harris fella come all the way to Ohio to try and sell a piece of Mexico when he lives right there in Texas?"

"What he told me, Mr. Bender, is he figured it might be a hard sell because, well, you know . . . it's in Mexico." He said this with raised eyebrows and a little shrug. Something in his eyes led Caleb to wonder if maybe there was something he wasn't saying.

"Besides, everybody wants electric lights these days, and this place is out in the middle of nowhere in the mountains where, who knows, they might *never* get electricity.

But Marlon Harris, being an enterprising young man, knew this wouldn't be a concern for the Amish. Since he was heading to Canada anyway, and his train would be passing through Amish country, he figured it wouldn't do any harm to put the word out."

Fiedler's explanation seemed sensible enough, but the land itself still sounded too good to be true.

"If the land is so gut, why would they sell it so cheap?"

Fiedler took a deep breath, blew it out through puffed cheeks. "That I honestly don't know, friend, but I try not to look a gift horse in the mouth. Maybe the owner is in some financial difficulty, who knows? But if it's anywhere near as fine a parcel as Marlon Harris claims, then I'd say their loss is your gain."

Caleb stood there thinking, holding the brochure open in his rough hands, studying it. There was even a crude map on the inside.

"What about schools?" he asked.

Fiedler scratched his head, winced. "I wouldn't know much about that," he said, "but I suspect they're not going to be anywhere near as good as what we've got in the States. Our neighbors to the south are a little behind us in some ways. For all I know they may not even *have* a school system."

"You don't say." A little smile relaxed Caleb's face, studying the brochure.

"Oh, wait . . ." Avery Fiedler said, and the light of recognition came into his eyes. "I read about the problems between the Amish and the school system. It was in the papers. Some of your people were arrested, weren't they?"

Caleb nodded. "I was one."

"Ahhh. *Now* I see. So you're wanting to know if there's any chance you might run into the same problems in Mexico. To be honest, Mr. Bender, I don't know what their laws are in that regard. But Marlon Harris can answer your questions a lot better than I can. If you're seriously interested, I might be able to arrange a meeting next week. When his train comes back through I can probably hold him here if you want to talk to him."

Caleb nodded firmly. "Yes. If you could do that, I would like it very much."

CHAPTER 8

Caleb Bender stopped off at four different farms on his way home from Kidron that Thursday afternoon, showing them the brochure and spreading the news of his discovery. He could hardly contain his excitement. The prospect of good, rich, cheap land in Mexico, where the government would not force its schools on Amish children, kindled a fire in him.

He said nothing to his neighbors about the other reason for his excitement — his wife, Martha. Caleb tended to keep such thoughts private, for he had been taught from birth that whether one lived or died was entirely in the hands of Gott. But Caleb adored his wife. He was terrified of losing her and he thought, just maybe, the brochure was Gott's way of telling him how to save her.

The meeting with the land agent from Texas was only a little more than a week away, but all he had to do was put out the word on Sunday and let the Amish grapevine do its work. The news spread like a prairie fire.

The following Saturday afternoon a line of buggies stretched down Caleb's back lot well past the barn. Chairs and benches from every part of the house were packed into the living room, and there was a great scraping of wooden chairs as Amishmen filed in and found seats. Precisely at one o'clock, as promised, Avery Fiedler's automobile pulled into the Benders' driveway and the two real-estate agents made their way into the crowded house.

Marlon Harris was a tall Texan, the biggest man in the room. He wore a strange-looking tan suit with wide lapels trimmed in a darker brown, a string tie with a clasp made of silver inlaid with turquoise and coral, and a hat with a flat brim and slightly rounded dome. Apart from the buckskin color and the narrow band proudly displaying the name Stetson, his hat looked an awful lot like something an Old Order Amishman would wear. Smiling, Marlon Harris seemed right at home, and indeed came across as the kind of man who would be right at home virtually anywhere.

After the introductions were done, Caleb quieted the crowd as best he could, and began. Uncomfortable as he was with speaking before such a crowd, his discomfort was doubled by having to do it in English for the benefit of his two guests.

"Brethren, what we come here to talk about today is our problem with the schools. I don't like it, and I don't think anybody likes it much that our *kinder* are made to go to the consolidated school every day, mix all the time with Englisher children, and learn things we don't want them to learn. So last week when I found out about this land in Mexico" — he held up the brochure, though most had already seen it — "I'm thinking mebbe it is an answer to prayer. But I don't know nearly so much about it as Mr. Harris here, who is from Texas and has been to see the land with his own eyes, so I'll chust let him talk."

"Well now," Marlon Harris said, rising to his impressive height, his booming voice a little overwhelming in the crowded living room. "Gentlemen, Avery here has told me all about your troubles with the schools in Ohio, and I've got good news for you. The government in Mexico couldn't care less where your young'uns go to school. Or even *if* they go. In Mexico you can do whatever

99

you like. You can run your *own* schools for all they care."

He rubbed his hands together, smiling a little too broadly. He had their attention now. "So let me tell you about this parcel of land for sale in Paradise Valley. I've seen it myself, and boys, it's a peach. We're talking about five thousand acres of rich black dirt at six thousand feet in the temperate belt of the lovely state of Nuevo León, the jewel of Mexico. You can grow wheat year-round on this place. The whole thing is flat as a cow pond and hardly a tree or a rock in sight — ready to plow, and so soft you could turn it with a boat paddle. And it's yours for a mere ten dollars an acre."

He spread his hands and looked around the room. "Questions?"

Caleb Bender looked around the room too, at the faces. Marlon Harris smelled of tobacco and cologne, and his flashy style made him look like a huckster, an outsider trying to sell them a bill of goods. Too many of them were already looking at him a little sideways, their arms crossed on their chests.

At first no one even ventured a question, but then a man from down near Maysville, sitting in the back, raised his hand and cleared his throat.

"Everybody knows Mexico is a hot, dry

place, full of rocks and snakes. You can't grow nothing but cactus. Why would a farmer want to go there?"

Harris put on the patient smile of a schoolteacher, shaking his head. "Now, I'm gonna tell you the truth — yeah, *some* of Mexico is like that, in fact a good bit of it, especially in the low country, but we're talkin' about a mountain valley, high up in the Sierra Madre Orientals. Just wait till you see it! I'm telling you it's an oasis, fellas, cool and green year-round."

There were skeptical glances. Jonas Weaver raised a hand.

"How far is the closest produce market?"

"Great question! Paradise Valley is about fifty miles from Saltillo, where they've got a real nice market. Now, I know that's a long way in a wagon, but the *good* news is, they're already drawing up plans to extend the rail line down from Saltillo to where it'll run within a few miles of Paradise Valley. You can see it for yourself on the map in the brochure. The dotted line represents the proposed route for the new rail line. When that goes in, why, the market will only be an hour away by rail. You'll be able to haul your goods to Saltillo and be back home the same night."

Harris seemed to be gaining a little ground

until a cabinetmaker from up around Wooster raised his hand.

"What about the war?" he asked.

Marlon Harris threw his head back and laughed. "Where you been, boy? Why, the revolution's been pretty much over for two years now! Things are calm as can be."

Even Caleb raised an eyebrow, and the cabinetmaker persisted.

"Mr. Harris, I'd like to know how a revolution could be 'pretty much' over. Is there war or not?"

"Well, truth is, the war ended a while back, but some of the revolutionaries didn't go home. The thing is, Pancho Villa's army in the north was made up mostly of rabble from the border towns — brigands and thieves even *before* the revolution — and some of them enjoyed the looting and pillaging so much they kept on doing it after the fighting was over. So now they've got a slight problem with little groups of bandits roaming around, but the new government is working on it. From what I hear, it's quieted down a lot just in the last year or so."

This was news to Caleb. He'd heard rumors, but nothing this concrete. There were skeptical glances, and some of the men began to whisper among themselves in Dutch. Fortunately, the rest of their questions were all about the land itself. It was, after all, a roomful of farmers. In the end, Paradise Valley sounded almost too good to be true, aside from the rainfall issue, which they all assumed could be remedied with irrigation.

The serious questions came only after Harris and Fiedler left. Although in general the Amishmen didn't trust the big Texan, what they gleaned from his answers was that this was indeed a decent and potentially productive tract of farmland in a place where they could raise their families without interference.

"We'd have to learn a new language," one of them said.

Caleb shrugged. "We already have Dutch, High German and English," he argued. "One more language shouldn't be so hard."

"What about the church?" another wanted to know. This was the big question and everybody knew it. For an Amish settlement to last, they would need a minister to lead church services on Sunday. More important, unless a bishop was willing to make the yearly pilgrimage to the colony, they wouldn't be able to baptize anyone, no marriages would take place, and they couldn't hold communion.

Caleb deferred to his minister, who had remained silent through the whole meeting up to now. Half of these men were members of his church.

"If enough of you decide to do this," the minister said, "and you go down there and build homes in this Paradise Valley, and you're able to thrive there, then jah, I'm thinking we could find a minister who would agree to come and live. I wouldn't make a promise, but I might even do it myself. Mebbe we would have a selection and draw lots to find a *new* minister. Now, I can't speak for the bishop, but as long as his health is good, I don't see any reason why he wouldn't be able to make a trip down there for a visit once a year."

This was a great relief to Caleb, a major hurdle overcome. His people would never move to a place that had no hope of a church structure. The church was at the center of their lives.

"Fifty thousand dollars is a lot of money," John Hershberger said, ever the pragmatist.

Caleb nodded. "Jah, it is, but they said they would sell us as much or as little as we want of the land. Our farms here are worth a good bit more than ten dollars an acre, and the agent said they will give us time to find people who want to go in with us."

"Well, I think mebbe that will be the real problem," John said. "Finding people. I don't care what that Harris fella says, none of us has ever *seen* this place. Not even you, Caleb."

Caleb nodded solemnly. "That's the plain truth. Only a mighty foolish man would spend all he had on a piece of land without first looking it over." He'd seen this one coming, and there was only one answer to it. "One of us will have to go and make a start in this Paradise Valley so we can know what it's really like down there. That's the only way."

It would be hard. Pulling up stakes and leaving behind everything familiar, breaking ground in a new country without the help of neighbors, learning a new language, building a home, digging a well, feeding livestock, putting up barns and fences, all while planting crops to fend off next year's hunger — it would be a massive undertaking. But it was, in Caleb's mind, exactly the same price paid by the Amish pioneers who had first come to America in search of religious freedom. They had borne it stoically, in the sure knowledge they were doing the right thing. That was all that mattered. The man who accepted such a calling would need all the courage and conviction of his forefathers and, like them, the help of a benevolent Gott. He would have to be a man of vision, entirely convinced of the ultimate rightness of the task.

And it wouldn't hurt anything if it was a man whose wife needed a dry climate to survive.

Caleb Bender took a deep breath and looked John Hershberger in the eye.

"And that man ought to be me."

Chapter 9

Dat told the family about it over dinner, while they were all gathered around the long pine-plank table in the kitchen. They were moving to Mexico, and they would have to move quickly to take advantage of the rainy season. They would leave in two months.

The news hit Rachel like a thunderbolt.

Jake!

Her first thoughts were all about her secret boyfriend. She'd stolen enough time with him to know already, Jake Weaver was *the one.* Some things a girl just *knew,* right from the first moment. She knew in her heart, without the slightest doubt, she wanted to spend her life with Jake, but she was quickly learning that such knowledge could be a curse. She wasn't even old enough to date, and now her father was going to haul the family to Mexico, a thousand miles away.

In two months!

Right after she reached courting age.

Rachel was quiet all through supper, and said very little while she helped clean up the kitchen afterward. When the dishes had all been washed, dried and put away, she went quietly to the back door, put on her heavy coat and slipped outside into the cold and dark. She didn't even take a lantern.

It turned out she didn't need one. A full moon hanging above the barn was so bright it cast shadows at the feet of trees and fences. The night sky was achingly clear, a billion polished stars winking at her as if all were right in the universe. The wind had quieted. The night was eerily still, and very cold. Rachel shrugged deeper into her coat, buried her fists in her pockets and angled across the yard toward the back lane. She had to be alone, to think. Her father's news had left her reeling.

She walked past the barn and the smoke-house, on out the lane along the pasture fence all the way to the back of the Bender property. There she came upon an old familiar stump where she had often gone to play with her sisters and cousins — back when she was just a child. For a while she sat on the stump thinking of Mexico, and Jake. No matter how mature Jake was, she didn't really believe any boy would wait for a girl so far away. Not for long, anyway, and she didn't know how long it would be.

In the end, thinking about these things only made her feel worse, so when the cold began to creep into her bones she got up and trudged back down the lane toward home.

As she passed the barn lot she heard a noise and stopped. It came from behind the smokehouse, across the lane from the barn. At first she only heard a little whisper of a sound, like a sniff, but as she drew nearer and walked softer she could hear it more clearly. Someone was crying. Rachel tiptoed to the corner of the smokehouse and peeked around behind it.

Emma sat huddled against the wall, her face in her hands, weeping softly. In the shadows, wearing a dark coat and wool scarf, she was hard to see at first, but the moonlight lit her face when she looked up and saw Rachel peeking around the corner at her.

Rachel rushed to her sister's side, knelt down with her and threw her arms around her shoulders.

"What's wrong, Emma? What is it? Why are you crying?"

Emma's eyes were red and swollen. Tears covered her cheeks. She buried her face in

Rachel's shoulder and wept anew, as if someone had died.

The sight of Emma crying shocked Rachel out of herself and filled her with compassion. Emma had always been the strong one, not given to tears or self-pity of any kind. Rachel had not seen her sister like this since her favorite colt died. Emma wept so fiercely she could not speak, so Rachel held her. She just held her, locking her arms about her sister and crooning to her that whatever the problem was it would be all right, that everything would be all right, that there was no storm they could not weather together. For the first few moments Rachel's mind raced, until she realized that her father's news must have hit Emma even harder than it had hit her. Emma was twenty and unmarried. If Levi didn't offer marriage, and quickly, the move to Mexico meant leaving him behind.

After a few minutes Emma cried herself out. The wave passed and she raised her head, dabbing tears from her face with a handkerchief.

"Rachel, you just don't know," she rasped, hoarse from crying, locking onto her sister's eyes in the moonlight, shaking her head slowly. "My whole world is about to end." Emma's voice grew smaller at the last, like a little girl. Her fingers covered her mouth and her face contorted again, fighting back another wave of crying.

"Silly child," Rachel said, and she suddenly heard Emma's voice coming from her own mouth. Her older sister had called her a silly child a thousand times, usually when she was being irrational, as Emma was being now. Their roles had reversed. Rachel took her sister by the shoulders and looked her in the face.

"Listen to me, Emma. You must talk to Levi. What sort of man is he, anyway? If he's the kind of man you want to marry, he'll understand and he'll find a way to make you happy."

Emma's head tilted, and now a look of compassion came into her eyes as she reached up and brushed her fingertips lightly down Rachel's cheek.

"Oh, Rachel," she said, shaking her head slowly. "Poor, dear, innocent Rachel. I have already spoken to Levi about marriage. He is a good man, an honorable man, and he loves me as much as I love him. We will marry. But right now, I am in trouble."

This was confusing. "Trouble? Emma, if Levi has asked you to marry him, what kind of trouble could be bigger than that? All your troubles —"

"I am with child," Emma said.

Rachel recoiled. She was literally knocked backward onto her haunches by this thunderbolt, her hands flying unconsciously to cover her mouth as she stared at her sister's face in shock and horror.

This could not be true! Not Emma. Her hero, her shining saint of a sister, the heartbeat of the family, the only person in the world Rachel had ever wanted to become.

Emma had fallen.

At the speed of teenage thought, Rachel's mind began searching, scrambling for an alternative — *any* alternative. *Anything* but this.

"Emma, you can't be certain of this, can you? How do you — ?"

"I know the signs, Rachel. I just . . . *know.*"

Rachel looked into her sister's eyes and saw truth. Suddenly her own world came crashing down in ruins alongside Emma's. She had seen this happen before, and the effect was devastating. It would mean scandal and ruin, reputations forever tarnished. Emma and Levi would be hauled before the church and condemned, shamed, cast out and ostracized, at least for a time. After a few weeks they would be allowed to reappear before the church to publicly repent of their sin, whereupon they would be reinstated so they could be married, but their sin would never be forgotten. The people of their church — their whole world — would bear a portion of the public humiliation, and no one would look at either of them the same again. All these pictures rushed across Rachel's mind in one great wrenching torrent, and the flood swept away the ordnung.

This was *Emma.*

In the end, all the rules and regulations and traditions, the nuances of right and wrong so ingrained in the fabric of her people's day-to-day living — all of it was swept away in a single instant, and Rachel was left empty of judgment. What she saw before her now was a sister she loved perhaps more than anyone else in the world, and she was suffering.

Rachel reached out to Emma and pulled her close, hugging her tightly and whispering into her ear as they wept together, "Everything will be all right in the end. I love you. I will stand by you. Oh, Emma, if I could take this away and bear what is coming myself, I would do it. For you."

Her words jolted Emma and she wept harder than ever, wracked by the kind of remorse only love can cause.

After a few minutes, when Emma had calmed herself again, Rachel backed away to look into her eyes.

"What about Levi? Have you told him?"

Emma nodded, wiping away tears. "Yesterday. He was crushed. Now he will have to face his father with this news, and you know how Uri Mullet can be."

This was well known. Uri Mullet was an upright man, but sometimes with his sons he was known to be a bit *too* upright, a little too harsh, even for an Old Order Amishman.

"He said he will marry you?" Rachel asked, just to be sure.

"Jah. Levi loves me, Rachel — as much as I love him. Of this I am sure. I suppose that's how we came to be in this mess in the first place."

"When?"

"As soon as we are reinstated, I'm sure."

"Emmaaaaa!" Mamm's voice called out from the back door. Emma looked up, dabbing at her face with a handkerchief.

"EMMA!" Louder this time. There was an uncommon urgency in the way Mamm shouted.

Emma rose to her feet, shook the dust from her dress and took a few deep breaths, steeling herself.

"This might be it," she said, looking into Rachel's eyes with the grim fatalism of one bound for the gallows.

"EMMM-AAAAA! Come IN! You have visitors!"

It was too late to do anything about the red eyes or the puffiness, so Emma held her head high and walked primly around the corner toward the house.

"I am here, Mamm," she said.

"Come, come, come! Come *in,* child," her mother said quickly when she heard Emma's voice, waving her in with one frantic hand and holding aloft a kerosene lantern with the other.

Emma marched into the house slowly with her chin up, and with a dignity all the grander for having been dented. Rachel shadowed her, apprehension growing with every step.

Ignoring her mamm's nervous urging, Emma took her time hanging her coat in the mud room and exchanging her scarf for a prayer kapp, then took one last quick swipe at her eyes and cheeks with her handkerchief before she followed her mother's lantern through the kitchen.

"Do I look okay?" she whispered, glancing back at Rachel.

"Fine," Rachel lied. It was too late anyway.

Dat and Levi Mullet stood waiting for her in the living room. They had risen when they heard her come in, the hickory rockers behind them still swaying a little. Between them stood the minister. A fire crackled in the potbellied wood stove, and two kerosene lanterns hissed from the tables by the chairs. All three men wore wooden expressions, revealing nothing.

Levi was a little taller than the two older men, probably because years of hard work had bowed their backs and legs a bit while Levi was still young and straight and strong. At twenty-one he was a serious man, fervent in following the ordnung and known for being a hard worker.

Rachel, watching closely, saw the look that passed between Levi and Emma, but could read nothing from it. Levi only nodded, his face revealing nothing except that his brows furrowed and he breathed through his mouth as if he was very nervous.

"This is grown-up business," Dat said, brushing fingertips in the direction of the younger daughter. "Rachel, you can go. *Out.*"

Rachel felt a little wave of relief when her father excused her from witnessing what was about to happen, and she turned quickly to leave. But it was not to be.

"No," Emma said, grabbing Rachel's hand before she could get away. "Please let her stay."

Normally calm and congenial, Dat's eyes were hard. An uncomfortable anger seeped from their edges, but he said nothing more to Rachel. She stayed, half hidden behind her sister.

"This young man," Dat began in a gruff voice and words oddly formal given his long and intimate knowledge of Levi Mullet, "has asked me for your hand."

Rachel's heart raced. Her hand went all by itself to Emma's back for support — both ways.

Emma glanced briefly at Levi, shaky fingers covering her lips. She nodded grimly, and her gaze fell to the floor. She said nothing.

The minister remained mute as well, his hands clasped behind his back, but everyone knew why he was there. Levi would not have engaged in such talks without a minister present. This was serious business.

"I told him we were going to Mexico very soon," Dat said, "and would not be here for the wedding season in the fall. Levi said he already got that news from his father, this afternoon, and this was why he wanted to go ahead and be married right away. So he

117

can go with us."

Rachel blinked. Her head recoiled in shock, and her hand involuntarily clenched the cloth in the middle of Emma's back. Was *this* what Levi had told them? Rachel watched as Emma's head came up slowly and looked into Levi's eyes. She saw both the question and the answer pass between them as Levi met Emma's questioning gaze with the briefest frown and an almost imperceptible shake of his head.

He had not told them about Emma's predicament! Levi was using the imminent Mexico trip as an excuse to get married right away.

"I told him it would be a long road we travel," Dat continued. "There will be much toil and many hardships. He said he don't mind work, and hardship is what makes a man.

"I told him there would be talk, that people would think it was a scandal. Why, everybody knows the only reason couples get married out of season is they're in trouble. Levi said let the tongues wag as they will."

The minister didn't blink, even at this last, though over the years his church had seen a few scandals. Under the circumstances

Levi's answer was not only bold, but shrewd.

Now Dat sounded a little less angry. A smile crept slowly into the corners of his eyes.

"So I told him yes, I would be thankful to Gott if my daughter Emma would marry a man with such a backbone."

Levi took a deep breath and seemed to relax for the first time. After watching him stand there so stiffly the whole time Dat talked, it now dawned on Rachel that Levi must have been holding his breath for fear of what Emma might say. One wrong word and his gambit would have failed.

But it had not failed, and now Emma would be saved from humiliation, at least for a while. The minister smiled for the first time and shook Levi's hand. Dat came and hugged Emma briefly, then spun Rachel around and herded her toward the door.

"I don't care what your sister says, get out of here and leave them alone," he growled.

Rachel left the room reeling, battered by conflicting emotions, the terrible anguish of Emma's secret sin warring against the relief of knowing that it would remain a secret, at least for now. Balanced against the joyous news of Emma's pending wedding was the ominous cloud of Mexico and the certainty that no matter what else happened she would soon be leaving the only home she had ever known.

And Jake.

She started to go up the stairs to the privacy of her room, but there was never any real privacy in a house with so many others. Her two younger sisters would be there and they would want to know what had happened downstairs — why the minister had come with Levi at such a late hour. She could not face questions just now. She knew too much.

She paused there for a moment with her hand on the stair rail before she turned toward the back door. In the mud room Rachel had only a rectangle of moonlight to see by as she took her heavy coat down from the hook, slipped her arms into it and tied a wool scarf snugly under her chin.

The full moon had risen higher, lighting the yard and the barn even brighter than before. Angling across the yard, she walked slowly down the back lane and slipped around behind the smokehouse. Growing up every day in a family of thirteen they'd always said you couldn't even be alone in the outhouse, but right now, in the still of the night behind the smokehouse, Rachel had never felt so utterly alone in all her life.

She sat down on the cold ground, huddled against the wall, and cried.

The next day's dawn found Rachel and Emma in the barn together, doing chores as if nothing had happened. As soon as they were alone, milking cows back to back on their stools, Rachel glanced about to make sure no one else was near and then whispered over a shoulder, "What did Levi say?"

The steady *rip, rip, rip* of milk against the galvanized pail never changed its rhythm. Once already this morning Emma had slipped off behind the barn to be sick, but now she seemed fine.

"About what?" Emma asked.

Rachel stopped milking and turned around. "About why he chose not to tell them about . . . you know."

Now Emma stopped too, and turned to face her sister. "You know why."

It really didn't need to be said. There was no greater humiliation than what Levi and Emma faced.

"Jah," Rachel said, "I know the first why — that he wanted to avoid a scandal. But I don't know Levi nearly as well as you, and the reason he wanted to avoid a scandal is the second why. The second why would tell me a lot about who he is. About his heart."

Emma smiled and touched her forehead to Rachel's. "You are far too wise for such a young girl," she said softly, and her eyes shined, remembering. "When we were alone he told me what anguish he'd been through the last two days, thinking of what I would have to endure. *Meidung*."

The shunning. Excommunication. All the people who mattered would turn their backs on her.

"He said to me — and you mustn't repeat this to anyone, Rachel, for these are the words of a man to his betrothed — he said I was the moon in his night sky, and he could not bear to see my light dimmed so. He said he would abandon all he knows, move heaven and earth, pour out his last ounce of blood and spend his last breath before he would let me suffer such pain."

Now tears came to Emma's eyes. Turning away from her sister to keep from crying, she said, "I think it is because he knows the pain of dire punishment and humiliation, of being made to feel small, that he cannot bear to even think of such a thing happening to me. His father . . . you know. So when Levi learned that we were going to Mexico very soon, the plan took shape in his mind and he acted upon it quickly before I had a chance to tell anyone else."

Rachel pondered this for a moment. Sooner or later it had to be said.

"But you can only hide from people. Gott still knows, Emma, and sin sometimes casts a long shadow."

Emma nodded, and met her eyes. "Jah, that may be, sister, but Gott is more forgiving than men. Does not our Lord say that there is no greater love than to lay down your life for a friend? Levi has never known real love until now. How is it wrong, now that he has found it, for my Levi to love so deeply that he would risk everything to protect the one he loves?"

CHAPTER 10

At Caleb Bender's age, starting over again would be very difficult, but he didn't mind hard work. Life had always been hard; this was the price of Adam's fall, that man should toil for his daily bread. But now that he was committed to uprooting his family and moving to Mexico, he was filled with regret.

His goodbyes to his land came upon him unannounced in odd moments of startling remembrance, each one stealing away a little piece of his heart. His fingers ran down the barbed wire stretched tight between a row of fence posts and he saw his long-dead father's face, focused intently on his work while he cut and split chestnut logs to make the posts. When he stroked the bristly forehead of a Guernsey cow it brought to mind the day his grandmother taught him to milk — the three-legged stool and oak bucket, the warm smile, the smell of the barn, the sense of accomplishment and belonging. In the misty gray dawn he gazed long across his quiet fields remembering the rattle of the traces and the lurch of the plow, and he knew in his bones that he did not really own the land, nor did the land own him. They were just old friends. The land accepted him as a friend because it had known his father and his grandfather. Their faithfulness and kindness to the land had built, season by season, year by year, a mutual respect into which Caleb had grown naturally and always believed he would enjoy for the rest of his days. Until now. Now life was forcing him to part company with the very earth from which he was made, and into which he had always assumed he would one day be planted.

He sold his farm to his son-in-law Andy Shetler, husband of his daughter Lizzie. So far, Lizzie and Andy had three children; the Bender farm would give them room to grow.

His daughter Mary would be coming with him to Mexico, along with her husband and their two small boys, hoping to make a new start. Emma and Levi Mullet, after they were married, would round out a total of fourteen people — at least that was the plan in the beginning.

■ ■ ■ ■

Ada, the eldest daughter, was to remain behind with the farm, and Lizzie would look after her. Ada was twenty-seven, and simpleminded. She was very sweet most of the time, but she had never been right in the head. Mamm said she had the mind of a small child. A large girl, Ada cried often, spoke little, and moved with a ponderous clumsiness.

Much as she hated to leave her eldest daughter behind, Mamm said it was for the best. As difficult as everyday life was for Ada, her routine was extremely important to her. Mamm said it would help a great deal if she could continue to live in the same house and sleep in the same bed every night. Although the departure of her mother and sisters would undoubtedly cause problems for Ada, Mamm felt they would be nothing compared with loading her on a train and hauling her off to Mexico.

But as it turned out, it was her mother and sisters who defined "home" for Ada, not the house. When Mamm and Emma were finally able to get through to her and explain what was about to happen in a way that Ada could understand, she went wild-eyed and wailed off and on for the better part of two days, most of the time sitting on the floor in a corner of the living room, rocking back and forth, her kapped head banging against the wall. Afraid for her daughter's life, Mamm finally pinned her down, wrapping arms and legs about her while she cooed and whispered in Ada's ear that she could go to Mexico after all, that her mamm would never, ever, abandon her. Only after an hour of this did Ada's struggling cease.

Mamm held on, in the end whispering over and over again, "Shhhh, little one. Gott knows. Shhhh." Finally, still snuffling, Ada laid her head on her mamm's shoulder and fell fast asleep.

Ada's inclusion would bring the number of the Bender party to fifteen.

After the youth singing the next Sunday evening Jake and Rachel were able to slip away and talk for a bit.

"Good news about Emma and Levi, jah?" Jake said. Emma's engagement had been "published" that morning at the service.

"*Wonderful* news. I'm so happy for her. And Dat will be glad to have another man along, I expect." Rachel guarded her words, her thoughts. Already it seemed like a thousand times she'd been forced to watch what she said.

"In Mexico, you mean."

Rachel nodded. "There will be so much work to do. . . ."

Jake sighed, staring off into the darkness. "I wish we could go, too," he said.

"Why don't you? Your brother William has three whole years of school yet, so it looks like your dat would want to go with us right away. Can't you talk him into it?"

"Well, he does want to go, just not now. He needs more time to find someone to buy our farm and to put another crop in the barn. Anyway, he said he's not in any big hurry to die in Mexico."

Jake recoiled as soon as he realized what he'd just said, but it was too late.

She tried to see his eyes in the near darkness.

"He thinks we're going to die in Mexico?"

Jake shook his head and tried to backtrack. "Well, no, I think he probably meant, you know, it'll be hard going for a while, and people have accidents all the time on the farm. Why, just last week little Abe Petersheim stood up on the seat at the wrong time, the horse lurched, and he fell back into the manure spreader. Broke his leg all up and laid his jaw open before his big brother could get it stopped. Dat says there probably wouldn't be any doctor in the middle of the mountains."

Rachel didn't believe that was what Jonas Weaver meant at all, so she pressed her point. "Tell me the truth, Jake. Does your dat think it will be dangerous in Mexico?"

He thought for a long moment before he answered. When he raised his eyes to hers he nodded and said, "Well, he's afraid it *might* be. There's a lot of talk about the revolution — soldiers and bandits and such. He won't take his family down there until he sees what things are really like. It's the same with most of the men. But it's all just talk, Rachel. They'll listen to your dat. After you've been there for a year, if he says it's okay, then everybody else will come."

She was near tears.

"Jake, what if he doesn't change his mind? What if your dat decides *never* to move down there?"

"Ach, that won't happen. We'll be down next year, you'll see."

"But what if you don't come?"

He took a deep breath and thought for a minute, then shook his head. "I don't know, Rachel. I don't know what I'll do, but I have faith it'll work out. Things always work out."

"Well, it doesn't sound that way to me,"

she said softly, her gaze dropping away from his face. "It sounds like your dat might not ever move to Mexico. It sounds like maybe you should find another girl."

She didn't really mean it. What she wanted was an argument. She wanted for him to say no, that he would never be happy with anyone else, that she was the only one and that he would wait as long as it took, that he would wait his whole life for her if necessary. But he didn't say that. What he did say made perfect sense, but somehow it wasn't very satisfying.

"Well," he said, "we can write letters, and we'll come down before you know it. You'll see."

"But what if you don't?"

Jake took her hands in his and held them lightly, his thumbs stroking the backs of her fingers. "Then we'll have to decide what to do about it, but we don't have to decide right now. In time, we'll see a way."

Rachel had always known that Jake's greatest strength was his level-headedness. Now she was discovering that his greatest weakness was that sometimes he could be so maddeningly level-headed.

As if the Benders weren't busy enough with preparations for the wedding and the move, winter was nearing its end so that every week there were more things to do.

Rachel went to the Weaver farm every day after school to help make syrup. Syrup making always began with the first sign of spring thaw. Every year, the smoke from the stovepipe on the Weavers' sugar shack on the hill in back of the barn signaled the coming of spring.

Nearby families always pitched in and fanned out through the woods to tap all the maple trees. The older Bender kids spent mornings gathering sap from their own trees and took what they'd collected down to the Weavers' on the hack after lunch. Rachel and her younger sisters raced Jake's brother home from school every afternoon to help the women strain, boil down and bottle the sap.

There was also the off chance that she might get to see Jake — maybe even talk to him for a minute or two.

It was a lot of work. The sugar shack had to be wiped down frequently to remove the sticky layer built up from the cooking process, the floors scrubbed clean of the inevitable spills. It took forty gallons of sap to make just one gallon of syrup, but for Rachel it was worth the mess and bother. She loved the whole process — working

131

together with lots of people in the warm sugar shack, the talk and laughter that went around, and especially the smells. Some of the women didn't care for the sweet smell of syrup cooking down, but Rachel loved it. Syrup making, for her, with all its smells and mess, was the ritual that marked the end of winter and the beginning of a new year.

It was going to be a very interesting year.

"So how long have Emma and Levi been planning their wedding?" one of Jake's older sisters, Laura, asked. She had just put a fresh pan on the stove and was pouring sap into it from a bucket.

Rachel stood by one of the tables helping with the bottling. "They haven't," she said, flipping the laces from her kapp back over her shoulders to keep them from dangling in the syrup. "Dat's Mexico plans came about so suddenly they haven't had time to do anything. They wanted to get married in the fall like everybody else, but now we're leaving and they wouldn't be able." Carefully measured words, at least half true.

"They haven't done *anything?* My word, they've missed all the fun!"

It was a tradition. A couple's engagement was kept secret until it was published in the church by the bishop, one month prior to the wedding. Couples would spend months secretly preparing to set up housekeeping, so a quick, unplanned wedding left a young couple without many of the things they would need. To a girl, the loss of that wonderful romantic time of secret anticipation and cooperative effort was an even greater penalty.

"Jah, that's a shame for sure," Rachel said, "but it couldn't be helped. They never knew we would be moving to Mexico."

"Well, I guess if you have to marry quickly, you must take what comes," Laura said. She glanced over her shoulder at Rachel as she said this, and there was a hint of a sarcastic smile on her face. Laura was one who had always loved a juicy bit of gossip, and she clearly remained unconvinced of the reason for the hasty wedding.

Rachel set down the bucket she was holding and fixed Laura with an iron stare.

"There is more than one reason to marry out of season," Rachel said as calmly as she could. "And we must all take what comes. None of us knows what Gott has in store for us."

CHAPTER 11

The week before the wedding was a wild, happy, busy time. The men moved all the furniture out while the women scrubbed the house from top to bottom, for tables would have to be set up in every room for the reception.

Rachel was washing walls one afternoon when Emma rushed in, grabbed her by the arm and said in an excited whisper, "Rachel, come with me! We have to go borrow dishes, and I have a surprise for you!"

She was positively giddy, but before Rachel could ask a single question, she flitted back outside. Rachel dried her hands, grabbed a coat and went out to find Emma already waiting in the buggy, reins in hand, waving impatiently. Borrowing dishes from neighbors and trying to match place settings was a fun part of a wedding, but hardly reason for this level of excitement. This had to be something big.

As soon as they were out on the road breezing toward the Hochstetters', Emma leaned close — as if anyone could hear — and said, "Can you keep a secret?"

Rachel raised an eyebrow. "I'm *already* keeping a secret," she said dryly.

"No, but this is a good one!" Emma was beaming.

Rachel nodded, a little suspiciously. "Okay. What is it?"

"You and Miriam are going to be my *navahuckers!*"

Rachel gasped and sat back hard against the seat, staring straight ahead with a world of conflicting emotions rushing through her. The bride was allowed to pick two unmarried couples to be her navahuckers — her attendants for the wedding — and they would be together all day, as couples, greeting guests as they arrived and sitting on either side of the bride and groom at the reception. It was the bride's right to pick them, and the names were held in strictest secrecy right up until the wedding.

"But I'm too young," Rachel muttered, still in shock.

"You'll be sixteen before the wedding, Rachel, and anyway I just spoke with Dat about it. He gave his approval."

Now she understood Emma's excitement.

It was a great honor, not to mention that Emma was her best friend in the whole world. Still, this was a complete surprise and it left her with a burning question.

"Who will be my escort for the day?" she asked timidly, unable to prevent a slight wince from flashing across her face. There was only one name she wanted to hear, and she dared not hope.

"Well, Dat and I talked about that," Emma said pensively. "There are lots of boys I could ask. I thought about Yost Schlabach, but he's too old for you — I'm thinking I'll give him to Miriam. That blond-headed Miller boy is your age, but he's too tall."

"And dull," Rachel added.

"Dat said maybe Eli Stutzman, but he smells funny."

Rachel giggled at this. There were stories.

"Anyway, we went through a whole list and none of them seemed right for you, so I told Dat I guess we'd just have to settle for that little neighbor boy, Jake Weaver."

Rachel's jaw dropped, and tears came into her eyes.

"And Dat said okay to this?"

Emma nodded, grinning from ear to ear. She knew. Emma knew everything, except perhaps how to keep a buggy straight in the road when her younger sister suddenly leaped upon her in a wild joyful hug.

On the morning of Emma's wedding the entire family rose at four, rushed through the day's chores, ate a quick breakfast and dove headlong into cooking for the wedding feast. Even the men helped in the kitchen — something that only happened, ever, on a wedding day. Rachel teased Harvey about doing women's work, but he just rolled his dark eyes and smiled. He would get even.

Emma slipped away to the privy several times that morning, and Mamm noticed. "Is Emma feeling all right?" she asked Rachel.

"Butterflies," Rachel said. "She's very nervous."

Mamm nodded. "Jah, I was the same on my wedding day."

The wedding service was to begin at eight thirty in the barn. It was a "banked" barn, meaning it had been built into a hillside, giving the cows and horses who lived on the ground level extra protection from wind and weather while simultaneously allowing drive-in access to the second level from the driveway. The heavy oak floor of the second level had been scrubbed and scoured for the occasion until the grain of the wood stood out, and church benches had been set up on both sides of the wide central aisle.

At seven thirty the bridal party would take up positions beside the barn door and begin greeting guests, so at six thirty the girls slipped away to change. A new navy blue dress awaited Emma upstairs, with a fresh white cape and apron. She had sewn it herself in the last two weeks, along with the dresses of both her attendants, but apart from being new, and perhaps made with a little extra attention to detail, the dress was not noticeably different from her usual Sunday attire. In fact, after the wedding the same dress would *become* her Sunday dress for as long as she lived. When she was done — Amish shorthand for "done with this life" — the dress would be used for her funeral.

As Emma's attendants, Rachel and Miriam got new dresses, too. When Emma was washed and dressed and ready she took a twirl in front of her sisters.

"Well, do you think I'm a suitable bride?"

Rachel smiled, even as her eyes pooled — it was going to be an emotional day. "You, sister, are surely the prettiest bride I have ever seen."

Miriam gave Rachel a cautionary sideways glance, eyebrows raised. "Best not let Dat

138

hear you talk like that," she warned. "That's just vanity. Pure vanity." Then her dark eyes crinkled with mischief as she leaned close to Emma and whispered, "Easily. *By far,* the prettiest bride ever."

Emma beamed, the flush in her cheeks and the excitement in her eyes putting the finishing touches on a naturally radiant face.

At seven thirty, in their new dresses and spotless white capes and aprons, the three sisters went downstairs to meet the rest of the bridal party.

Jake was there, strikingly handsome in his Sunday clothes. His eyes lit up when he saw Rachel. He shook her hand with proper reserve, then leaned close when no one was watching and whispered, "You look wonderful. I've been looking forward to this."

Miriam's escort, Yost Schlabach, looked good too, though Miriam seemed to be keeping her customary distance. He was nice enough, but Miriam had already confided to Rachel that she didn't think he was terribly bright. Sometimes it seemed to Rachel that, for someone with no prospects, her sister was awfully choosy.

It was a fine golden morning lit with radiant flowers and the eager gossiping of birds. The bridal party sat in a row of kitchen chairs outside the barn, with Levi and

Emma in the center, Miriam and Yost on the right, and Rachel and Jake on the left.

Rachel took great delight in just being with Jake, only now there was the added joy of seeing people's faces as their buggies drove down the lane and they got their first glimpse of her and Jake sitting together. It was a kind of declaration.

By eight thirty the crowd had filled the benches in the barn to capacity, and the singing began while the bridal party waited outside. Until now, Emma had shown nothing but the normal nervous anticipation common to any young bride, but when the singing began Rachel saw her older sister biting her lip. Angst had crept into her eyes.

Emma knew what was coming next.

So did Rachel, and at such times she could read her sister's mind. She reached over and laid a hand on top of Emma's, and when Emma turned to look at her she mouthed the words, "It will be okay."

Emma smiled thinly, but the worry didn't leave her eyes. Two lines into the first song, one of the ministers came outside and said to Levi, "It is time."

Rachel and the other navahuckers stayed where they were, watching silently as Levi and Emma rose and followed the line of ministers to the house. The clutch of visiting preachers accompanied the bride and groom upstairs to the *abrode,* a bedroom that had been set aside and prepared for a closed-door session of counseling and prayer before the actual wedding could commence. Rachel had no idea what would be discussed there, what questions might be asked.

Nor did Emma. That's why there was fear in her eyes.

Sitting outside the barn waiting for Emma and Levi to return, Rachel fretted about it herself. What would happen if they asked Emma and Levi the wrong question, point-blank? Neither of them would lie to the ministers — and then what?

Jake touched her shoulder and whispered, "Why does she look so worried?"

Rachel forced a smile. This was one of the things she liked about Jake. He paid attention.

"She's all right. It's just a serious step — marriage. They're going to be fine. A wonderful couple. They love each other very much, and Levi is very good to her."

Jake pondered this for a moment, frowning with thought.

"What does that mean, exactly?" he asked.

"What?"

"That he is good to her. I mean, I know a

man is supposed to be nice to his wife and provide for her, but surely there is more to it than that. There must be some special thing a man does that makes a woman say he is good to her, but what is it?"

"It's not complicated, Jake. He just gives her what she wants."

The singing from inside the barn intensified, and Jake leaned a little closer to be heard over it.

"Well, okay," he whispered, "then tell me. What does she want?"

A shrug. "What every woman wants."

"And what is that? What does a woman want from her husband?"

"She wants him to know what she wants."

There was a trace of frustration in his voice. "But how would he know if she didn't tell him? I'm not sure a woman even *knows* what she wants. Why, I bet even *you* don't know what you want."

She nodded emphatically, a slight frown creasing her brow. "Jah. I know."

"Okay, tell me then. What is it that you want from me?"

"I want you to know what I want."

He slumped back in his chair, staring straight ahead. A slightly sardonic smile crept onto his face. As much as she liked him, Jake was still a man. He could be a little thickheaded at times.

And then, slowly, without looking, his hand came over and gently took her hand from her lap. Holding their hands down between them where no one could see, Jake's fingers intertwined with hers.

Perhaps he was not so thickheaded after all.

The prayer and counseling session in the abrode lasted thirty minutes, during which time the navahucker couples waited outside while the congregation in the barn sang hymns from the *Ausbund,* led by men chosen from the families of the bride and groom. Then Levi and Emma rejoined the wedding party, and the six of them marched into the barn and took their reserved seats.

Emma's face was serene and relaxed, and Rachel breathed a sigh of relief. Things had gone well in the counseling session and only joyful celebration lay ahead.

Staring across the aisle at Jake Weaver, Rachel found herself constantly thinking about the future, about what her own wedding day might be like. His eyes twinkled when he looked at her, and she was dying to know if anything of the sort had crossed his mind.

Probably not. He was, after all, a man. Perhaps she would find a way to pry into his thoughts a little later. There would be plenty of time for that — it was going to be a very long day.

The bishop began his sermon in the Garden of Eden, when Gott himself noted that it was not good that a man should be alone, and worked his way through the Great Flood, carefully pointing out that the widespread evil which ultimately caused Gott to destroy the world was the inevitable result of mixed marriages. After about an hour he finished by driving home the point that marriage was a binding promise witnessed by Gott himself, never to be taken lightly, and never, *ever,* so long as you both shall live, *ever* to be broken. Among the Amish, there could be no divorce.

Most of Emma's family had remained in the house to finish preparing the feast, but near the end of the sermon they all moved silently into the barn and took seats to witness the wedding vows.

When the bishop finished his sermon he turned to the bride and groom and bid them come forward.

It was a moment that would be forever etched in Rachel's memory, Emma standing there straight and tall in her crisp new dress, all eyes watching as she smiled up at the man she loved, their future as bright as the striped sunlight angling across a barnful of hushed, expectant faces.

"Can you both confess and believe," the bishop asked solemnly, "that Gott has ordained marriage to be a union between one man and one wife, and do you also have the confidence that you are approaching marriage in accordance with the way you have been taught?"

"Jah," they both answered.

"Do you have confidence, brother, that the Lord hath provided this, our sister, as a marriage partner for you?"

"Jah," Levi said.

He asked the same of Emma, to which she answered, "Jah."

"Do you promise your wife that if, in bodily weakness, sickness, or any similar circumstance she should need your help, that you will care for her as is fitting for a Christian husband?"

"Jah."

The bishop repeated the same question for Emma.

"And do you both promise together that you will live with each other with love, forbearance and patience, and not part from each other until Gott separates you in death?"

"Jah," they both answered.

"Then let us rise and pray for those about to be married."

Everyone stood and the bishop prayed.

Then he took Emma's hand and placed it in Levi's, saying, "May the Gott of Abraham, Isaac and Jacob be with you and help you together, giving his blessing richly unto you, and this through Jesus Christ — amen. You are now one flesh, and will remain so until death do you part." Then he looked them solemnly in the eyes and warned, "To do otherwise would be a great sin."

Many of the women wiped tears as the congregation sat down. Only the navahuckers remained standing. The newlyweds returned to them, and all six marched out stiffly in single file, boy girl, boy girl, with Jake and Rachel bringing up the rear. The congregation remained seated, watching silently until the whole wedding party had filed out of the barn.

Lunchtime was upon them, stomachs were grumbling, and mouthwatering scents drifted across the yard — fresh-baked bread, *hingleflesh,* mashed potatoes, gravy, ham, an army of casseroles, plenty of cakes, cookies, pies, tubs of tapioca pudding, trays of cookies and a hundred other delights. The bishop dismissed the crowd and the festivities began.

The wedding party took up their places of honor at the corner table with Levi and Emma in the center and her attendants on the wings.

Rachel was in heaven. Seated beside Jake as everyone filed past to offer their congratulations, she was thrilled by all the teasing winks and raised eyebrows they gave her and Jake in passing. For today at least, they were a couple, and everyone knew it. Even more than that, on this day Emma had married the man she loved and the newlyweds would be going to Mexico with the family.

That Showalter girl came through the line, and when she shook hands with Jake she smiled a little too brightly. She was pretty, but a shameless flirt, and Rachel had heard rumors. Jake smiled back at her and made a little joke. After the girl had passed out of hearing Rachel leaned close to his ear and whispered, only half joking, "I saw that."

"What?" His eyebrows went up in mock surprise and he suppressed a grin.

"You *like* her?"

He shrugged. "She's friendly, and nice to talk to . . . if you like talking about tabby kittens." He frowned then and added, "But I don't much care for her tapioca pudding."

Rachel lowered her face and gripped her

147

stomach, trying to squelch hysterical laughter. One of her more spirited cousins, known for her loose tongue, had once famously quipped that the bubble-headed Mary Showalter didn't know road apples from tapioca.

By the time Rachel got herself under control and sat up straight again she knew she was falling in love.

CHAPTER 12

Most of the adults went home after the evening meal, and the teenagers held a late singing. Afterward, as usual, the remaining grown-ups sat around inside the house talking with Levi and Emma, ignoring the teenagers for a good long time.

Rachel and Jake went down the lane to be alone. Jake had fallen quiet, and she could see that something was bothering him. They were walking slowly, very close, almost touching.

"What is it, Jake? What are you thinking?"

It was so dark she couldn't see his face, but she could tell that he looked away for a moment as if he were making up his mind about something. Then, without warning, he turned back to her and kissed her right on the lips. He'd never done that before. It was a very light kiss, and it only lasted a second before he turned away again. Even in the dark she knew he was blushing.

"I'm sorry," he mumbled, and then, "No I'm not."

Suddenly she felt it necessary to defend her honor. "What kind of girl do you take me for, Jake Weaver?"

Very quietly, he answered, "After today, spending so much time with you, I *know* what kind of girl you are. That's why I wanted so badly to kiss you."

"And what is *that* supposed to mean?"

Again he hesitated, trying to find words. "I don't know how else to say it. I guess it means I *choose* you."

He took her hand and drew her with him down the lane away from the house.

Being fairly new to the romance business, she didn't quite know how to take this. They were walking slowly, going nowhere in particular, and now they were holding hands. Some Amish boys went hog-wild the moment they reached dating age, and girls had to be careful around them. Others were awkward and reticent, unlikely to even speak to a girl without a lot of prompting and goading.

Jake wasn't either of those.

"You *choose* me?" she said, once she'd had time to think about it. "You mean like a mule at the auction? Wouldn't you like to look at my teeth and hooves first? What do you mean, *choose* me?"

He laughed a little, but not too long. He seemed almost embarrassed, a good sign.

"I'm not sure, exactly," he said. "I just know it took forever to be sixteen, so I been thinking about girls for a time now."

"*Most* of the boys I know have been thinking about girls for a while. Some of them, why that's *all* they think about."

"That's not what I meant."

Rachel waited, giving him the benefit of the doubt.

"I guess Emma's wedding made me think about it, that's all. It's got to happen sometime. I mean, sooner or later a boy has to choose a girl, jah? He starts dating when he's sixteen, and almost everybody is married off by the age of nineteen or twenty. In those few short years he has to pick who he'll be with for the rest of his life. After baptism, I'm thinking it's the most important choosing a boy ever does."

"A girl, too," she said. "But, Jake, surely you're not saying already you want us to be married. I'm barely old enough to court." She was having trouble keeping her voice from quivering, and she was glad for the darkness. He would not be able to see her eyes pool.

"No, I'm not that hasty. But if choosing is

important, why would I waste time being with a girl I would never marry?"

She pondered this, her heart pounding, but only for the few seconds it took to see that it was a natural extension of Jake's level-headedness.

"Jah," she said, clearing her throat. "That makes sense, I suppose."

"So why do so many get it wrong? I've watched lots of boys choose, including my two older brothers, and sometimes it don't work out so good."

"What do you mean? Your brother Noah married Linda Traeger, the prettiest girl in the district."

"That's *exactly* what I mean. Just between me and you, she's sometimes not so easy to get along with."

Rachel had heard the rumors. But Jake didn't stop there.

"I seen it before," he continued. "It's like if Gott puts too much pretty in a girl, He has to make up for it, so she has a shortcoming somewhere else."

Her face darkened. She let go his hand and crossed her arms on her chest. "I see. So you 'choose' me because I'm not pretty. You don't want a pretty girl; you want plain little redheaded Rachel Bender."

Most of the boys she knew would have

gotten defensive at that point and started blustering, trying to squirm off the hook. But not Jake. Out in the open, in the moonlight, she could see that he was laughing quietly. He shook his head as if this was such nonsense he would not dignify it with an answer. Then the grin faded and he became very serious.

Stopping and turning to face her in the path, he said, "Do you remember one day raking leaves last fall with Miriam? It was a fine crisp day with a deep blue sky and a little wind, the leaves all bright red and gold, a good crop harvested and another year of good health behind us. Miriam threw some leaves at you and pretty soon the two of you were chasing and laughing —"

"Wait," Rachel said, "I remember that, and you weren't there. We were in our own backyard, away from the road and prying eyes. Were you *spying* on us, Jake?"

"Well, no, but we were hunting pheasant that day and I saw you from down in the pasture on the other side of the creek. Your kapp came off, you remember?"

He made motions with his fingers on either side of his head, like rain. "Your hair got loose and came down all around you. I could hear you laugh when Miriam tackled you into the leaf pile, and it was a sound like silver. Then you got up and chased her, all that red hair dancing and the sunlight flashing off of it like . . . like spun copper."

He paused then, and she peeked at his face. He was searching for something — the right words, or maybe the courage to say them. She'd never known an Amish poet before, and she wasn't about to interrupt him. She waited.

"In all my life," he said softly, shaking his head, "I have never seen a sunset more beautiful than that."

She averted her eyes. Suddenly short of breath, she unconsciously pawed and tucked at her hair. What kind of boy was this who could so easily stir such feelings within her, frightening and embarrassing and wildly exciting all at once?

He must have sensed her discomfort, or shared it, because he took her hand and continued down the path. Walking side by side it wasn't necessary to look at each other.

"But deep down," he went on, "I knew it wasn't so wise to let one little minute of sunshine decide my whole life for me. And *that* is what I meant when I said a boy shouldn't choose for pretty.

"I even asked my dat about it," he chuckled. "Anybody can see how he is with my mamm, so I asked him what was the secret to choosing the right girl. We were out haying. He looked up at the house, where Mamm was hanging out the wash, and I will never forget what he said — 'Why, it's easy, son. Just remember when you choose a girlfriend, don't choose so much the girl. Choose the *friend*.'

"I've known you all my life, Rachel, and you've always been a good friend. I watched how you are with a baby calf or a baby boy, how you work and how you play, how you treat your mother and how you take such care with Ada. I used to think you were maybe a little too timid until you stood up at the children's home, pretending to be dumb, and drew the nurse away so I could get my little brother out of there. And then I knew — *here* is a friend I will be able to count on when things don't look so good."

The ground suddenly seemed uncertain of itself. Somehow she kept putting one foot in front of the other, but the spaces between steps felt like falling from the hayloft. She didn't know it was even possible for a boy to have this much inside him — so confident and so vulnerable at the same time. On second thought, maybe it *wasn't* possible for a boy. Even at the tender age of sixteen, this was no boy. And Rachel knew, given the things he had said to her and the way he made her feel, she would never be a little girl again, either.

She stopped walking and tugged at his hand, forcing him to turn and face her in the lane. Then she put her hands on his waist and drew him closer. Looking deeply into his eyes she bared heart and soul in one burning gaze and said boldly, "I choose you too, Jacob Weaver."

It was nearly midnight before all the guests finally cleared out and Levi and Emma dragged themselves upstairs to bed. Yet there were other traditions still to be addressed, because a couple of Harvey's cousins had stayed over to help him with wedding night mischief. They'd already taken care of all the usual pranks, like putting potatoes under the mattress and hiding the chamber pot. After the newlyweds retired and blew out the lantern the boys found a broken strand of jingle bells in the tack room, tied them to a long cane pole and ran past the house every ten minutes or so, slapping the bells across the upstairs bedroom window.

For an Amish couple there would be no luxurious vacation like an Englisher honeymoon. Levi and Emma rose early the next morning to help finish cleaning up from the previous day's festivities. Emma's first chore was to gather her husband's clothes and wash them together with her own, symbolic of their intermingled lives. She needed to get it done quickly because by evening they would load a buggy and start off on a three-day jaunt to relatives' houses.

Their church district had voted just last year to allow a wringer-type washing machine to be hooked up by belt and pulley to a small, separate rope-start motor, and Caleb Bender had been among the first to rig such a contraption on his back porch. To ease his wife's workload, he would do whatever was allowed.

The morning sun was peeking through the treetops when Emma went out to pour the first pot of hot water into the washing machine. A minute later she came storming back into the kitchen, where Rachel was helping her mother clean up from breakfast.

"Where is Harvey?" Emma demanded, hands on hips, head forward.

Mamm looked over her shoulder, drying a bowl with a dish towel. She was having one of her good days, not coughing too much. "I think he's in the barn. Why?"

"Because somebody has taken the motor and I can't wash clothes! I have a lot to do today. I'm not about to rub my fingers raw on a washboard, and anyways I don't have time for foolishness."

"The motor with the little pulley?" Mamm asked. "The one for the washing machine?"

"Jah, Mamm, that's the only motor we have."

Rachel bit her lip to keep from laughing out loud. Wiping her hands on a towel, she said, "I'll go and see if I can find out what became of the motor, Emma. You should maybe calm down a little bit before you get your blood pressure up." She winked at Emma on the way out.

Rachel found Harvey rummaging around in the tack room and stuck her head in the door.

"You might want to saddle a horse and make a run for it," she said. "Your newlywed sister is on the warpath."

When he looked up from the workbench there was not a trace of innocence in his devilish smile. "Why? I haven't done anything."

Neither of them heard Emma coming until she shoved her way past Rachel and barged into the tack room holding a piece of board like a baseball bat, threatening Harvey with it.

"Give me that motor or *say your prayers,*"

Emma hissed.

Harvey threw his arms up in front of his face. He and Rachel were both laughing.

"You can't hit me with that board, Emma — it has a nail in it."

She lowered the board to look at the end of it. She'd picked it up from a scrap pile by the barn door where the boys had torn down an old shed last week, and it did, in fact, have a rusty nail sticking out of it.

"Good!" she said, cocking the board as if she would really swing it, though she too was biting back laughter.

"But I'll get lockjaw," Harvey said, "and then I won't be able to tell you where I hid the motor."

Emma's face teetered between rage and laughter, but before she could say anything else, Harvey got off the stool and hugged her. Chuckling, he kissed her cheek and said, "It's up in the mow. I'll go get it and put it back for you."

The board with the rusty nail was still cocked in her hands when Harvey went out the door. Lowering it, she looked at Rachel and both of them burst out laughing.

"I know what you're going to say," Emma said. "He wouldn't work so hard to drive me crazy if he didn't love me."

Rachel shrugged. "It's true."

"I know that," Emma said. "We are blessed to have such a family."

By late afternoon the newlyweds had dressed and packed, loaded their freshly cleaned clothes into a buggy and headed out to visit each other's kin. Watching their buggy rattle down the driveway and out into the road, a quiet new melancholy descended upon Rachel.

Emma was gone.

Yes, she would return, but in many ways she would not. She was Levi's wife now. Emma would never again be quite the sister she was before, and the thought left Rachel with a lingering ache. Life was changing entirely too fast. Dat had always said, *"If you don't like the way things are, just wait,"* but Rachel had always taken him to mean that familiar things would change the way leaves change from one season to the next, not that she would have to abandon everything familiar and move clear to Mexico.

Even after a celebration — *especially* after the noise and clamor of a celebration — the odd quiet that fell in Emma's absence was palpable. Until now the impending trip had been an abstract, a storm on the horizon, but Emma's sudden marriage rumbled through Rachel like echoes of distant thun-

160

der. Soon now she would be leaving her home. This was the only home Rachel had ever known, and she might never see it again.

Soon now.

Chapter 13

Rachel was walking home from the store one afternoon, full of ominous, brooding thoughts, and was half a mile past the school when she heard a wagon coming up from behind, matched horses clopping happily along. As the wagon drew near, the clip-clop of hooves slowed and a familiar voice called out to her.

She turned to see Jake hauling back on the reins and bringing a pair of dapple Percherons to a shuddering stop. Beside him on the wagon seat was his brother William with his lunch pail on his lap. Her own two younger sisters waved to her from the back of the wagon.

"Would you like a ride?" Jake asked. His wide-brimmed hat was pushed back on his head and his sleeves were rolled up for work, the muscles in his forearms straining against the reins. "I was on my way back from town and thought I'd pick up the young ones from school," he explained as she put her parcels into the back and climbed up onto the seat.

She settled on the bench next to William, but Jake gave him a look, whereupon William rolled his eyes, climbed over the seat and sat down with an audible huff in the back of the wagon with the girls.

Jake glanced over his shoulder, laughing gently as he snapped the reins, nudging the horses into action. "Thanks, little brother. Someday I'll return the favor."

Rachel stayed where she was, sitting primly on the other end of the seat from Jake with her hands in her lap. After all, they were in an open wagon in broad daylight, and her sisters were right there in the wagon.

"I love this time of year," Jake said, watching a four-horse team plow a field as he passed. Along the road little blades of green appeared, daffodils and jonquils raising their dainty heads to see if spring had arrived.

"I love the smell of fresh-turned earth, the warm sun on the back of my neck. Look at those birds."

A pair of red-tailed hawks wheeled and hovered in the sky above the farmer and his plow, waiting to pounce on displaced field mice.

"This is the best time of the year," Jake said quietly. "The time of beginnings."

"Or endings," Rachel muttered, even now besieged by an uncharacteristic melancholy. "It's the worst time to think of leaving, when home shines its brightest."

"Cheer up," he said with a warm smile. "Think about something else."

"It's hard to do that when everything reminds me all the time. Every day, Andy is bringing his tools to the house and plowing our fields — *his* fields now. There's sadness in Dat's eyes, just watching. Mamm is already packing, my sisters are making canvas tents for us to live in until we get a house, and Dat spends his days sorting his tools, choosing what to take and what to leave behind."

"You mean there's not enough room on the train?"

"Oh no, there's room on the train, but when we get there we have to cross the mountains. We can only carry what fits on our wagons. It could be worse, though. Dat got a letter from that Mr. Harris the other day, saying a German neighbor is going to come guide us over the mountains, and he's bringing an extra wagon. Now we can take Mamm's mattress and the washing machine at least, so we won't have to use a scrubbing board." She sighed heavily. "I'm already homesick and we haven't even left yet."

Reaching across the seat and lifting her downcast face with a gentle finger, Jake said, "Everything will be fine, Rachel. You'll see. Your dat is a good man, a *strong* man. He'll take care of his family."

She nodded. "Jah, he always has. It's just hard for me because I'm only a girl." Her thoughts had plagued her for a long time, and now they surrounded her. "A girl has no say over her own life, that's all."

His brow furrowed as he listened, but he said nothing. He waited.

"Like school," she said. "Men in the government — men I don't even know — decided I should go to school every day, and so I go, like it or not. Because of this, my father decides we should move to Mexico, and so I'll go, like it or not. One day I'll get married, and then my husband will decide everything for me, like it or not. A girl has no more say-so than a dandelion seed. It's just not fair, that's all."

Jake pondered this for a long time with a wry smile, then said quietly, "Whether it's fair or not depends a lot on the man you marry. My dat decides things in our house, but never without taking my mamm's feelings into account. Dat says a man who is strong in his heart is gentle in his hands."

She read between the lines, heard the promise in Jake's words, and it brought her great comfort. Riding on the bench seat next to Jake in the fine spring weather, with the smell of freshly plowed earth in the air and a cool breeze blowing across the country road, the melancholy melted away and before she knew it Rachel was smiling.

Jake was right. The right man could make all the difference. Emma had been distraught about everything until she married Levi, but she seemed happy enough now, as if she knew things would be all right so long as Levi was there. Even Mamm didn't seem terribly upset by the idea of leaving the house where all of her children were born. She had her quiet regrets, but even though she did not possess Emma's boundless energy and inherent courage, Mamm managed to take everything in stride — so long as Dat was there. Looking back over the frequent misfortunes of farm and family that Rachel had seen in her short life, she saw that the women remained unshaken so long as the men were there, standing between them and total disaster.

She had seen it in her mamm's eyes the year of the drought, when they lost the corn crop. Mamm watched the men huddle and squat, plucking straws from the ground and chewing the ends as they talked in the shade, figuring out what they would do, and as she watched her husband's face, the worry left her and a look of relief came into her eyes. Rachel had seen it plain as day. Mamm trusted Gott, but she also trusted Dat.

There was a kind of comfort in knowing that someone else was in control so long as it was someone faithful, someone who cared for his wife as Gott cared for His children. Someone strong enough to be gentle with his wife. Someone who not only would *allow* his wife to be everything Gott intended her to be, but *wanted* it so. She had seen the other kind too, in the downcast eyes of women whose husbands ruled with an iron hand that squeezed the dreams out of them. If the right man could complete a woman, the wrong one could crush her. The choosing, as Jake himself had said, was everything.

Rachel stole glimpses of Jake's face now, and saw the same thing Mamm had seen in her father — the peace and patience of a self-aware man, confident that he could deal with whatever came. And as she looked at his gentle face, the face of a friend, she heard again the words he had said to her that first night.

"I would do a great many things for you."

She slid a hand across very slowly and gripped the front edge of the seat halfway between them. A moment later his fingers came to rest on top of hers. For now, it would have to do. For now, it was all she needed.

CHAPTER 14

Caleb rented the railcars and paid for them in advance. The railway agent went with him and marked the cars, sitting among a string of others on a siding in Fredericksburg. It took three days to get everything packed up, hauled into town and loaded on the cars.

It was a week of long and tearful good-byes, as one by one Martha and Caleb Bender's brothers and sisters dropped by the house with their surrey-loads of children and grandchildren.

The Sunday before they were to leave they attended gma — church services — in Abe Byler's barn loft. A soft rain fell during the service, and though they were all thankful for the spring rains, the steel gray sky only added to the already somber mood. Even the youth singing that night, usually upbeat, fell victim to the overcast. The Benders would be pulling out the next morning. They had lived in Salt Creek Township as far back as anyone could remember, and their departure would rip a gaping hole in the fabric of the community. What was worse, everyone suspected the rift would grow larger over the next year or two as more families migrated south.

The rain stopped in late afternoon, and after the singing Jake and Rachel slipped away behind the buggy shed. They didn't talk much; anything worth saying had already been said, so they just held each other. Rachel made him promise to write, and then he left her with a kiss that she would long remember.

They left home on a cool, breezy morning under a bluebird sky, the previous day's rain having washed the air and fed the newly awakened earth to bursting. Everywhere the world was drunk with sunlight and succulence, shouting out that rare spring green that makes new grass and budding leaves seem lit from within. Beside the house, the kitchen garden had exploded into bloom overnight, and along the front fence a garish army of tulips stood at starched attention, beaming.

The day was bright and perfect — cruelly so, for it broke Rachel's heart. It nearly killed them all to leave on such a day.

No one came to see them off. Their church friends had all said their goodbyes the day before, and today they would all be busy with washing and farming. Jake would be working somewhere on his father's place. Rachel could only cling to the hope that she would get a glimpse of him one last time as her family paraded past the Weaver place. On a morning like this, she knew for a fact that everywhere they looked as their odd caravan wormed its way down country roads toward Fredericksburg, Amishmen would be out in the fields working.

Jonas Weaver stopped his team and stood up on the back of his harrow waving and shouting.

A quarter mile farther along, there he was.

Jake. She would have known the shape of him from any distance, and there he was, standing on the back of a steel-wheeled planter holding the reins of two draft horses. When he saw them Jake took his hat off and waved it wildly over his head, a huge grin on his face.

The whole family — strung out along the road in two surreys, a hay wagon, a produce wagon and a hack — waved and shouted to him as they passed. All except Rachel. She knew his eyes were on her alone as she sat beside Harvey in the hack. Very slowly, hoping none of her family would notice or know what she was doing, she raised the fingertips of her right hand to her lips and held them there for one brief second. He saw. She knew that he saw because after he put his hat back on, his own fingers paused at his lips. It was such a fleeting gesture that she was sure no one else could have noticed it, a secret message passing just between the two of them in the middle of a crowd.

Rachel watched him as long as she could, wondering if this would be the last she would ever see of him, and then she turned and faced the road ahead hoping Harvey would not see the tears in her eyes, for she could not take his teasing just now.

But Harvey surprised her. As far as she could tell he never took his eyes off the wagon ahead, but his hand came up and gently squeezed her shoulder. Today, even Harvey's heart was soft. Rachel wiped the tears away and clutched her arms against her stomach trying to quell the terrible ache.

At the railway station the men loaded the surreys into a cattle car and put up the horses while the women arranged things in the boxcars that would be their home for the next several days. An hour later the big door rumbled shut. Couplings clanked and cars lurched as the train hooked them up.

The engine chugged and strained and grumbled, belching clouds of smoke, and slowly they began to pull away. Mary and Ezra's little boys stood with their fingers hooked in the boards, tiny Amishmen in their wide-brimmed hats, suspenders and dark coats, hair down over their ears, peeking through the cracks as Fredericksburg slid past and the train gained momentum. Mamm was busy holding Ada, who had sunk into despair, crying even before they boarded the train. By the time the train got under way, Ada had curled into a fetal ball on top of the bedding at the front of the boxcar, and all Mamm could do was to lie up against her and wrap her arms about her, whispering over and over, "Shhhh, little one. Gott knows. Shhhh."

Harvey and Aaron and the two youngest girls rode in the cattle car with the livestock for now, watching over the animals.

In late morning they rumbled through the outskirts of Columbus, the first real city Rachel had ever seen. She couldn't believe so many people could live so close together, and she scarcely believed there could exist a city even larger until she saw Cincinnati. In the early afternoon they passed over the wide river, through Louisville and on down into the rugged hills of Kentucky. In the open country between cities the whole earth was bursting with buds and blooms, promising a bountiful year.

While the train took on water at a whistle-stop in the hills, Rachel carried lunch back to her brothers and sisters in the cattle car — cold sweet potatoes and leftover roast chicken. She stayed there with them because she could see so much better from the slatted sides of the cattle car. Harvey was his usual exuberant self, endlessly optimistic and unfazed by the trials that lay ahead. The younger girls were flush with excitement — too young to see it as anything but a grand adventure. Aaron said nothing, watching through the slats, his eyes drinking in the sights. When Rachel took him his lunch he stayed where he was, refusing to sit down even to eat.

Rachel understood. The others ignored him, figuring Aaron stayed at his post looking out through the slats because he didn't want to miss anything, but Rachel looked in his eyes and she knew. Every mile carried him farther away from Amos. She didn't say anything; there was nothing to say. Aaron understood that his twin brother was gone and that Gott had allowed it, but leaving Amos's body so far behind and going so very far away felt a little like a betrayal nonetheless. She stood beside him for a long time holding on to the slats and looking out just as he was doing, her forearm barely touching his. But touching.

A hundred times since leaving home Jake's face had come to Rachel and twisted a knot in her heart, but it occurred to her after a while that when she touched the edge of Aaron's pain it helped her forget about her own hurts and desires.

As the steam engine struggled up a grade in western Tennessee, trailing a plume of smoke, an endless mist of deep pink blooms lined the forests overhanging the tracks.

"Redbuds," Aaron said. "I never seen so many in my life."

"Everywhere I look, I see new things," Rachel said quietly, the passing wind ruffling her skirts.

Aaron nodded, and said with an oddly regretful smile, "This is a truly beautiful country."

The next time the train stopped, Rachel went back to the boxcar where her mother and sisters stayed most of the time. Miriam was there, sitting in a corner watching through a crack as the green hills rolled past. Rachel sat on a nail keg beside her, not saying anything at first, just watching through the same crack. But Miriam barely acknowledged her, and after a while Rachel began to sense a melancholy even deeper than Aaron's. She touched her sister's knee.

"Miriam, are you all right?"

Miriam nodded and forced a small smile, but she didn't look at Rachel. The train rocked gently, wheels clacking rhythmically as the daylight faded and a sifting rain obscured the landscape. Ada, who had finally stopped crying for a little while, sat holding a skein of yarn while her mother knitted. She was humming a simple children's song, and even then the worry never left her puffy eyes. Mary napped beside her boys. Emma and Levi were sitting in the far corner of the car where a small table and chairs had been arranged, studying a book of Spanish phrases together. Rachel looked again at the suppressed sorrow in Miriam's eyes. Gently, she touched her sister's shoulder.

"Talk to me, sister. What's wrong?"

And then she waited. She knew her sister well. Miriam was quiet and studious, but underneath she was fiercely independent, scrupulously honest, and too smart for her own good, which went a long way toward explaining why she didn't have a boyfriend. Rachel knew Miriam would eventually say what was on her mind, but she would always choose to think first, to arrange her thoughts and understand them clearly before she put words to them. In a moment Miriam turned to look at her, and there were lines of silver in the bottoms of her eyes.

"Mary has Ezra," she said softly. She turned away to look outside again, but she kept talking and Rachel knew she had looked away because she didn't want the tears to come. "Lizzie has Andy. Now Emma has Levi, and even you have someone, Rachel. Though you can't speak of it, and you won't be with him for a while, you have him yet. At least you have hope." Now she turned again to look Rachel in the face, and a tear trickled down her cheek. "What hope do I have?"

She had never come right out and said this before, though even Rachel knew she had to be thinking it. Miriam was almost eighteen. She'd been eligible for nearly two years. A few boys had tried to court her, but Miriam had dismissed each of them in turn, saying only that they "played games" and their interest in her was for all the wrong reasons. After a while the others shied away, somehow intimidated. And that was *at home,* where there were lots of boys. Now she was moving off to another country, where the only Amish people within a thousand miles would be the ones in her family.

"They will come," Rachel said gently. "In a year or so there will be lots of others. You'll see. Oh, Miriam, we'll have a *fine* community in Mexico! Why, they'll be standing in line to court a beautiful girl like you."

Miriam looked down at her lap and a tear clung to her nose. "I'm not beautiful."

Rachel stared at her in disbelief. She had always envied Miriam's dark complexion, her coal black eyes and natural plum lips, her silky raven hair. Especially the hair. Rachel, with her mop of red, had always loved her sister's hair, though no one else ever saw it let loose outside her kapp. And then she remembered what Jake had said that night, walking in the moonlight, about seeing her own red hair flashing in the sun like spun copper. What it proved to her was that, like Miriam, her image of herself was shockingly different from the way others saw her.

"Miriam," she said, putting an arm about her sister, "Gott made someone for each of us, didn't He?"

A sniff, a shrug.

"Well, I believe it," Rachel said. "The man Gott made for you has a heart that will search and will not be satisfied until he finds you. Only you. When he sees you he will know. You will take his breath away, and he will say he has never seen a sunset more beautiful."

Miriam didn't answer for a long time. Finally she said, "Those are pretty words. I would love to meet that one, but no boy has ever taken the trouble to know me."

"He will," Rachel said.

But Miriam only sighed and kept staring out the crack, watching the world grow dark.

Rachel found a private corner that night and did some crying of her own. Her heart ached for Miriam, and trembled in fear for Emma. She cried for Aaron, for poor confused Ada, and lastly for herself. Already she missed Jake and feared she would never see him again. In the wee hours, somewhere near Memphis, the train car finally rocked her to sleep.

When she awoke the train was sitting still, taking on water and switching cars in the humid low-country air of New Orleans. Everyone did their chores, and after breakfast Harvey and Aaron found a pumping station where they refilled the water barrels before the train got under way again, heading west.

In the afternoon the lowering sun swept ever more to the right as the train curved southward. Just after sunset the steam engine hissed and slowed and lumbered into the freight yard at Laredo, an expansive flat on the edge of town with cattle pens all around it, packed with hordes of longhorn steers that made a great lowing racket through the night.

Caleb paced and fumed for two days while they were stuck on a siding in hot, dusty Laredo. It took one day for the Mexican customs officials to show up and inspect their livestock and passports, and another to come back with official papers saying the Benders would be allowed to pass into Mexico.

Still, there was a promising sign. Mamm's cough had worsened almost immediately as they were leaving Ohio in the drafty train car, and she had to sit upright all night in the humid air of New Orleans to relieve the pressure in her chest. By the time they reached Laredo her eyes had sunk into her face and she was weak, barely able to stand. But in the dry air of south Texas, parked on a siding in Laredo, for the first time in a week she slept soundly and awoke feeling a little better. Maybe the doctor was right.

The morning they left, an American customs agent showed up and reinforced

Caleb's nagging sense of foreboding. The agent, making his rounds in a dark blue uniform, came to check their papers and peek into the cars. His great big handlebar mustache reminded Caleb of the policeman who had escorted him to jail — was it only three months ago? The agent carried under his arm a black leather book where he wrote their names and whatever else he thought was important.

"That's some fine draft horses you got there," he said, eyeing Caleb's Belgians, absently twisting the end of his mustache around a finger. "Looks like you're planning on farming."

Caleb nodded. "Jah. That's about all we know how to do."

"Got folks down there?"

"No. It's chust us, yet."

The agent bit his lip, frowning. "Mind if I ask whereabouts you plan to settle?"

"Paradise Valley," Caleb said with a touch of pride.

The agent squinted. "Never heard of it. What's it close to?"

"Agua Nueva."

A blank stare. "Don't know that one, either."

"Well, there's another town — Saltillo."

"Ah! Now, Saltillo I've heard of. Decent

181

little place from what I hear. Not as rough as the border towns, but it's still Mexico. South of the border, things can get a little scrappy sometimes." He eyed Caleb and his family closely, and a worried look came into his eyes. "How you fixed for firearms?" he asked, his gaze sweeping at waist level across the men in the group.

"You mean guns?"

A nod.

"Well, we got a shotgun for rabbits and squirrels, a rifle for deer."

"No side arms?"

Caleb had already noticed several cowboys on horseback that morning, riding around the stockyards wearing pistol belts. They had *all* noticed. The customs agent's question made Caleb a little uneasy.

"We have no need of a pistol," he said flatly. "A rifle is better for hunting."

The agent eyed them all again for a long moment without saying anything, taking in the plain clothes, the prayer kapps and aprons, the wide-brimmed farmer's hats. He shook his head, took a deep breath, blew it out and offered Caleb a parting handshake.

"Best of luck to you, then, Mr. Bender. I sure hope you make friends easily. I expect you'll need 'em."

Chapter 15

The Mexican National Railway hooked them up and dragged them across the trestle into another country. Soon they were breezing along through the Mexican countryside, but as the sun rose higher even the wind of the train's passing did little to blunt the oppressive heat. What lay around them was a desert, pure and simple. It wasn't perfectly flat; the land rolled gently, and they crossed an occasional small canyon or creek gorge, but it was all terribly hot and dry, a place of sagebrush and cactus, snakes and scorpions.

In midmorning they passed through Monterrey, a fair-sized city on the edge of the mountains. Great, long ridges of jagged rock loomed over them in the west, mostly green on the lower slopes, with patches of red rock showing through near the peaks.

"We still have a ways to travel," Emma's voice said. She had come up behind Rachel and laid a hand on her shoulder as she stood looking up at the mountains through the slats of the cattle car. "But we're headed up into the mountains now. Soon we'll be a lot higher up, where it's cooler."

"I sure hope so," Rachel said, fanning the neckline of her dress in a vain attempt to cool off.

"How are you holding up?" Emma asked.

"Me?" Rachel tried to act surprised. "I'm fine, why?"

Emma's head tilted and she smiled gently. "You must miss him very much."

She could never fool Emma. Rachel studied her toes for a minute, determined not to cloud up. The best she could manage was a weak nod.

Emma put her arms about Rachel's shoulders, touched her forehead to Rachel's temple and said, "You won't believe this now, but the time *will* pass and you'll be together again before you know it. I'm sorry it's so hard for you right now. I wish there was something I could do, but when you're sixteen time just moseys along like a tired old horse, doesn't it?"

Rachel nodded weakly. "But you're only four years older than me, Emma."

Emma chuckled softly. "Yes, and already, for me, the horse has begun to canter. Grossmammi says when you're old the years go by like fence posts."

"Well," Rachel said with a sad smile, "I wouldn't mind a quick trot just now."

Emma's arms tightened about her younger sister's shoulders. "The year will pass soon enough, Rachel. Keep yourself busy and before you know it the others will come, and Jake with them. Gott knows your heart."

It helped a little. It wasn't so much the things Emma said that made Rachel feel better, it was just that she was always there. She was always Emma.

"And how are *you* doing these days?" Rachel asked, glancing at Emma's belly.

"Oh, not so bad. I've been a little queasy on the train, but Mamm thinks it's motion sickness. In another month or two I'll start to show a little bit, but I think I can hide under this dress for a while yet."

The train climbed steadily, its steam engine laboring sometimes on the grades. They passed through tunnels and along the edges of steep cliffs, through a world of cleft and chasm like nothing Rachel had ever seen, a world apart from the rolling green hills of home.

The train made a brief stop in Saltillo to pick up mail and unload coal; then the engine hissed and chugged and climbed even higher. In midafternoon they pulled into the station at Agua Nueva, where the three cars of the Bender family were uncoupled for the last time on a siding at the far end of the little station.

The towns had gotten smaller and poorer at every stop since they left Laredo. Monterrey was smaller than Laredo, but still a city. Saltillo was half the size of Monterrey, and Agua Nueva half the size of Saltillo. There were no grand government buildings here, only a few small stores, a blacksmith shop, and a scattering of houses along the tracks and up the sides of the hills. Most of them were mere shacks of adobe, gray unvarnished wood and rusting tin, a few with makeshift goat pens in back. There were chickens running loose everywhere. One or two rangy dogs paced warily along the dry dirt streets, and half-naked children stopped what they were doing to watch every move the foreigners made.

They were deep in the Sierra Madre now, and the air had cooled noticeably with the altitude. Rachel had been wearing her coat since they left Saltillo. She busied herself helping her mamm and the other women pull all their belongings together and box everything up, all the hundred little necessities that had gotten them through the days and nights on the train. And they were

Amish women. It was a point of honor to leave the boxcar cleaner than they had found it.

While the men and boys hauled out the wagons and began putting them together, Dat went up the platform to the little ramshackle station to inquire about Herr Schulman. While he was gone, a big mule-drawn wagon turned a corner and rumbled down the service road beside the tracks. When the wagon drew even with the Benders the driver hauled back on the reins and stopped.

"Sind sie Herr Bender?" he said to Aaron, who only now looked up from pinning the tongue onto the front of his own wagon. Rachel was already up in the wagon, catching and stacking.

Aaron straightened up and hitched his suspenders, eyeing the newcomer warily.

"Er ist mein Vater. Ich bin Aaron," he said, trying not to sound too Dutch. Rachel smiled, for she knew High German didn't come easily to her brother's tongue. *"Er ist dort."* He pointed toward the station, where Dat was just emerging from the door and coming down the platform.

As he tied off the reins, the German looked back over his shoulder and spotted Dat. He jumped down from the wagon and pulled off his hat, a shapeless felt thing, badly frayed along the edges and corners, deeply stained with sweat. Standing on the ground next to Aaron, Rachel could see that Herr Schulman was a big man, broad in the shoulders, with a shock of light brown hair and a ruddy-cheeked, distinctively German face. He wore heavy wool trousers, a brown corduroy coat and hobnail boots that looked like they'd spent plenty of time behind a plow.

Herr Schulman stuck a big hand out to Caleb Bender when he walked up. "Herr Bender? Ernst Schulman! *Wie gehts?*"

Dat was far more comfortable with High German than his son, and he told Ernst Schulman all about the trip from Ohio while the whole family lined up shoulder to shoulder to meet their new neighbor. Dat introduced them all, one by one, and each of them gave Herr Schulman a good, stiff, one-pump Amish handshake.

A cart about half the size of Schulman's wagon rumbled down the service road and came to a stop behind the other one. The cart was drawn by a small slow-footed ox — a relative rarity at home, though a few people kept them just for fun — and driven by a young Mexican. The driver jumped down and stood by the wagon, one hand casually draped over the front wheel, watching Schulman, waiting. He didn't say a word, nor did he make any move toward any of the Benders. He didn't even look at them.

Rachel stared. The Mexican's loose-fitting pants had once been white, made from some sort of heavy native cotton, and the waist was tied with a piece of thin hemp rope. He wore a dark brown hat with a flat brim just like an Amish hat, only with a taller crown. His jet-black hair was long like a woman's, and it hung straight down past the shoulders of a threadbare poncho and a shirt made from the same heavy cloth as his trousers. There were dusty sandals on his feet instead of boots. He was taller than many of the local people, longer of leg than the average. But something about him struck Rachel wrong. He seemed relaxed almost to the point of boredom, yet his dark eyes were alert and focused. There was just something arrogant in the way he carried himself.

"Pelao!" Schulman yelled, switching to Spanish. "Don't just stand there. Get up here and help load the wagons! Quickly!" Schulman shook his head. "One thing I cannot get used to in this country, Herr Bender — everyone moves like molasses. These

189

people are so incredibly lazy. They just don't care."

Pelao remained motionless for a moment, just long enough for his inertia to become a statement. When he was good and ready he sauntered casually over to one of the boxcars to help Aaron haul out the riding plow and heft it up onto the hay wagon. Even then he didn't speak.

With Schulman's help, all the wagons were loaded and tied down in less than two hours. While Levi and Ezra brought out the draft horses and hitched them to the larger wagons, Pelao led one of the standard-bred horses out to where Harvey was assembling one of the surreys. Rachel watched as he backed the horse into place and hitched it up, his movements unhurried but precise. At least he knew what he was doing. When all was ready he leaped back up onto his oxcart and sat holding the reins loosely, waiting, a faint smirk on his lips.

Rachel went with her father to the hay wagon, as the surreys were overcrowded. Dat was about to climb up to the driver's seat when he looked over his shoulder at Schulman, nodded in the direction of Pelao and whispered in German, "Is he mute?"

Schulman spat, glanced at the Mexican. "No, he can talk when he wants to, but like most *Chichimeca*s he's a bit stubborn. They're like mules — they'll work, but you have to get their attention."

Schulman took his hat off then, and looked purposefully at the western sky where the sun was beginning to dip toward the mountaintops. "We won't make it all the way home tonight," he said, "but we should put some distance between us and this town. It's not safe here."

The ragged caravan trundled slowly up a dirt road for two hours, climbing gradually to the northeast along the face of a ridge. Pelao's oxcart took the lead, being the slowest of all the wagons. The others paced themselves behind him, Rachel's father constantly fretting and muttering to her about the top-heavy hay wagon with its load of farm equipment on these rutted, rocky, uneven mountain roads. But the pace suited the cows, plodding along, tied behind the wagons. Several miles up the ridge, when they were out of sight of Agua Nueva, they came to a crossroads. Pelao's oxcart led them to the right.

As they were making the turn Schulman looked over his shoulder from his position in front of Dat's recalcitrant hay wagon. Pointing to the mountain pass in the east he shouted, "This is the last turn, Herr Bender! From here, the road takes us straight to your property!"

On the other side of the pass, a long curving valley opened out in front of them, and in the gathering dusk Rachel could see a ribbon of road winding ever upward and out of sight at the top of the southern ridge. She wondered how much farther they could go before dark, but ten minutes later her question was answered. As they neared the base of the ridge Schulman shouted something up ahead to Pelao, who threw up a casual hand to acknowledge that he'd heard and then slowly pulled his oxcart off the road, heading for a level spot up the hill a little ways in a stand of oak trees.

Schulman called back to Dat, "We camp here for the night!"

The campsite had been used many times before, evidenced by a shallow depression full of ashes and blackened earth in front of a log worn smooth by so many having sat on it. While the women built a fire and put together a makeshift supper, the men took care of the livestock, seeing that the horses and chickens and cows and pigs were secure for the night, with plenty of food and water. Harvey and Rachel saw to the milking. Even here, the cows needed milking. Schulman had picked the spot because he knew of a small spring a stone's throw up the hill where the water was always fit to drink. Aaron fetched water, and the women made a big pot of soup with potatoes and canned vegetables. Levi and Ezra untied one of the wagons and brought down hickory rockers for the women, and when the chores were done everyone gathered around the campfire for dinner.

While they ate, Dat and the others began peppering Schulman with questions about their new home.

"It's a fine piece of land," he assured them. "This road runs right through the middle of it. There are hills on three sides to keep the worst of the winds out, and the topsoil is black and rich. Best of all, you have me for a neighbor!" He laughed heartily at his own joke, as did everyone else.

Except Pelao. Turning his bowl up, he drained the last of his soup without so much as a smile. Mamm noticed, and asked him — through Schulman, because she had barely begun to learn Spanish — if the soup was to his liking.

Pelao nodded once, uttered a low grunt, then put his bowl down beside him on the log. Schulman said one clipped word to him in some strange language. The Mexican nodded curtly, rose and walked out of the circle of firelight. Pulling a ratty gray blanket and a Winchester rifle from under the seat of Schulman's wagon, he propped the rifle on his shoulder and disappeared into the darkness.

"What was that about?" Dat asked.

"I told him to keep watch," Schulman said. "He has the eyes of a hawk and the ears of a wolf, that one. And the good thing about a Chichimeca is he can go for days without sleep."

"But what was it you said to him? I didn't know the word. Was it Spanish?"

"Oh, that." Schulman shrugged. "I know a few words of his native tongue. He's easier to get along with if I make the effort once in a while. A little less . . . *insolent*."

Dat's eyebrows went up in surprise. "He doesn't speak Spanish?"

Schulman chuckled. "Of course he does. Everyone here speaks Spanish, but he *prefers* Nahuatl. You have to know a little of their history to understand how things work down here. There are three kinds of Mexicans — people of pure Spanish descent, mixed-blood mestizos, and Indians. The Indians are a difficult bunch — backwards, illiterate, and hopelessly superstitious. Completely incomprehensible. The Spanish, at least, are civilized. Some of the Spaniards have mixed and interbred with the Indians over the centuries, but a mestizo is never the equal of a Spaniard. Señor Hidalgo, the man whose land you are purchasing, is a gentleman of pure Spanish descent."

While the women washed up, the men dragged out one of the homemade cabin tents and erected it by lantern light without too much difficulty. The women would enjoy the privacy and comfort of a tent, at least, while the men slept under the stars.

CHAPTER 16

The next morning dawned bright and fair and cold. The Benders' unwieldy caravan got under way at first light with the sullen Pelao once again leading the way in his ox-cart. Twice that morning they passed little groups of Mexicans going the other way, peasants dressed in the same kind of loose cotton clothes Pelao wore, except that most of the men wore floppy straw sombreros. Nearly all of them wore multicolored ponchos or blankets draped over their shoulders. Each of the parties was towing a burro laden with burlap bags of what appeared to be beans of some kind.

The washed-out dirt road led a winding course, climbing gradually along the face of the ridge until they reached the crest, a lofty place of barren rock where they could see for a hundred miles in every direction. Rows and layers of bald mountain peaks stretched into the blue distance on both sides. Below them at the tree line a coyote dashed from a patch of scrub brush to pounce on a small rodent, and Rachel pointed out a herd of mule deer flashing through the piñon pines.

"It will be good hunting here," Caleb said, pressing his hat down tighter on his head after a stiff gust of wind nearly tore it away.

Rattling along the rocky crest, the air felt almost cold enough for snow, even at mid-morning. Rachel buttoned the top button of her coat and tucked herself as well as she could into her father's wind shadow.

Around noon, when the sun hung directly overhead, Pelao halted his oxcart and sat looking out over the valley ahead as the others pulled to a stop behind him.

"Come see!" Schulman shouted, jumping down from his wagon.

Everyone swarmed out of the wagons and buggies to gather in front of Pelao, who remained seated on the oxcart. They had reached the end of the crest. In front of them the road turned and fell away precipitously. Below, beyond the foot of the ridge, lay a broad valley bracketed by two lower ridges like parentheses, their upper reaches half covered with pine and oak thickets. The road ran like a crack through the middle of the valley floor, where the earth, though uncultivated, shone as green as the pastures of heaven with wild grasses.

"Your new home!" Schulman said with a flamboyant sweep of his arm.

Caleb stood still, looking out over Paradise Valley, and it seemed that a great weight lifted from his shoulders in that moment. He stood a little straighter, a cold wind ruffling the hair covering his ears and the long wisp of beard hanging from his chin. The hope that had festered and burned within him for so long found instant vindication in what he now beheld with his own two eyes, and he felt ten years younger. The young couples — Levi and Emma, Ezra and Mary — hugged each other, laughing and chattering rapidly to the children in Dutch. Mamm snugged against Caleb's arm, a rare display for her, and, her eyes shining, whispered to him, *"Vas danksht?" What do you think?*

A hush fell over them all as they looked to the patriarch, eager to hear his first impression.

Caleb pursed his lips. "I think," he said, nodding solemnly, "it is beautiful. I think we may have found the promised land. Let us hope it flows with milk and honey."

An hour later they reached the valley floor, and the Bender caravan clattered and clanked slowly through the heart of the wild pasture. Rabbits hurried across the dirt road in front of them and darted into the brush as a golden eagle wheeled overhead, hunting.

When they came to what he judged to be the center of the valley, Caleb called ahead and brought the caravan to a halt. Climbing down from the hay wagon he walked out through hip-deep prairie grass dragging his fingertips across the seed heads, surveying the land with a farmer's eye. It wasn't perfectly level; there were long, shallow waves in it, noticeable only from ground level, which was good. The fields rose gently toward the ridges on either side, breaking into little grassy knolls as they neared the slopes, and Caleb noted that any of those knolls would be a perfect spot for a house.

A hundred yards from the road Caleb stopped and stood for a long time with his hands on his hips, seeing a farm in his mind's eye. There, on that knoll in the shadow of the ridge, he could see a good solid house with smoke coming from a stovepipe and a spread of colorful flowers off to the left, where Mamm's kitchen garden would be. Behind, from a second little rise, grew a splendid barn with a silo and whitewashed horse fences all around. The fields to his right and left came alive with waves of wheat and forests of corn. As he turned full circle he saw with a clear eye the houses and silos and slender spires of windmills dotting a sea of fine, rich, cultivated land, and he knew in his heart that he would make the dream come true. Paradise Valley was real.

He got down on his knees, yanked up a handful of grass and sniffed the roots. He stuck a hand down into the depression, scooped out a little topsoil, squeezed it in a callused fist to gauge its moisture and sand content, sniffed it, tasted it.

A contented smile came to his eyes as he spat out the dirt and wiped his hand on his pant leg. He remained there, kneeling, while he removed his hat, lowered his head and closed his eyes.

His kin had all followed him silently into the grass and gathered around him, waiting. When he lowered his head, they all knelt with him while Caleb voiced a brief but fervent prayer, thanking a benevolent Gott for His blessings and for bringing them all so far without calamity.

When Caleb rose to his feet and snugged his hat back on his head, the others rose with him. Turning to face his family he waved his arm toward the knoll behind him and proclaimed, "We build *here*. Tonight we make camp at Hacienda El Prado. Tomorrow is the Sabbath and we will rest, but on Monday we will return to this place and begin digging our well."

Señor Hidalgo had offered to let them pitch camp at the hacienda for now. The hacienda lay two miles farther down the road beyond the end of the valley, but until they could get a well dug and build some kind of pen for the animals they would not be able to live on their land.

Ezra, Levi, Aaron and Harvey all gravitated toward Caleb at that point, drawing into a huddle to talk about the land — what they each saw in it, the problems and possibilities. The women separated naturally into another group to talk about an entirely different set of problems and possibilities.

While Ezra and Levi debated about the best place to find water, Caleb looked up to see someone coming on a horse. A big black Friesian loped straight toward them across the prairie grass, ignoring the road, and as it drew nearer they could see the rider was a middle-aged Mexican. Schulman, too, strode purposefully toward the group from the direction of the wagons.

The horse slowed his pace and stopped next to them, stamping his large hooves nervously and tossing his long mane. Caleb had not seen such a fine animal since they entered Mexico. The rider, sitting atop a silver-studded western saddle, wore a narrow brimmed hat like city folk wore back home, a fine new hunting coat and fancy leather chaps. The toes of newly polished cowboy boots peeked through the stirrups. Raising his hat with his free hand, the Mexican smiled broadly.

"*Buenos días!* Señor Bender?"

Caleb stepped forward, removing his hat, and reached up to shake the hand of his benefactor.

"I am Caleb Bender," he said, in his uncertain Spanish. "Are you Señor Hidalgo?"

"*Me llamo* Diego Fuentes," the man said, reaching down from his perch on the tall horse to shake Caleb's hand. To Caleb's relief, he switched abruptly to English. "I am the administrator of Señor Hidalgo's estate. The *haciendado* is away just now, but we have been expecting you. I watched your progress from the hacienda for the last hour and have come to greet you. So!" He swept an arm over the valley, a proud glint in his eye. "What do you think of our little valley?"

Caleb smiled, nodded. His Spanish was precarious at best, and he was greatly relieved to hear that Fuentes's English was quite good. *"Muy bien,"* he answered. "It's a fine piece of land, and I think we will do well here."

"I imagine you are all very tired and ready to end your long journey," Señor Fuentes said. "We have a place prepared for you at the hacienda, and I will be happy to guide you the rest of the way." The big Friesian shivered and reared a bit, anxious to get moving. Fuentes gripped the reins and calmed his horse with a few low words.

Caleb gestured toward the wagons and asked, "Could we leave the hay wagon here? There's only farm equipment and tools on it. We will need the tools here when we come back on Monday."

Fuentes shook his head. "No, Señor Bender, you must not leave the wagon out here. Not if you are going to stay at the hacienda."

"But why? This is our land, is it not?" He had, after all, made the down payment and signed the letter of intent.

Fuentes shrugged apologetically. "Well . . . because it won't be here when you come back."

Caleb stared blankly for a minute, trying to comprehend. "Are you saying someone might steal it?"

"Yes, this is exactly what I am saying. You

must not leave anything out here on the open plain, unguarded, or it will not be here when you return."

"They would steal our tools?" Caleb's face twisted in confusion. "From our own land? What kind of people — ?"

"There are bandits who pass through here," Fuentes said. "Also, most of the people around you are very poor. Mestizos, Chichimecas. They live in squalor, and to them you are outsiders, people from another world. *Yanquis.* The rules are different here. If you leave something unattended, someone will assume you don't want it anymore and they will take it. Señor Bender, you are not in Ohio anymore."

Despite her momentary joy at finally reaching Paradise Valley, Rachel couldn't help feeling a little discouraged sitting on the front of the hay wagon with her father as they followed Señor Fuentes to Hacienda El Prado. It seemed to her they had entered a strange world where new and unanticipated threats loomed just beyond every turn.

The road out of Paradise Valley bent southward once they cleared the end of the southern ridge, and on the open plain she could see Hacienda El Prado from a long way off. In the middle distance lay a few small farms, if they could be called that — they seemed very poor farms by Amish standards. There were a few adobe hovels like the ones they'd seen in Agua Nueva, some with crude stables and rickety barbed-wire fences to corral a milk cow, a handful of goats or a burro. The fields around them had been cultivated, but poorly — hand-sown in oats and winter wheat. Each of the houses had its own small vegetable patch at its feet, usually with a natural fence of prickly pear cactus planted around the perimeter. There were none of the tall, fork-shaped saguaro cactus here, and very few of the little round barrel cactus. Occasionally, she did see a tall, spiky thing that looked for the world like some kind of yucca. Some of them were higher than a man's head.

At the feet of the hacienda lay a fair-sized village. Everything Rachel had learned in her Spanish studies had led her to believe a hacienda was just a big house, but she was unprepared for what she saw when they approached the real thing. The house itself dominated the landscape by its sheer size and grandeur, sitting atop the largest hill this side of the ridges, but at its feet lay a small town. They drove right on into the middle of the town amid the stares of a hundred peasants who stopped what they were doing to watch the parade. Riding down the main street Rachel proudly demonstrated to her dat that she had learned enough Spanish words to read many of the signs over the shop doors.

"Look! *Mercado,*" she said. "That's a grocer, and next to it is the *carniceria* — the butcher shop. And there's the *oficina de correos* — the post office."

Everything was here that a proper town should have. She identified the blacksmith shop, a tannery, and a small textile mill of some kind. At the far end of town, in the shadow of the hacienda itself, stood a beautiful little Catholic church with walls of stone and stained-glass windows. The grounds around the church were neat and clean, and beyond it lay a large fenced-in cemetery shaded by two huge old oak trees.

A little ways beyond the church stood the entrance to the grounds of the hacienda, a pair of massive arched wrought-iron gates in a smoothly finished adobe wall with decorative vines growing across the top. Rachel expected their wagons to keep going right on through the gates, but she was wrong. Just short of the church, Fuentes's big Friesian took a left turn and led them through a winding little dirt street to the outskirts of the town.

"I thought we were staying at the hacienda," she said to her father.

"Well, if I understand it right, *hacienda* has two meanings in Spanish. It means the big house, but it also means the estate — the whole of Señor Hidalgo's property. If I'm not mistaken, everything in this town belongs to Señor Hidalgo, as well as all the ranch land for miles around."

"Everything?"

"Sí," her father said, and he was smiling. *"Todo."* She had not seen him in such a light mood since before he was arrested.

She looked about her at the adobe shacks of the peasants on the outskirts of town. Here, in the heart of Mexico, it appeared there were only two kinds of people — the very rich and the very poor.

"Señor Hidalgo must be a very, very wealthy man," she said.

Diego Fuentes guided them to a little ranch where they found a tidy little adobe lean-to structure with a corral attached where they were able to turn out the livestock. There was even a watering trough with a hand pump next to it where they could draw water for themselves. The building itself had only three walls and was open on one long side as though it might once have served as a stable. Now it held a stove at one end, which hinted that it may have become a summer kitchen or a place to do canning during harvest season. The men tied up one of the tents over the opening and dragged in an empty trough they found outside. Tonight, finally, they would all have a hot bath.

Chapter 17

Their first full day in Paradise Valley was a Sunday, so they decided to hold a church service — as best they could without a minister. Emma, Miriam and Rachel put on their new dresses from Emma's wedding, but nothing seemed quite right. The bells of the Catholic *iglesia* in town tolled while they were rearranging the makeshift benches and kitchen chairs in their temporary hovel, and everyone straightened up to listen. The bells echoed a loneliness they all felt too deeply in this strange new place. They took their seats, men on one side and women on the other, and Caleb stood before them to speak.

"I am no minister," he said. "I'm sorry for that, but it is a sacrifice that someone had to make. If you think about it, I guess this makes us a little like Jesus when He said, 'I go to prepare a place for you.' We have come here to Paradise Valley to prepare a place so that others may come. Our work begins tomorrow. Today will be a day of rest and prayer. We must ask Gott to help us, to bless our hands and backs that we may not falter in our work, to keep us safe from harm . . . and to bring us a real minister. For now, as poor a shepherd as I am, you will have to make do with me."

Caleb read from the Bible, a long passage about Moses and how his people were delivered from bondage by the hand of Gott. And then he just talked for a little while, though he didn't go on for an hour like a minister was supposed to do, and he didn't even pretend to adopt the singsong cadence of a good preacher, the rising and falling of the voice like waves. He just talked.

"We must obey Gott rather than men," he said. "Government — any government — is but Gott's way of keeping godless men from devouring one another like fishes. It is a necessary evil, but it has nothing to do with the children of Gott. We have a higher law, and we should have nothing to do with government. The men who rise to become rulers in this world will always be those who know the secrets of worldly power, and how to tickle the ears of godless men. As children of Gott we must live in this world, among worldly men, yet always remember that our citizenship is elsewhere. We must live not by power or might, but by the Spirit of the Lord of hosts. We are foreigners not just in Mexico, but also on Earth. Our time here is short, and if we are to be about our Father's business we must learn to be *in* the world, but not *of* the world."

Well before daylight on Monday the family rose to get their chores done. By dawn the wagon was loaded, the horses hitched, and the men headed out to the valley to begin digging a well. Since they were shorthanded, Miriam and Rachel went with them while the married women and Ada remained behind at the hacienda to finish settling in and wash the clothes.

Caleb had stayed up late Saturday night talking to Schulman about the right way to dig a well that would give them enough water for irrigation, and during the ride out to the valley he explained to his sons and sons-in-law what he had in mind.

A square cistern the size of a living room could be dug out, Schulman said, and then a number of small holes drilled straight out horizontally near the bottom like the spokes of a wheel. The holes would empty into the cistern, effectively gathering water from a wide area. Meanwhile, the dirt from the dig could be used to make adobe bricks, which they would need for building houses. The idea was brilliant in its simplicity.

As soon as they arrived at the shallow depression Caleb had chosen for the well and unloaded the digging tools, he sent Harvey and Levi up to the ridge to start cutting timber.

"You're our two best loggers," he said. "That ridge is not on our land, but Señor Fuentes has given us permission to harvest a few trees. Be careful to take only what you need and don't leave a mess. Try to find a few big logs because we'll need to set aside some lumber to cure, for when we're ready to build the house. We will have a saw pit dug before you get back."

With axes and crosscut saws, a couple of stout log chains and a pair of Belgians, the boys would make short work of a tree. Aaron and Ezra set about digging a saw pit while Rachel and Miriam, in their long dresses and prayer kapps, took turns with a scythe cutting prairie grass and spreading it out to dry.

As promised, the saw pit was finished by noon, and Caleb had used the precious few planks they'd brought with them from Ohio to build a trestle over it. It was all hard manual labor, but after a week of sitting in a train car they found the work wonderfully invigorating. It was a fine clear day with a light breeze and temperatures in the seventies, a perfect day for working. When the sun was directly overhead Caleb looked up and saw the wagon returning from the ridge with six straight pine logs, and from the other direction, Emma bringing lunch in the hack.

He wanted to sing for joy. Selfish pride was a trap, but there was nothing selfish about Caleb's pride in his family. There was nothing worth doing in this world that could not be accomplished with common sense, hard work, and the help of a strong family.

After lunch they started digging the well. One pair of men manned a pick and shovel while another pair went to work ripping logs into lumber. The pit saw wore them out quickly, so the digging and sawing crews swapped places frequently and a friendly competition soon developed between them to see who could get the most done.

They wasted nothing. When they squared up a log with the two-man saw they saved the slabs from the four sides. With a few pegs drilled into them the half-round slabs would make excellent benches.

By the end of the first full day's work they had dug two feet of the massive hole required for the irrigation well, piled up a considerable mound of dirt, and built five ladder-like molds to be used for producing four-inch-thick adobe bricks, six at a time.

Near sunset they loaded everything back onto the wagon, including the new lumber and the brick molds, and headed back to the hacienda. The trestle over the pit was too unwieldy, so they left it in place.

Sitting beside Rachel on the back of the bouncing wagon, filthy and exhausted, swinging her legs and watching the red sun kiss the mountaintops, Miriam said, "It feels so strange, having to start over again."

"I know," Rachel said. Miriam was a year and a half older than Rachel, so starting over had to be even harder for her. "Having to build from scratch all the things we already had back home. But maybe Dat's right when he says it makes you appreciate the simple things more."

"Like a drink of clean water."

"Or a warm bed."

"Oh, yes! A bed where you don't have to check for scorpions first," Miriam said, beginning to chuckle.

"An outhouse," Rachel contributed. "I never thought I'd miss it so much."

"We'll have one soon," Miriam said. "At

least I think we will. I don't know for sure if you can build one out of adobe."

"I bet it'll be hard to move," Rachel said.

Miriam laughed out loud then. Harvey and his friends had been known to move an outhouse back a few feet on a dark night when they thought someone deserved a major prank.

"But you know, Rachel, I have to admit I feel much better today. Sometimes all it takes is a little hard work to make you forget your troubles."

"Well then, we're in the right place. With all the work ahead of us it may be ten years yet before we have another minute to think about our troubles."

The sun dipped behind the mountains, leaving the western sky streaked with colors they had never seen back home — brilliant turquoise fading into orange, orange into deep red, and deep red into a velvet black already dotted with eager stars.

That evening the boys used a few of the freshly cut pine planks for a makeshift dinner table, and for the first time in a week they were able to gather the whole family around one table for a meal. It was a small thing, but now that they had arrived in Paradise Valley, found the place to be viable and seen the work of their hands already changing the landscape, a new kind of optimism had begun to sprout. There was a palpable feeling that each day's work would restore a little bit more of the civilized life they had known before.

During dinner, Mamm asked casually, "Did you plow a place for my kitchen garden today?"

Dat stopped a fork halfway to his mouth and put it back down. He had not failed to notice that his wife had been sleeping better, and her cough seemed already to have abated a little. Now she was giving orders and planning her garden, perhaps the best sign of all.

"Mamm, you know we didn't take a plow on the wagon. We had plenty to do already, digging the well, making a saw pit and cutting timber. Anyways, if you plant a garden before we move onto the land, who will watch it to make sure no one steals your vegetables?"

She was ready for this. "We can move tents onto the land and set up housekeeping as soon as we have a little fence and a well. This will save you the trip back and forth each day, plus you will have all your tools at hand. How long will it take to dig a well?"

She asked it innocently, almost sweetly, but he knew he was trapped. His pride would not allow him to say his well might take longer than two weeks.

"Oh, probably not more than a couple weeks," he said, sensing defeat.

"Well then, there won't be any vegetables ready yet, so no one can steal them anyway."

It was decided. Tomorrow they would take the plow.

After dinner, perhaps as a kind of apology for her little victory, Mamm brought in the trough for baths and put huge pots of water on the stove to heat. It was a rare occasion indeed when they took baths on a Monday night, but after a day of digging they were as filthy as pigs.

Everyone used the same bathwater, so by the time Rachel got her turn there was a layer of grit in the bottom of the lukewarm brown water, and still it was heaven.

After her bath Rachel sat at the table and wrote a long letter to Jake by lantern light. She told him about the train trip and all the wonderful sights she had seen. She described Paradise Valley for him, and the grand hacienda of Señor Hidalgo. Keeping the letter light and friendly because she knew his mother would probably read it, she ended by saying simply, "We wish you'uns were here." Jake would understand. He would read between the lines, instinctively replacing the plural with the singular.

And he would not fail to hear the ache in her voice.

CHAPTER 18

The first thing Caleb noticed when his wagon pulled up to the homestead the next morning was that the crude trestle he'd built over the saw pit was gone. Someone had come during the night, disassembled it and hauled away the planks.

He stood there for a long time staring at the naked pit, his hands on his hips, his jaw working.

"Why would anybody want to steal something like that?" he asked Levi, who knelt beside him pondering the same question, his fingers probing the footprints. The tracks in the soft dirt around the pit were small, for men, and barefoot. The big toes splayed out in the manner of someone unaccustomed to shoes.

Levi shrugged, picking his teeth with a pine sliver. "It was good lumber. I guess they could use it for fencing, or framing a roof, or mebbe just firewood."

Caleb nodded thoughtfully. "Well, we learned our lesson, didn't we? I won't be leaving nothing else behind anymore."

"But what do we do with these people?" Levi asked, rising. "How can we live among thieves?"

"It will be hard, but I believe we have to make friends of them. Like Fuentes said, they steal because they are poor — they don't have anything. Maybe we can help them learn to live better."

"Generosity is wasted on a thief," Levi said. "He will take the chicken you give him and smile and say thank you, and then when you're not looking he will steal your horse, too."

Caleb chewed on this for a moment and replied, "I didn't say we should *give* to them, I said we should *teach* them." He turned a wise eye on his son-in-law. "And I said it would not be easy. We must be patient. Anyways, it's not so bad. We can build another trestle."

It was a horrendously busy week. The whole family, even the women, came to the site at dawn each day and worked until dusk. Harvey turned over a half-acre garden plot with the plow, and it was nearly as easy as Harris had said it would be, the topsoil rich and soft as butter. There were hardly any rocks, and no stumps. As always, the biggest problem with newly cultivated ground would be keeping down weeds and wild grasses. Normally, such a field would be turned several times in the winter to expose roots and kill all the weeds, but they didn't have time for that. Caleb hooked up the spring-tooth harrow every day and dragged it over the garden plot, but after only five days Mamm said, "Enough. I'm planting my garden."

"It will be overrun with weeds," Caleb warned.

"That can't be helped," she said. "It's new ground. We'll just have to use the cultivator to get rid of the weeds when they come up."

By the end of the week the massive central cistern for the well was finished, rows of damp adobe bricks stood like dominoes on planks just up the hill, and huge mounds of dirt stood waiting for more to be made. Even Ada and the children had helped out. They seemed to have a natural talent for brickmaking — it was, after all, a lot like making mud pies. And the work was good for Ada. She was no less depressed in the evenings but at least she was too tired to cry all night. Mamm planted her garden, and the boys made a good start on turning over a large section where Caleb planned to put in a corn crop.

Late on Saturday afternoon a rain shower popped up and drenched everyone as they were loading the wagon to go home. Standing at the edge of her new garden watching the ground darken, Mamm paid no attention to the downpour soaking her dress. Alarmed at the sight of his sick wife in the rain, Caleb grabbed a piece of oilcloth from the back of the wagon and ran to cover her, but as he drew near she did something that stopped him in his tracks.

Raising her work-reddened, dirt-stained palms toward the heavens, Mamm closed her eyes, lifted her face into a driving rain and said quietly, "Thank you."

On Sunday afternoon, after prayer and Bible reading, the Benders ate lunch and then hitched up the buggies and drove over to Schulman's place. Everyone went except Levi and Emma, who stayed behind at the hovel to keep an eye on their belongings.

"I don't know why Emma would have to stay behind," Caleb grumbled as he drove away. "Levi could watch by himself."

Mamm's eyes smiled. She leaned close to her husband's ear and whispered, "Shhh. They are newlyweds yet, Dat."

Where the road from the hacienda bent westward into Paradise Valley, another road forked off to the north around the tip of the ridge. This was the road to Saltillo, fifty miles to the north, the same path that the railroad would follow when the new spur was built down through Paradise Valley. Schulman's farm lay only a couple of miles up Saltillo Road, on the other side of the ridge from where the Benders were building their home.

Schulman's house and outbuildings — all made of adobe, including a low barn and stable — sat a hundred yards back from the road. When the buggies turned in and headed up the driveway a pair of German shepherds charged out to sound the alarm. Caleb kept a tight rein while the dogs circled the two buggies barking, their hackles raised.

Schulman came from the stable to see what the fuss was about, and when he saw the buggies, his face broke into a huge grin. He waved and shouted, "Wilhelm! Augusta! *Kommen sie!*" The two dogs instantly stopped, pricked their ears and looked, then bolted toward their master.

Ernst Schulman was so delighted to have company he had one of his hired hands go out and kill chickens for dinner, and then took the Bender men out for a walking tour of his farm while the women got to know each other. His wife was a tiny blond woman, lively and quick to laugh. She and Mamm took to each other right away.

Walking over Schulman's place, Ezra pointed out something strange. Behind the farmhouse lay a twenty-acre pasture fenced in with barbed wire. In the middle of the pasture lay a full acre of freestanding bushes as high as a man's head, and arbors laden with vines. A huge longhorn bull grazed in the shade of a lone cottonwood tree not far from the vineyard.

Ezra squinted. "Are those blueberry bushes?"

"Oh jah!" Schulman said, breaking stride to look with them. "And grapevines. Blueberries do very well here, and they bloom early because of the mild winter. In fact, the blueberries are ripe right now, if you'd like to pick some."

Ezra and the boys looked to Caleb, who shook his head. "No, not today."

"Really, I don't mind," Schulman said. "I'll have Oquendo saddle a horse and put away the bull, then you can pick your hats full of blueberries."

"*Danke,* but no," Caleb said. "We don't pick on Sunday."

"Ohhhh, I see. Sorry, sometimes I forget about your religion. Well, that's all right then, you can come back another day or send the women up here — anytime."

Ezra pointed, curious. "Why would you have to lock up the bull to pick berries?"

Schulman laughed. "Satan is the meanest animal I have ever known. If he gets the chance, he will kill you and trample your corpse."

"Then why would you have him loose around your vineyard?"

A devious smile stayed on Schulman's face as he pointed at the vineyard. "Would you go in there with Satan, on foot, for a handful of berries?"

Ezra shook his head, his eyes wide. "Noooo."

"Neither will the Mexicans. He makes an excellent watchdog."

Schulman's fields were thick with oats and wheat, and at dinner they learned that not only did his garden yield a bounty of vegetables but his wife was an excellent cook.

"Oh!" Schulman said suddenly, his mouth full of chicken. "By the way, Augusta has pups! There are four left, already weaned, and you must choose one to take with you." He pointed at Caleb with his fork. "You will need a good dog, Herr Bender, to watch your chickens."

Schulman's table, built only for him and his wife, would not hold them all, so the younger ones were eating in the kitchen. All of them broke into excited chatter over the new pup, rushing through the rest of their dinner so they could hurry out and pick their new dog.

After dinner the grown-ups strolled out to the stable, where the younger ones had already gathered around the pups. Walking across the backyard Caleb said, "I have not seen Pelao since we came. Is he not here today?"

"Pah!" Schulman spat, glowering. "I chased him off. Two days ago I found one of my peons sleeping in the barn when he was supposed to be working, and I woke him with a buggy whip. Pelao snatched the whip away from me and threatened me with it, so I ran him off. Good riddance. I never trusted him anyway. There's nothing worse than an uppity Chichimeca."

The four shepherd pups bounded and tumbled in a furious heap with the children.

"Sammy! Paul!" Mary shouted, bending to snatch her sons' Sunday hats from the dirt, but Schulman's booming laugh overruled her.

"They're boys!" he said. "Let them play."

There were three male pups and only one female, the smallest of the four. Miriam and Rachel squatted among them, running fingers through the rich puppy fur and getting scratched by needle-sharp puppy teeth, testing their personalities. The little female took an instant liking to Miriam, who clutched it to her chest, heedless of her new white apron. She looked up at Caleb and said, "I want this one."

"Ach, that's the runt," Schulman said. "You can have the big one if you want. He's going to be a fine dog."

Rachel intervened. Like Emma, she knew her father's mind. "A female can have puppies," she said. "We have only to find a suitable mate, and then there will be more dogs to come."

Caleb's eyes softened, and she knew she had him.

"All right," he said. "The female it is."

On the ride home, in the purple light of a mountain dusk, Miriam held her new puppy on her lap and hugged it to sleep. By the time they reached the hacienda she had given it a name.

Hope.

CHAPTER 19

"Schulman said when we finish the well we can borrow his diesel pump for irrigation until we can get a windmill," Caleb said, thinking out loud as he drove the wagon out to the homestead in Paradise Valley with the sun just beginning to rise behind him.

Levi nodded, sitting beside him on the wagon seat. "We can probably buy a windmill in Saltillo."

"Jah, but it will take most of my cash, and if we use his pump for a while we can put off the windmill until we can raise a cash crop to sell. In the meantime, I'm thinking we need to hire a couple of the locals to help us build the house and fences. Already we don't have enough men to put up a house, dig a well and work the fields all at the same time. It's a hard question. If we don't get a cash crop in the ground soon, we won't have enough money to make it through the year, but on the other hand I don't know if it's wise to spend money on hired hands."

"The train wasn't cheap, either," Levi said. He had paid his share of the passage, as had Ezra. "But me and Ezra have a little money put by yet. We can pay the Mexicans. Anyhow, they will work for almost nothing . . . if we can get them to work. Schulman says they are lazy."

As they drew near to the farm they saw a lone figure at the base of the ridge overlooking their property. He was sitting on the ground with his knees drawn up and a blanket about him, but they recognized the wide, brown flat-brimmed hat even from a distance.

Pelao.

"I wonder what he's doing here," Levi said. "After what Schulman told us I hope he doesn't think we're going to hire *him*."

"Well, let's not be too quick to judge," Caleb said to his young son-in-law. "He seems able enough, and there's two sides to every story."

Caleb halted the pair of Belgians near the well site and climbed down to start unloading. While he was untying the ropes at the back of the wagon a low voice behind him said, "Señor Bender?"

Pelao was standing behind him, the moth-eaten blanket still draped over his shoulders.

"I come to work for you," Pelao said in Spanish, then glanced around at the well, the saw pit, the half-plowed field. "You need help."

Caleb chuckled. "I never heard you speak before. I wasn't sure you could."

This, Pelao did not answer. He stared blankly.

"What about Schulman?" Caleb asked. "I thought you worked for him."

Pelao's head turned sideways momentarily. He spat on the ground, and then his steady gaze came back to Caleb.

"*Veo*," Caleb said. *I see.* He thought for a long moment, trying to find the Spanish to say what he wanted. "It's true, we do need help. Your troubles with Señor Schulman need not follow you here, but I expect you to do as I say and work as I work. Do that, Pelao, and you will be treated with respect."

Pelao's eyes narrowed. "My name is not Pelao," he said in Spanish, speaking slowly, apparently having heard enough to know the language was still difficult for Caleb. "That name was a gift from Schulman, a callous word for someone with no education. It is his way of calling me an ignorant savage. My people are the Nahua, and in my native tongue my name is Tlacayaotl. It is a proud name, a warrior name."

Caleb tried it, but stumbled over the first syllable.

The native smiled. "Nahuatl is difficult for a Yanqui tongue. My mother's Spanish name for me was Domingo, because I was born on Sunday."

"Domingo," Caleb repeated. "That I can pronounce."

Rachel and Miriam, unloading the shovels and hoes they would need for their brick-work, watched Domingo climb down into the cistern with Aaron and Levi to begin drilling the radial holes.

"Did Dat just hire him?" Miriam whispered. "I thought Schulman said he couldn't be trusted."

"Jah, but you know Dat," Rachel said, hefting two shovels onto her shoulder. "He makes up his own mind about people. Anyway, Dat's a good judge of character."

Harvey and Ezra unloaded the plow and switched the Belgians over to it. Domingo had taken Harvey's place in the cistern, freeing him to plow the cornfield.

Not more than a half hour later, mixing mud, Rachel stopped to wipe her brow and saw the Belgians standing idle at the far end of a freshly plowed furrow, and Harvey wading off through the uncut prairie grass beyond them.

She nudged Miriam and pointed. "There goes Harvey. Doesn't matter if it's Ohio or Mexico, as soon as he starts work in the morning he has to stop and go," she chuckled.

Then she saw her brother leap into the air sideways, falling, losing his hat. He popped up from the grass immediately and bolted toward them, snatching at his left pant leg, running with a pronounced limp over the soft, plowed field, shouting and waving.

"Dat!" she cried out, pointing. "Something's wrong with Harvey!"

Caleb and Ezra dropped what they were doing and ran toward Harvey, who fell to his knees as soon as they reached him.

Rachel and Miriam ran to see what happened. Harvey was screaming, and she knew pain would not have done that. It was fear — Harvey was in a panic.

"Schlange!" he cried. *Snake!* "It bit my leg!"

By the time she reached the little huddle in the field, her father had pulled up Harvey's pant leg and rolled him over onto his stomach. There were two puncture wounds in the center of his calf, the skin around it already red and swelling. Aaron, Levi, and

Domingo had climbed out of the hole to see what the fuss was about and now leaned over Harvey. Ada came puffing up to the group last and squeezed in between them to look. Her eyes went wide when she saw Harvey's calf and heard the word *snake.* She flung her hands in the air and bolted back the way she came, screaming, Miriam hot on her heels to make sure she didn't fall into the well or run off to the ridge.

Rachel's heart froze. The locals had told them the nearest doctor was thirty miles over the mountains in Agua Nueva, and no one in the family had any experience with snakebites. The thing that scared her most was the fear in her father's face.

Dat looked up, and his eyes swept the little circle. "What do we do?" he cried, near panic himself.

Domingo knelt beside Harvey. He'd left his own hat in the back of the wagon, and his long black hair hung loose, hiding his face.

"What kind of snake?" he asked, in Spanish.

Lying on his stomach, Harvey had to turn his head and look over his shoulder to see Domingo. At the moment, Spanish words escaped him. He held up a forefinger, twitched it back and forth rapidly and

233

hissed between his teeth. A rattler.

Domingo's hand slipped behind his back and reappeared with a knife in it. Without a word he slit quickly into the flesh of Harvey's calf, straight across the two puncture wounds.

"Leave him be!" Levi yelled. Unsure of the native's intentions and unwilling to wait and see what else he would do with the knife, Levi grabbed Domingo by his shoulders, pulled him off of Harvey and sent him sprawling backward.

Dat snatched off Harvey's suspenders and began winding them around the leg just below the knee.

The leg was bleeding profusely now, from Domingo's cut. Dat slid his own pocketknife, closed, under the loop of suspenders and twisted it several times, cinching the tourniquet tight. Then he sat back on his haunches and looked up at the sky.

"Gott, what do we do?" he prayed, anguish written on his face. Rachel knelt and prayed. Levi glowered. It was Ezra who first heard a noise and looked back toward the wagon.

"Is he stealing our horse?"

After coming to the site in the surrey that morning the girls had unhitched the buggy horse and left it tied to the back of the empty wagon. Domingo, apparently taking advantage of the diversion, had untied the horse, leaped on its back and was now spurring it to a full gallop, racing away toward the ridge.

Levi glared after him. "I knew that Indian couldn't be trusted."

"There is no time to worry about that now," Dat said. "Is there a doctor at the hacienda?"

Rachel shook her head. "No, I heard Señor Fuentes say the doctor only comes when Señor Hidalgo is here. He travels with the haciendado, and right now they are in Europe. There is no doctor in the village."

"Well, we have to do *something*. Bring some kerosene!"

Ezra ran to the wagon and fetched a gallon can from the toolbox. Dat opened the can and poured kerosene directly into the knife wound on Harvey's calf, washing out the blood and revealing red meat. Harvey didn't even flinch.

"Maybe that will wash the poison out," Dat said, but he didn't look convinced. When he noticed that Harvey's ashen face was lying on the dirt, he took his own hat off and placed it gently under the boy's head. "We will wait and see. It's no good to move him yet. Let him calm down and slow the poison a little bit."

They heard hoofbeats and looked up to see Domingo charging toward them from the ridge, gripping the horse's mane in his fists and hauling back on it as he drew near. He leaped off the horse and landed nimbly on his feet, so close by that his momentum carried him running into the little circle, where he brushed Levi roughly aside.

Kneeling by the stricken boy, Domingo leaned over, put his hands on both ends of the cut and squeezed, opening the wound like a change purse.

Then he spat.

A big mouthful of some viscous yellow substance splattered right down into the cut on Harvey's leg — something Domingo had been holding in his mouth, chewing. He wiped his mouth on his sleeve and then, without a word, pulled a bandanna from around his neck and wrapped the wound with it, tying it tightly when he was done.

It all happened so fast, none of them had time to object. Rachel could only stare openmouthed at Domingo as he rose to his feet.

"Que es?" Dat asked, proper Spanish eluding him in the heat of the moment.

"Raíz negra," Domingo said, pointing a thumb back toward the tree line at the base of the ridge. *Black root.* "Nahua medicine

for snakebite." He pointed at Harvey's leg. "If I was quick enough, he will walk in two days. You will see."

Dat took a deep breath, staring hard at Domingo. "Sí," he said. "We'll see."

There was nothing else to do now but send the boy back home and let his mother tend to him, so they loaded him into the buggy and hitched up the horse. Rachel drove. Harvey lay in the back, nauseated, sweating profusely. Miriam held his head and prayed.

Caleb took over the plowing, fretting constantly about his son and glancing a million times down the road toward the hacienda wishing for news, but there was nothing he could do. It would have been a waste of time for all of them to stop work, and it would only worry Harvey. If all the men of the family came home to stand over his bed, Harvey would think he was dying.

Rachel and Miriam returned in the buggy at midday, bringing lunch. They also brought good news.

"Harvey's feeling pretty good," Rachel said. "His leg is swelling really big, but it's not turning black around the wound anymore. It's not even as red as it was before."

"And the fever is almost gone," Miriam

said, casting a curious glance at Domingo, who was leaning casually against the wagon wheel.

"The Nahua have lived with the rattlesnake much longer even than they have lived with the Spaniard," he said, as if the two were synonymous. "When it comes to snakes, maybe savages are not so ignorant."

Driving home that evening in the purple twilight, Caleb eavesdropped on his son and son-in-law, who were riding behind him on the wagon.

"He's a pretty good worker," Aaron said. "Almost like an Amishman."

Levi, lying on his back utterly exhausted and covered in mud from head to toe, had to raise his hat from his face to reply. "I hate to admit it, but you're right. He's not so bad, once you get used to his ways. I still don't like him much, but he sure knows how to work. Why, that Indian worked almost as hard as I did, and mebbe *twice* as hard as you." Levi lowered his hat back down over a wry smile, waiting for Aaron's comeback.

It didn't take long.

"You're forgetting, Levi," Aaron said quietly. "I was there."

Everyone on the wagon got a chuckle out of this inside joke. A few years earlier, Aaron and his twin brother, Amos, had gone on a fishing trip with some of their cousins to a river up beyond Akron. When they returned, Amos told everyone at the dinner table about how they'd gotten bored and started skipping rocks, and he was the only one who could skip a rock all the way across the river.

"Why, that river must have been a quarter mile across!" the irrepressible Amos said, to doubtful stares.

In the ensuing silence Aaron quietly pointed out, "The river I saw wasn't more than a hundred feet at the widest place."

When Amos saw he was caught in a lie he hung his head and muttered darkly, "Oh, jah. I forgot you were there."

Amos's flawless deadpan delivery made the moment enormously funny. They laughed about it for three days, and the line became a standard among the family, a sly rebuke for wild exaggeration.

Aaron's gentle rebuttal to Levi brought a smile to all their faces, but it also reminded them of Amos, who had always been the life of the party. They were quiet the rest of the way home.

Harvey didn't make it to dinner that night, and everyone else was almost too tired to eat. Around the long pine-plank table in the little stable, every head drooped. Their elbows were on the table and their cheeks resting on their palms, all of them, as they picked one-handed at their potatoes and peas — until Mary livened things up.

"Looks like I'm going to have another baby," she said.

Heads came up, and smiles lit tired faces.

"Well, that's a fine thing!" Caleb said, beaming. "He'll be the first Amish baby in Mexico."

"Maybe not," Emma said, smiling at her older sister. "It seems I'm going to have a baby, too. We can race to see who's first."

The whole mood in the stable changed then, and an air of celebration took over. When Emma went out to feed and water the pigs an hour later, Rachel went with her to talk. Emma dumped the slop bucket and hung it on a fence post while Rachel pumped water into the trough.

"Emma, what made you decide to go ahead and tell?"

Emma shrugged, admiring the stars. "I didn't have any choice, really. Pretty soon now this dress won't hide it."

Harvey's lower leg was swollen to twice its normal size that evening, and he was in considerable pain, but by morning the fever abated and he wasn't sick anymore. By the

next night the swelling had begun to sub-
side. After two days, just as Domingo had
said, he was able to walk on it. After breakfast on the third morning, Harvey put on
his hat and coat and limped out to the
wagon, ready to go back to work.

Rachel and Miriam were fast becoming
experts on the making of adobe. With their
crew of Ada and the two little sons of Mary
and Ezra, they were turning out bricks at a
prodigious rate. Even Hope got into the act,
though she mostly provided a riotous diversion. Twice she fell into the cistern, and the
newer bricks all had paw prints in them
until Miriam finally tied the dog in the
shade of the wagon with a bowl of water.

During lunch Domingo wandered over to
their adobe brickworks just uphill from the
well. He had taken off his hat and shirt to
work in the well. His upper body was lean
and muscular, his shoulders broad and his
waist narrow, though at the moment he
looked like a savage — covered in mud from
head to toe, his long hair matted and his
pants plastered to his legs. The only clean
spot on him was his right hand, which he
had wiped off to eat. He took a bite from a
big hunk of bread as he inspected the brickworks.

Rachel and Miriam, having finished their lunch, came over and stood on either side of him, proudly surveying their handiwork.

"Bueno, no?" Rachel said.

Domingo jammed the hunk of bread in his mouth and held it in his teeth while he reached down and hefted one of the driest bricks from its plank. He held the forty-pound brick in front of him at eye level for a second, and then let go.

The brick crashed down on the plank, landing on a corner and shattering into a half dozen big chunks.

Both the girls gasped, their mouths flying open in outrage.

"Es tú loco?" Rachel said, figuring it was probably not the right words, but he'd get the idea from the tone of her voice.

Domingo pulled the bread from his mouth, chewing while he toed the remains of the destroyed brick.

"Demasiada paja," he said.

Miriam and Rachel stared at each other, their faces twisted in confusion. Miriam's Spanish was better than Rachel's, but even she didn't understand what he'd said. They turned their palms up, the universal sign for *Huh?*

"Demasiada paja," he repeated, nuzzling the rubble with a bare muddy toe, pointing at it with his bread.

"No entiendo esa palabra," Miriam said. *I don't understand that word.*

Domingo rolled his eyes. *"Zu viel stroh!"* he said, raising his voice. *Too much straw.* In High German.

They were stunned. It took a moment, but Rachel recovered first.

"You speak German?"

A casual nod. "Jah. I worked for Herr Schulman three years. I may not read or write, but I can hear and I pick up language quick. I have a good ear."

He spoke with a heavy Spanish accent, but the words were right and they could understand him quite well.

"Does Schulman know you speak German?" Miriam asked. This was on Rachel's mind too, but they had listened to Schulman enough to know it was unlikely.

Domingo flashed Miriam a devilish grin and stared at her for a moment before he shook his head. *"Nein, cualnezqui.* It was a great advantage, knowing what he said to his wife. He would never have spoken his mind if he knew I understood."

Domingo then went on to explain about the straw. The drop test was normal, he said, a way to know if the mixture was right. If there was too little straw in the bricks, they

243

would crack during the drying process. Too much, and they would crumble. A proper adobe brick could be dropped from shoulder height and not break — *most* of the time. It was not an exact science.

"Well then," Rachel said, "we'll cut down on the straw."

Miriam was still gaping in astonishment. "Your German is pretty good," she sputtered. "How could you work for the man three years and never tell him you learned his language?"

A sly smile lit his dark eyes. "There are two things you must know if you are to thrive in this land, cualnezqui. The first is, never tell anyone everything you know."

Miriam's brow furrowed and she looked at him a little sideways. "Cualnezqui," she repeated, sounding out the syllables. "Twice you have called me this. I don't know this word. Is it Nahuatl?"

"Sí."

"What does it mean?"

He chuckled. "Friend," he said. "Or neighbor. Whichever you like."

"Thank you," she said, blushing. "It sounds nice."

Domingo shoved the last of the bread into his mud-smeared face and went back to the cistern without another word. Lesson over.

"Nahuatl, Spanish, and High German," Miriam mused. "An ignorant savage who speaks three languages?"

"That we know of," Rachel said. "And he has a sense of humor, too."

Miriam's eyes followed Domingo until he went out of sight down the ladder.

Chapter 20

Rachel sat up late Sunday night writing a letter to Jake at the makeshift table in the hovel, a kerosene lantern hissing and guttering beside her. The others had all gone to bed, most of them in the tents outside, a few in the hovel. Ada was having one of her bad nights, and Mamm lay against her in the corner, cooing to her and trying to get her to sleep. "Shhhh, little one. Gott knows. Shhhh."

Rachel dipped her pen in the ink and paused, trying to sort out everything that had happened lately and choose the most important. She had planned to write Jake at least once a week but it just hadn't been possible — there wasn't time.

Dear Jake,
 Gott has been good to us. The weather here is wonderful for mid May, with sunny days in the sixties and chilly nights. It only

rained twice since we came, but the well is almost ready. Gma was good today, though we miss having a real minister, and of course all the others. We pray that a minister comes soon so we can have a real church.

She stopped writing at that point and sat dawdling with her loose hair and staring into space. There were thoughts she could not express because she feared Jake's mother might read the letter — *oh, how I miss you and long for you to hold me, to look into my eyes* — and there were other things she would not say even to Jake. Some things were only for dreaming, but dream she did. Anyway, marriage was not even possible so long as no minister came to Paradise Valley.

Men are busy with the well, digging a basement for the house, and planting. The sweet corn is in already, and they are plowing for the field corn. Dat says the sweet corn is from that new seed Danny Chupp gave him. Danny told him if it gets good water it would be ready to pick two months from planting, but Dat says he'll believe when he sees. If Danny was right, we'll have ears to sell by August. Pretty good.

Everyone is working daylight to dark, coming home worn out and sleeping like the dead. There's hardly even time to write. Last week Dat hired a Mexican named Domingo to help out. Two days later Domingo brought two of his cousins from San Rafael and Dat hired them, too. We all enjoy learning Spanish from them even though sometimes they laugh at how we say things. The way they really talk is not like in the book.

She paused again to wipe a tear from her eye because she could not write that there was only one voice she longed to hear, and his words were not Spanish.

Mamm's feeling a little better. She stays busy with her kitchen garden, with Mary and Emma to help. Her garden is coming up nice and green but right now we have to carry water to it and weed it every day.

Emma says she thinks she is going to have a baby, and Mary too! Our little colony will be growing soon.

Emma. Lucky, lucky Emma. Life was easier now that they didn't have to be quite so careful of their words. What must it be like for Emma, to be united with the man she loved and able to start a family together?

And what would *Jake's* children look like?
Would they have his eyes, his easy smile?

Harvey was out plowing and got bit by a rattlesnake! Praise Gott, he is fine now, and back at work. He says it still aches a little, and he will have a scar but it could have gone much worse. Answered prayers!

Miriam and I have become the best adobe brick makers in all of Mexico, with Ada and the little ones helping out — Mary's boys like to mix the mud and straw with their feet.

Oh, and we got a new pet, a fine German shepherd pup named Hope. She loves Miriam, a good thing because Miriam needed a friend just now.

Miriam. The one girl in all of Mexico with hopes slimmer than her own. Miriam hid it well, with busy hands and a placid, inscrutable face, but Rachel saw the pain in her sister's eyes sometimes late at night, after prayers, and she knew what prayers Miriam had not spoken aloud.

Well, I'll stop since it's getting late. We miss you'uns terribly and count the days until you come.

Your friend,
Rachel

We. You'uns. Yes, Jake would read between the lines and hear the words *I miss you.* There was so much behind the words. She missed his voice, his touch, the way he looked at her. She missed the mere *fact* that he looked at her, that his eyes watched for her alone, and she fervently hoped, against all the natural angst and doubt that came with being a teenage girl, that somehow, across a thousand miles, his eyes would continue to look only for her.

In the end, she trusted Jake. He would read between the lines. Jake would understand, and smile at the closing words.

Your friend.

Indeed.

CHAPTER 21

The weeks passed and the corn sprouted, shooting up out of the ground as if it shared Rachel's impatience. The men finished digging the well and lined the sides with rock hauled from an outcropping in the nearby ridge. Water poured in from the radial holes at a surprising rate, filling the cistern halfway to the top. They installed Schulman's diesel pump for irrigating the fields and a hand pump for personal use, then built a tin-roofed shed over the whole thing.

By the time the corn was knee-high the men had finished digging the basement for the house. They hauled more rocks from the ridge and built the foundation walls with a wagonload of surplus lime mortar Señor Fuentes had graciously sold them from the hacienda warehouse, saving Dat a trip to Saltillo. Meanwhile, Rachel and Miriam and Ada and the children stacked up adobe bricks by the hundreds.

As soon as the well was finished the whole family moved their tents from the stable to their land. By keeping all the farm implements at the homestead instead of hauling them back and forth they gained nearly two hours of work time each day.

The weather had warmed to what passed for summer in the mountains, but still the temperatures seldom climbed into the eighties.

Late one Saturday afternoon Dat took a walk down through the field to see how the sweet corn was coming, taking his time for once, admiring the deep green stalks higher than his head. Emma and Rachel walked with him, a rare moment of calm.

"Gott is good," he said, reaching out to rub the tassels between his callused fingers. "The earth here is very fertile, and Danny Chupp's seed grew as quick as he said it would. This field is almost ready for harvest." Then he glanced at Emma's swollen belly and smiled. "Emma, I guess mebbe you'll be bringing in a crop of your own soon."

Emma blushed, and only Rachel knew why. Her time was closer than it should have been, and Emma couldn't help being a little afraid of what her father would think if she delivered a baby in early fall when she'd only gotten married in March. Even a man could count. She changed the subject.

"Your big well has done mighty gut too, Dat. No more rain than we get, I don't know where we'd be without that well."

He nodded, stroked his graying beard. Rachel watched her dat's eyes, and she could see how proud he was. Things had gone well. The Benders had gained a foothold in a new land in a remarkably short period of time.

"In a couple weeks the corn will be ready to pick and we can take a load to sell in Saltillo." Dat looked up the hill at the half-finished adobe walls rising from the knoll. "We can buy tin for the roof and some glass for the windows while we're there — plus the windmill. Emma, I'm thinking I'll need you to go with me so you can sell corn in the market while I go to buy what we need."

Emma glanced at Rachel, and a sly smile turned up the corners of her mouth.

"Dat, I don't know if it would be so good for me to go bumping all the way to Saltillo in that old wagon." Emma patted her belly, flashing her eyes at her father. "Maybe you should take Rachel and Miriam instead."

Dat stared at her from under his hat. Rachel saw the tiny smile in both their eyes and understood. Emma wasn't worried at all about riding in a wagon to Saltillo — she would ride bareback to Boston if she had a mind to, and Dat knew it. But she also knew how monotonous it must be making bricks all day, so she was suggesting to her father that he give Rachel a little break. All this passed between them in one silent glance.

"Jah, well, Rachel, you have been working mighty hard, so mebbe Emma's right. You need a little rest, and a chance to see some of the country."

A shiver of excitement went through Rachel. She actually clapped her hands in delight. "Can Miriam go, too?"

He nodded. Lifting one of Rachel's hands, he ran a thumb over the calluses, and a little sadness came into his eyes. "I'm sorry you and Miriam have to do men's work," he said. "Things will be better when the others come, but for now we're on our own here and we have to make do with what we got. Soon our friends will be here, and everything will be better."

Rachel squeezed his hands in hers. "It's all right, Dat, we don't mind. Me and Miriam are happy to do whatever is needed, and think how proud we'll be when the house is done! Anyway, the work is making us very strong."

Emma laughed that golden laugh of hers. Pregnancy had filled her with joy, once she got over being sick in the mornings, and heightened her natural glow. "Jah, pretty soon the two of them will be wrestling with the boys in the haymow!" she teased.

Dat pointed a warning finger at his silly daughters, but there was laughter in his eyes. And pride. He walked away shaking his head, chuckling.

"Emma, I hope your little one can hold off for a while," Rachel said, once her father was out of hearing. "I mean no offense, but you really have gotten big."

"Ach, this is nothing," Emma said, walking aimlessly through the corn, dragging a hand across the stalks. "Have you looked at Mary lately?" Her eyes bulged and her cheeks puffed out as her hands mimed a belly the size of a washtub. "I'm wondering if it's twins this time, she's so huge."

"Oh, I hope so!" Rachel cried, giggling. "The more the merrier. When is her bundle supposed to arrive?"

"She says December, but I'm not so sure the *buppela* will wait that long." Her smile faded, and Rachel saw the lines of concern crease her forehead.

"What's the matter, Emma? What are you

thinking?"

"Oh, nothing. It's just I hope nothing goes wrong."

"What do you mean? Are you talking about your baby or Mary's?"

"Both," Emma said. "Now that my time is getting close it worries me. And Mary, too. As big as she is it *could* be twins, and there is no doctor here."

"Jah," Rachel said, "but there was never a doctor at home, either. The closest one was in Kidron." A grasshopper buzzed into her hair, and she bent over suddenly, snatching her kapp off and raking frantically at her hair until it came out.

"But at least there *was* a doctor in Kidron," Emma said. "If something wasn't right, we could send for him anyway. The doctor in Agua Nueva is a day's ride away, and the one in Saltillo even farther. Rachel, do you realize that until the others come, we don't even have a midwife here?"

Rachel honestly hadn't thought about it, though she didn't have as much invested as Emma did.

"Well, it doesn't seem like such a great worry to me," Rachel said, trying to cram her unruly hair back into her kapp while Emma waited. "I helped lots of cows and horses have babies, and it always goes good.

There's never any problems."

"Cows and horses are one thing," Emma said, worry carved plainly on her face. "Women are another. Lots of things can go wrong. Sometimes the baby is breech, or the cord gets tangled. Mary lost both of her last two babies, so I know she's worried. Things just happen."

They walked on between the cornstalks in silence for a minute, and then, out of the blue, Emma turned to Rachel and said, "I want you to be my midwife."

"What?"

"When I have my baby," Emma said. "I want you to be my midwife."

"*Me?*" Rachel's mouth hung open. "But, Emma, I'm only sixteen. I'm not even married! I've never even been in the *room* with a woman having a baby. I don't know anything about it!"

"I still want you there." Emma's eyes were determined, smug. She'd made up her mind.

"But what about Mamm?"

"She'll be there too, but you know how she is — Mamm is steady as a mule until something goes wrong, then she gets all flustered and befuddled. You're just the opposite. You always worry and fret like a little girl, but when things go crazy you keep your head. Rachel, there's nobody in the world I trust more than you. Not even Levi. I want you there."

Rachel looked long into her sister's face, astonished, but Emma's eyes attested to the truth of what she had just said.

"Then I will be there," Rachel said. "With Gott's help, I will be there for you."

"And you can be there for Mary, too."

"But —"

"No *buts.* I have a very good feeling about this, Rachel. Something tells me you'll be a fine midwife."

There was no arguing with Emma once her mind was made up. Rachel nodded numbly. "Okay."

The round trip to Saltillo would take three days. It was still dark when Caleb hitched the Belgians and headed north in the wagon with a huge mound of sweet corn in the back and his two daughters beside him on the bench seat. All the money Caleb had left in the world was sewn into a hidden pocket under the waistline of his handmade trousers, and he wasn't sure it was enough.

At six thousand feet the mornings were chilly, even in late summer. Miriam and Rachel wrapped themselves in blankets, waiting for the day to warm. The sun was just cracking the eastern horizon when they stopped to pick up Domingo, who waited for them by the road outside the village of San Rafael.

The girls climbed into the back and sat on the food box in front of the pile of corn to let Domingo sit up front with Caleb. A short while later, as they rumbled slowly past the farm of Ernst Schulman, Domingo kept his eyes straight ahead. He never even glanced to the left.

A mile or two down the road, with Schulman's farm gone from sight, Caleb turned to Domingo and asked, in High German, "Why do you hate that man?"

Domingo didn't say anything for a long time, and Caleb waited. Finally, keeping his eyes on the road ahead, Domingo said quietly, *"Ich hasse ihn nicht." I don't hate him.* "Hate, among the Nahua people, is reserved for a respected enemy. Herr Schulman I do not respect."

Caleb pondered this. "Why? He seems like a decent man to me."

"He is a fool," Domingo said. "Herr Schulman knows everything about a man by his clothes, or the color of his skin. It's easy. A European like himself is best. An American like you is only a little lower, and a haciendado, with all his land and money, is a little lower than an American because a haciendado is still, after all, only a Mexican. But even the half-breed mestizo is better than a Chichimeca. To him, we are cattle, not men." He glanced at Caleb. "He told you about the whip?"

"Jah," Caleb said, his eyes on the road. "He told me you took it away and threatened him with it."

Domingo nodded. *"Es ist wahr." It is true.* "The man Schulman found sleeping and beat with the whip had walked all night to another village to get medicine for a sick child, then went to Schulman's farm to work. He fell asleep when he stopped to eat at midday, and I let him lay for a few minutes."

"Maybe Herr Schulman didn't know about this."

Domingo shook his head bitterly. "It would make no difference. To him, this was not a man, it was a burro. If a peon doesn't do what you want, you run him off and get another. Peons are cheap."

An old man passed them as he spoke, going the other way in a tiny wooden-wheeled cart pulled by an ox. The Mexican lifted his hat and flashed a toothless grin as he passed. Caleb nodded. "Buenos días."

"The man who just passed us," Domingo

said, "his name is Pablo Garcia. He has raised five children on tortillas and beans. He owns nothing, though he has worked hard all his life. His three grown sons all died fighting in the revolution."

Caleb nodded, waiting, assuming this was leading someplace.

"Pablo Garcia has worked for Schulman longer than I have, yet Schulman does not know about the five children, the lost sons. Schulman does not even know his last name. He only calls him Pablo, even though the man is old enough to be his father."

"Why are you telling me these things, Domingo?"

"Because you asked me about Schulman."

"Yes, but why are you telling *me?* You wouldn't even *speak* to Schulman. Why me?"

Domingo looked Caleb in the eye and said, "Because you are not arrogant. Schulman came here to escape the storm he knew was coming in his own 'civilized' country, but he's just another rich European, like the haciendados. My people lived here for thousands of years before the Spaniards came and took everything. Now they call a man a thief if he steals a chicken to feed his children. Schulman *scoffs* at men like Pancho Villa and Emiliano Zapata, calls them

261

petty thieves, but he forgets that at the same time, in the Great War in his own 'civilized' country, people slaughtered each other by the millions in the trenches. To someone whose family has known nothing but hunger for generations, these *petty thieves* were heroes who rose up against the tyranny of the haciendados."

Caleb was a little surprised at the vehemence of Domingo's tirade. He had never heard the young man speak this way before.

Miriam and Rachel were apparently listening as well, because they had turned and stood up on the box behind Caleb. Now Miriam asked a question.

"So you think Pancho Villa is a hero?"

Domingo glanced over his shoulder and shrugged. "To the common people he is a legend. Pancho Villa was a peon once, working on a hacienda. When he was only a boy the master of the hacienda raped his sister, so Pancho killed the haciendado and fled to the hills, where he became a very successful bandit. In the revolution he raised an army and fought against the oppression of the rich men who own grand haciendas, drive around in automobiles and rule over their little kingdoms. He became a great general, and then, because he had learned to read and write, he became governor of a province and grew very rich. Now Pancho Villa owns a hacienda, drives an automobile and rules over his own little kingdom, but to the people he is still a hero. I only hope he has not forgotten what it was like to work fourteen hours in the sun to bring food to a fat man and then go to bed with an empty belly. Pancho Villa is a complicated man."

Caleb studied his young friend's face. "Villa is not the *only* complicated man," he said. "How old are you?"

A shrug. "I don't know. My uncle says I am twenty."

CHAPTER 22

Their wagon crawled along over gently rolling humps and swells, generally following the dusty valley floor between and around a maze of overlapping ridges. Thin pine and oak forests covered the lower slopes but never quite reached the red-rock ridgetops. Nor were there many trees down in the dry valleys of prairie grass and sage, where the occasional stunted, wind-rustled corn patch of a mestizo farm huddled against the road, or the mangy dogs of a native village ran out to pester the horses. But even in the afternoon when the road began to climb, winding through gaps in the craggy mountains toward the town of Arteaga, Caleb noted that it was a much better and smoother road than the one from Agua Nueva.

"That is why the railroad will come this way," Domingo said. "The tracks are already in Arteaga, and the road down this way is much smoother than the pig trail from Agua Nueva."

"When do you think they will build the rail line through El Prado?" Caleb asked.

A shrug. "This is Mexico. Who knows?" They were approaching a narrow mountain pass and Domingo tensed, watching the tree line ahead.

"Men on horses are coming down to the pass," he said. "On the back side. I can't tell how many."

Miriam and Rachel heard, and stood up to look over their father's shoulder.

"Will there be trouble?" Rachel asked.

"I don't know. If they stop us, be careful what you say to them." He caught Caleb's eye as he said this, and jerked his head toward the girls.

Caleb turned to his daughters. "Sit down. Don't move and don't talk. Don't do anything to draw attention and maybe they will leave us alone."

"I didn't see a rifle or shotgun in the wagon," Domingo said. "If you have a pistol, hide it now."

"I am unarmed," Caleb said.

"Good."

As they rounded a bend in the deep notch of the mountain pass, a group of eight or ten men emerged from the woods in front of them on horseback, all heavily dressed and heavily armed. Most wore sombreros; the others wore the sweat-stained hats of cowboys or farmers. Almost every one carried a bandolier of bullets across his chest, a pistol on his side and a rifle in the saddle scabbard. Their faces were leathered from sun and wind, and most of them needed a shave. The bandits — for even Caleb knew bandits when he saw them — laughed casually, bantering among themselves as their horses fanned out in the road ahead, but their eyes were hard, and when they laughed their eyes did not laugh with them.

The leader, a thin man with prominent cheekbones and slit eyes, held up a hand, palm out, as they neared the wagon. Caleb pulled back on the reins and brought the wagon to a halt. The pair of Belgians stamped nervously as the bandits slid past, reaching out to run their hands down the sleek flanks of Caleb's draft horses.

Most of the men clustered around the back of the wagon, ignoring the girls at first and chattering excitedly about the pile of corn, but the leader stopped right beside Caleb. His horse was larger than the others, a fine big Appaloosa whose front half was liver colored, the back half white with leopard spots.

"Buenos días," the man said, a gold front tooth showing in a grin that was almost a sneer. There was nothing cordial about the look in his eyes. Up close, Caleb could see that one of his eyes was all milky. A purple crescent scar ran down across the eye from the middle of his forehead almost to the corner of his mouth.

Caleb nodded nervously. "Buenos días."

The bandit rested his palms on the pommel of his saddle and leaned closer. "Señor, my men have ridden a long way today, and they are hungry. Can you spare a few ears of corn for weary soldiers, *por favor?*"

Caleb looked over his shoulder. The bandits were already busy, leaning far out from their saddles, plucking ears of corn from the back of the wagon and stuffing them into pockets and saddlebags. They were also ogling his daughters and muttering between themselves, grinning.

"Sí," Caleb said. "I am always ready to feed the hungry."

The bandit leaned even closer, reaching out to steady himself by gripping the back of the wagon seat by Caleb's shoulder. His eyes flitted over Caleb and Domingo, checking the space between them and under the seat. Caleb sat straight and stiff, trying not to recoil from that gaunt face, mere inches away, radiating pure and remorseless evil.

"Señor, we do not wish to trouble you," he said, his eyes cutting for a brief second to the girls in the back, "but perhaps a man as generous as yourself can spare a few pesos so we can buy feed for our horses, no?"

Caleb opened his mouth to answer, but Domingo's voice intruded. He spoke in an even tone to the bandit, but Caleb didn't understand a word of what he said. The bandit's eyes widened in surprise and he pulled up, now focusing entirely on Domingo. He made some reply to the younger man, but Caleb didn't understand that, either. He realized suddenly that what he was hearing was not Spanish at all, but the strangely harsh language of Nahuatl, Domingo's native tongue.

The bandit's eyes narrowed and his right hand crept to the butt of a pistol in a cross-draw holster on his hip. His thumb ticked against the hammer as he studied Domingo's face.

Caleb didn't move, didn't twitch. He hardly dared breathe.

The bandit asked Domingo a question in Nahuatl, and Domingo answered him calmly, never wavering.

Neither man raised his voice, but an

electric tension crackled between them, as if at any second one of them might spring at the other without warning. A challenge of some kind had been made, and Domingo had answered it. Whatever had passed between them, Caleb felt sure that his fate, and the fate of his daughters, hung in the balance.

A cry came from the back of the wagon — a girl's voice. Caleb spun around and saw that one of the bandits had snatched the prayer kapp from Rachel's head. He'd apparently grabbed a fistful of hair as well, because the pins flew out and red hair cascaded down around her shoulders. Rachel hid her face in Miriam's lap while Miriam covered her younger sister's head and shoulders with her arms, glaring at the bandit.

"Leave her alone!" Miriam hissed.

The bandit held the kapp aloft, grinning triumphantly, pointed to Rachel and shouted, *"Pelo rojo! Muy bonita!"* All of his cohorts were laughing.

Caleb started to rise from the bench, but Domingo's hand pressed on his shoulder and held him down. Domingo said a few sharp words to the leader, and that gaunt face relaxed. His hand came away from the pistol and he laughed — a harsh, dry laugh.

Leaning back in his saddle and spreading his hands in feigned apology, he said in Spanish, "Never mind about the pesos, señor. A little corn will do."

Then he barked an order at the man with the kapp in his hand. The bandit's grin melted. Keeping his eyes on his leader he leaned over and flung the kapp into Rachel's lap.

"Muchas gracias," the leader said, but he was glaring at Domingo when he said it and he spat the words like a threat. And then, yanking his reins away, he turned the big Appaloosa around and galloped off. His men, suddenly losing interest in Caleb's daughters, followed their leader. The gaunt, one-eyed bandit swiveled in his saddle and pointed at Domingo as he rode away, shouting something in Nahuatl. This too sounded like a threat.

Domingo waited until the whole troop disappeared into the woods, then let the dust of the road settle before he gently took the reins from Caleb and started the horses plodding along again.

Caleb took a deep breath and tried to steady his shaking hands. He turned to check on Rachel. She was still crying, but Miriam had already helped her pin her hair up and cover it with the kapp.

He leaned down and laid a gentle hand on his daughter's shoulder.

"Are you hurt?"

Rachel looked up from her perch on the food box and shook her head. "No, Dat, I am not hurt."

He glanced over the pile of corn in the back of the wagon. They may have lost a bushel or two, but it could have been worse. Much worse.

A little ways down the road, after Caleb had calmed down, he said to Domingo in High German, "I don't understand what happened back there."

Keeping his eyes on the road ahead, Domingo said, "These men are mercenaries who rode with the División del Norte — Pancho Villa's army. Their leader is a very dangerous man. He is a full-blooded Nahua and a great warrior, but he is a man with no conscience. Even his own people fear him. They call him El Pantera."

"You know him?"

"Jah — or at least I know *about* him. My father knew him well. They fought together at the battle of Zacatecas, the fiercest battle of the war. There is a rumor that my father fell because El Pantera abandoned him at the wrong time. My father, too, was a great warrior."

Caleb did not know quite how to answer this without offending the memory of Domingo's warrior father, but in the end, as always with Caleb, the truth won out.

"Our people do not fight," Caleb said evenly. "We will not take up arms against men, and we do not honor warriors. We believe it is wrong to kill."

Domingo raised an eyebrow and his head backed away. "You don't *fight?*"

"No. We are Amish," Caleb said.

"Amish. Is that your tribe?"

"In a way, jah. We are plain folk. We live simply, in a way that honors Gott."

"So, this *Amish* . . . it is a religion?"

"Jah, but also a way of life."

"This is why the women dress the way they do?" Domingo's forefinger circled his head, a reference to the white kapps the women wore.

"Jah. The men, too," Caleb added, thumbing his suspenders.

"And you don't believe in fighting, no matter what."

"No."

Domingo rolled his eyes. "Well then, I hope your god is very strong, because if he is not, you won't last long in Mexico. If it weren't for a warrior, you might be dead already."

"What do you mean?"

"Back there, in the pass . . . El Pantera. You have a wagonload of corn, those big fine horses, and . . ." Domingo's eyes flitted for a second toward the girls, and Caleb understood the unspoken fear. "Anyway, everyone knows a gringo would not go so far to the market without money in his pocket."

Caleb shook his head sadly. "I don't understand this. Does everyone here just take whatever they want? Is there no law in this place?"

"Jah, there are the Federales — government soldiers — but they cannot catch a man like El Pantera in these mountains. They don't even try anymore. He does as he pleases in the Sierra Madre. You would have been lucky to only lose your money and your horses."

"He would not have found my money," Caleb said.

Domingo laughed out loud. "Herr Bender, how long would he hold his knife to your daughters before you found it *for* him? He might have let you live if you did not resist, but who is to say? There is no telling what would have happened if I had not been there to stop him." Domingo's tone was not boastful. He said this matter-of-factly, and

273

Caleb knew he spoke the truth.

"What did you say to him?" Caleb asked.

"I asked him if he would rob the son of Ehekatl. He did not know who I was until I said that. He answered no, he would not rob the son of Ehekatl, but he *would* rob a gringo if the son of Ehekatl did not mind. I told him the gringo was my friend, and to rob the gringo El Pantera would have to *kill* the son of Ehekatl. This he was not prepared to do." Domingo shrugged. "So he left."

Caleb stared at the young native's face for a long moment. "You risked your life for us," he said quietly. "Thank you, Domingo. It was a brave thing you did."

Domingo chuckled. "Oh, he would have paid a price. If someone wishes to take my life, Herr Bender, believe me, I will put up a fight."

That evening they made camp in a grove of oaks overlooking Arteaga with the mountains behind them and only ten miles of flatland to go before they reached Saltillo. The girls cooked over a small campfire and then made themselves a bed on the back of the wagon. Dat took his bedroll underneath the wagon, and Domingo disappeared into the darkness to keep watch. Long after nightfall Rachel and Miriam lay awake listening to the sound of singing drifting up to them from a cantina somewhere in the town below, warbling voices mixed with trumpet, squeeze-box and guitar.

Rachel lay on her back with her hands behind her head, staring up at the stars. She could hear her father's soft snores from under the wagon and she spoke in a hushed voice so as not to wake him.

"I thought we were going to die out there today," she said.

"Me too," Miriam answered. "It was horrible. Those men were savages."

"And they smelled bad, too. Did you see the look in the eyes of that one who took my kapp? There is no telling what they would have done if Domingo hadn't stopped them. We are helpless in this country. Only Gott can defend us against men like that."

Miriam was silent for a moment, and then she raised up on an elbow to stare out into the dark landscape and said quietly, "Sometimes Gott sends a helper to guard His children."

"Jah, sometimes," she said, wondering at the odd, wistful tone in Miriam's voice. "Miriam, why does he always call you 'cualnezqui'?"

Miriam lay back down flat, staring at the stars beside her sister. "I suppose because I am his friend."

"But he only calls *you* that. Never me, or Dat. We are his friends too, aren't we?"

"Jah, I noticed. Maybe it's just a pet name — his way of being nice to me. I think he feels sorry for me, his little friend."

"Mmm. Maybe," Rachel said sleepily.

As the moon rose above the mountains the music from the cantina stopped, leaving them with only the distant yipping and keening of coyotes.

CHAPTER 23

When they rolled into Saltillo early the next morning Caleb drove straight to the market and unloaded the sweet corn. Miriam and Rachel had brought a few spare boards and adobe bricks to set up a makeshift table where they piled as many ears of corn as they could. They piled the rest on the ground, because Caleb and Domingo needed the empty wagon.

The open-air market was really nothing more than a great long wide street, made considerably narrower by the booths and tables and carts and barrows of peddlers lining both sides of it, hawking their wares. There were vegetables — tomatoes and squash and onions and all sorts of peppers — and fruits, from apples and oranges to melons and even bananas. There were live chickens and live goats, and hanging from hooks under a little awning, dead plucked chickens and dead skinned goats, fish and rabbits and beef and wheat. Almost anything could be found here. Domingo mingled with the people in the market for only a few minutes before he came back and told Rachel and Miriam what their corn was worth, by the ear or by the bushel.

"But don't give them that price first," he warned. "If someone asks how much, you double it, and let them talk you down to the real price."

"But why not just give them the real price to start with, and stick to it?" Miriam wanted to know.

Domingo looked at her like she was crazy. "Because they want a bargain, and you must not cheat them out of it!" he said. "If they have to pay full price, where is the dignity in that?"

"But they *are* paying full price," she said.

"No they're not!" Domingo pointed a finger at her and raised his voice a little. "Only a *foreigner* pays full price. The local people know better, cualnezqui."

He climbed up onto the wagon with Caleb, and then, as they were driving away through the crowd in the bustling market, Domingo turned, cupped his hands around his mouth and shouted, "Watch out for the *niño*s!"

Rachel turned to Miriam. "What did he

278

mean by that?"

Miriam shrugged. "Maybe he meant for us to care for them. When the children come around, to look out for them and be kind to them."

They did a brisk business in the morning. The toothless old woman in the long dress and colorful head scarf selling apples and summer squash from an oxcart right next to them said the morning was the busiest time. When the sun grew hot at midday most people would go to find shade, she said. In the afternoon it would be busy again, but not like the morning.

Women came in a steady parade of twos and threes with big hand-woven sacks on shoulder straps, buying what they would need for the day's cooking.

At the busiest time, around nine o'clock, four little hatless barefoot kids came knocking down the street, laughing and hooting to each other, running here and there, peeking over edges and looking to see what was in the carts. The toothless old woman handled them roughly, squawking at them, calling them "gutter dogs" and chasing them off with a piece of kindling she'd been swishing over her apples and squash to keep the flies from loitering.

The children's clothes were ragged and

dirty, but they had the faces of angels —
black eyes with long lashes, raven hair and
impossibly white teeth.

One of them, the cutest little boy, ran over
to Miriam.

"Beautiful señorita," he said, flashing her
a smile full of sunlight and mischief, "you
have such a kind face, surely you must have
brought candy in your pockets for the children."

"No, I'm afraid I have no candy," Miriam
said, smiling, bending down to talk to the
little boy. "What is your name?"

"Me llamo Maximilian de la Cholla," he
said, thumping his chest. The name was bigger than the boy. "But you may call me
Pepé."

One by one, the others saw Pepé talking
to Miriam, and when they saw that Miriam
was not squawking at him or calling him a
gutter dog or swinging at him with a stick
of kindling, they drifted over and crowded
around her, tugging at her skirt, calling her
"beautiful señorita" and asking for candy.

"Well, Pepé," Miriam said, "if you're
hungry I will give you an ear of corn. It's
not so good raw, but you can take it home
to Mama and she will boil it for you."

A dark-eyed little girl peeked around
Miriam's skirts at Pepé. "Come on, let's

go," she said impatiently. "Maybe the carnicerio will give us a *salchicha*." She ran off, and then the others, laughing and slapping, ran after her.

Miriam watched them chase each other down the street, and the smile lingered on her face right up until she reached into the deep pocket in a fold of her dress where she'd been keeping the money from the corn she'd sold. She pinched the bottom of the pocket, turned it inside out and shook it to make sure. The pocket was empty.

She was still standing there with her arms folded on her chest glaring down the street when the toothless old woman shuffled up from behind, slapped a stick of kindling into her hand and shuffled back to her apples and squash, muttering to herself. Miriam hefted the kindling and swung it a time or two to hear the *whoosh* it made in the air, then looked over her shoulder and said, "Muchas gracias, señora."

Rachel, who had been busy with a customer, watched the whole episode unfold without saying a word. She walked up behind Miriam, who was still staring down the long street smacking the kindling against her palm, and whispered over her shoulder, "Miriam. Watch out for the niños."

■ ■ ■ ■

After they left the girls behind at the market, Caleb and Domingo threaded their wagon through the crowded streets of Saltillo toward the industrial corner of town, stopping twice to ask directions to the foundry. Once they found the place and determined that they could indeed buy the windmill they needed, Domingo took over and haggled with the merchant for ten minutes, driving the price down by almost half. Caleb paid, and then they waited, sitting in the shade of a tin awning while the parts were located in the warehouse and brought to the wagon.

Caleb opened his pocketknife and slowly curled off shavings from a stick to pass the time. "I keep thinking about that El Pantera fella," he said idly. "Something about him felt . . . *evil*. He never harmed us, yet I was still very afraid of him and I don't know why."

"Your instincts are good," Domingo said. "There are bandits who will take your food and your horse, and others who will take your life, but there are a few who will do worse things. El Pantera is one of those. I would have told you this yesterday, but the girls were there, listening."

"What do you mean, Domingo? What could be worse than taking my life?"

Domingo took his hat off and fanned his face with it — the morning had grown warm.

"They say El Pantera takes young women."

Caleb stared at him, his pocketknife paused mid-stroke. "What do you mean, *takes* them?"

"I mean he steals them. Kidnaps them. Always the young ones. The stories are all about Mexican girls, but I think it is only because there are not many white girls. I'm pretty sure a white girl will bring a higher price."

"Price. You mean a ransom?"

Domingo laughed softly. "No, Herr Bender. If El Pantera takes a girl, he will not ask for ransom. Not from her family anyway."

"What then? Does he take them for his . . . *pleasure?*"

Domingo shook his head. "He takes them to sell. Have you never heard of the white slave trade?"

Caleb shook his head. "Slaves? There *are* no more slaves. You cannot buy —"

"If a man is rich enough, he can buy

whatever he wants," Domingo said. "And we are not talking about the kind of slave who picks his crops or scrubs his floors."

Caleb stared at him for a long time before it began to sink in.

"You mean to say there are men who will buy young women and keep them for their pleasure?"

Domingo nodded. "Jah. My father told me about this. There are men in Europe, Herr Bender, and even some in the East, who have so much money they can buy anything. *Anything.* It is said that some of these men, if you know how to find them, will pay a king's ransom for a young girl. It is also said that El Pantera *knows* such men."

Caleb's pulse quickened, thinking of Rachel and Miriam, alone in the street market. The world had grown colder and darker. Suddenly there was more evil in the world than he had ever imagined. He stirred, and started to rise.

"We must go," he said. "We must get to my daughters."

Domingo shook his head, put a steadying hand on Caleb's arm. "They are safe, for now. El Pantera always stays in the hills, where he cannot be caught. Your daughters are safe in Saltillo, and he will not bother you on the road as long as he knows I am with you."

"Are you sure?"

Domingo shrugged. "This is Mexico. Nothing is sure."

Caleb sat back down, thinly reassured. He stared straight ahead, his jaw working.

"I am curious, Herr Bender," Domingo said, his eyes narrowing. "Would you fight *now*?"

Caleb's brow furrowed. "What do you mean?"

"I mean, you say your people do not fight. You told me before that you would not fight even to save your own life. But after what I have told you, Herr Bender, would you not kill El Pantera to save your daughters from such a fate?"

Caleb pondered this for a long moment, staring at his hands. This young man had risked his life to protect Caleb and his daughters. He had earned an honest answer.

Finally, he took a deep breath and shook his head. "No, I would not. Though it cost me an unthinkable price, I could not defy Gott. I would not risk hell."

"Never?"

He shook his head sadly. "We do not live by power or might, but by the Spirit of the Lord of hosts. It is better to suffer in this brief life than for all eternity. If it is sin to kill, who do I serve by killing? I will accept whatever Gott allows." Caleb meant what he said, and he would live by it, but such thoughts crushed him with the weight of the sea.

Domingo flashed him a curious sideways smile.

"But you did not mind when *I* stood against El Pantera. Is it not hypocrisy to approve of this?"

"I didn't say I approved, I only said 'thank you.' Anyway, the law I cling to is for my own instruction. I do not judge you by it."

Domingo smiled, shaking his head. "Herr Bender, you are either the most honorable man I have ever met or the most foolish. I have not decided which."

Caleb pondered this for a second and shrugged.

"Neither have I."

By midday the streets of Saltillo were much warmer than the lofty fields of Paradise Valley. Miriam and Rachel found a patch of shade under the upturned end of a produce wagon and sat down to eat lunch.

"Dat's right," Miriam said thoughtfully as she munched on an apple. "Right now I'd like to swat every niño in this whole country with a piece of kindling, but it wouldn't do any good. It won't change anything. Dat's right, the reason they steal is because they are poor."

"We're not rich ourselves," Rachel said absently, polishing her own apple on a sleeve. "Anyways, I've seen some Amish who were really poor, but they wouldn't steal yet."

Miriam shook her head. "They were rich compared to these people. This is a different kind of poor. For generations the mestizos couldn't even buy a piece of land. The haciendado owned everything, and everyone had to work for him or starve. They never had a chance."

"I thought the revolution was supposed to change all that," Rachel said, twisting the stem from her apple.

"How? There is land for sale now, but no one has the money to buy it, and most of them still can't read and write. They can't even read a newspaper. What will they do?"

"I don't know," Rachel said. "All I know is, in Mexico things have been this way for hundreds of years. Are you going to change the whole country all by yourself?" She took a bite of her apple and looked absently down the nearly empty street.

"Maybe I can't change the whole country," Miriam said, "but I can do my little bit."

Rachel turned to stare at her sister, a chunk of apple bulging in her cheek.

"How?"

"I'm thinking Mary's boys will be old enough to start school in the fall, and there will be many more little ones in the spring when the others come."

"Jah," Rachel said, "but there's no school here. That's why we came in the first place."

Miriam nodded. "I'm talking about an *Amish* school, Rachel. In Mexico we can do what we want."

Rachel lowered her apple. "What do you mean, Amish school?"

"I mean reading, writing and arithmetic. Just the basics, and only once a week, or maybe two times for half a day. Rachel, I could teach the little ones to read and write. *I* could do that."

Rachel shrugged. "Okay. So teach the little ones to read and write. But what does that have to do with . . . ohhh, *now* I see."

"Right!" Miriam grinned, gesturing with a half-eaten apple as she went on. "The children will have to learn Spanish. If I can teach an Amish child to read and write Spanish, why, it ought to be easy to teach a *Mexican* child to read and write Spanish.

Why can't I start a school for whoever wants to learn to read and write? I can *do* that!"

"Do you really want to be a teacher? I'm glad to see you excited about this, but *school?* I don't even like to *go* to school. I certainly wouldn't want to teach it."

"But don't you see? Didn't you hear what Domingo said about Pancho Villa?"

Rachel shrugged, shook her head.

"He said because Pancho Villa learned to read and write he became governor of a province. In a country like this where so many are poor, a little thing like that can make a big difference."

Rachel stripped the seeds from her apple core, tossed away what was left and stood up, wiping her hands on her dress. "Well, just remember it's probably not so easy. Domingo said Pancho Villa was a bandit first, then he learned to read, and *then* he became governor. Just because a man learns to read and write doesn't mean he will become governor. He probably has to be a bandit first."

Business in the market that afternoon turned out to be every bit as slow as their toothless old neighbor had predicted. The few shoppers who were there took their time, strolling along at a leisurely pace, enjoying the day, but the ones who stopped took time to admire the girls' corn. They pulled back the shucks and ran a thumb over the plump yellow kernels and showed it to each other and nodded with appreciation. There were fewer customers, but those who came through bought corn by the bushel instead of only a few ears. By late afternoon, when Caleb and Domingo returned with the wagon, there were only two bushels left.

As they were pulling away, the toothless old woman in the next booth was threatening two niños with her kindling. Miriam waved to her and shouted, "Muchas gracias, cualnezqui!"

The old woman didn't answer. She just tilted her head and frowned quizzically as they drove away.

"You should have just said *amiga*," Rachel said. "Obviously, she doesn't speak Nahuatl."

An hour later the wagon — carrying four people and a heavy load of steel parts, piles of angle iron and pipe, boxes of bolts and nuts, and sheets of corrugated tin — trundled slowly down the road toward the collection of adobe and terra cotta that was Arteaga. A tall church steeple rose above the town, a white cross at its top.

Holding the reins loosely, Caleb looked over his shoulder at the westering sun. "I'm thinking there are two hours of daylight left," he said to Domingo, riding beside him up front. "We can make a few more miles before we have to stop for the night. It will put us closer to home, but it will also put us in the mountains. Is it safe?" El Pantera was very much on his mind, though he didn't say it out loud.

"I know a place," Domingo said quietly, and his tone let Caleb know that he understood what hadn't been said.

By the time the sun dropped below the western peaks, their wagon had skirted Arteaga and climbed up into the edge of the mountains, once again connecting with the main road south, toward home. Domingo took the reins and drove off the road, down into a little arroyo for a few hundred yards and then turned into the neck of a narrow canyon where they could not be seen from the road.

"We will camp here," Domingo said, taking off his hat and staring up at the strip of purple sky between the rocky cliffs. "There are no clouds. If a storm came to the mountains, we could be washed away in this place, but the sky is quiet. I think we will be safe here for the night."

When they had made camp and fed the horses, Domingo built a small fire in a smooth place under the overhanging rock, and they ate a meager dinner in silence while their shadows danced on the red rocks overhead.

"We will need to get an early start," Domingo said to Caleb, stirring the embers of the fire with a stick.

Caleb nodded, worry written plainly in his weathered face. "I just hope we don't run into any more bandits."

Domingo shrugged, shook his head. "I don't know about the others, but they say El Pantera never moves at night if he doesn't have to."

This brought another fear to Caleb's mind, a chilling thought. "How would we know he hasn't gone to Paradise Valley?"

"He won't go there," Domingo said, shaking his head.

Miriam's head tilted. "Why not?"

Domingo plucked a straw from the ground, pinched off the end and used it to pick his teeth. "Because, cualnezqui, he is Villa's man. Did you never wonder why Hacienda El Prado still stands?"

"I have wondered about this," Miriam said, leaning forward and resting her elbows on her knees. "I read everything I could find about the revolution, about how most of the grand haciendas were sacked and burned, and it occurred to me — why not El Prado?"

Caleb stared at his daughter's face, shining in the firelight. Miriam normally would never have spoken up in front of a man like this.

"Did Señor Hidalgo perhaps *bribe* Villa?" Caleb asked.

Domingo chuckled. "How do you bribe a man whose army can kill you and take everything you own anytime he pleases? Nein. I don't know what passed between them, but it seems to me that Señor Hidalgo must have once done something to help Pancho Villa, some great kindness for which Villa was grateful, a kindness he never forgot. For some reason Hacienda El Prado has his protection, and out of respect — or fear — his men leave it alone. Others may come, but Villa's men will not."

"There are others?" Caleb asked.

"Jah, many of them, though most are not so fierce — or so evil — as El Pantera."

"And these others — they will come to Paradise Valley?"

"They already have. I am surprised you have not seen them."

"Then perhaps we should appeal to the

government for protection," Caleb said. "Maybe they will send policemen to our valley."

Domingo rose to his feet, yawned, stretched and kicked dirt on what was left of the fire. His voice came from the darkness as the last of the flames flickered out.

"Do you trust the government?"

CHAPTER 24

At first light they were back on the road, and before noon they had descended from the rugged northern mountains. The thought of his wife and daughters back home in Paradise Valley without him lay on Caleb's mind like a weight so that he leaned forward a little on the bench seat, shaking the reins often and urging his sturdy draft horses on. They seemed to understand, shouldering the load and picking up the pace without complaint. Caleb's head turned constantly left and right, watching the ridgetops, hoping he would not see men on horseback — especially the big bicolor Appaloosa with the leopard spots.

As the sun settled into the western mountains they dropped off Domingo at the village of San Rafael and rounded the end of the ridge into Paradise Valley. A great weight lifted from Caleb's tired shoulders when he came to the long driveway and turned his wagon toward the half-built adobe house up near the base of the ridge. In the dusk, the tents already glowed soft yellow from the lanterns inside.

The whole family turned out to welcome them home. Aaron and Harvey saw that the horses were fed and watered and brushed and put away while Caleb and his daughters washed up for dinner. It was Saturday night, so Mamm asked Emma and Mary to draw big pots of water and set them on the stove, which for now sat in the open behind the tent with only a short section of stovepipe out the top.

Mamm laid out dinner for Caleb and the girls while they told the story of their trip, and they could hardly eat for having to answer the eager questions fired at them from all directions. Everyone crowded into the tent to listen to Rachel as she told them all about the market street, the toothless old woman and the pickpocket niños.

Caleb filled them in on the rest of the trip, but he intentionally left out the part about the bandits. The women need not worry about such things, and Domingo had assured him El Pantera would not come this far south.

"So, you had no trouble on the road?" Emma asked. It was an innocent question

— on such a trip it was not uncommon for a horse to pull up lame or an axle to break — but Caleb paused too long. He and Rachel and Miriam were all sitting at a little table with plates of beans, fresh tomatoes and onions in front of them, and when Emma asked about difficulties on the road they all hesitated and glanced at each other in a way that Emma's sharp eyes would surely not miss. Besides, her question was too direct. If he said they'd had no trouble at all, it would be a lie.

"Well," Caleb finally said, "there was a few fellas met us on the road asking for something to eat."

"Fellas?" Mamm asked. "What kind of fellas?"

Caleb spooned up some beans and tried not to look her in the eye. "Oh, just fellas. Domingo said they used to be soldiers in the war."

"Soldiers! Oh my!" Mamm's eyes widened and her hand flew up to cover her mouth. "Did they have guns?"

The two youngest daughters stood on either side of Caleb, watching his face, hanging on every word. When she heard that soldiers had stopped her father, the eleven-year-old blurted out, "Did they try to kill you?"

Everyone laughed except Rachel and Miriam. Rachel suddenly seemed to be very intent on her vegetables, while Miriam simply stared at her father. Mamm saw this, and bored in on her husband.

"Caleb, tell us what happened. What did these men do?"

Caleb knew he was trapped then, so he proceeded to tell the whole story of how they had been stopped on the road by eight or ten rough-looking men who claimed at first to only need a few ears of corn.

Miriam thumped her spoon down on the table, glaring at him.

"They were *bandits,* Dat, and they would have robbed us if not for Domingo. Or worse," she said flatly, interrupting her father. Everyone in the tent sat very still and stared at her. Caleb stared the hardest. She had spoken out of turn and contradicted her father.

She looked around at the frozen faces, all turned toward her.

"Well, they *would* have," she said, standing her ground no matter the cost. "That's what Domingo told us, and one of them pulled Rachel's kapp from her head, too. We were afraid we would be killed."

Mamm's face had gone ash white. "How did you get away?" she asked weakly.

Caleb dismissed the issue with a little backhanded wave as if he were brushing away a fly. "It was not so bad as all that. Domingo knew their leader, a man who was with his father in the war. Domingo asked the man to leave us be, so he did, and his men left with him. We were never in any real danger."

CHAPTER 25

The Bender men never slowed down. Over the next two weeks they bolted the windmill together and got it working, hooked the pipes to it, and returned Schulman's diesel water pump. Meanwhile, Aaron and Harvey laid the last few courses of bricks, topping out the walls of the two-story house.

Caleb and Ezra made cabinets and doors and windows while the others built the roof. The finished house was smaller than the one they'd left behind, but standing alone at the base of the northern ridge with no other buildings for miles around except for a few meager palm-thatched huts, it was an imposing structure.

Their new home was nicer than they had ever imagined a mud house could be. Once they'd been whitewashed, the walls were just walls — it was easy to forget they were made of dirt. They still had to watch out for scorpions in the house, but thanks to the tight-fitting doors they would no longer have to worry about a snake crawling under the covers with them.

This had actually happened once, to Aaron, when they were still sleeping in the tents. It was a chilly night, and the snake just crawled in and stretched itself up against Aaron's nice warm back while he was sleeping. Inevitably, Aaron rolled over, pinning the frightened black snake underneath him and causing it to thrash about, waking first Aaron, and then everyone in roughly a five-mile radius. The snake wasn't poisonous, but in the pitch-dark middle of the night there were any number of ways someone could have been killed, heart attack not the least among them.

Sitting at the head of the table one evening in September, Caleb helped himself to the green beans and said, "I got a letter today from John Hershberger. He said so far they got eight families planning to come down here. There's bound to be more, though. There's a bunch in Kentucky who said they wanted to come, and another bunch in Lancaster. So far, all John's counting is around home and a couple up in Geauga County."

Rachel and her sisters all started talking

at once, drowning Caleb in questions until he held up both hands for them to stop.

"Well, all right, lemme see if I can remember the names he wrote. He said the Shrocks are coming —"

"Enos or Ira?" Rachel asked.

"The Ira Shrocks. But not the grossmammi. She'll be staying with her other daughter . . . um —"

"Linda," Mamm reminded him. "Bill-Linda, Hochstetter." This was a Dutch abbreviation for Linda, wife of Bill Hochstetter. There were several Lindas in the Amish community; it was customary to differentiate between them by prefacing Linda with the husband's name. There was a Bill-Linda, an Enos-Linda, and a Jake-Linda just in the Benders' circle of friends.

"Bill-Linda, jah. Then of course Jonas Weavers are coming, but not Eli Stoltzfuses. I never did think they would come. The two families from up Geauga County are Roman J. Millers and Mahlon Yutzys."

He named them all. Caleb never forgot a name. Then he told them the rest of the news.

"They won't all be coming right away, though," he said. "John's are coming this winter, sometime after the new year, but only the Shrocks are coming with him this time. He said most of the others plan to be down in the summer."

Amid all the excitement over the pending arrival of the Hershbergers and Shrocks, Rachel noticed a curious thing — Miriam didn't really seem interested. The married folks were genuinely excited about their new neighbors, the people who would sit with them in church and work alongside them at harvesttime. The unmarried young people, a group which at this point only included Aaron, Harvey, Miriam, and herself — well, and Ada — would normally have been very keen to know whose faces they would be seeing at the singing on Sunday night. It mattered a great deal to Aaron and Harvey, though Rachel herself had already made her choice and her interest was mostly for show. But Miriam, the one who should have cared the most, never uttered a word. She didn't seem to care who would be coming, and in fact hardly seemed to be paying attention.

After dinner Miriam went off into a corner by herself with a kerosene lantern and her Spanish book. Lately, she'd been spending every spare minute studying. Rachel wandered out into the front yard to watch the dregs of a watercolor sunset drain into the western mountains. There was still that last little bit of pearly light in the valley when she saw the horses.

They were coming down the road from the west, the direction of Agua Nueva, pacing along in that steady way of horses and dogs that are accustomed to traveling for days at a time. It looked like six or eight of them, but at such a distance in the half-light she couldn't tell for sure. When they came to the driveway of the Bender farm they stopped and sat tall in their saddles, studying the two-story adobe house with its new tin roof and inviting windows full of the yellow light of lanterns.

In a moment the horses turned in and sauntered casually up the long drive. Rachel went back up the steps and stuck her head in the door. Dat was still sitting at the kitchen table, talking with Levi, Ezra and Aaron.

"Dat," she said, "there are men coming up our driveway. On horseback. Mexicans."

"How many?" Dat asked, rising.

"Six, I think."

He picked up a lantern and his hat as he went out the door, the other three men right behind him. Rachel followed.

The six trotted up the driveway in single file, but when they came to Dat and his lantern, their horses fanned out six wide and stopped in front of him. He raised his lantern and his practiced eye swept over their horses. He didn't say it, but Rachel knew he was looking for that big liver-and-white Appaloosa. It wasn't there. This was not the same bunch.

"Buenas noches," the one in the middle said. He wore a gilded sombrero. A huge black mustache hid his mouth and half his chin. Two bandoliers of bullets crossed his chest, and he wore pistols on both hips below his waist jacket.

Dat nodded. *"Hola."*

They were hard-looking men, just as lean and hungry as El Pantera's band, especially about the eyes. Dangerous men.

The leader pulled off his sombrero, wiping his forehead on his sleeve in the same motion. "Señor, my men and I have traveled far today, and we are very hungry. I wonder if we could trouble you for a crust of bread and some water."

"We will feed you," Dat said. "Your horses are tired, too. My boys will feed and water them while you come inside and eat, but I will have you leave your guns out here."

The leader leaned back in his saddle and muttered something to his men. His words were too quick and slurred for Rachel to understand, but his men laughed among themselves. He wiped his smile away with the back of a hand, then put his sombrero back on his head. None of them moved to get down from their horses. The chickens cackled suddenly out back, and the man on the right craned his neck, trying to see the coop. Another leaned forward onto his pommel, leering at Rachel until she was forced to lower her face.

Their leader used his sombrero to shade his face from the lantern for a moment while he studied the ridge they had just come down — as if he half expected to see someone following them.

"We are very sorry we must decline your kind invitation," he said, "but we are in a little bit of a hurry just now. We will water our horses at your trough, but if you could only give us a little bread and whatever else is handy, we will eat while we ride."

Caleb nodded to Rachel. She ran back to the house for food.

"The trough is over here," she heard her father say, and the lantern moved off toward the corral.

Five minutes later Rachel went out to the corral with two big loaves of fresh bread, three ears of boiled corn and some tomatoes. The bandits divided the food between themselves, muttering "Gracias" over their shoulders as they turned their horses about and trotted down the driveway.

"They didn't seem so bad," Levi mused, watching them leave.

"Jah, maybe, but you only saw them on their best behavior," Rachel said, staring at her splayed hands. They were still shaking when she heard distant shouts and looked up to see a larger band of horses charging hard down the road from the west — the direction the bandits had come from.

The bandits turned into the main road and spurred their horses into flight. As the second group flew past the farm, leaning forward in their saddles and galloping flat-out in pursuit, Rachel counted a dozen men. They were all wearing dark uniforms. Federales.

The desperate chase had passed out of sight in the darkness to the east when they heard the unmistakable echo of distant gunshots from somewhere near the end of the ridge.

They all ran for the house then, but halfway across the yard the front door flew open and Miriam's head popped out.

"Rachel!" she shouted. "Come quick! Something's wrong with Emma!"

CHAPTER 26

Levi outran her to the house and bolted down the steps into the stone-walled basement. His and Emma's bed lay almost underneath the stairs — they occupied the front half of the space, while Ezra, Mary and the boys slept in the back half, which had been sectioned off for privacy by hanging a tent-canvas curtain from wall to wall.

By the time Rachel ran down the steps Levi was already there, sitting on the side of the bed, leaning over his wife, still wearing his hat and coat. Mamm stood by the side of the bed holding a handkerchief to her face, coughing. She'd been much better lately, but her cough returned sometimes when she was stressed. Rachel put an arm around her mother, who glanced at her with tears in her eyes but said nothing.

"It's too early," Levi said, leaning over his wife, face-to-face, and speaking to her as if he was giving orders. "You can't have it now; it wouldn't be ready yet."

Mamm shook her head and leaned close to Rachel, whispering, "No. The baby can't live if it comes so soon."

Emma lay on her side on top of the covers, still in her dress and kapp, holding her abdomen and breathing hard through pursed lips. Her head turned when she saw Rachel, and she held out a hand, beckoning.

"Is the baby coming *now?*" Rachel asked, kneeling to take Emma's hand.

"I hope not. I'm trying to calm him down."

"It's not time!" Levi said, his face twisted with anxiety, confusion, and maybe a little anger. Emma looked at Rachel when he said this, just a brief glance, the slightest turn of her head, but Rachel saw the pleading in her eyes.

"Don't let it come now!" Levi commanded, his fists gripping the sheets in frustration, his eyes fierce.

Rachel put a hand on his shoulder and leaned a little lower to look up into his eyes. "Levi," she said gently. His eyes didn't move from Emma's face, so Rachel said his name again. "Levi."

This time he looked at her.

"Please," she said. "Go upstairs with the

men. It's better if you leave this to the women. Everything will be all right, but you must trust us. Let us take care of her." The words sounded ridiculous to her own ears, knowing she had no experience at all.

Her sister Mary had tiptoed down the stairs with a lantern and stood on the other side, the lantern up-lighting her swollen belly so that the shadows made it look twice the size of Emma's. Levi looked up at Mary, who nodded. His hat turned and he looked up at Mamm, who also nodded, her hand-kerchief pressed to her mouth.

"You're right," he said, appearing to deflate just a bit as he said it. "It's not good a man should be here just now. I'll go and pray." The anger drained out of his face, leaving only a pitiable desperation as he stared into his wife's eyes. "I must beg Gott not to take this baby," he said very softly, then shoved himself to his feet and hurried up the steps without looking back.

"We were at the table cutting out squares for a new quilt when she doubled over and grabbed her belly," Mary said as she untied Emma's kapp. "She had another pain after that, but they're a long ways apart yet, so I'm thinking maybe it's just false labor and she'll get over it."

"It's too soon," Mamm whimpered.

There was fear in Emma's eyes, and Rachel counted months in her head. Emma had been married a little less than six months. The baby couldn't be more than eight months along, at the most. It *was* too early — not nearly as early as Mamm thought it was, but still too early.

Suddenly, Emma squeezed Rachel's hand tightly and gasped. "I think my water just broke!"

"Oh, my stars!" Mamm cried, her eyes wide. "Now the baby *must* come! What will we do?"

Rachel's resolve nearly melted then, knowing that with a few well-chosen words she could relieve the panic in her mother's heart, but she didn't dare. She stared across the bed at Mary's horrified face, yellow in the pale light.

"It will be all right," Rachel said calmly, and even as she said the words she saw a question come to Mary's eyes. Perhaps she had spoken *too* calmly. Mary knew something was not right about this. She could count too, and she was no fool.

Mary glanced down at Emma, who nodded ever so slightly. Mary's head tilted, her lips parted and the flash of shock in her eyes melted quickly into a vague sadness. Without a word passing between them the three sisters now shared Emma's secret, a secret none of them would utter in front of their mother.

They helped Emma undress and got her into a clean gown, even as her contractions grew stronger and the time between them shortened. Rachel watched her writhe, feeling helpless and utterly useless, desperately wishing she could do something, anything, to relieve the spasms of horrendous pain contorting her sister's face. And yet, at the same time she began to feel an inexplicable but unquenchable thirst for knowledge, to learn all she could about what was happening.

"What does it feel like when that happens?" she asked meekly during a lull.

Emma's eyes opened. "You mean the pains?"

She nodded.

Emma closed her eyes again and didn't answer right away. In a minute she muttered, "Remember the other day when you had a really bad charley horse in your leg?"

"Jah."

"It's like that, only ten times worse. My lower back cramps really bad, then it spreads around to the front, and then it goes all over like a wave."

Emma's pain, and her mother's fears,

seemed to grow deeper with each wave. Mary had taken over while her mother watched, crying quietly, at the foot of the bed.

Mamm could barely contain her growing terror. "This cannot end well. It's too soon!" she moaned.

"It will be a long night," Mary said. "Rachel, why don't you go upstairs and make preparations — put a log in the stove and draw a big pot of water to boil. Also, put the iron on the stove and make ready to iron some baby blankets. You'll find them in that trunk over there."

Rachel was all too glad to have work to do, to have something to occupy her hands and mind while they waited. Patience was not one of her strengths to begin with, and endless minutes of waiting punctuated by convulsions of pain was almost more than she could bear. A thousand times she wondered if perhaps Emma was wrong about her. While she stoked the fire and ironed the blankets, a million random thoughts swooped through her mind like bats.

Will Emma be all right? Will Mamm figure out her secret? Will the baby live? How, oh how, Gott, can I help? What can I do?

As the hours passed and Emma's time drew near, Mamm grew increasingly despondent, pacing and coughing and weeping quietly, certain that she was witnessing the loss of Emma's first baby. She was just too tenderhearted.

Even so, not one of them had the heart to tell her that it might not be so.

In the wee hours of the morning Emma gave birth to a tiny baby boy, not much bigger than Rachel's hand. Though her hair clung together in damp rivulets and her gown was soaked with sweat, even during the worst of it she made no noise louder than a groan.

But the infant lay limp in Mary's hands while she rubbed him and massaged his chest in vain. He did not cry, nor did he move. Mamm broke down, wailing with grief. Mary, too, was on the verge of giving up, her hands trembling with panic. Her last two babies had been lost in much the same way, and the memory haunted her now.

Rachel stood mute on the other side of the bed, her heart pounding, her hands clasped over her mouth, and her eyes full of tears. This could not be happening — not to Emma!

Suddenly, Emma turned. Her eyes bored into Rachel, a lightning bolt of desperation. The voice in Rachel's head screamed, *Do something!* She did not understand her sister's faith in her, yet she had never doubted it. Such faith would not be denied.

Rachel said a brief, silent prayer as she rushed to Mary's side and, gently but firmly, took the baby from her. Putting her mouth over the tiny infant's whole mouth and nose, she breathed carefully into him and then pressed his chest with her thumb. The third time she did this he flung his tiny arms out and arched his back, his face crinkled in a soundless cry.

Rachel almost dropped him in astonishment, and in the next instant found herself laughing hysterically out of boundless joy, mountainous relief, and the sheer absurdity of it all. *That was me?* No one in the room was less prepared or more shocked than Rachel herself by what they had just witnessed.

Watching closely, forgetting to breathe herself, Mamm blinked and recoiled.

"He *lives?*" She looked again to be sure, then took a deep shuddering breath and raised hands and eyes to the heavens. "He lives! Oh, thank you, Gott!"

Rachel gently kissed the baby's forehead, handed him over to a stunned Mary and stepped back out of the way while they cleaned and wrapped him and laid him on his mother's breast.

Now that the crisis had passed, Rachel's

emotions overwhelmed her. In the space of five minutes she had felt a new life quicken in her hands, and a new Rachel quicken in her soul. It was a watershed moment. As long as she lived, she would remember her life in two parts — life before the birth of Emma's baby, and life after. She sank to her knees, laid her forehead on the edge of the bed, cried and prayed, and prayed and cried.

Emma's face relaxed into a contented smile. The anguish of the last few hours melted away, entirely forgiven and forgotten in the presence of new life.

"A handsome new son," Levi said when he was finally allowed into the room. He sat on the side of the bed, full of quiet gratitude that Gott had granted his wish, though he did not deserve such grace. He would only watch, afraid to touch the tiny infant.

Mamm gazed tearfully at the little bundle. "So small. Will you name him Uri, after your father?"

Levi's face darkened for a second. Everyone knew he and his father were not on the best of terms. No one talked about it openly, but they all knew it was one of the reasons Levi wanted to leave Ohio in the first place. His decision to move with the

Benders to Mexico had done nothing to heal the rift between him and his father.

He shook his head. "No, Mamm. His name will be Mose."

Emma nodded, smiled. "Mose. That's a good strong name."

Mary had fallen silent. She had barely said a word since Rachel took the baby from her and breathed into it, and she kept staring at Rachel with a trace of puzzlement in her eyes.

Finally, Rachel asked, "What is it, Mary? What's the matter?"

Mary frowned as if greatly confused. "How did you know, Rachel? You've never even seen a baby born before. How did you know what to do?"

"Other than God's grace, I don't know. It was just there when I needed it, that's all."

"You don't know." Mary shook her head in quiet amazement. "Well then, it's a gift. That's the only explanation."

In her heart Rachel was thrilled and terrified at being filled with a sense not her own. That Gott had given her that sense at the very moment when Emma needed her was indeed a gift.

CHAPTER 27

An air of cautious celebration tiptoed around the Bender farm for the next few days — cautious because both Mary and Mamm said that the premature baby's first few days, perhaps weeks, would be as perilous as his birth. The women of the family all hovered over him for days. Little Mose was very small and frail, but they soon learned that he was also very tenacious. He fed well and grew quickly. He had a headful of copper hair a little darker than Rachel's, and curly.

Caleb was proud of his new grandson — the first Amish baby born in Mexico — but the timing worried him. Over the years he had heard enough about birthing babies to know that one could not live at six months. Caleb could count, yet he did not entirely trust his instincts where womanly matters were concerned. He said nothing to Emma or Levi, but one morning he came to Martha while she was alone in her kitchen garden.

"Little Mose is doing well, isn't he?" he said.

She straightened up with a big yellow squash in one hand, a paring knife in the other. "Jah," she said. "He grows stronger every day. I think he is going to be fine."

"A miracle," Caleb said, scratching his cheek. "I don't believe I ever heard of a six-month baby living more than a day or two before."

She watched him cautiously, and when their eyes met she looked away. She knew.

"Jah, a miracle," Martha said, bending down to put the squash in her basket with the others. "Or maybe it wasn't so early as we thought." She said this without looking at him.

His eyebrows went up, his suspicion confirmed. "An eight-month baby can live," he said. "Maybe sometimes even a seven."

She nodded, still not looking at him. "But not a six-month baby. It's just not finished yet."

Neither of them said anything for a minute. They stood mute in their garden, two statues, one with her head lowered and the other gazing solemnly at the horizon.

"They deceived us, Martha. They deceived

everyone. This is wrong." His voice was heavy with sadness, for he loved Emma greatly. "So what will we do?"

She bent over to put her paring knife into the basket, then dusted her hands on her apron as she high-stepped over the vines until she stood facing him. She raised her round face to his.

"Why must we do *anything?* They are married yet, and we are in Mexico, a thousand miles from our church."

"There has been sin. There should be repentance."

"Do you not think they suffered? Do you not think they repented to Gott? Must we shame them before men?"

He took a deep breath, his eyes level. "They sinned before Gott and man — they should *repent* before Gott and man."

"And what would be the point of that? Nothing would change, except that they and their child would bear the shame for the rest of their days. *What is the point of that?*"

"It's what is right," Caleb said. "It's the truth."

Hanging her head, Martha pulled a handkerchief from her pocket and dabbed at her eyes.

"And what of love?" she said softly, without looking up. "What of Joseph, who, when his betrothed was with child, sought to put her away privately to spare her from the shame? Is not love greater than the law?"

"Our daughter is not the Virgin Mary," he said, "and anyways, an angel came to Joseph if I remember right." But he felt his resolve slipping. Like Jonas Weaver, in his youth Caleb Bender had been wise enough to marry a friend. Now that friend was asking for a favor.

She didn't touch him, or even look up. She was folding that handkerchief, folding and folding again until it became a tight little cube between her fingertips. He barely heard her when she said, "Can't I be your angel?"

A cool breeze rippled over the fields, swept through the garden and tugged at the brim of Caleb's hat. Even now, when he looked at his Martha he could still see the lovely, slender eighteen-year-old girl who captured his heart so long ago. He kept his eyes on the horizon, but his rough hand came up to stroke the back of her arm.

"Jah," he said quietly. "You surely may."

CHAPTER 28

As soon as the house was finished the men set to work, digging into the side of the knoll for the ground floor of a banked barn while Rachel and Miriam turned the loose dirt into bricks. Mary's little boys worked with them, stomping and sloshing in the mud, but Ada stayed balled up in bed crying with one of her headaches.

Somehow Ada had made a connection in her muddled mind. It finally got through to her as they were nailing the last of the roof on the house that this was permanent. They wouldn't be going back to Salt Creek Township anytime soon. Rachel watched as the revelation slowly melted the corners of her oldest sister's eyes, and then her mouth, and then her shoulders. The finishing of the house, the very thing everyone else celebrated, seemed to extinguish the last of Ada's hope.

Miriam took the screed and scraped the

top off of a fresh row of wet bricks. Rachel came behind her with a flat shovel, clearing away the excess mud, tossing it back into the mixing pit.

"So, when are you going to start your school?" Rachel asked.

Miriam stopped and leaned on the handle of the screed, staring off into the distance. "I don't know. In the beginning I would need you to help me, and right now we are too busy — when would we have time? Maybe in a month or two, after the harvest."

"Are you going to teach English?"

Miriam wiped sweat from her forehead with a wrist — her hands were too dirty. Then she looked at her sleeve to see if she'd smeared mud on it from her forehead.

"I don't see any reason for it. We only learned English in Ohio because it was America and people speak English there. Here, everyone speaks Spanish. It wouldn't make any sense to teach these little ones English when we live in Mexico." Mary's little boys had not learned any English yet because they had not started school. They spoke only Dutch.

"Are you still planning to teach the Mexicans, as well?"

Miriam shrugged. "Why not? It will be easier for our own children to learn Spanish

323

if there are Mexican children in the class, and they can all learn to read at the same time."

As they talked, Domingo trundled a wooden wheelbarrow down from the barn and dumped a load of fresh dirt ten feet away.

"But you don't even have teachers' books," Rachel said.

"I don't need them. In the beginning I will only teach how to read and write and add and subtract. I know how to do those things. Later, someone else will come."

"But you're not a teacher, Miriam. Do you really think you can do this?"

Miriam smiled. "What harm can it do to try? Anyway, how do we know I'm not a teacher if I never tried to teach?"

Domingo set his wheelbarrow down and straightened up, staring at Miriam. "You're going to teach school?"

"Jah," Miriam said, "but you mustn't tell anyone, Domingo. It's a secret. I haven't asked Dat about it yet."

Domingo shrugged, and Rachel looked a little sideways at her sister. "You haven't talked to Dat about this?"

"Not yet. I will. There hasn't been a really good time to bring it up."

Rachel chuckled. "You're afraid he will say no."

A puzzled frown crossed Domingo's face. "Why would your father say no to a school?"

Miriam almost grinned, sheepishly. "Well, we're thinking he might not be too crazy about the idea of Amish children being in school with outsiders. After all, he brought us all the way to Mexico so we wouldn't have to go to school all the time with Englishers, and the subject might still be a little tender with him. But I don't think Dat minds learning, so long as it's just reading, writing, and arithmetic. He knows how important it is to be able to read."

"Outsiders," Domingo said, his head tilting. "You mean Mexicans?"

"Sí."

"You're going to teach *mestizo* children to read?"

Miriam nodded. "That's what I was thinking, yes — but only if they want to, of course. I just thought since —"

"They will want to, cualnezqui," Domingo said. There was a new light in his eyes.

"Well," Rachel said, "it's a month or two yet before the end of harvest — plenty of time to talk Dat into it. If you're afraid, you can always get Emma to ask him. She can talk him into anything."

Miriam shook her head. "I might think about that if he says no, but this is really important to me, Rachel. I want to do it myself."

CHAPTER 29

The field corn was finally ready. Caleb's boys had barely finished building a crude corncrib when everybody took to the fields to bring in the ears. Though the crib looked like a leaky Noah's Ark, thrown together out of leftover slats and floating on knee-high posts to keep the rabbits out, it was their only way of drying corn for feeding the animals over the winter. Caleb didn't know for certain what their first Mexican winter would be like.

Domingo worked alongside Caleb and Aaron, pulling the field corn, tossing ears into the wagon as a pair of draft horses eased along, guided only by whistles from Caleb.

"The bandits I've seen so far don't seem that bad," Caleb said. "The only thing frightening about them is all those guns. The ones I've seen around here didn't scare me nowhere near as much as that El Pantera fella. Most of them are even sort of polite."

Domingo chuckled. "Those are the ones who were raised as peons on haciendas. From the time they are born they are taught to be respectful of anyone they don't know, and it becomes a habit. Life is easier that way. They will smile at you and mind their manners right up until they cut your throat and steal your horse."

"Anyway," Caleb said, tossing an ear of corn into the wagon, "the bandit problem doesn't seem so bad. I have only seen two groups of them since our trip to Saltillo last month."

Domingo laughed out loud. "Then you need to train your eyes, señor. In the last week I have seen four different bands passing by or watching us from the ridgetops, and two others late at night in San Rafael."

Caleb stopped to roll up his sleeves, as the afternoon had grown warm. "You talk as if the whole country is full of bandits. How many are there?"

"How many men are in an army?"

"So you're telling me, now that the war is over, everyone who fought in the revolution has become a bandit?"

"Not all of them, but many. You have not seen the last of the *bandido*s, Señor Bender."

■ ■ ■ ■

Domingo's prophecy proved true. As the days cooled and the hardwood trees on the ridges began to turn, more bandits drifted down out of the hills, though they were not always seen. Chickens went missing, the kitchen garden was regularly plundered, and sometimes the coop yielded no eggs when there should have been a dozen.

About once a week some ragtag clutch of armed men would wander up the driveway in the evening to water their horses. Almost always they came from the hills, out of rough, mountainous terrain, and the Bender place was the first farm they saw when they came down into Paradise Valley. From the ridgetops it must have looked very inviting with its neat quilt of irrigated fields. The Benders were quickly turning a barren prairie into an oasis that nomads could not resist.

The bandits always wanted food, and before they left they would usually ask for a sack of oats for the horses. It was an unexpected strain on the meager stores put by in one short growing season. Already Caleb feared there would not be enough to last the winter, but if his family tightened their belts a bit they could get by somehow, and next year would be better. Next year the others would be here to share the burden.

Up to now the bandits had never openly threatened anyone at the Bender farm, and so long as they harmed no one Caleb saw no reason to take action against them. He said the Bible was clear on this — when someone asks you for something, give it to him.

But then, in October, something happened on the road from the hacienda that changed his mind.

Rachel and her sisters milked four cows twice a day, which supplied the families with more than enough milk. Every day one of the women would run the fresh milk through a hand-cranked cream separator and then store the cream in the well house to let it cool. After a couple of days they would take the cream out and churn it into butter. Once a week one of the women — usually Emma or Mary — would take the surrey into the village at the foot of the hacienda and trade butter for a bag of salt or sugar or whatever they needed from the mercado. While there, they would run errands and stop by the hacienda post office to drop off the week's letters and pick up mail. It was a pleasant little half-day excursion, and sometimes Rachel or Miriam got to go along as a treat. Dat was reluctant to let his daughters go to town unescorted at first, but the hacienda village was within sight of home, only a few miles away, and he needed his boys on the farm.

On a glorious fall day in October Rachel took an afternoon off to go to town with Emma. A little wind rustled the dry brown prairie grass and the air felt cool. Swallows dipped and dove after bugs, and a pair of large gray hawks hung almost motionless against a crystalline sky, hunting. Emma carried Mose in a cloth sling, but Rachel got to hold the baby while Emma was driving the buggy.

Everyone in the village was in a festive mood that day. Señor Hidalgo had returned to the hacienda less than a week ago to oversee the harvest and immediately declared the first three days a fiesta, during which he visited among his peons and gave them gifts. Rachel spent a wonderful day with her sister, and to cap it off there were *two* letters from Jake waiting for her at the post office. Rachel read them in the buggy while Emma drove out of the village, but the first letter made Rachel smile and blush so much that Emma teased her to read it aloud.

"Nooo, I couldn't do that, even for you," Rachel said, folding the letter back into its envelope.

The second letter brought a frown to her face.

"What is it?" Emma asked. "Come on, I can see it in your eyes. What's wrong?"

Rachel lowered the letter to her lap and stared off into space.

"It's his dat," she said. "Jake says there are rumors of bandit trouble down here and his dat is wavering. They are afraid."

"So write him back and tell him yourself, there is nothing to fear. Jah, there are a few bandits roaming around, but mostly they are just hungry. They have done us no real harm, and they have never taken anything of great value. *Tell* him."

Rachel read both Jake's letters over again as Emma drove back toward Paradise Valley, the surrey rattling and rocking gently over the rutted dirt road. As they topped a shallow swell near the fork where Saltillo Road veered off to the north, Emma tapped Rachel's knee with a fist.

"Look," she whispered.

Up ahead at the fork, four men stood huddled next to their horses. One of them held a left front hoof between his knees, the horse standing patiently on three legs. The other three men leaned in, examining the hoof with him. Even from a distance there was no mistaking the pinto ponies, the layered clothes plastered with road dust, the bandoliers and pistols.

Bandits. Rachel and Emma couldn't have run into them in a worse place. There wasn't even so much as a thatched hut within a mile of the Saltillo fork. A cry for help out here in the open would not be heard by anyone.

Emma slowed the buggy to a walk, but it was too late to turn around. They had come too far even to dash back to the hacienda village. The four men looked up at the same time, sombreros turning toward the surrey like sunflowers to the sun.

She tried to hold the buggy to the left side of the road and keep moving, but one of the bandits stepped out and raised a hand. When the horse came close he reached up and deftly caught hold of the bridle, halting the nervous horse in its tracks. The bandit who'd been looking at his horse's hoof stayed where he was and held the reins of all four horses while the other three men surrounded Emma's buggy.

The one on Emma's side lifted his sombrero and slid it off the back of his head, letting it hang from its neck cord behind him while he smiled up at her. He was a wiry little man with a face like a weasel, badly in need of a shave and a bath.

"Buenos días, señorita —" Then he noticed the tiny baby Rachel cradled in her arms, and the empty sling around Emma's neck. "Pardon me. *Señora*," he said. "Please, I do not wish to trouble you, but my amigo's horse is injured — not badly, mind you, only a little." He held his thumb and forefinger an inch apart, smiling apologetically. As he was saying this, one of his friends kept a tight grip on the buggy horse's bridle while the other ran a hand down its slick flank.

"Porfirio's horse has only a little stone bruise in the soft part of his hoof," the weasel said. "But this is a big problem for us, beautiful señora. It would not matter so much, but we must get to Arteaga before morning. We have work to do there."

The other man, the one who had been appraising their horse, now slipped back to the buggy and fixed Rachel with an openly lascivious gap-toothed grin. She tried very hard to keep her eyes straight ahead and not look at him at all.

The weasel-faced leader spoke with the exaggerated sincerity of a huckster. "Now,

Porfirio's horse is a *fine* specimen. He was once a rodeo champion, no?" He held out a hand to the other three men for affirmation of this outrageous lie.

They all nodded vigorously and said, "Sí, señora, a champion!"

"So I wondered, if it would not trouble you greatly, if perhaps Porfirio might trade horses with you — only for a few days," he said, holding up both hands and rushing his words when he saw the rebellion in Emma's eyes. "Only for a few days, señora, or perhaps a week, until we can come back to retrieve Porfirio's champion stallion. Then we will return your old mare as good as new, I give you my word."

Appraising him coldly, Emma opened her mouth to say something to him, but Rachel squealed.

The bandit standing next to Rachel had reached into the buggy and laid a hand on Rachel's knee. Her face flushed crimson. She shrank away from his touch, clutching Mose close to her chest, but there was nowhere to go.

"Como una fresa!" the man said, grinning, pointing at her face. *Like a strawberry!* "I would like to take this ripe strawberry home with me. I would make the lovely señorita the queen of my hacienda!"

Emma tried to stare him down, but he had eyes only for Rachel. She appealed to the weasel.

"Señor," she said sharply, "surely your companion knows he should treat the friends of the haciendado with respect here in the shadow of the hacienda, especially when Señor Hidalgo is on his estate." It was a calculated bluff. Señor Hidalgo kept a small army of bodyguards with him on the estate, and the bandits knew this.

The weasel, glaring at his man through the open front of the surrey, said to him in a dangerously quiet tone, "Go and help Porfirio with the horses."

The gap-toothed bandit tensed. His grin vaporized, and his eyes narrowed in unmistakable challenge. But when he saw the weasel's hand slip down to the butt of his pistol he broke the stare and stalked away.

"You must forgive my friend, señora — he has no manners," the weasel said, but his hand remained where it was, a forefinger tapping ominously against the side of his leather holster.

"Take the horse," Emma said slowly through gritted teeth. Rachel muttered something, but Emma shushed her and continued. "Put Porfirio's horse in the traces for us. Then we will go, no?"

The bandit smiled broadly, pointing a bony finger at Emma. "I *knew* you would understand! You are very kind, señora. And do not worry. You will have your horse back in a week, wait and see!"

The buggy horse was as smooth a trotter as Rachel had ever seen, a prize standardbred mare, well-trained and in her prime. The broken-down pinto that replaced her stood a good two hands shorter and his head drooped. Thin and lethargic from hard use, his ribs poked through a dull, patchy coat. Emma let him limp along at his own pace the last two miles to the house.

"Dat will be furious," Rachel said as the lame nag grudgingly negotiated the turn into the driveway.

"Not with us, he won't. We did the only thing we could."

"Do you think they will bring our horse back?" Rachel asked.

Emma sighed, shook her head. "No. We have seen the last of her. I hope they treat her well."

Dat, as Rachel predicted, was furious. He met his daughters in the driveway a hundred yards shy of the house, demanding to know exactly what his buggy was doing strapped to a half-starved painted pony and precisely what had become of his best buggy horse.

When they told him, he snatched his hat off and paced back and forth a few times, then stalked away and waded far out into the thigh-deep oats, where he stood with his hands on his hips staring off in the direction of the hacienda, talking vigorously to himself.

Emma snapped the reins and marched the half-dead plug on up to the house, leaving her father to his rantings. It was his way. He would get out all of his reckless words in the open field where no human would hear, then apologize to Gott for his anger and return to civilization with his usual placid demeanor.

CHAPTER 30

The next morning before daylight Caleb dressed himself in his Sunday clothes, saddled his one remaining buggy horse and rode off to the east. It was high time he introduced himself to Señor Hidalgo.

He was met at the gates of the hacienda by two armed guards who asked him his business. When he told them he wished an audience with the haciendado, they made him get down from his horse. While one of the guards poked around his saddle, the other actually frisked Caleb's person, looking for concealed weapons. Once they decided he was not a threat they directed him through the gates and up around the curving drive to the stables, where his horse was taken from him and a stable hand led him to the back entrance of the hacienda. There he was met by another armed guard who turned him over to a butler, who took him down a maze of polished hallways to a small room with a large window and eight wooden chairs, six of which contained Mexicans who sat quietly with ragged hats on their laps, obviously waiting for an audience.

Caleb sat down and waited his turn.

After a few minutes a door opened at the far end of the room and a barefoot Mexican worker emerged, followed by Diego Fuentes, Señor Hidalgo's administrative chief. When Fuentes saw Caleb his face lit up and he came straight over to shake hands.

"Señor Bender! Buenos días! It is good to see you again. I have heard very good things about your farm. Everyone says you are doing very well indeed!"

"Muchas gracias," Caleb said. "We do what we can as hard as we can and trust Gott to do what we cannot."

Fuentes waved an arm toward the door. "Please, Señor Bender, we must not keep you waiting. Come into the library and let me introduce you to the haciendado."

The half-dozen Mexicans who had been there before him said nothing as Caleb walked between them into the library and Fuentes closed the door behind him.

Caleb had never seen anything remotely like the grand library at Hacienda El Prado. Three walls of the cavernous room were lined with ornately trimmed mahogany bookshelves twenty feet high with a narrow balcony halfway up, its delicate handrail supported by hundreds of curved spindles of exquisite design. The outer wall held a solid bank of windows facing east over a splendid garden that must have covered five acres, with lawns and shrubs and ponds and shade trees and vine-laced trellises over neatly paved walkways. The frescoed ceiling of the library looked like something out of a museum, each of its gilded sections framing a different painting, indecipherable scenes that Caleb figured must have been drawn from Mexican folklore. Persian carpets covered almost the entire polished stone floor.

A man who looked to be in his forties stepped out from behind a massive cherry desk at the far end of the room as Fuentes bowed slightly, made a sweeping gesture in Caleb's direction and said grandly, "Señor Hidalgo, may I present to you Señor Caleb Bender. Señor Bender, Don Louis Alejandro Hidalgo."

The haciendado greeted him warmly with a firm handshake. Hidalgo was ten years younger than Caleb, and slightly smaller. Señor Hidalgo's clothes were nothing like those of a farmer; he wore a perfectly fitted three-piece wool suit, tailor-made white shirt, and an ascot in place of a tie. Clean-shaven, with dark hair slicked down and neatly parted on one side, he looked like the pictures of movie stars that Caleb had seen on the covers of glossy magazines in the store racks.

And he was well-spoken. He offered to speak English or German if Señor Bender preferred, but Caleb politely declined, explaining that he lived in Mexico now, and though his Spanish was very coarse, it would only improve through use.

Señor Hidalgo offered him a cigar. When Caleb declined, Hidalgo lit one for himself and puffed away as he made small talk. Hidalgo wanted to know all about the farm and how the irrigation system worked, and then he asked after the others — when they would come and how many. When he finally asked if there had been any problems with the local people, Caleb took a deep breath and drew himself up.

"Well, sir, that's what I came here to talk to you about." He informed Hidalgo of the increase in visits his family had been getting from small groups of outlaws of late, the pilfering of eggs and chickens and vegetables. Then he said, "But that's not the worst of it. Yesterday, they took one of my horses and threatened my daughter."

Hidalgo pondered this with a frown, a fist containing a huge cigar pressed against his cheek in thought. "What kind of horse?" he asked.

"Standard-bred," Caleb said. "Best buggy horse I had, a mighty good trotter."

Hidalgo's eyes lit up. "I have heard of those! There is no talk of them here, but in New York everyone knows about the fine, fine, standard-bred trotters of the Amish in Ohio and western Pennsylvania. I would love to have seen this horse."

"I have another almost as good," Caleb said. "It is in your stable as we speak."

"Well then, let's go! I must look at it. Come, Diego!"

Diego Fuentes and Caleb Bender followed, hat in hand, behind the haciendado as he hurried down the labyrinthine hallways of his palace and out the back door to the stables. They found Caleb's horse housed in a paddock right next to the splendid Friesian he'd seen Fuentes riding that first day. Hidalgo opened the barred door and went right up to the horse, patting and rubbing it, talking to it in soothing tones.

"You can ride him if you want," Caleb said. "He's kid broke."

Within minutes the impeccably attired master of the estate was gliding around the show ring beside the stables, putting Caleb's horse through his paces and grinning from ear to ear with that cigar clenched in his pearly white teeth. When he was satisfied he dismounted and turned the horse over to a stableboy, saying, "Give this excellent animal the royal treatment."

He found the ride invigorating, and rather than going back into the library Hidalgo decided to show Caleb around his gardens. He was profoundly impressed with the horse, and in fact tried to buy it, but Caleb refused to sell.

"It's the only buggy horse I have left. I don't see how we could get by without it," he explained. But the horse had left a deep impression, and Hidalgo treated Caleb as an honored guest.

"So, what can we do about these bandits?" Caleb finally asked as they strolled past a pond full of some kind of bright orange fish.

Hidalgo's face fell. "Alas, my friend, there is little I can do anymore. There was a time . . ." Then he shook his head as if to clear it and said, "Ah, but those days are gone, my friend. Mexico is in a time of change, a time of chaos. Old things are passed away, but new things have not yet come. I'm afraid the day of the hacienda, as glorious as it once was, is past. For centuries the haciendas ruled the land, and the pure-blooded Spaniards who owned them brought peace and morality and culture to this impoverished country."

He sighed heavily, glancing up the hill toward his grand mansion. "But all things must pass, Señor Bender. History tells us that there will always come a day when the peasants band themselves together — as they did in Russia a few years ago, and in Europe before that — and arm themselves and overwhelm the nobility. Now it has happened here. This misguided egalitarianism has spread like a plague through Mexico, and now the hacienda will go the way of the plantation in the American South. The passing of our way of life is a shame, but we must face the fact that the revolution has come and things have changed. We are entering a new, more democratic time. This is why I have sold part of my pastureland to you and your people. I have decided to liquidate some of my family's estate and invest in anonymous business and industry. Oil is the future of Mexico."

With his hands clasped behind him, Hidalgo strolled slowly down a brick-lined path between high banks of exotic flowers and pampas grass, into the shade of a towering oak whose autumn-browned leaves fluttered lightly down to collect in little drifts on the path.

"I have said all this to say I am sorry, my friend, but I cannot help you with the bandit problem. I can no longer defend my own lands for fear of triggering an uprising. Hacienda El Prado only stands today by the favor of Francisco Villa, who once swore an oath of friendship to my father. Now that the war is over, there are far too many armed men scattered through the mountains for me to risk provoking them and uniting them against me. My advice to you is to make peace with them as best you can."

"But there must be *law*," Caleb said. "There must be some police or sheriff or soldiers *somewhere* who will protect us. Surely we will not be left at the mercy of these criminals."

Hidalgo shrugged. "Well, you can appeal to the government, but I don't know if they will help you. When we get back to the library I will give you the address of an official in Monterrey who controls the allocation of government troops in Nuevo León. Perhaps you can persuade Señor Montoya to send a detachment to live here in the valley, and then the bandidos will go away.

They will become a thorn in someone *else's* side."

"Well, I'm not the best letter writer," Caleb said, glancing sideways at Hidalgo. "I'm wondering if it might be better for this letter to have *your* name on it. After all, this government official wouldn't know me —"

"But that is the problem, Señor Bender. He *would* know me. As I said, times have changed. For the men who now rule Mexico it is not politically expedient, and may even be perilous, to be seen as friends of the haciendados. I am afraid my name might do your cause more harm than good."

CHAPTER 31

Miriam, with her intense studies over the last couple of months, had become the family expert on the Spanish language, so it came as no surprise to her when her dat asked her to help him with a letter. The two of them sat up late at the kitchen table, by lamplight crafting a letter to Señor Montoya, the government official in Monterrey. Even the actual printing of the final draft fell to her, as her dat doubted that anyone could decipher his herky-jerky farmer's hand. When she had finished, he signed it.

"Mebbe now they will help us," he said as Miriam sealed the envelope.

Everyone else had gone to bed. It was just the two of them bending over the letter at the table. Dat yawned and stretched and started to reach for the lantern, but Miriam stayed his hand.

"Dat, I need to talk to you about school." This would be as good a time as any. He was tired, and she had just done him a great service.

"School?" He settled back onto his bench, directly across the table from his daughter.

"Jah, for the kinder. I would like to start a school."

He pondered this for a minute, rubbing the back of his neck. His eyebrows went up. "Well, little Sammy and Paul are old enough to learn their letters, and Leah and Barbara could use help with Spanish. I don't see why you couldn't teach them if you want to."

Miriam hesitated, not sure how to lay out her plan. "I will need some things. I will need to take a little time away from work once or twice a week, and I'll be needing some space for the school."

Dat shrugged. "There's only just the four of them. You could teach them Spanish here at the kitchen table after evening chores."

"But when the others come there will be more children, and I'm thinking I could teach them not just Spanish but reading and writing and numbers," she said, watching his face. "I might need more time than that."

Dat's head tilted and he stared at her a little too long. She squirmed a little, and he read her like an open book.

"What is it you really want to say, daughter? Just say it."

He was right; she should just get to the point. Her father always said what he meant in as few words as possible, and he expected the same from his children.

"I want to start a school," she said, fidgeting with her kapp strings, "but not just for Amish kids. For the Mexicans, too."

He leaned back a little, and his eyes widened in surprise. Then, as if there was a chance he hadn't heard her correctly, he squinted and said, "For the *Mexicans?*"

"Jah. They have no school." It was almost a whisper. She knew this was dangerous ground. The main reason the Amish had fought so hard to keep their children out of the consolidated school in Ohio was that they spent too much time mingling with outsiders, being influenced by them.

He looked away for a minute, his hand first covering his mouth and then wringing his beard.

"They have no school?"

"No, Dat. That's why most of them can't read and write their own language." Sensing an advantage she pressed her point. "I thought maybe since the way they really talk isn't like in the book, the Mexican children could help the Amish children to speak real Spanish, and we could teach them to read."

"But are you *sure* there is no school?

Schulman is always saying the mestizos are illiterate, but I thought he meant they just wouldn't go to school, or could not be taught. Why, just today Señor Hidalgo said to me that Spanish landowners like him were the ones who brought culture to this poor country. I thought surely there were schools of *some* kind."

Over dinner Dat had described Hacienda El Prado to his family — the flowing gardens and manicured walks, the soaring library with its acre of books and gilded ceilings covered with paintings.

"No, Dat. The haciendados keep their fancy libraries to themselves, and they hire tutors for their own children. I've heard that some of the Catholic churches have schools, but the one at El Prado does not. There is no school for the poor. Maybe things are different in the cities, I don't know, but out here in the country the only ones who can read and write are wealthy landowners, Catholic priests, and foreigners like us."

Her father sat for a long time staring at the edge of the table, thinking. She could hear him breathing. After a while he began to nod slowly. He had reached a decision.

"Then your school is a good thing, Miriam. It is a *very* good thing. What will you need?"

"First, I will need time. I'm thinking one or two days a week. And then, I don't know how many will come, but we'll need a place to meet."

He scratched his bald head. "The barn wouldn't be too good. It's too crowded already."

This was true. Since large timber was scarce on the nearby ridges, they had built the walls of the barn with adobe and put a gambrel roof on it to make a loft, but the adobe walls limited them to a space half the size of a normal Amish barn. And it was harvesttime — the barn would soon be packed with hay and oats.

"I guess you'll have to have your school in the house," he finally said, "if there's not too many people. I hope to get a buggy shed built by spring, but I don't know if it will have doors on it yet. Or a wood stove."

"We'll need paper, too. Lots of paper and pencils, and a place to write."

"A desk?"

"No. Well, we can make benches and tables from wood scraps, but I was talking about a blackboard. And chalk." Miriam was bursting with energy and ideas now that her dat was on her side.

"We will have to see about that. I wouldn't know where to look for something like that in Mexico. Maybe we can get them to bring one from Ohio when they come."

As he was saying this he yawned, and in the same instant from the next room Miriam heard Aaron's soft snore. She was keeping her father up past his bedtime.

"It's very late, Dat," she said, rising. "I should be getting to bed. Thank you for letting me do this . . . for understanding."

He didn't make a move to get up right away. He was leaning on his elbows, his chin in his palm, looking to the side with his fingers covering his mouth. There was a peculiar sadness in his eyes.

"Dat?" she said, pausing, three fingertips resting on the end of the table. "Are you all right?"

He looked up at her then, the sadness clinging. "Yes, child, I'm all right. Just a little ashamed."

Her head tilted. Shame was not something she associated with the image of her father.

"Ashamed? Why, Dat?"

He shook his head. "I don't know if I have the words. It's just . . . I try my best to be honorable, to keep Gott's laws, live in peace with my neighbors and forgive those who wrong me, but I'm finding out it's mighty easy to be honorable until a man steals your horse.

"My mouth says 'I forgive,' but my heart wants soldiers to come and do away with these bandits. All of them. That's why I wanted to send this letter; I wanted those men to pay for taking my horse. I don't want to see harm come to my family, and that's good, but in my heart I *do* want to see harm come to the bandits. And that's not right."

His eyes wandered as he struggled to put words to his thoughts. "All these laws we try to follow, Miriam . . . they are Gott's laws, and in my heart I believe what they're for is to keep me humble and remind me not to be selfish. I always thought that if I could do that, why then my one short little life can mebbe push the whole world one inch to the good, in the direction Gott wants it to go. That's all. One inch. But the change one man makes in the world is so little we wouldn't even see it, and that's why we need faith. If a man lives without faith, he pulls the world toward himself — only an inch, mebbe, but he makes it hard for people around him to live in faith because they learn to fear him. They are afraid to be without. If a lot of men live selfish lives for a very long time, they move their world a lot of inches the wrong way, and they end up with a country full of hungry people who steal because they are afraid."

He waved a hand at the envelope lying on the table. "My answer to this problem is to ask the government for soldiers. Your answer is to teach them to read. It's only an inch, but which is Gott's way?"

Lifting the letter from the table he held it in his rough hands for a moment, feeling the thickness of it with his thumbs, and then tore it in half and dropped the pieces on the table.

"Not by power or might, but by the Spirit of the Lord of hosts," he said. "A father is never prouder of his children than when they make him a little bit ashamed of himself."

Chapter 32

When the first fall cold snap came to the fields around their thatched huts, the Mexicans began working from daylight to dark, pulling up bushes by the roots and piling them to dry. While the Amish farm slowly turned to shaved ground dotted with orderly rows of oat shocks, the mestizo fields yielded little mounds of uprooted bushes, tangles of leaves turning from green to gold, drying and shriveling in the autumn sun.

One day, when the men had come in from the harvest for lunch and Miriam was helping to clear the table afterward, she asked Domingo about the piles of bushes.

"They are beans," Domingo said. "After the bushes are all pulled and piled up, you will see families in the fields every day turning the piles over to make sure the beans dry all around. It is a lot of work."

"I have seen them. They work as if their lives depend on it," Miriam said as she brought another pitcher of water to the table. Sometimes when the men came in for lunch they were not very hungry, but they were always thirsty.

"Our lives do depend on it," Domingo explained, emptying his glass and reaching for the pitcher. "In bad years the beans are all we have. Sometimes rabbits are scarce in the winter, or we have no luck finding deer and javelinas. One year the coyotes took all our chickens, and another there was not enough rain for the corn to grow. But no matter what else happens, the family can live as long as we have beans stored up. With a little cornmeal or flour and some dried beans, we survive."

Caleb held up his last bite of sweet potato and pointed at Domingo with it. "Have *you* got beans?"

"Sí," Domingo said. "Everybody does. The three of us — me and my cousins — we have a few acres outside of San Rafael that we work together."

"Well, you've been working here every day. When did you harvest your beans?"

Domingo gulped water, wiped his mouth on a sleeve and shrugged. "We haven't yet, but they are ready. We need to take a few days off."

Caleb laid his fork down, glowering.

"Why, that's just not acceptable, Domingo. That's not the way we do things here."

Domingo's eyes met Caleb's hard glare. "Señor . . . you are a farmer. You know the beans won't wait — the pods are starting to crack."

"I know that," Caleb said flatly. "So tomorrow morning at first light my boys will be at your place with a team and a spring-tooth harrow. They'll have your few acres of beans out of the ground in a couple hours, then you can all come back here for the rest of the day. The next day we'll all be there with pitchforks. How long does it take before they're dry enough?"

"Three, four days if there is no rain." Domingo and his cousins all sat motionless, staring at Caleb, not sure what to make of this.

"A couple hours every morning — with enough hands, that's all it'll take to turn them. Then we can bring in the oats in the afternoon. It's not that big of a field." Caleb paused, his brow furrowed. "And after the beans are dry, you separate them by hand?"

"Sí. Put the pile on the cart, take out the beans, then throw the chaff back on the ground and get another pile. It takes a long time."

"Hmm. Shame we don't have a thresher for that. We can all help with the shelling, even the women. Many hands make light work."

Domingo shook his head. Carlos and Paco stared at him in disbelief. "Señor Bender, we have no money to pay for your help."

Caleb's eyebrows went up. "I didn't ask for money. I told you, that's not the way we do things. When neighbors need help in the fields, we help them." He pointed at Domingo with his fork. "*That* is how we do things here."

By late October the kitchen garden was spent, all except for the potatoes. Rachel had never seen so many potatoes, and so big. She'd never dug them up this time of the year either, but obviously the late start had done them no harm. The potatoes clearly loved the soil of Paradise Valley.

She was prying a tangled mess of potatoes and roots out of the ground with a stout fork when she spotted Emma coming up the road in the surrey. Emma saw her from a long way off, smiled and waved, and held up a letter. She'd made the weekly run to the hacienda village and brought back a letter from Jake. With a little twinge of excitement Rachel dropped the fork and trotted down the driveway to meet her. Emma stopped to let her climb up.

"Dat's right up there behind the house putting hay in the loft," Rachel said, and Emma understood. She would hold the buggy still long enough for Rachel to read Jake's letter and put it away before they went up to the house. Rachel had been careful not to let her father find out about the boyfriend she was not supposed to have, and Emma was dependably complicit in the deception.

While Rachel devoured the letter from Jake, Emma gazed around her at the stubbly fields dotted with shocks of bundled hay.

"This place needs trees," Emma said, almost to herself. "I miss them so, especially in the fall. Back home there were so many trees — not just the woods but shade trees by the driveway and the house and the barn. Even when the fields are ripe, this valley seems barren without trees in it. I'm going to write Lovina and see if they'll bring saplings when they come." Her eyes brightened with a vision of the future.

"Yes! I know just what I'll do. I'll plant poplars all down both sides of the driveway and one day they'll make a lovely shady lane for anyone who comes to visit Dat's house." She spread her hands against a backdrop only she could see, and her eyes shined. "There will be great big oak trees on both ends of the house to hold off the summer sun, and I'll plant a grove of fruit trees along the base of the ridge. And maples! Why, that whole ridge will blaze like fire with maple leaves in the fall. Rachel, could you and Miriam make me some adobe for a sugar shack?"

Rachel didn't answer. The letter lay crumpled between her fists in her lap. She kept her face away from Emma, staring out over the fields and biting her lip to keep the tears from coming. It wasn't working.

"Rachel?" Emma reached out very gently and hooked Rachel's chin with a finger, turning her head. When their eyes met, Rachel's freckled face crumpled like the letter and she sobbed.

"Rachel, what's wrong?"

Rachel pressed her face into Emma's shoulder and her sister's arms closed about her.

"What is it, child? What's happened?"

"He's not coming," Rachel whimpered, her shoulders shaking.

"*Jake's* not coming? But why?"

Rachel didn't answer. She couldn't. Without moving her face from Emma's shoulder she held up the crumpled letter. Emma took it, smoothed the paper against her knee with her free hand and read over Rachel's shoulder. She skipped over the first part of the letter, but when she came to the middle paragraph she began to read aloud, her soft voice now sharing her sister's grief.

" 'Everyone here is talking about the bandits who stole your horse. I know you must have been frightened out of your mind, Rachel, to have to face such men. I only wish I could have been there with you. Don't know what I could have done, but I wish I was there all the same.' "

She stopped reading for a few seconds and muttered, "Why would Dat tell them about the horse?" And then, with hardly a pause, she answered herself. "Because he is Dat. They sent him here to find out the truth about the bandits, and he will tell them the truth even if it costs him everything he has. He is Dat." Then she picked up reading where she left off.

" 'There was also an article in a magazine a little while ago about all the trouble in Mexico and how bad things are right now. Everyone was talking about it. I don't know how to say this, Rachel, but Dat is telling everyone he can't take his family to such a place because it's not safe. I asked him myself, and he said no, we are not going right now. Maybe later, if things calm down, he said, but not now. Sometimes I think I will die if I cannot see you, but Dat will not budge. I am very, very sorry, Rachel, but we won't be coming to Paradise Valley anytime soon.' "

Emma didn't read any further, nor did she say anything. Rachel didn't need words anyway — what could be said? Emma just wrapped her arms about her, pressing Jake's letter to her back, and held her for a long time while they wept quietly together.

Rachel pulled away at last. While wiping her eyes on a sleeve she made a little backhanded motion toward the house.

"Go on," she said.

As the surrey reached the house, Rachel jumped out and stalked across to the kitchen garden, head down, fists clenched, doing her best to hide her face. Perhaps it was an extension of her father's stoicism that even in a family dominated by daughters — perhaps *especially* in a family of daughters — self-pity was not tolerated. Rachel and her sisters had been raised to believe that though each of the Bender women had her own personal trials and struggles, there was never a problem that couldn't be overcome by some combination of hard work and faith. Ada was the only one in the entire family allowed to wallow in self-pity, and then only because she couldn't help it; she was, and always would be, a child.

Naturally, at a time when Rachel would rather not face any of them, most of her family was right there in front of the barn with the hay wagon, right next to the garden. To make matters worse, she had to cross in front of the house to get there. She nearly ran into Mary when she came out the front door with the slop bucket in her hands on her way to the pigpen. Mamm's voice rang through the open front door, telling Mary to rinse out the bucket and bring more water. Ada swept a pile of dirt out the door as Rachel stalked past, dusting her skirt with it. Beyond the house, her father was standing by the hay wagon, and Rachel passed within fifty feet without speaking to him. She dared not look up for fear that he would notice her puffy eyes and red nose, and ask why she had been crying. She did not want to lie to her father just now. Still, it seemed to her that he stopped what he was doing and watched her. Keeping her back to him, she picked up the potato fork and went back to work.

Fighting back the urge to cry, Rachel worked her way down the row, jamming the fork into the soft earth a little harder than necessary, shaking the dirt and clumpy roots from the potatoes with a bit too much enthusiasm, and throwing the potatoes into the pile a little too hard. But when she reached the far end where the dry remains of the pole bean vines hid her from view, she sank to her knees in the middle of them and gave in to self-pity. Holding on to the shaft of the fork with both hands as if it were a rope to Gott, she cried her heart out. Hope came to her all awaggle, thrashing through the vines, ducking under her arms and licking her face until Rachel swatted her away.

And then she heard the last thing she wanted to hear — the rustling of dry vines and the sound of soft footsteps behind her. Not now. There was nothing she could say to her father, no way she could even attempt to explain that she was wasting time weeping over the loss of a lover she was not supposed to have in the first place, a lover she had lost because *he* told Jonas Weaver about the bandits taking the horse.

She tried, but she couldn't stop crying. She remained where she was and waited for the inevitable, for her father's voice to ask what was wrong, and then she would have to stand and face him. But it didn't happen. Instead, a hand lay softly on her shoulder and squeezed; then someone — a woman, Rachel could tell from the rustling of skirts — sank to her knees behind her and wrapped loving arms around her, gently enfolding her. Rachel did not look up as a white-kapped head pressed itself to her shoulder, and then Ada's childlike voice cooed to her.

"Shhhh, little one. Gott knows. Shhhh."

CHAPTER 33

In early November Dat loaded the wagon with cabbage and made another trip to Saltillo. This time he took Domingo and Aaron with him. He claimed he wanted his son to learn the way to Saltillo so he wouldn't have to go himself every time, but Rachel knew the real reason he chose not to take any girls along. She remembered too well the incident with El Pantera, and the bandit pulling the kapp from her head.

When he returned three days later with the cabbage still piled on the back of the wagon, Rachel could tell by the set of his jaw that something was wrong. Dat was scowling and holding his head a little sideways the way he did when he had a headache. Rachel thought surely he'd been accosted by bandits again until her mother ran out to meet the wagon and Dat barked at her.

"Make sauerkraut!" he snapped. "Make

as much as the barrels will hold and we'll feed the rest to the pigs. What the pigs don't eat, we'll plow under."

Mamm tried to appease him. "What's wrong, Caleb? Why didn't you sell the cabbage in Saltillo?"

"I *tried!*" he shouted. "Mexicans don't eat cabbage!"

"I tried to tell him," Domingo said, working hard to suppress a grin.

Dat glared. "They came by the stand and poked their fingers at it," he said, miming the action with a comical look of disgust. "They asked us what it was, and then they said our lettuce was too hard and turned up their noses. I even peeled some off and ate it to show them, but when they tasted it they just made a face and spit it out! What kind of people don't eat cabbage?"

"Mexicans," Domingo said dryly, and then suddenly decided he would be wise to go help Aaron unload the cabbage and pile it by the back door.

Miriam had come from the house wiping her hands on a rag, and heard part of the conversation.

"Dat, were you able to buy paper?" she asked carefully.

Some of the frustration melted from his face then. "Jah, I had a little money left over yet, from the corn. I didn't get as much as you wanted, so you'll have to be sparing with it. I got pencils too, and Domingo even found an old blackboard someplace. He paid for it with his own money, and he wouldn't tell me how much he paid. He got chalk, too."

Mamm broke out the cabbage cutter, and the women set to work filling three big barrels with shredded cabbage. Sammy and Paul had great fun stomping it down in the barrels, but they were not happy about having to scrub their feet when it wasn't even Saturday.

Miriam put out the word, and the following Monday she held her first class in the living room. Leah and Barbara, the two youngest daughters, helped her set up the benches from the kitchen and bring in the long crude writing tables the boys had nailed together in the barn.

"I don't know what to expect," she told Leah. Miriam was literally wringing her hands, trying to figure out how to hang the little blackboard on an adobe wall.

"Calm down," Barbara said. "If they see you're afraid of them, they'll take advantage." She knew this from her own classroom experience. "I'll get Harvey to fix the board for you."

While Harvey was driving a wooden wedge into the adobe and screwing the blackboard to it, Rachel ushered in Domingo with four small boys from San Rafael. Long-haired, hatless, barefoot and dirty, terrified of the strange surroundings, the boys stood mute against a wall at first, but when Sammy and Paul ran in from the barn the new boys loosened up. Shortly after that a couple of young girls showed up, having walked the two miles from a tiny village at the end of the opposite ridge.

Miriam did her best to get them seated, but she had let them go a bit too long and the children had gotten rowdy. She clapped her hands and shouted. Sammy and Paul heard her, stopped running around and eased into their seats — they had, after all, been trained to sit still and pay attention for three hours in church all their lives. But Miriam couldn't get the Mexican boys to quiet down and stop chasing each other around the room until Domingo snagged one of them by the back of his shirt and lifted him off his feet the way he would have picked up a puppy by the scruff. The others all froze in place, watching to see what terrible fate would befall Juan.

Domingo dangled the petrified boy from

one hand and turned him so that their faces came very close together. The room was deathly quiet when Domingo looked straight into the boy's frightened eyes like a wolf and spoke in a low voice that rumbled through them like thunder.

"*Esto es un regalo de Dios*, Juan," he said. *This is a gift from God.* "You will treat the señorita with respect, no?"

Little Juan's eyes were white with fear as he nodded fervently, his lip quivering. "Sí" was all he could manage.

Domingo twisted the child about like a weather vane and lowered him gracefully onto a bench, facing Miriam.

Standing at the front of the room, Miriam now had their full attention, and it took only a nod and a small gesture of her hand for the rest of them to file calmly into the rows and seat themselves.

Rachel leaned close to Domingo's shoulder and whispered, "Maybe you should stay."

Domingo switched to German so the Mexican kids would not understand, and said, "They are *outside* children, accustomed to running free all day. They will learn quickly, but you must have a firm hand."

Miriam began with introductions. After

they had all said their names she asked, "How many of you can *spell* your name?"

The kids looked at each other, shook their heads.

"By Christmas," she said, "you will all be able to write your names, I promise."

Doubtful stares.

"Ahhhhhhh," she said, drawing a great big A on the blackboard, then waited a beat and explained, "Letters make sounds. First we will learn the letters, and what sounds they make."

She made a game of it, asking them for words they knew that began with "Ah."

Sammy and Paul looked at each other and then over their shoulders at Rachel. Miriam's Spanish had already lost them.

Rachel knelt behind them and translated. "Words that begin with an *Ah* sound," she whispered.

"Apfel!" Sammy blurted. The Mexican kids all leaned forward frowning at him, confused; then one of the little girls raised her hand and said bashfully, *"Agua?"*

Miriam was stumped for a second, but then she just went with the flow. Turning to the blackboard she picked up the chalk and wrote.

Apfel.

Agua.

"German or Spanish," she said, "it doesn't matter. The letter makes the same sound."

Juan pointed a thumb at Sammy and asked, "Do they not speak Spanish?"

"Not yet," Miriam said, smiling. "You are going to teach them."

Paul's face lit up, suddenly seeing what was required. Placing a hand on Juan's shoulder he beamed up at Miriam and belted out, "Amigo!"

"See?" Miriam said. "They are learning already." She added *Amigo* to the list.

Domingo never left the room. Rachel thought at first he was being very kind to volunteer his services as classroom disciplinarian, but then she noticed he was paying very close attention to everything Miriam said. When the kids belted out words and Miriam added them to the list his lips moved with them. Then he began to add words of his own. Focused and intense, he whispered, "*Aquí, adiós, año, arena, azul . . .*"

They only worked until noon that first day, but by the end of the session all of the children had made a connection between letters and sounds, formed a few crude letters with their pencils, and learned to count to five. The two Amish boys had even picked up a few words of Spanish. Leah and Barbara, who already knew their letters, had been a great help.

At the end of the class Miriam pulled a little black New Testament from the pocket of her dress, opened it to the ribbon bookmark and read aloud, " *'Porque tanto amó Dios al mundo, que dio a su Hijo unigénito, para que todo el que cree en él no se pierda, sino que tenga vida eterna.'* "

The children listened in silence and then bowed their heads while she said a brief prayer.

Miriam explained to them that she couldn't let them take the paper home because they would need to use it again next time, but that they should help each other remember their letters, practice writing them in the dirt with a stick and come back on Friday ready to learn more letters.

Miriam's first day as a teacher had flown past. Mamm was in the kitchen putting lunch on the table for the men, so the benches had to go back right away.

"That," Rachel said, lifting one of the benches to take it back to the kitchen, "was amazing. All this time I thought you were just a brickmaker. Now I find out you're a teacher. Miriam, you were wonderful with those kids. Did you see how they listened to you?"

"I saw," Miriam said, wiping the board

clean with a rag. "And I'm as surprised as you are. It all seemed so natural, so easy. Even that little troublemaker Juan, after he settled down, turned out to be my best student."

Coming back for the other bench, Rachel stopped in the doorway and said, "No, I don't think so. Not even close."

"No? Who then?"

"Domingo. Didn't you see him? He hung on every word."

"Oh my . . ." Miriam spun around, her eyes widening and her fingers covering her lips. "He was *listening?* You think he was trying —"

"Miriam, I can't believe you didn't notice. While the children were making letters on the paper he was leaning over them watching, and the fingers of his right hand were imitating what they were doing."

Miriam sat down heavily in her mother's hickory rocker, stunned. "Oh my. Of *course* he wants to learn to read. Why did it never occur to me? Well, we'll just have to include him in the school."

"You'll have to be careful about that. I think he may be too proud to sit on the little bench with the kinder," Rachel said.

Miriam nodded. "Oh jah, we'll have to figure out a way that's not so obvious. I know what we'll do — we'll make him an assistant. Next time we'll move the small table from the kitchen and put it in the back of the room. You and Domingo can sit there in real chairs and I'll put the supplies on the table. That way you can help him and it'll look like he's just there to watch the kids. You know, Rachel, you were great with the children, too. When the others get here you may end up teaching a class of your own."

Rachel scowled and shook her head. Glancing at the kitchen where Mamm was flitting back and forth from stove to table, she glided across the room to Miriam and whispered, "I don't think I'll be here that long."

Miriam's lips mimed *What?* Rising, she grabbed Rachel's arm and dragged her out into the yard, closing the door behind her.

"What do you mean, you won't be here? Where are you going?"

"Back home," Rachel said, lowering her face. "I miss Jake, and if he's not coming here, then I'll go there. I can go right back home and live with Lizzie and Andy in the same house, like I never left."

"You can't do that, Rachel. Think of your family. What would Mamm do without you, or *me,* for that matter? Will you leave me to

376

make bricks all by myself? And don't forget you promised you would be midwife for Mary when she has her baby."

Rachel shrugged. "Mary's baby will come anytime now, and I'll wait until after. But I'm going home, Miriam. I won't stay here if Jake's not coming."

Miriam's eyes narrowed. "I see. So, if there's no one here for you, you can't stay, is that it? Because there are no prospects in Mexico? You would use this excuse with *me?* You were the one who told me everything would be all right. Now you're *leaving?*"

Despite her best efforts, Rachel clouded up and started to cry.

Miriam wrapped her arms around Rachel's shoulders and drew her in. "Oh, it's all right. You were right, you know — what you told me about how everything would turn out okay in the end. It will, you'll see, but you can't leave your family. Not now. Not when we all need each other so badly. Rachel, nothing on this earth is so important as family, especially now, here in a strange land with so much work ahead of us. What would we do without you?"

Rachel sniffed, wiping at her eyes with her fingertips. "It's just . . . *Jake.* I miss him so. I want to hear his voice, feel his arms around me."

"I know, I know. But, Rachel, you can't leave your family. Family is *everything.* You must be patient. Trust Gott and see what happens. No matter what, you must never, *ever* leave your family." She gripped Rachel's shoulders and held her at arm's length, trying to look her in the eye. "Okay?"

Rachel nodded meekly, still refusing to look up. "Okay."

CHAPTER 34

It was Mamm who brought up Thanksgiving one night while they were gathered around the table for dinner.

"I was wondering if we should invite Herr Schulman and his wife," she said.

"And let's not forget our Mexican friends," Miriam added. "Domingo and the other farmhands, at the very least."

"What about your school kids?" Rachel asked. The excitement had spread through Caleb's daughters like a virus.

Mamm frowned. "Oh, I don't know. How many students do you have?"

"Twelve," Miriam answered. Her class had grown over the last couple of weeks.

"Hold on now," Caleb said, his hands up, palms out. "Thanksgiving is an American holiday, and we live in Mexico now. Why, I bet these people never even heard of Thanksgiving. Even Schulman has never lived in America."

Mamm was on the verge of sulking. "That's why I want to do it," she said. "I'm American, and I miss it."

"She's right," Emma chimed in. "It would be like home again, and I'm thinking we're all a little bit homesick just now."

"I don't know," Caleb said. "I'm not sure we have the stores to make it through the winter as it is. A big feast like that . . . I don't know."

Emma reached across and laid her hand on his. "We need this, Dat," she said softly. "It will lift everyone's spirits, and besides, how can we not set aside a day to thank Gott for all our good fortune in this new land?"

"But it's an *American* holiday."

"No, Dat, it's a *Gott* holiday. We should thank Him for coming with us to Mexico."

Caleb smiled then. He could never resist his Emma. "Schulman has turkeys," he said, and the planning began.

It would be a memorable feast. Dat traded Schulman a shoat for two large turkeys, and when he invited them to the feast, Schulman's wife insisted on bringing pies. By some miracle Emma found a big sackful of dates in the hacienda mercado for date pudding, but there were no cranberries to be found anywhere.

Mamm and her daughters stormed the kitchen early on Thursday morning, and when the weather turned out to be fine the men nailed up long rows of tables in the front yard.

Domingo was among the first to arrive, his oxcart loaded with the four boys he always brought to school. He also brought with him a young Mexican woman with dark eyes, long silky hair as black as a crow and a demure but captivating smile. Miriam was carrying a stack of plates out to the tables when he pulled up near the barn, and she stopped in her tracks to watch as Domingo helped the young woman down from the wagon.

Rachel was right behind Miriam, and nearly bumped into her when she stopped to stare.

"Who is that?" Miriam asked.

Rachel followed her gaze. The young woman wore a colorful Aztec sarape over a dark print peasant skirt and blouse. She was stunningly beautiful. Domingo was very careful of her, deferential, and there was a proud smile in his eyes. Rachel glanced at her older sister's face and saw a faint but unmistakable trace of jealousy.

"Oh, Miriam, please tell me that look in

your eye is not what I think it is. *Domingo?*"

Their eyes met. Miriam turned away without answering, confirming Rachel's suspicion.

"Well," Rachel said to her back, "I hope for your sake she's his *wife*. It would save you from a great deal of trouble."

There was nothing Miriam could say at this point. She marched toward the tables without looking back.

Ten minutes later the sisters were carrying food from the house when Domingo rounded the corner and called out to them.

"Miriam! Rachel! There you are. I was looking for you."

They stopped in the yard, each of them holding a bowl of potatoes, and waited while Domingo and his dark-eyed beauty caught up with them.

Domingo's eyes went straight to Miriam.

"This is Kyra," he said proudly. "She is the mother of two of your students."

"Sí, Benito and Juan are mine," Kyra said, pressing Miriam's hand between her own. "I cannot tell you how grateful I am that you are teaching them to read. I only hope they do not worry you too much. That Juan, he is full of the devil." She grinned at Domingo then, and added, "Just like his uncle."

Miriam's eyes widened in surprise — and,

Rachel couldn't help noticing, a fair dollop of relief. "So, Juan and Benito are your *nephews,* Domingo?"

"Sí. Why do you think they are so afraid of me?" he said, smiling.

Rachel could only shake her head in amusement at how quickly Miriam's attitude toward Kyra changed. Kyra offered to help set the tables, and within minutes she and Miriam were laughing and chatting like old friends.

Later, she thought, *we will have to have a talk, my sister and me.*

Miriam had already invited all her students before she learned that they assumed the invitation included their families. By noon there were over fifty people in the front yard — a truly international gathering of Mexicans, Germans, and American Amish.

Dat raised his hands and took command of the situation, in a loud voice explaining how things would go. First the men would serve themselves, then the women and children, but before anyone was allowed to eat he would offer thanks for Gott's bounty. It was not his custom to pray out loud at mealtime, but for the benefit of his guests he did so on this occasion, and he did it in Spanish.

There was more food here than many of these people had ever seen in one place. Turkey, chicken, roast beef, mashed potatoes and gravy, sweet potatoes, loaves and loaves of fresh-baked bread, Mamm's special pumpkin butter, corn on the cob, all kinds of salad and greens — including cabbage, which Rachel noted with considerable amusement that the Mexicans indeed would not touch — and then the desserts.

Afterward, Miriam helped the women with cleanup while the men retired to the new horseshoe pits beside the barn. While she was washing dishes, Harvey ran in to tell her that he and some of the Mexican boys were saddling horses for an impromptu race around the cornfield.

Miriam dried her hands and walked down to the field with Rachel and Kyra to watch. She saw Domingo already trotting down to the field on the little pinto the bandits had traded them. She had personally nursed the horse back to health, tending his foot until it was sound, fattening him up and brushing out his coat until he looked presentable. And with Domingo sitting tall in the saddle, the little pinto held himself like a champion.

Domingo put on a surprising burst at the start of the race and pulled ahead. Miriam tried, but she couldn't take her eyes off of him — that chiseled bronze figure straining forward in the saddle, his cotton shirt flapping in the wind, and his long black hair flying. She told herself this was only a childish infatuation, that it was wrong, that he was not Amish. That it would pass.

Anyway, she thought, *when he looks at me he sees only an old maid schoolteacher.*

But in that one brief moment, flying over the field with the grace of a deer and the raw power of a mountain lion, he took her breath away. He was *beautiful.*

By the time they rounded the last turn the pinto had begun to lose steam so that Harvey, riding the larger standard-bred stallion, pulled away. He won by three lengths, and Miriam laughed and clapped and cheered along with Rachel and Kyra, though she fervently hoped that her little sister hadn't noticed that she wasn't watching the winner.

As the girls strolled casually back up toward the house Rachel patted Kyra's back and raved, "That pinto sure loves to run, and your brother handles him like he's known him all his life!"

Kyra nodded, smiling proudly. "*Your* brother rides like the wind, too." Then she turned to Miriam and said, "You know, Señorita Miriam, Domingo admires you very much. It is a wonderful thing you are doing, teaching the niños to read." She leaned closer, as if it was a secret, and said, "And Domingo, too. He has always wanted to learn, but when he was a boy my father would not let him go to the Catholic school."

Miriam's head tilted. "There is a school here? At El Prado?"

"Oh no. Not anymore. The government closed down most of the Catholic schools five years ago after the new constitution outlawed them, including the one in the iglesia at El Prado. Domingo could have gone there when he was little, but our father would not allow it. He said the Catholic Church was only a tool of the imperialist Spaniards."

"But you wear a cross around your neck," Miriam said, pointing. "I thought you were Catholic."

"I am," Kyra said, pinching the cross from her chest and touching it to her lips. "My mother is mestizo, and a Catholic from birth, but my father was full-blooded Nahua and he held to the old ways. He let my mother do as she wished with me because I was a girl, but Domingo answered only to him. When Domingo was born all my father's brothers and friends brought weapons and laid them in his crib. He was trained from childhood to be a Nahua warrior."

"Domingo?" Miriam said, genuinely shocked. The Domingo she knew did not seem like a warrior at all. "He has never spoken of this. Did he fight in the revolution?"

Kyra shook her head. "He was planning to go, but then my father was killed at Zacatecas, along with my husband."

Tenderhearted Rachel was almost in tears. "Your husband died in the war? I'm so sorry, Kyra."

"He was a good man, and I miss him," Kyra said softly. "But many families were torn apart in the revolution. My mother begged Domingo not to go then, because he was the only man left to provide for us. He made a promise to her, and he has honored it. My brother is an honorable man," she said, her dark eyes shining with pride.

"I'm really surprised to hear this about Domingo, though," Miriam said. "I have never seen him raise a hand to anyone, and he always seems so gentle with children and horses."

"He is," Kyra said, drawing aside her heavy hair to watch her brother pull the saddle from the pinto and hang it on the corral fence. "He is very gentle . . . until someone he loves is threatened."

"Rachel, get up."

Someone was shaking her shoulder.

She sat up too quickly, banging her head against Emma's lantern.

"It's the middle of the night," she mumbled. Cold.

"Come quick," Emma whispered. "Mary's having her baby."

Rachel grabbed the quilt from her bed, flung it around her shoulders to cover her gown and stumbled down to the basement behind Emma and her lantern. They passed Mamm in the kitchen, in her gown with her hair down, a rare sight. A pot of water sat on the stovetop, and Mamm was bending over, shoving firewood into the cold stove.

"Ezra woke me just a few minutes ago," Emma explained on the way down the basement steps. "She's having regular pains. He said he counted and they're about five minutes between."

The canvas divider glowed yellow from a lantern on the other side. Levi was still asleep in the dark near the stairs, little Mose bundled next to him. Underneath the stairs was the potato bin, and in the corner stood the barrels of sauerkraut, fermenting.

Beyond the curtain they found Mary alone in her bed, with Ezra standing at her side. Her dark hair was loose around her, and the mound of her belly swelled the blankets. Ezra took one look at Emma and Rachel and said, "I think I'll mebbe see if I can get a couple more hours' sleep before chores."

Then he left. In a hurry.

Mary's face was ghostly pale and covered with sweat despite the cold.

Emma sat down on the edge of the bed, handing her lantern to Rachel and taking Mary's hand. A second lantern hissed and guttered on the nail keg next to the bed. The air smelled of hot kerosene, a comforting scent.

"How do you feel?" Emma asked, which struck Rachel as a rather odd question under the circumstances.

"Like I'm going to have a baby," she grunted.

Emma wiped sweat-damp hair out of Mary's eyes. "Is there anything we can get you?"

She shook her head and, against all reason, chuckled. "I only wish I hadn't eaten so much turkey this afternoon. Most of it is in the chamber pot now."

The curtain parted and Mamm swept into

the room, now fully dressed, her prayer kapp neatly pinned in place. Of the four women present she was the only one wearing her kapp. Having borne thirteen children herself, Mamm knew there was no great rush, so she had taken the time to dress. She breezed around the bed to sit on the other side and hold Mary's other hand.

"I put the scissors and some rags on the stove to boil," she said, patting Mary's hand. "There's lots of time, yet. Rachel, I laid out some baby blankets on the kitchen table. When the stove is good and hot you should go up and iron them."

"I'm ironing blankets again?" she asked.

"Heat cleanses," her mother said. "Everything has to be clean, you know."

Shoulder to shoulder with Emma, scrubbing her hands over a pan of water on the kitchen counter while the sterilizing pot began to tick and steam on the stove lid, Rachel said, "I feel useless. I want to be more than a blanket ironer."

"Hush," Emma said. "Always in such a rush. Anyway, mark my words, the moment will come when you are needed, just like when I had my Mose. And if not, then watch and learn. Even if all you do is iron blankets, at least you get to witness the miracle of birth."

Emma was right. It was an honor just to be there, to see what was about to happen, to be there when Mary's baby was born. If Emma wanted her to observe, then Rachel would observe.

Later, when she returned with the blankets and the boiling pot, Mary looked up at her, fresh from another contraction, and asked, "Where are my boys?"

Rachel smiled, setting the pot on a trunk in the corner. "Upstairs with their dat on the living room floor next to Aaron and Harvey. They're all snoring."

"Men."

"Oh, child, this is no place for a man," Mamm said. "It's good they can sleep."

The three of them hovered over Mary for the next two hours while the contractions intensified and the intervals grew shorter.

To her surprise, when the time came Rachel learned that she was no longer just a blanket ironer. Mamm stepped aside and made way for her to actually take part in the delivery. Rachel wrapped her new niece in a freshly ironed white blanket and held her still while Emma cleared the nose and mouth. The infant shivered, flung its arms wide in surprise, and a rusty little cry came from its mouth. Mamm wrung out a cloth from the pot and began wiping the baby's face.

"She's a fine-looking girl," Mamm said, smiling. "Her color is very good, and just look at that headful of hair!"

Everything had gone smoothly, but the night was not over yet.

CHAPTER 35

The baby's eyes were open, gazing at her mother's face, inches away. Mary ticked the little nose with a forefinger.

"We need to clean you up real good," she said, "so you can meet your father. Oh, Ezra is going to be so proud. He so wanted a little girl to —"

She didn't finish the sentence. Her head rocked forward suddenly and the smile flew away, replaced by a twisted grimace.

Mamm grabbed the newborn baby and handed her to Rachel, who tucked the bundle inside her quilt to keep her warm.

"Another pain," Mamm said, furrows forming between her eyes. "She's not done."

Footsteps crossed the floor over their heads as the household began to move about their morning routine, getting dressed and seeing to their chores. Outside the window the black of night had faded to dark gray.

The new contraction finally eased, and Mary lay back against the pillow breathing heavily. "What's happening to me?" she gasped.

Mamm sat on the side of the bed and pressed her palms to Mary's abdomen. As her hands moved, fear came into her eyes. "You're having twins," she said, her voice shaking.

Rachel saw the look in her mother's eyes. There was something they were not saying in front of Mary. Something ominous.

"What's wrong, Mamm?"

"It's just . . . you know, I had twins, once. Mine went fine, but not all of them do. Everyone says the second one is tricky because sometimes it lays the wrong way."

This made perfect sense to Rachel. If there were two babies in a crowded space and their heads were the biggest part of them, it made sense they would lie in opposite directions.

Ezra poked his head through the curtain, grinning sheepishly. "Did I hear a baby cry?"

Mary looked up, smiling bravely at her husband.

"I have given you a daughter," she said weakly.

Rachel opened her quilt and showed the

bundle to Ezra, who stood just inside the curtain beaming over his new baby girl.

"Amanda," he said, with a kind of reverence. "We wanted to call her Amanda if it was a girl."

Emma nodded. "It's a girl. Trust us. But you should get out of here now. We're not done yet."

Ezra looked from Emma to Mary, puzzled.

"She's having twins, Ezra. Go. We'll call you."

"OH! I'm sorry, I thought she was finished. I'll just —" Wincing, he backed through the curtain, and they heard him run up the stairs shouting to the rest of the family, "Twins! My Mary is having twins!"

But forty minutes passed and the baby still refused to be born. It wouldn't budge. Mary was losing strength, and Mamm was starting to fall apart. Her splayed fingers pressed gently against Mary's abdomen.

"I can feel it," she said, her voice high-pitched and quavering. "The head is over here. No, no, no. It's not lined up good."

"What can we do?" Rachel asked. "There must be something we can do."

Mamm was wringing her hands and rocking back and forth now, the way Ada did when she was upset. "We can try to turn it mebbe, I don't know. Oh, this is bad. Rachel, go upstairs and tell them to pray. Do it now."

Rachel took Baby Amanda with her and did as she was told.

Emma followed her to the top of the steps.

"There's more to it," Emma whispered. "Mary's life is in danger, too. If the baby doesn't come out, they both will die."

Rachel entered the living room feeling as if she'd been kicked in the stomach by a mule. The family had all gathered around the wood stove, where they had a roaring fire going. They had not gone out to do chores, all of them wanting to meet the new baby first.

"The second one is turned wrong," Rachel said, holding back tears, but deciding on the spur of the moment not to burden the men with Emma's ominous words. "Mamm says *pray*."

All their faces were lined with worry even as they peeked at the newborn baby girl, but when Aaron heard there was a problem with the second infant the color drained from him and he wobbled for a second as if he might collapse. His head wagged, and his eyes were full of fear and sorrow. The others hit their knees right where they were, but Aaron turned and stumbled out the back door. Rachel didn't have time to talk to him then, but she knew the only thing that could have made him run away like that was embarrassment. Aaron was a grown man. He couldn't let them see him cry.

When Rachel returned she saw a flicker of movement outside the narrow little casement window at the top of the wall, where the coming day had turned the world a lighter shade of gray. A pair of booted feet passed back and forth, back and forth, pacing.

Aaron. *This must be killing him,* Rachel thought. *To him it must be as if Amos is dying all over again. And he doesn't even know yet that he may lose a sister, as well.*

Another forty minutes passed and nothing changed. Mary was beginning to weaken, gasping like a fish from one pain to the next with never a chance to fully recover.

"It won't *move!*" Mamm cried, her voice rising to a fever pitch. "I can feel where it is, but it won't move! Emma, what are we going to do?" Her hands covered her face and she started to cry.

"I want . . . to pray," Mary said, a hoarse whisper between gasps. Her voice was gone. "Get me up on my . . . knees so I can . . . pray."

"Mary, dear, you can pray right where you

are," Emma said. "You don't need to waste energy getting up. I'll pray with —"

"No!" Mary growled. "Get me up!"

Emma looked to Mamm for support, but she was falling apart — she would be no help. Emma's eyes turned to Rachel.

The eyes of a prophetess, Rachel thought, with Emma's words ringing in her ears.

"When things go crazy you always keep your head . . . nobody in the world I trust more than you . . . the moment will come."

That same trust was in Emma's eyes even now, and once again her faith awakened something inside Rachel, a new sense. It wasn't as if she understood *everything*, and yet there was no longer a shred of doubt in her mind about what needed to be done.

Rachel opened her quilt and handed Baby Amanda to Mamm, who took the bundle with shaky hands, weeping openly.

"Mamm, why don't you take the buppela upstairs and clean her up good," Rachel said calmly. "Keep her near the stove where she will be warm."

Mamm hesitated, confused.

"Go!" Rachel said firmly.

To everyone's surprise, Mamm got up, sobbing, and left.

A short while later Mary held a fine, healthy

son in her arms. He wiggled and squirmed, scratching out a frail newborn wail of anger and surprise while three sisters laughed, and cried, and laughed again. Mary was completely exhausted, but relieved — and proud.

After the room had been straightened up and Mary was resting comfortably with her new son, Mamm returned with Baby Amanda. For the first time, Mary held both twins in her arms.

With eyes full of wonder, Mamm looked at Emma suddenly and asked, "What happened? How did you do this?"

"Oh, it wasn't me," Emma said. "It was Rachel's idea. We helped Mary up to her knees, and somehow it was easy after that."

Mamm's eyes turned to Rachel, the question still hanging.

Rachel smiled, shrugged. "I got her up to pray," she said. "It was what she wanted, and sometimes I think maybe a woman's body tells her mind what it needs."

It was then that a flicker of movement in the window caught Rachel's eye and she looked up.

Boots, still pacing. She had forgotten about Aaron.

"Mary, could I borrow the boy for just a second?"

"Jah," she said hesitantly, "but only a second."

Rachel took the bundle in the crook of her arm and, crossing the room, reached up and rapped a knuckle on the little windowpane.

Aaron's bearded face appeared upside down as he bent low to look through the glass. His eyes were red.

Smiling broadly, Rachel held up the newborn boy so he could see it. The sadness and worry vanished instantly from Aaron's kind face, and then his face went away entirely so that only his booted feet were visible through the window. Then, suddenly, his feet disappeared too as he leaped straight up in the air.

When those big boots came down again they *danced* in the pearly light.

Rachel's heart leaped as well, and she fought back tears of joy as she returned the baby to his mother's arms. "It's time he met his dat," she said.

Only now did Rachel become conscious of the waterfall of red hair that had hung wild about her shoulders throughout the whole ordeal. Gathering her unruly hair in her fists and knotting it behind her neck, she pulled the quilt tight around herself and went to look for Ezra.

In a moment she held the curtain back for the proud father, who tiptoed into the stone-walled room as if it were a church and knelt beside his wife's bed. He kissed Mary's hand and reached out delicately to brush his son's red forehead with a rough fingertip.

"It's a boy," she said, her features finally at peace, the pain already forgotten.

"A son!" he whispered, his eyes bright with joy. "Mare, did we ever decide which name we would give him if it was a boy?"

"No," Mary said. "I was hoping for Caleb, and you wanted Eli, but now that I see him I don't think either of those is right."

"No?" Ezra squeezed her hand, frowning. "All right, then. What would we name him?"

Mary stole a brief glance toward the window, and then, smiling down at her brand-new son, said softly, "His little eyes remind me of Amos."

CHAPTER 36

"We need to get busy building your house," Levi said to Ezra at breakfast. "If we work hard, we might be able to get both of them done this winter before the others arrive." By both, he meant Ezra's house and his own. There were currently three families living in one house, and now, counting Emma's new baby and Mary's twins, the basement alone slept nine people. The others would be arriving in a few months. Two more houses would be a great relief.

Bone-weary from months of hard labor, they should have resisted, should have wilted at the mere suggestion of building two more houses so soon. And yet, all around the table that morning, heads lifted and eyes lit with excitement. Even Rachel, who had slept very little, felt rejuvenated by the miracle that had come to them in the night. She was ready to make more bricks.

As soon as she finished eating, Rachel carried a plate downstairs for Mary. Emma was still there, wrapped in her quilt by the bedside holding the baby boy while Mary suckled his twin sister. Rachel set the plate on the nail keg and took the sleeping baby boy from Emma.

"You should go up and eat something," she said to Emma, "and then maybe get a little rest."

"I could use a bite," Emma said, rising, yawning. Rachel had dressed herself before breakfast and corralled her hair under her prayer kapp. Now Emma nodded at Rachel's clothes and said, "But I need to get dressed first, and I have to take care of Mose. I won't be sleeping today; there's too much work to do."

Clutching her quilt about her, Emma leaned down and kissed Mary on the forehead. She did the same to the twins, and then gave Rachel a hug. Smiling into her eyes Emma said, "I am so very proud of you, little sister. I watched you grow up last night." And then she left.

The tiny infant in Rachel's arms opened his eyes and gazed up at his freckle-faced aunt. Rachel smiled. "You know, the whole family was talking about you at breakfast," she said to the baby. "They're already calling you Little Amos."

Mary glanced up. "Aaron sneaked down here to visit a little while ago," she said. "He's beside himself. He thinks I had that one just for him."

Rachel chuckled. "Maybe you did. Gott works in funny ways, Mary. I haven't seen Aaron smile so since Amos died. It's like part of him was missing, and now it is restored."

Mary reached out to Rachel with her free hand, and Rachel took it.

"What about you?" Mary asked.

"What do you mean?"

"I mean, are *you* restored? I've watched you these last weeks . . . since the letter came. Emma told me about Jake. It hurts me to see you so sad. I'm so sorry, Rachel."

Rachel's gaze fell to the child in the crook of her arm and she didn't answer.

"Emma's right about what happened last night. I couldn't talk then, but I could *see*," Mary said. "Something came over you. Something happens when you come into your gift, Rachel. You found your strength, and it was wonderful to see."

Rachel blushed, shook her head slightly, still averting her gaze. "It was just common sense, is all. Besides, it was your idea to get up on your knees. I just figured sometimes a woman's body is telling her what to do, but nobody is listening."

"No one but you. You have a gift."

Rachel wiped a tear from her eye. She was glad she had the baby in her arms because it gave her an excuse not to look at her sister just now.

Mary checked the baby at her breast. "I think this one's asleep. Here, let's swap."

Rachel exchanged babies with her, and Mary settled Amos on the other side. Amanda snuggled contentedly in Rachel's arms. Rachel inhaled deeply the distinctive scent of a newborn infant.

As soon as Amanda was settled in, Mary looked up at Rachel again. "I guess what I'm trying to say is, don't be in such a rush to find a man, Rachel. I know when you're so young it seems like the whole world turns on such a thing, but it doesn't. You have lots of time to find the right man. Don't rush. Now is the time you should be discovering who *you* are, and not trying so hard to be part of someone else."

And then, for no apparent reason, she started laughing. For a moment Mary laughed so hard she embarrassed herself, covering her mouth with her fingers.

"It came to my mind last night," she said, "when the pains were on me, and if Mamm hadn't been in the room I would have been screaming at you, Are you *crazy?* Have you taken leave of your senses? What on *earth* do you want a *man* for?" Then Mary gazed down at her baby with wistful eyes and said, "But the anguish is soon forgotten. The thing is, you're only sixteen, Rachel, and if last night is any sign, you're only now finding out who Rachel Bender is. You have your whole life in front of you, and you have all the time in the world to find a good man. Most of all, he needs to be a man who will let you be who you are, but to find him you must first *know* who you are. Have patience. Gott knows what He's doing."

Rachel still couldn't look at her sister. Almost everything she'd said was right. Almost. Gott *did* know what He was doing, and she *did* need to be patient, and she *did* need to know who she was. But she had already found a good man.

"I would do a great many things for you," Jake had said, and his words rang in her ears even now. Words from the heart of a good man, a strong man who would not only let her be who she was but help her and support her and defend her while she did it. Rachel carried these thoughts in her heart, but she did not speak them aloud.

CHAPTER 37

Homesickness nagged her as Christmas neared. Rachel felt more keenly than ever the thousand miles that stood between her and all her friends in Ohio — one of them, especially — and yet the three new babies in the house laid a veneer of bright optimism over the melancholy. A growing family, after all, was the surest sign of prosperity.

Winter in Paradise Valley was very different from Ohio. The sun shined and the days were warm and mild — nothing at all like Christmas back home, but she missed the sledding. It rarely snowed here. Even if it had been cold enough, she could not have gone ice skating because there was simply no pond. The sparsely timbered red-rock ridges, the mountains in the blue distance, Paradise Valley itself — these were all beautiful in their own way, but for Rachel they still did not feel like home.

She spent Christmas Day with her family,

quietly, in prayer, Bible reading, and fasting. Mamm had decorated the mantel and the doorways with pine boughs, and Rachel and her sisters had even made tallow candles for the windows. In the evening they lit the candles and sang Christmas songs, and Rachel would have thought the occasion as beautiful and serene as any in memory had it not been for the thin blanket of homesickness that accumulated on her like snowfall.

The next morning the family exchanged small gifts, mostly handmade items and tools, useful things. They had drawn names, so each person received only one gift, with the exception of the three new babies. Everyone wanted to spoil them, so Emma and Mary were still opening presents long after everyone else had finished. The very last gift in the pile was a small package wrapped in plain brown paper and tied with baling twine. The name *Amos* was scrawled on it in a crude hand.

When Mary peeled away the paper to reveal a shiny new harmonica she paused and just sat there cradling it in her hands, staring at it. Aaron bit his lip, trying in vain to hold back an eager pride. His hand made a little pushing motion toward Amos, who appeared to be clapping his little hands while he rested with his twin sister in the

408

wood box at Mary's feet.

Mary clearly didn't know what to do, for the harmonica was a musical instrument and such things were forbidden. Speechless and flustered she looked to her father, who sat off to the side in a kitchen chair with his arms folded across his chest, watching. Everyone's eyes turned to Dat, waiting for his verdict.

Dat contemplated the thing for a moment, his long beard moving slightly as his chin worked. In the silence Rachel heard the faint moan of a harmonica floating over distant fields, mingling with the silver laughter of a lost brother, and it brought a tear to her eye. Dat must have heard it too, for his eyes grew soft. Apparently, his son's illicit harmonica had not escaped his attention after all.

"Well, aren't you gonna give it to him?" Dat said gruffly, and Mary smiled.

She tried to give it to Little Amos, but the month-old infant's hands were too small and weak yet to hold a harmonica.

"It's all right, Little Amos," Aaron whispered, lowering himself to sit cross-legged next to the wood box and taking the harmonica from his sister. "You'll grow into it."

Leaning close so that the baby fastened

his eyes on the shiny instrument, Aaron coaxed the tiniest note through the harmonica. Little Amos's fingers clenched, his arms shook, his feet pedaled, his face crinkled into a smile, and his uncle Aaron shuddered from head to toe with pure joy.

Schulman and his wife joined them for the midday feast, a lavish affair almost as grand as Thanksgiving had been. The menu included smoked ham and venison, for the boys had gone hunting on the ridge Christmas Eve and brought down a deer. And the menu included sauerkraut. They would be eating a lot of sauerkraut this winter.

After too much lunch Schulman unbuttoned the top button of his pants and insisted on going for a walk. Caleb went with him, and as they were passing the corral Schulman stopped to stare at the pinto pony trotting around the fence line next to Caleb's standard-bred buggy horse.

"Caleb, is this the same pinto that bandit traded you a couple months ago?"

"Oh, jah," Caleb said. "Miriam took a liking to him and made a pet of him. He turned out to be a sturdy little saddle horse after all, and sometimes they use him to pull the hack. Still a little rough with a buggy, though."

The pinto ran alongside the taller standard-bred, precisely matching his speed if not his aristocratic gait. The horse's ribs no longer stuck out. He held his head high, prancing, his brushed coat sleek and shiny in the slanting winter sunlight.

Schulman shook his head, leaning his forearms on the fence. "If I'd been there, I would have shot that bandit, Caleb. I'd have shot all of them."

Caleb studied his friend's face for a moment, the hard eyes, the set jaw. Ernst Schulman's wagon never left home without a lever-action rifle and a side arm on board, and he meant what he said.

"You would kill four men? For a *horse,* yet?"

Schulman nodded. "Vermin," he said. "No great loss to the world."

Caleb shook his head. "Ernst, these men were not meant to be as they are. Look at this horse," he said, watching the pinto prance. "Why, we could have shot him three months ago and you would have said the same — 'no great loss to the world.' But look at the difference when we treat him with respect for just a little while."

"Jah," Schulman said, "but horses have more sense than men. Men are stubborn."

■ ■ ■ ■

The real highlight of the day was the Christmas program put on by Miriam's school children that afternoon. All of her students came, and the Mexican kids brought their families with them to watch. Domingo brought half of them from San Rafael, and his sister Kyra came with him to watch her two little sons perform. She immediately sought out Miriam.

Rachel watched from a distance as her sister shared laughter and secrets with her beautiful Mexican friend, and it struck her that Kyra looked more like Miriam than her own sisters. It warmed her heart to see that Miriam had found such a friend.

The kids had been practicing for weeks. With their families present, plus the Schulmans, it was a packed house — standing room only. It was a rare treat for Amish kids to participate in such a public performance, and they reveled in the attention.

Rachel laughed until she cried as the children put on their Christmas play, wearing grown-up robes that piled around their ankles and hats that kept falling into their eyes, muffing the lines of kings and shepherds alike. But they finally got the Christ child born, and then they sang songs of the season and recited poems they had written themselves, little arms miming trees and ocean waves. Afterward, as darkness fell and Mamm lit the candles in the windows, a houseful of people from three different countries sang Christmas songs, a cappella, in Spanish.

And it was beautiful. Rachel particularly loved listening to Schulman. He had a rich baritone voice, and his eyes reflected the genuine pleasure he found in the rare opportunity to sing among a group.

Before the guests left for home Caleb read the Christmas story from a Spanish Bible, said a prayer of thanks for the year behind them and hope for the year to come, then sent them on their way with his blessings — and a good many leftovers. When Schulman got back to his wagon he found that someone had loaded a barrel of sauerkraut onto it.

Laughing, he clapped Caleb on the back and said cheerfully, "Jah, Herr Bender, I will be more than happy to help you dispose of your cabbage!"

As the Schulmans disappeared into the night, Miriam came outside wrapping a shawl about her shoulders, looking for Domingo. She spotted him helping his sister and the others climb into his rickety oxcart. Clutching a big book against her chest Miriam started toward the wagon, but halfway there she slowed and stopped, mesmerized by what she saw.

Two of the adults held lanterns aloft, and Kyra's youngest boy flashed through the pool of light as Domingo tossed him into his mother's arms. For a split second the lanterns illuminated both their faces — the dark-eyed child giggling hysterically in mid-flight, and the strong, graceful man whose eyes laughed with him. The sight, fleeting though it was, stirred something deep within her, something profoundly akin to a memory, and it seemed to her that the earth trembled. She waited till the last of the children were on board before she composed herself and called to him from the darkness.

"Domingo, could I see you for a moment, please?"

He had already braced a leg to climb up, but when she called to him he turned and came to her.

"Sí? What is it?" He stopped two feet away, but she couldn't see his face. Silhouetted against the lanterns with his wide-

414

brimmed hat, it struck her that he could almost have been mistaken for an Amishman.

"I wanted . . ." She found herself suddenly flustered for no apparent reason, and words tripped over themselves in unwarranted embarrassment. "I wanted to thank you for helping us with the school."

"It is my pleasure."

"I have a gift for you," she said, hastily unfolding her arms to show him the book. "A woman from the village came to me with this. She could not read, and she wouldn't say where the book came from, so I can only guess that it was looted from someone's hacienda by one of the men in her family. I traded a shawl for it."

She held the heavy book out to him, but he made no move to take it.

"I have nothing to give you in return," he said quietly.

Miriam shook her head and shoved the book closer. "Owe me if you must, but take the book. I have watched you in the class. I didn't want to say anything in front of the children, but —"

"I know," he said. "You have pretended not to notice. It was kind of you to say nothing."

"It's perfectly all right, Domingo, but

415

learning to sound out words is only the beginning. Now you must read and read until the words come easily. This book will help."

His hands came up slowly and embraced the book with a kind of reverence. Turning a little to one side to catch the light from the lanterns, Domingo muttered along with his forefinger as it traced slowly over the gilded title.

"*Don . . . Quijote de la . . . Mancha.* What is it about?"

Miriam shrugged. "I'm not sure. I haven't had time to read more than a few pages, and what is said about it in the front, but I think it's a story about a crazy man. Anyway, it doesn't really matter. What's important is that you get plenty of practice reading. Practice, practice, practice, and before you know it, you will read as fast as you can speak."

Domingo hefted the book in his hands. "There should be enough words in here to last a lifetime, and if I can't read it, I can use it as a club."

Miriam snickered. Her fingers covered her mouth and she suddenly found herself trying to remember a time when any Amish boy she'd dated made her laugh.

"Muchas gracias," he said, running his

fingers over the cover of the book. "In my whole life, no one has ever given me such a great gift."

Something in the reverence with which he said this struck her as so solemn and so deeply personal it pierced her like a sword. Was he that poor? Her gaze dropped to the book in his hands, mostly because she could not bear it.

"It is only a book," she muttered.

The tilt of his hat told her he had raised his face to look at her, though she could not see his eyes. His hand rose up until his fingertips lightly brushed her cheek, and his voice came softly from the darkness.

"I was not speaking of the book, cualnezqui, but the gift of reading . . . and the respect you give me by pretending you are not teaching me. To a Chichimeca, respect is the rarest gift." She could hear the smile in his voice as he added, "But thank you for the book, too. I will treasure it."

He turned away without another word, leaving her to watch from the darkness as he mounted his oxcart and snapped the reins.

"You are welcome, my friend," she whispered as her fingertips drifted up to the place on her cheek where he had touched her.

CHAPTER 38

The Bender family ate sauerkraut for New Year's because it was tradition, but it seemed to Rachel that a tradition didn't mean much when it was exercised every day. She ate sauerkraut the day *before* New Year's and she would eat it again the day after, but she would not complain. It was food, and she had been raised to understand that she was never to complain about what kind of food was put in front of her so long as Gott provided food.

After dinner, but before anyone had gotten up from the table, Dat pulled out the latest letter from John Hershberger and read it aloud to the family.

" 'Well, Caleb, I hope you'uns are ready for company because it looks like we'll be down there before too long. The first of us will arrive at the station in Arteaga on Friday, February 2nd.' "

"I told them they should stop in Arteaga,"

Dat explained, "since it's only a little farther than Agua Nueva and the road is much better for buggies and wagons."

And then Dat read down the list of names John Hershberger had written in his letter. The Hershbergers and Shrocks were the only two families that would be coming down in February, but six more families from Wayne and Holmes Counties planned to come the following summer, and a couple more even later than that. All the names were familiar. Oddly, though, of the four men who had originally been arrested along with Dat, the only one still planning to come to Mexico was John Hershberger himself. The other three had all backed out.

Rachel hung on every word, hoping to hear the name Weaver, praying that by some miracle Jonas Weaver had changed his mind and decided to bring his family anyway. Of course she'd already been told the Weavers would not be coming, but hearing her dat read the list out loud and come to the end of it without saying the name Weaver drove a spike through her heart all over again. It was all she could do to keep from breaking into tears right there at the dinner table.

The first of the newcomers would be arriving in four weeks, and she couldn't care less. By the end of summer the Mexico settlement would number well over a hundred people, many of whom she knew and loved, as well as a few strangers that in time she knew she *would* come to love, yet none of it mattered one bit. There was only one name she really longed to hear, and it wasn't on the list. She excused herself and took her plate to wash. There hadn't even been a letter from Jake in the last month. He had given up.

Maybe it was time she did, too.

The men stayed busy for most of January finishing the other two houses, putting windows and doors and kitchen shelves in them, and running pipe to a spigot from the big well at Caleb's.

There was always something to do. They were all so busy the month flew past, and before they knew it the day came to go get the newcomers from Arteaga.

At supper, the night before he was to leave, Caleb made a surprise announcement.

"I've decided to let Miriam and Rachel go with me to Arteaga to meet the train," he said. "Lovina Hershberger will be there, and I'm thinking she'll be glad to see some girls after riding on the train with all those boys."

The two girls were delighted, but Mamm

glowered.

"Do you think it's safe?" she asked.

After a year in the dry climate of Paradise Valley, Mamm had nearly stopped coughing and regained some of her strength. Able to resume many of her chores, she had even lost weight and put some color back in her cheeks. She was slowly returning to her old feisty ways.

Caleb smiled at her and said, "Jah, Mamm, it will be all right. Schulman is going with us — he always carries his rifle on his lap to warn bandits away. Anyways, I don't think we have anything to fear when there are so many of us. And Domingo will be there, too."

She stared, a look of intense worry on her face.

"I'll need somebody to cook for me," he argued.

"The Hershberger and Shrock women can cook," she countered.

He sighed. "The girls need a break, Mamm. They've worked very hard."

Reluctantly, she gave in, but the worried frown did not leave her face.

Levi and Emma had settled into their new home already, but on the morning Dat was to leave for Arteaga the whole family came down to Mamm's house to see him off.

After breakfast Rachel and Miriam loaded a box of food to put on the wagon. Emma helped clear away the breakfast dishes while Mary laid Little Amos up on the table to change his diaper. He took advantage of the opportunity to pee in his own face. Seeing this, and the look of utter shock in the infant's eyes, Emma laughed so hard she nearly lost the plates. As she set the stack of dishes on the counter she gasped and dropped to her knees, one hand gripping the edge of the counter and the other clutching at her stomach.

"Emma?" Mamm and Rachel both rushed to Emma's side, kneeling with her, supporting her. "What is it?" Mamm asked.

"I don't know," Emma said, wide-eyed, as she drew a breath through clenched teeth and tried to straighten up. "I have a sharp pain."

"Here?" Mamm said, placing a hand on top of Emma's. "Do you think . . . is it possible you are with child again so soon?" Mamm asked. Ada stood behind her mother, eyes wide with fear and her teeth clamped tightly over four fingertips, moaning and swaying.

Emma nodded weakly. "I think so, Mamm. I've been sick in the mornings lately. But something is not right."

"We have to get you to bed," Rachel said. "Maybe if you get off your feet for a while, whatever is wrong will pass." She looked at Miriam. "Can we get her down the stairs?"

The basement of Dat and Mamm's house was now unoccupied, though one of the beds remained. The Hershbergers would soon be sleeping there.

"No." Emma winced. "If I have to be laid up, I want to go home, to *my* house."

Miriam bolted out the door and in a moment came back with Levi. He lifted his wife from the floor, carried her out back to the surrey and drove home while her sisters held her in the back seat. Mamm stayed home to mind the three babies, and Ada.

When they got to Emma's house Levi brought her in and laid her on the bed, anguish carved into his young face. He knelt at her bedside stroking her forehead.

"Are you gonna be all right?"

"I'm fine," she said, glancing up at Rachel, Miriam and Mary, but her face was pale and ash gray. "This is nothing, you'll see."

"Okay, then." Levi pointed a thumb nervously over his shoulder. "I left the team out. I guess I better . . ."

"Jah," she chuckled. "Go to work, Levi.

There's nothing for you to do here. My sisters will tend to me."

Rachel looked at Miriam and said, "Go with Levi back to the house. Tell Dat I'm staying here with Emma. Mary is here, and Mamm will be up in a bit. We'll take care of her."

Emma rose up on an elbow. "No, Rachel. You go on. I know you were looking forward to the trip. Don't stay here for me. I'll be fine."

There was a strange twinkle in Emma's eye, despite the pain, but Rachel held her ground. "No. If I'm to be a midwife, then it's important for me to be here at a time like this. I'm not leaving. But one of us should go meet the train, for Lovina. Go, Miriam! Dat won't wait long."

Miriam hesitated, glancing back and forth between her sisters, but she got no support. "Oh, all right," she said. "I'm sorry, Rachel. I know how excited you —"

"GO!" Rachel waved her off.

As soon as Levi and Miriam were gone, Rachel and Mary undressed Emma and put her gown on her.

"Was there blood?" she asked as Mary pulled the covers up and tucked her into bed.

Rachel nodded, biting her lip. "A little."

"What can I do?"

"Nothing," Rachel said. "Be very still. Give your body time to rest and maybe whatever is wrong will heal itself."

"That's right, I remember now!" Mary said. "This same thing happened to Ezra's cousin in Maysville a while back, only she went to the doctor with it. He made her stay in bed for a *month.*" She gave Rachel a curious sideways look. "You're so sure of yourself, child. How do you know these things?"

"Did the cousin get better?" Rachel asked, ignoring Mary's question. Emma's eyes said she wanted to know, too.

"Oh, jah," Mary said. "I heard she had a new son right before we left Ohio, and they were both doing well."

Domingo sat up front with Dat while Miriam bumped along in the back of the wagon by herself all the way to Arteaga. It was just as well, as she felt she would have been too flustered to talk to Domingo right now anyway. She sorely missed Rachel.

Late that afternoon they rolled into the station in Arteaga. On a siding in the rail yard, six cars had almost finished disgorging two large families of Amish along with all their worldly possessions. Dat's arrival made the chaos momentarily worse as all

425

the newcomers converged on him, shaking hands and being formally introduced, one by one, to Schulman and Domingo.

Miriam found Lovina Hershberger, and they hugged each other fiercely, a truly happy reunion. When Miriam looked up she got the shock of her life.

Jake Weaver was standing there watching, hat in hand.

"*Jake!* Oh my goodness! Where did *you* come from? *OH MY!* I thought you weren't coming! Rachel said —"

"I know," he said, smiling. "But at the last minute your dat convinced my dat to farm me out to John Hershberger so I could come down by myself."

"Dat did this?" Miriam looked around instinctively for her father. He was talking with John and Ira, paying no attention to them. "Why?"

Jake chuckled. "I think Emma talked him into it — for Rachel's sake."

"Emma knows you're coming? She didn't say a word."

"Jah, she knows. I guess she and your dat wanted to surprise Rachel. I might have ruined the surprise, though. I sent a letter a few days ago, as soon as I found out. Didn't she get it yet?"

"No. The mail is slow here. If she knew

you were coming, I would have heard her crowing from the rooftop. Oh, Jake, you just don't know. She'll be beside herself when she sees you. It'll be the happiest moment of her *life*."

Little clusters of Mexicans watched as cows and horses and mules and men and women and children and buggies and wagons and crates and chickens and pigs and barking dogs clogged the little railroad yard with uncommon busyness, but in the presence of so many Amish, chaos is doomed. In two hours' time the horses were all hitched, the wagons loaded and strapped down, and the parade had begun streaming through the narrow streets on its way out of town.

John Hershberger rode with Caleb on the lead wagon so they could talk. As the string of wagons pulled out of town Caleb glanced up at the small orange ball of winter sun about to kiss the western mountaintops.

"There's not much daylight left," he said to John. "It gets dark quick in the mountains. I'm thinkin' we best make camp in the foothills just outside town." They could have made a few miles yet, but he couldn't bear the thought of spending the night in the high mountain passes where El Pantera lived.

"That will be fine with us, Caleb. I think nobody really cares where we camp, so long as it's not on that train. I'll be hearing those wheels in my sleep tonight."

Caleb chuckled. "Did you bring any firewood? Might be a little chilly after the sun goes down."

John Hershberger busted out laughing at this. "Jah, we got a little firewood, but if you think this is chilly, why then, you've already forgot what an Ohio winter is like, Caleb."

The men talked around the campfire for a long time after supper, catching up on all that had happened since they last saw one another. Domingo sat with them but he didn't say much, probably because Schulman was there.

Well after dark a high-pitched scream echoed down from the mountains. All of them turned and looked.

"What was that?" Caleb asked.

"Panther," Domingo answered. "There are still a few of them in the high country."

Caleb nodded, casting a meaningful glance at the young native. "Jah . . . and not all of them walk on four legs."

Ira and John both shot questioning looks at Caleb, but he would say no more. There were girls within hearing.

"Where did the boys get to?" Caleb asked, looking around.

"Oh, they got their own campfire going — over there on the other side of the wagons," Ira said, his ruddy face shining in the firelight. "I imagine they're wrestling. They like to do that whenever they get a chance."

"Jah, I forgot how much your boys like to wrestle. Especially that Micah. He's even bigger since I saw him, Ira. Filled out like a plow horse. I guess a little wrestling is good for 'em after being cooped up in that train for so long, but it's getting late. We probably all need to turn in."

Domingo rose to his feet, stretched, tossed a stick into the fire, settled his hat on his head and said, "I will go tell them. After that, Herr Schulman, if you don't mind I'll take your rifle and keep watch on the hill."

He said this in flawless High German, and a vengeful little smile flashed across his face.

Schulman looked up in surprise, but then he just nodded and said nothing.

Hershberger watched him go, and when Domingo was out of hearing, he leaned close to Caleb and asked quietly, "Do you trust that one?"

"With my life," Caleb said evenly. "I don't travel nowhere without Domingo."

Schulman gave him a hard look, but Caleb didn't need the German's approval. He had always been one to make up his own mind about people.

When Domingo emerged from between the wagons the boys were all in a loose ring off to one side of the campfire. Micah stood in the center of the ring, breathing heavily, swiping dust and straw from his clothes. His coat lay across the nearest wagon wheel, his shirttail was out and one of his suspenders hung loose around his knee. Jake Weaver, four years younger and a head shorter, stood among the other boys with his hands on his hips, grinning, trying to catch his breath.

"You might have pinned me," Jake said, panting, "but I made you earn it."

"Jah, Jake," Micah laughed, pulling the errant suspender up onto his shoulder. "I'll admit you're mighty stout — for your size. Who wants to be next?"

They didn't see Domingo until he walked into their midst.

"What about you?" Micah said, turning to Domingo. "Want to try me?"

"No," Domingo answered flatly. "Caleb said to tell you it's time to bed down."

"Oh, come on — one quick round, just

for fun."

Micah was twenty-one, the same age as Domingo, but he had indeed filled out like a horse — big square shoulders and stout legs, feet like a Clydesdale. He was fifty pounds heavier than Domingo and six inches taller.

"Play is play, and fighting is fighting," Domingo said. "I don't fight for fun."

The ring of boys broke apart and they started to walk away. Everyone put on their hats, picked up their coats and headed for the wagons — all except Micah. As Domingo turned to walk away, Micah grabbed him from behind in a bear hug, pinning Domingo's arms to his sides. There was no malice in the big Amishman — he was laughing when he did it. But what happened next shocked him. It shocked them all.

Quicker than thought, Domingo shrugged and dropped, leaving Micah's big arms holding only his hat. An elbow crashed into Micah's stomach, knocking the breath out of him. In the same instant Domingo's feet spread and he reached between them to snatch Micah's leg out from under him. Micah went down hard on his back, and in a split second he found himself pinned to the ground with Domingo's thin sandal pressed against his throat.

Domingo leaned down so their faces were only a foot apart, in the flickering firelight fastening the eyes of a wolf on Micah, his arm still locked around that thick leg so the big man couldn't move or roll away.

"I tried to tell you," Domingo said calmly. "For me, fighting is not play." He removed his foot from Micah's throat and tossed the leg aside casually. "We start early tomorrow. Get some sleep."

He turned his back on Micah, picked up his hat, dusted it off and snugged it on his head as he walked out of the firelight without looking back.

CHAPTER 39

Emma asked Rachel to spend the night. Levi gave up his spot in the bed for her and made himself a pallet on the living room floor.

When the lanterns were snuffed the two sisters lay side by side in the darkness for a long time, listening to the distant yipping and keening of coyotes and the occasional hoot of an owl. After about an hour Rachel could hear Levi's soft snoring from the other room, and she rose up on an elbow to face Emma.

"Are you awake?"

"Jah."

"Is Levi okay?"

She heard Emma's head turn toward her. "Sure, he's all right. It won't kill him to sleep on the floor for one night."

"I didn't mean that," Rachel said. "I just meant he seems so . . . *upset* about all this. You didn't see him at the supper table. He didn't hardly touch his food, he was so worried. I could see it in his eyes."

"Oh, that," Emma said quietly, and then she turned her head and held still for a long moment, listening for Levi's steady snore, making sure he was asleep. "He is very afraid, Rachel. Levi has a strong conscience, and his father raised him to believe that no sin ever goes unpunished — not only in the next world but in this one, too. Levi believes my troubles are Gott's punishment for our sin. He fears that Gott will take this baby."

Silence hung between them for too long, and then Rachel asked the question.

"Will He?"

Emma reached out in the darkness and caressed the side of Rachel's face. "Oh, child, it's not for me to say what Gott will allow. I've seen great tragedy befall those who have done nothing wrong, and blessings showered upon a few who did *plenty* wrong. But whatever Gott allows to happen, Rachel, it is for the good. It is our duty — our *place* — to accept what comes, and to grow from it. I have repented and asked for Gott's forgiveness. I can only hope He has forgiven me, not because I deserve it but because He is a merciful Gott."

Rachel pondered this for a long time, for it was a heavy question and she was reluctant to even put words to such thoughts. She spoke hesitantly.

"But, Emma, if you were to lose this baby . . . would you believe it was Gott's punishment?"

She could hear the smile in Emma's voice. "Sister, how would I know such a thing unless Gott himself tells me? In the end, I think I am probably just one of those unlucky women who isn't very good at having babies. I do everything too quick — I conceive too easily and I have babies before they are ready. But if this is my lot, then I will accept it humbly and remember how I have been blessed in so many other ways."

Rachel found this a bit puzzling. She waited a beat before she whispered, "Blessed? Emma. You're living in a mud house in Mexico, with nothing."

Emma shook her head, and laughed. "Child, you're going to have to learn to stop counting what you *don't* have. Jah, it's true I'm living in a mud house in Mexico, but with a devoted husband, a great big loving family, lots of neighbors coming soon, plenty of good land to farm, more than enough food to eat . . . and my best friend at my side."

CHAPTER 40

By dawn the next morning the Shrocks and Hershbergers were all loaded up and ready to make the daylong trek to Paradise Valley. A dozen wagons, hacks and surreys turned about and began to form a line, but before Caleb could take his place at the front of the line his rear wheel bumped up over a large rock. The wheel dropped over the back side of the boulder with a bone-jarring jolt and an agonizing crunch came from underneath the wagon. The back end sagged.

Caleb stopped and climbed down to inspect the damage. The others stopped too, and Hershberger came over to see what was wrong.

"The axle is broke," Caleb said, letting out his frustration in a long sigh. "All that weight was too much when it fell off that rock."

"What can we do?" Hershberger asked. "We don't have a spare axle with us."

"I can get one from town, but it will cost us a whole day," Caleb said.

"All right. I'll go tell everybody to pull off and make camp again."

Caleb shook his head. "No. There's no need for everybody to lose a day. Schulman can take the lead. No one will bother you as long as there are so many, and Schulman has guns with him to protect you."

Hershberger's eyebrows went up. "But who will protect you?"

"We'll be all right — we have Domingo. The worst of the bandits won't bother us as long as he is with us. I could use another strong back, though, to fix the axle."

"Micah can stay with you," Ira Shrock said. He had come over as they talked and had heard most of the conversation. "He's an ox. Would you want us to take Miriam with us?"

Caleb thought for a minute, then shook his head. "No, she'll be useful to us. She can stay."

Ten minutes later the wagon train was snaking up toward the pass, leaving Caleb behind with Domingo, Miriam and Micah.

Caleb bought an axle from a smith in Arteaga, and by evening the wagon was good as new. Miriam made camp and cooked dinner while the three men worked, and after dinner they reloaded the wagon and tied everything down.

CHAPTER 41

Emma's pain came and went throughout the day, but each time was a little easier than the last. By late afternoon the pain had disappeared and she was feeling a lot better.

"Perhaps tomorrow I can get up from this bed and get some things done," Emma said. Her mother and sisters were there when she said it, a bedroom full. They all berated her at once, creating such an uproar that none of them could be understood. In the end, she held her palms up in surrender, laughing.

"All right. I get the message," she said. "But you'll be sorry. I'm going to lay here like a queen and order all of you about until you're sick of it. Rachel!" she commanded, pointing, "Bring my child to me! But clean him up first — I'll not have a dirty diaper in my presence. Mary! A glass of water, please, and be quick about it!"

Both of them did as they were told, laughing hysterically. They would have done the same even if Emma's feigned pomposity had been genuine, but it wouldn't have been nearly as much fun.

The others took the surrey back to Mamm's house shortly after that because they were expecting Caleb to arrive anytime now with the caravan from Arteaga, and they wanted to be there to greet them. Rachel alone stayed behind to cook dinner for Levi and Emma and take care of Mose.

After dinner, when all the dishes were washed and dried and put away, and Mose was fed and cleaned and put down for the night, Rachel lay down behind Emma. She moved her sister's luxurious honey-colored hair out of the way so she could rub her shoulders and massage her back.

Emma moaned with pleasure, and then laughed. "I could get used to this," she said, "lying in bed with my little sister pampering me like this. This is a memory we'll share for the rest of our lives, Rachel. Someday, when we're just two old biddies rocking in the shade with a hundred grandchildren doting on us and bringing us cookies, we'll look back on this and say, Remember the night the Hershbergers came to Mexico, and we were piled up in bed like queens?"

"We'll sit under one of your shade trees

out in front of this very house. Oh, they'll be tall then."

"That's right, the *trees!* With all this fuss I forgot I asked Lovina to bring trees. She hasn't said another word about it in any of her letters, so I know she's going to surprise me. You know how Lovina loves to put on a show. Oh, I hope she brings maples! Rachel, I'll plant lots of maples, and at the end of winter the syrup will flow." Emma closed her eyes to savor a moment of bliss in her own bright future.

The light from the window had faded to dusky purple and the lantern had taken over when Levi burst into the room breathless with excitement.

"They're here!" he cried, pointing in the general direction of Dat's house. "I seen wagons coming up the road! They'll be at your dat's in a minute."

Emma raised herself onto her elbows, staring at the window.

Rising from the bed Rachel pointed sharply at her sister and barked, "You don't move! I'll watch for you."

Emma rolled her eyes and fell back against the pillow. "It's all right, Levi. I'll be fine with my jailer here. You go! Greet our new neighbors."

Levi nodded once and took off. They heard his footsteps running around the house, and Rachel watched from the window as he ran across the fields. He didn't even take time to hitch a buggy.

"I can see them," Rachel said. "They've lit their lanterns so we can see them coming."

She watched them the whole way, giving Emma a running commentary as the line of flickering lights turned in and strung out half the length of Dat's drive.

Ten minutes later her father's farm was as busy as a kicked anthill, lanterns swinging to and fro as people took horses to the corral, unloaded wagons, and some of the young ones erected tents in the field beside the Bender house. Someone started a campfire and the sparks flew upward on a slant, dancing on the ever-present breeze. Even from a distance, in the darkness, the air of jubilation was palpable. Their neighbors had arrived!

"A buggy is coming," Rachel announced. She could see it silhouetted against the lights, drawing near.

"I bet that's Lovina," Emma said. Lovina was a good friend to both Emma and Rachel; they knew she would come as soon as she could get away.

Moments later they heard the surrey pull up to the front of the house, accompanied by the laughter of girls.

Lovina Hershberger bustled into the room alone, grinning from ear to ear and carrying a sapling in her arms, the burlap-wrapped root ball nestled in the crook of an elbow as if it were a baby. Squealing with delight she ran straight to Rachel and gave her a big hug, then turned to Emma with a hand on her hip.

"What's this about you being sick?" she said, then plunked her sapling by the side of the bed and leaned down to give Emma a gentle hug. Then, pinning Emma's shoulders with her palms, she looked her in the eye and said, "You can't be sick, Emma. I won't have it."

"Oh, it's just this new baby," Emma said. "He's giving me a bit of trouble, but I'll be fine in a day or two, you'll see."

Lovina's hands flew to her cheeks, her mouth opened and she squealed. "Your baby! I have to meet Mose! Where is he?" Scanning the room, her eyes landed on the apple crate in the corner and she jumped up and ran over to it.

Rachel pulled the little quilt back to show Lovina the infant's sleeping face.

"Oh, he's beautiful!" Lovina cried. "And

such hair!"

"Yes," Rachel said. "I'm afraid the poor thing has my hair, only a little darker."

"Oh, he's handsome," Lovina said. "Listen, I almost forgot. There are others here and they want to meet Mose, too. Is it all right for them to come in?"

"Bring them all," Emma said, beaming. "We'll have a party. Where's Miriam? I thought she would come as soon as she got back."

"Oh no! I forgot to tell you. Your dat broke an axle early this morning, and Micah stayed behind to help fix it. Miriam stayed with them. If all goes well, they'll be home tomorrow night."

Lovina rushed to the door to signal the others, her mother and sisters and the women of the Shrock family. Each and every one of them brought a sapling with her and placed it on the floor beside Emma's bed. A hack pulled up outside. Mary joined the crowd, with more trees. The little room was filled with women and trees.

"You see?" Lovina said. "I told you, you can't be sick. You've got trees to plant."

It was a great reunion, full of joy and laughter, old friends reminiscing about old times. But after half an hour most of them left and those who stayed grew quiet, reluctant to leave, though they sensed that Emma and her baby needed privacy and rest. Lovina Hershberger and Emma's sisters remained to the last, standing among an impromptu forest of leafless young trees.

"You've outdone yourself, Lovina," Rachel said, shaking her head at the grove of saplings.

"Oh, it was fun! And this isn't all of them. We've been planning this for weeks, digging up saplings and wrapping the roots. Everyone was in on it — except for Jake, of course. He only joined us at the last minute. When we were on the train I told him about the trees and he laughed for two —"

"Jacob *Coblentz?*" Rachel asked, interrupting. "Eli's Jake?"

Emma glanced up at Rachel then, and there was a curiously sly smile in her eyes.

"Oh no," Lovina said, with the same sly smile. "Jonas's Jake. Weaver. His dat farmed him out to my dat and he came down with us on the —"

Rachel didn't hear the rest. She had already slipped out the door.

445

CHAPTER 42

She hurried around the front of the house, her pace quickening until she found herself gripping her skirts in her fists and running breathless through the dark fields toward the lights and commotion of her father's house.

Halfway there, she saw someone walking toward her, silhouetted against the lights. A wide-brimmed hat, broad shoulders. A man. She slowed as he approached, and then stopped, not sure who it was. There was no such backdrop of lights behind her, and she knew by the tilt of his hat that whoever it was had not seen her in the dark.

She waited, trying to slow her breathing.

He stopped, ten feet away. Perhaps he had heard her, or spotted the white of her kapp in the darkness. He stood still, a black figure against the light. And then she recognized his shape, for she had seen it often enough at the singings on Sunday nights, standing as he was now, with his back to the lights of home.

"Jake?" It was little more than a whisper, a frail hope.

"Rachel?"

His hand went to his hat and flung it carelessly away as he closed the last ten feet of a gap that only a minute ago had been a thousand miles. Neither of them said anything else for a long time — not with words, anyway.

The world suddenly and miraculously righted itself in Jake's warm embrace, and for the first time in a very long while, enfolded in his strong arms, Rachel felt warm and safe — and free. A weight of years left her shoulders, and a tightness vanished from her chest, a tightness that she had borne so long she had forgotten it was there. Unable to hold back tears of pure joy, she buried her face in his chest and prayed that this moment would never end.

After some minutes had passed she noticed that her face did not reach to the crook of his neck where it had fit so comfortably before. She leaned back to look at him, but it was too dark here in the middle distance between the houses.

"You've grown taller," she said.

"Jah. Two whole inches just this year."

Then, squeezing her in his arms and running his hands up her back, he added, "And you've grown into a woman yet, lean and strong. Different from the girl I remember. Even better."

She blushed, glad for the covering darkness. "It was the bricks. We have worked very hard, but now that more men are here maybe Miriam and I can go back to women's work again."

For the first time she noticed she was cold and remembered that in her flight she had left her coat behind at Emma's. She snuggled deep in his warm arms, clinging tightly around his waist, fearful of ever letting go. As long as she felt his arms about her, this could not be a dream.

"Oh, Jake, I really thought I had lost you," she said. "There wasn't even a letter for the last two months."

"I gave up the hope of ever seeing you again," he said, and then, hesitating, "I didn't see the wisdom in keeping you from finding another."

"What about now? Now that you're here and we're together again, do you feel the same for me as you did before?"

"No, I don't." And then his arms tightened around her. "I feel more. Much more. I would go to the ends of the earth for you,

Rachel. I have left my home and family behind for you."

"I would do a great many things for you."

His chin rested atop her prayer kapp, and his words made her scalp tingle. "At first I was heartbroken when you weren't there to meet me at your dat's house," he said quietly. "I had seen that moment in my head a thousand times, and longed for it to be so. But then Mary told me Emma was having trouble and you were up here with her. Mary is so proud of you, Rachel. She tells me you are a natural-born midwife." He chuckled. "And all this time I thought you were just a brickmaker."

"It's a gift from Gott," she said. "I never knew until it happened." It took a moment for her to put two and two together, but then, without moving an inch, she asked, "Jake, why would I be there to meet you when I didn't know you were coming? The last I heard from you, you said there was just no way."

He paused for a moment, confused, and then his chin moved against the top of her head. "Your dat didn't tell you I was coming?"

"No. I only heard five minutes ago from Lovina Hershberger that you were farmed out to her dat. After you were already here."

She pulled back and looked up at him. "Wait . . . you mean my dat *knew* you were coming?"

"Well, jah. Your dat arranged the whole thing. He worked it out with John Hershberger, and then he wrote my dat a letter and talked him into letting me come down with John."

Weeks. Such an exchange of letters meant that her father had known for *weeks,* yet he had said nothing.

"But this can't be. My dat doesn't even *know* about you and me. Why on earth would he arrange for you to come?"

"Oh, Rachel, you really didn't know any of this?" He laughed out loud. "*Emma* talked him into it! She said she couldn't stand seeing you so gloomy."

"Emma talked my dat into fixing it so you could come down, just for me? Then he *knows* about us?"

"Jah, I'm afraid he does. As a matter of fact, he knew all along — it was in his letter. Ask Emma."

"Oh, trust me, I will have a word with Emma. I can't believe she knew you were coming and kept it secret from me this whole time!"

"You'll thank her is what you'll do. She's the reason we're together right now. Your sister loves you, Rachel. She loves you so very much." He paused for a second, then added quietly, "And so do I."

It was she who kissed him, this time.

They stood holding each other for a long time, until Jake finally stirred and said, "We better get back. I should be helping with the work. Anyway, sooner or later people will start to miss us, and then there will be talk."

"I'm nearly seventeen," Rachel said. "Plenty old enough to court. Anyway, I've waited a hundred years for this moment, and I'll not be robbed of one second. Let the tongues wag."

And so they stayed longer, gazing together in blissful wonder at stars they now shared.

"There are more stars here," Jake said, looking up at the diamond-clustered night, "and they are so much brighter."

"Jah, they are," she answered, for she knew what he meant, though at the moment the stars all ran together in tear-washed eyes. At least they were *there* now. She had not noticed the stars in a very long time.

CHAPTER 43

The next morning, under a wide red dawn, Miriam sat on a crate in the back of the wagon as it struggled up toward the first mountain pass. She could tell that her dat was pushing his team a little harder than usual.

Micah sat on another crate near her. Already she had felt his eyes on her far too often. Micah was a good man, no doubt, but she didn't know him that well and still didn't feel very comfortable around him.

Micah leaned toward her and spoke quietly. "Why does he push the horses so?" he asked. "They pull a heavy load."

She knew why. She had seen El Pantera for herself, experienced the pall of evil surrounding him. Her father wasn't the only one who wanted to be well clear of the northern mountains before dark.

"It's not safe here," she explained. "There are bad men in these hills. *Very* bad men."

Micah smiled. He was not altogether unpleasant. "Well, if we meet them, don't worry," he said. "I will protect you."

Two hours later, beside a deep ravine in the middle of the mountains where the dense forest crowded against the road, it happened.

Miriam heard it first — the sound of hoofbeats approaching from behind. She looked back over the top of the crates and spotted two men on horseback coming up the road from Arteaga. She turned around to warn her father, but Domingo was already watching them so she said nothing.

The bandits overtook them quickly. Riding hard they blew past both sides of the wagon, then reined in their horses in the road ahead so that her father was forced to pull up. They trotted together to Domingo's side of the wagon and stopped.

The leader, a ferret-faced little man, raised himself up in his stirrups and craned his neck to look into the back of the wagon.

"Hola, señor!" he said cheerfully, grinning and tipping his sombrero to Dat. "What do we have here? Anything that might be of use to a pair of poor, tired soldiers?"

Dat shook his head. "Only a farmer's dishes and clothes," he said. "Nothing that would interest you, I am sure."

"Maybe we should take a look in your crates and barrels and see for ourselves," the weasel said, scratching his whiskered chin. But then, rising up in his stirrups and peering into the back of the wagon where Miriam sat, a sinister gleam came into his eyes.

"Perhaps you are right," he said. "The trails we must travel are too steep for a wagon, so we have no way to carry barrels and crates even if you are kind enough to give them to us. But I think there may be something here that our captain will find much more valuable than your dishes and rags, and it is not so difficult to carry."

Miriam squirmed uneasily as a cold fist gripped her heart. The weasel was hinting none too subtly at an unthinkable evil, and his eyes remained on her the whole time. Quivering in fear, she shrank down into a corner against the crates. She wanted to disappear. She wanted to run screaming the other way, but there was nowhere to run in these mountains.

"Porfirio," the man said casually to his accomplice, "take the girl."

Tears filled Miriam's eyes and she began to pray.

With a gap-toothed grin the second bandit

climbed down from his pinto and came straight to the side of the wagon where Miriam sat. He started to climb up.

Her fingernails dug into the sides of the crate and she cowered, whimpering. Afraid she would pass out from sheer terror, her eyes roamed, desperately seeking sanctuary, until she found Domingo's face.

Domingo's head was turned her way — still, calm, watching — but he made no move to intervene. His eyes, sharp and intense, fastened on Micah, who was sitting atop a crate near Miriam. When he caught Micah's eye he nodded toward the bandit hoisting himself up on the side rails to enter the back of the wagon.

Micah returned the nod, ever so slightly, and when the bandit had reached the top of the rails, he sprang. Grabbing the bandit by his upper arms Micah yanked him into the wagon in one swift motion, planting the surprised bandit on his face on top of a crate. His feet flailed and kicked against the side rails and his shoulders twisted and squirmed, but Micah held on. His big hands slid through the bandit's armpits, wrapped around and locked together behind that grimy neck. The bandit cursed and spat and fought, his arms waving like a trapped bug, but Micah's hold was unbreakable and he could not reach his weapons. Then Micah leaned back, pulling the bandit upright, exposing his pistols and bandoliers.

"Take his guns!" he shouted to Miriam.

She had no idea where the courage came from, but she saw her hands snatch the pistols from their cross-draw holsters. Then she just stood there, holding them daintily in her fingertips as if they were poisoned, waiting for further instructions.

The weasel laughed out loud, watching this little comedy from his saddle, but in the same instant he drew his pistol and raised it to aim at Micah's back.

It happened so fast Miriam saw only a blur from the corner of her eye. There was a flash and a shout, and the bandit was gone from his horse.

Domingo had launched himself from the front of the wagon like a spear. He clamped a fist around the gun barrel in the same instant that his shoulder crashed into the weasel's ribs and swept him cleanly off his mount, the gun firing harmlessly into the air. The wide-eyed bandit plunged to the ground with Domingo on top of his chest and landed flat on his back with a resounding *whump,* driving all the air out of him.

It was all over in a second. The two riderless horses bolted away in a swirl of dust, and when it settled, Domingo sat straddling the weasel's chest, pinning his arms to the ground with his knees. One hand held the bandit's head down by the hair while the other kept a very large razor-sharp knife pressed against his throat.

Domingo's jaw flexed and his knife hand tensed.

"Domingo, NO!" Dat shouted, and Domingo paused.

Slowly, without relaxing his grip, Domingo turned his head and looked up at Dat, fierce eyes staring through a loose curtain of black hair.

"Please, señor," the bandit whimpered. His eyes pleaded with Dat, but he dared not turn his head.

"Shut up," Domingo hissed without even looking down.

"You must not kill this man," Dat said. He spoke quietly now, the way he would soothe a spooked horse.

Domingo's head tilted, curious.

"Why not?"

"Because it is a great sin to kill a man."

Domingo stared at Dat for a few seconds more, then turned his eyes back to the weasel, the decision made.

"Not in *my* religion," he muttered. His arm tensed, and his knuckles whitened on the knife.

"Domingo!" Miriam shouted. She flung the pistols into the ravine and hung over the side rails so he could see her face. "Domingo," she repeated softly, "let him live. For me."

He hesitated for a second longer, but then in one swift motion he launched himself to his feet and sent a vicious blur of a heel-kick to the weasel's chin. The man's head snapped sideways and his eyes rolled back, unconscious.

Switching to German, Domingo snapped, "Then what would you have me do with him?" His knife disappeared into a sheath behind his back.

"Take his weapons and let him go," her father answered.

Domingo glared at him. "These are El Pantera's men, Herr Bender. Let them go, and in two hours he will know. In four, we will all be dead."

Dat sighed. "Jah, well, there is only one thing left to do then. If we cannot let them go and we cannot kill them, we will bind them and take them with us. Tie their hands and feet, and Micah can sit on them until we are far enough away."

Domingo shook his head in obvious disgust, but he turned back to the unconscious bandit and started stripping weapons. He took two pistols and a boot knife from the weasel, along with two bandoliers of bullets, and piled all of it under the seat in the front of the wagon.

"I know you won't touch these, Herr Bender," he said, "but they are mine now, and before the day is out I may need them."

Dat nodded.

The other bandit had ceased struggling and had become very docile when he saw what happened to the weasel. Without his guns he was no match for Micah.

Miriam heard a noise from the road in front of the wagon.

"Dat, look," she said, pointing.

One of the bandits' horses had returned. The paint had galloped out of sight around the bend, but the chestnut was ambling back toward them. As Dat turned to look, the horse shoved her head right into the wagon and nudged his arm.

The mare was dirty and thin, her ribs showing, her coat a dull mess. A gob of what looked like dried mud obscured part of her forehead, and only after Dat wiped it away with his palm did he see the little white mark that looked like a lopsided star.

"Star," he murmured, a touch of wonder in his eyes as he patted his horse's jaw. "I

didn't believe I would ever see you again. How have you been, girl?"

Five minutes later both bandits lay facedown between the crates in the back, tied hand and foot with baling twine. Dat left the Mexican saddle on Star and tethered her to the back of the wagon with a length of rope. She was going home.

It was two hours before Miriam's heartbeat slowed to normal. She sat staring at Domingo's back the whole time, deeply shaken. The sudden emergence of Domingo the Warrior had rocked her foundations like an earthquake, leaving them shifted and tilted. What troubled her most was the suspicion, deep down, that what Domingo had done was the right thing. That ferocity — that decisive and unapologetic *violence* — had saved Micah's life, possibly her own life, and her father's, too. Was there a time when violence was the right thing? Did not the Bible say there was a time to kill? She could see no way around it.

And then something came to her that Kyra had said the day of the horse race. She could still hear it, in Kyra's voice, word for word. *"He is very gentle . . . until someone he loves is threatened."*

Was it possible? Could it be that Domingo's claws came out because someone he *loved* was threatened?

Kyra's words haunted her.

There were cracks in her world, and through the cracks shined the light of a breed of man she had never encountered before.

Caleb pushed his horses perhaps too hard, but he feared for his daughter. He noticed that Domingo's sharp eyes constantly scanned the ridgetops, and every few minutes checked the road behind them.

But no one came. They passed Schulman's farm at sunset and pulled into Caleb's driveway in the purple hour of twilight. There were lanterns and campfires lit in the yard, and children ran to meet the wagon. He was home.

Exhausted, Caleb climbed down and met the throng of neighbors in front of his house, leaving the work of unloading and putting away the horses to his sons. Domingo took the pile of weapons with him rather than leave them unattended. With gun belts and bandoliers slung over both shoulders he looked like a bandit himself. All the newcomers eyed him warily and avoided him.

Children swarmed over the wagon, and as

Caleb talked with John Hershberger a little boy standing atop the mountain of crates cupped his hands around his mouth and shouted, "Mr. Caleb, there's a pile of *Mexicans* in your wagon!"

Caleb nodded wearily and said to John, "It's a long story, but I have one more little piece of business to attend to."

He had Harvey bring the painted pony from the corral and put the Mexican saddle on him while Micah and Aaron cut the bandits loose and escorted them down from the wagon.

All the Amish looked on in silence, most of them wide-eyed with terror. Word had spread quickly. These were real live bandits.

The weasel stood glaring at Caleb, rubbing his wrists.

"Thank you for returning the horse you borrowed," Caleb said. He nodded toward the pinto, already saddled. "This one is yours. Take it, and leave us be."

The weasel glanced at Domingo, who stood behind Caleb dripping with bandoliers, his hands resting on pistol butts.

"Can we have our weapons back?" the weasel asked. His eyes were angry, unfazed by defeat and unimpressed with Caleb's generosity.

"Spoils of war," Domingo answered coldly.

"You are lucky to be alive, *ladrón.*" The look in his eye made it plain that he would still prefer to change this one detail.

The two bandits muttered a steady stream of oaths and curses as they mounted the pinto and trotted away toward the east. A hundred yards into Caleb's wheat field one of the bandits twisted around and shook his fist.

"You have not seen the last of us, gringo! Now we know where you live!"

A gunshot shattered the air very close to Caleb. Women and children screamed, everyone ducked, and Caleb spun around to see where the shot had come from. Domingo still held a pistol aloft, smoke trailing from its barrel.

"Just a reminder," Domingo said, sliding the pistol back into its holster. "Something for them to think about. Look — now he has put the *spurs* to that pinto."

CHAPTER 44

A half hour later, after they had eaten supper, Domingo picked up his pile of weapons from the back porch and said to Caleb, "It is a long walk to my house, and these things are going to get heavy. May I borrow a horse for the night?"

Caleb pondered this for a minute, gazing toward the barn. A lantern cast a golden light on the interior of the barn, where Miriam was already brushing the burs and mats out of Star's coat while the mare fed from a trough.

"Just take yours," he said.

Domingo's brow furrowed. "But I *have* no horse."

Caleb nodded toward the barn, toward Star. "That one is yours. Take her, and be good to her. She is a fine animal."

"But this is *your* horse. I cannot accept such a gift."

Caleb's eyes turned to Domingo. "It is not

a gift, son, it is fair payment. I have enough horses, and I have my daughter yet. Because of you. In my mind . . . in my *heart,* I owe you much more than a horse. There are three saddles in the barn. Take your pick."

Domingo pondered this for a minute, then nodded slowly and said, "Gracias, Señor Bender. I will take good care of her." He hitched the bandoliers higher on his shoulders and turned toward the barn, but then he stopped and looked back at Caleb. "There is one more thing. I have made up my mind. I still think perhaps you are a little bit foolish, amigo, but you are *surely* the most honorable man I have ever met." Then he lowered his head and went on up to the barn.

Domingo's words stuck to Caleb's mind like cockleburs, and in spite of bone-deep fatigue he knew he would need to comb them out before he went back inside. His house and yard were full of life and light and clamor, and he wanted to be alone just now. A full moon had risen enough to light his way, so he buttoned his coat, turned up his collar and wandered up toward the dark ridge, trailing a callused hand on the top rail of the fence as he passed the barn lot.

"Cualnezqui."

Miriam jumped, startled. She didn't know the soft-footed native was standing behind her until he spoke.

"Your father has given me this horse," Domingo said.

She glanced toward the house and a little smile turned up the corners of her lips.

"Sí," she said. "That's my father."

Domingo picked out the oldest and plainest of the saddles. Miriam helped him cinch it in place, and then walked with him across the backyard, out to the edge of the wheat field.

"Domingo," she said, and he turned to face her in the moonlight.

"Sí?"

"I don't know how to say it. There are no words for what I feel after what happened today. Nothing in my life has prepared me for such a thing. It's just —"

"Gracias will do," he said. "I did only what I have been taught. I will not let harm come to my friends."

Friends. She wanted more, she knew that now. She wanted desperately to bridge the gulf between them, to declare herself, to let him know how she really felt, but it was a terrible risk — if he didn't share her feelings, she would look like a foolish child and the gulf between them would grow impossibly wide. She studied his face in the moonlight. His eyes betrayed nothing, but there might never be another moment like this, another chance. On an impulse she closed the distance between them, put a hand on his neck and reached up to kiss his cheek.

"Gracias," she said softly, and waited for his reaction.

But there was none. He was holding the reins in front of him, and his hands did not move to embrace her. His expression did not change, except for a slight blink that might have been only surprise. If anything, he backed away from her an inch or two.

He nodded stiffly. "You are welcome, cualnezqui. You and your family have become very dear to me. I swear to you, as long as I am able I will protect you with my life."

And then, with great tenderness and something very close to love, he looked up at the horse and stroked its face.

"It is late. I must go now," he said. With a heartbreakingly casual grace he swung up into the saddle, and then, looking down on her, said, "I forgot to thank your father for the saddle. Please let him know I am very grateful."

Then he spurred his new horse and trotted off across the field without once looking back.

Standing in the yard watching him ride away, Miriam's heart shattered like glass. He had been very gracious, and yet his words didn't satisfy her. Domingo knew nothing of this cauldron of feelings that roiled and steamed inside her, and he certainly did not share it. To him, she was only a good friend who taught him to read and granted him respect. In the end she was as devoid of hope as ever, only now she was hopeless *and* suffering — the penalty for her desire. She wanted to scream and cry, and at the same time she wanted to turn about and forget, to erase her feelings the way she erased a blackboard. Perhaps it was for the best. Perhaps in time, with Gott's help, the ache would lose its grip. Perhaps the longing would fade into nothingness one day and she would be content to be his friend, as comfortable and familiar as a worn-out shoe. Conflicting thoughts pelted and plagued her as she stood in the edge of the light from her father's house, fighting back tears.

"Miriam? Are you all right?"

Rachel's voice. Miriam was careful to put on a thin, non-committal smile before she turned around.

"I'm fine," she lied. "Just enjoying the evening air. The moon is lovely tonight." A full moon hung low in the east, big as a washtub and bright as a beacon. It mocked her. In its light she could still make out a tiny spot of white bobbing in the distance — Domingo, a half mile away and getting smaller.

Rachel came and stood beside her, hooking an arm in Miriam's. "Jah, it's very nice."

They stood that way for a long time, two sisters side by side contemplating the night sky, and then Rachel said very quietly, "You're in love with him, aren't you?"

Miriam weighed the question inside her for a moment. She did not wish to lie, to her sister or to herself.

"It takes two," she said. "I would rather have no hope at all than pine for a man who cannot see me. To him I am just a friend. His ugly little cualnezqui."

Rachel laughed. She actually covered her mouth with her hand and giggled. Miriam pulled away and turned to face her.

"This is *funny* to you? I have trusted you with the thoughts of my heart, Rachel."

Rachel laughed harder, shaking her head and holding a calming hand out to Miriam because at the moment she couldn't speak. Finally she managed to say, "No, wait. You don't understand."

"*I* don't understand? I understand my own sister is laughing at me when I have bared my soul to her."

"No," Rachel said, at last bringing her laughter almost under control, "it's not like that at all. Listen — let me tell you. Kyra came yesterday to bring Emma some native herbal remedy that's supposed to make her well. Kyra is our friend, so when she went to leave I said to her, '*Vaya con Dios,* cualnezqui,' and she turned around and gave me the strangest look. Her mouth opened a little, like she was shocked, and there were tears in her eyes. She asked me if I knew what I had said.

"I told her everybody knows 'Vaya con Dios' means 'Go with Gott.' But she said no, the Nahuatl word — *cualnezqui.* So I told her yes, I know what it means, because Domingo calls Miriam that sometimes; it means 'friend' or 'neighbor.' Kyra shook her head and laughed a little then, but she was crying at the same time."

Miriam's eyes narrowed. "You're saying cualnezqui doesn't mean *friend?*"

"No! She told me the Nahuatl word for friend, but I can't say it, it's too hard. It's not even close to the same."

Miriam harbored a profound suspicion

470

that she was being ridiculed, but Rachel's laughter was nothing compared to the humiliation she would feel if she learned that Domingo had been making fun of her all this time. She crossed her arms on her chest.

"So what does it *really* mean?"

Rachel's grin faded, and in the pale blue moonlight Miriam could see her eyes. There was a deep caring in those eyes, and a trace of fear.

"It's what Kyra's late husband always called her when he thought no one was listening," Rachel said softly. "Beautiful one. Miriam, cualnezqui means *beautiful one.*"

Caleb went only a little ways up the ridge, stopping at the first scattering of trees when he came to a waist-high outcropping of rock. A perfect spot. He sat himself down on the cold stone, took his hat off and laid it beside him.

Rubbing his bald head, he turned his face up to the stars and muttered, "Have I been *foolish?* Was it only blind stubbornness that brought my family, and now our friends, to a place half a world away where bandits roam the roads, my sons plow among snakes, our babies crawl among scorpions, and no one speaks our language or shares our beliefs? *What have I done?*"

A deep sigh welled up from the cold edge of doubt, and Caleb lowered his gaze. As was his way in quiet moments, he waited for Gott to answer — for that gift of clarity to descend like a dove and bring him peace.

But nothing came.

After a while a little rusty squeak distracted him, the vanes of his windmill nudged by a light breeze. His thoughts turned to irrigation, and his eyes roamed over endless rows of corn shocks and twice-plowed fields ready for planting. Fat cows and sleek horses grazed in a newly fenced pasture. A swell of laughter drew his eye first to the campfire in his yard, then to the yellow light spilling from his home and the lamplit windows of his daughters' houses, one to the east and another to the west, where three new lives had begun in the last year.

He heard the faint pounding of hoofbeats — his friend and protector Domingo riding home at the end of a long and eventful day, skirting a field thick with winter wheat. A prayer kapp glowed pale blue in the moonlight, a girl standing on the edge of the yard. He knew the shape and stance of his daughter Miriam, even at night and from a distance. A moment later the back door opened

— Rachel, venturing out to join her sister. He could see them quite clearly, his fine strong daughters arm in arm under the stars, and he sat contentedly for a long time, admiring them.

When he looked up again his eye was drawn to the dark ridge looming over the opposite side of the valley, and it occurred to him that the ridges and mountains wrapped themselves around his new home rather like the arms of Gott.

Only then did he remember what he had come here for. He hung his head, chuckling sheepishly.

"I *am* foolish," he muttered. He had come to this rock to be alone, to ask Gott an honest question, but like a child he'd gotten distracted and forgot to listen for an answer. And like a father, Gott had answered him anyway. His heart was full to bursting.

A shiver ran through him, the night air beginning to seep into his old work coat. Sliding to his feet, Caleb stuffed his hat back on his head and started down the hill, still smiling at himself, whispering a line from a psalm he'd learned in his youth, forty years and a thousand miles ago.

" 'If I ascend up into heaven, thou art there: if I make my bed in hell, behold, thou art there.' "

AUTHOR'S NOTE

In the early 1920s, five Amish fathers were arrested and jailed in Holmes County, Ohio, for violating the Bing Act of 1921. Their children were taken from them and placed in a children's home, had their hair cut and their Amish clothes confiscated. Later, the men actually did find a pamphlet advertising land for sale in Mexico for $10 an acre in a place called Paradise Valley, owned by Hacienda El Prado. The colony began with one pioneer family and grew to well over a hundred people. While in Mexico, the Amish built adobe houses, dug community wells, traveled three days round trip to market in Saltillo, learned to speak Spanish, went without a minister, were hounded by the remnants of Pancho Villa's army and later by Federal troops. These are facts.

The author's great-grandfather was the elder statesman of the colony; his grandparents lived in Paradise Valley, and his father was born there. However, written records are scant and few firsthand accounts have survived, so the author used the known history and geography of the colony to create a backdrop. But this is a work of fiction. While the historical context of the novel is fairly accurate, the characters and their stories are entirely the author's creation.

ACKNOWLEDGMENTS

This novel could never have been done without the generous help and gentle correction of friends and family. I owe a debt of gratitude to the following:

First, my wife, Pam, who has somehow endured the madness that is a writer's life and given me her unflagging support. When I began writing this novel I let her know I was in trouble. "It's about women," I said, "and I don't know the first thing about women." I'll never forget the compassion in her eyes when she looked up at me and said three words I've been waiting thirty-five years to hear: "You're absolutely right." She proofed the manuscript repeatedly, saving me from many a male blunder.

My father, Howard Cramer, shared a wealth of inside knowledge about Amish life and culture, and my cousin Katie Shetler did her best to keep me out of trouble with my Amish kin.

Marian Shearer, a local writer who grew up in Mexico, gently corrected my Spanish and graciously shared insights into Mexican life, culture and geography.

Lori Patrick, a freelance editor and friend, wrote the back cover copy. It's good to have talented friends.

Larry McDonald, Terry Hadaway, and Joe Nolan all endured hours of exploratory chats and brainstorming sessions, helping me work out the direction of the story, and a number of other friends read early drafts, offering encouragement and advice. I won't try to list all of them here for fear of forgetting someone, but they know who they are.

My long-suffering editor, Luke Hinrichs, and a host of others at Bethany House went above and beyond this time, showing me how to turn a lump of clay into a work of art.

My agent, Janet Kobobel Grant, always takes care of business, leaving me free to write. She's also a keen-eyed editor and wise counselor who always has my back.

Last, but certainly not least, this work owes a great deal to a book by David Luthy titled *The Amish in America: Settlements That Failed, 1840–1960.* To my knowledge, it is the only comprehensive written record of the Paradise Valley settlement, and it was instrumental in creating the backdrop for the novel.

ABOUT THE AUTHOR

Dale Cramer is the author of the bestselling and critically acclaimed novel *Levi's Will.* He lives in Georgia with his wife and two sons.

For more information visit Dale's Web site at *dalecramer.com,* and his blog at *dale cramerblog.com.* Or readers may write to Dale at P.O. Box 25, Hampton, GA 30228.